I0562962

The Bastard Sorceress

Verna McKinnon

TANSTAAFL  PRESS

If you purchased this book without a cover, you should be aware that it was an unauthorized sale. All books without a cover have been reported as "unsold and destroyed." As a result neither the author nor the publisher received payment for the sale of this "stripped book."

TANSTAAFL Press
891 PH 10
Castle Rock, WA 98611

Visit us at www.TANSTAAFLPress.com

All characters, businesses, and situations within this work are fictional and the product of the author's creativity. Any resemblance to persons living or dead is entirely coincidental. TANSTAAFL Press assumes no responsibility for any content on author or fan websites or other publications.

The Bastard Sorceress

First printing—TANSTAAFL Press
Copyright © 2022 by Verna McKinnon
Cover art: WGOULART or @wgoulart_designer

Printed in the USA
ISBN: : 978-1-938124-71-6

Book layout by Hydra House Books

CHAPTER 1

An unexpected shipment of mystical books arrived by post this afternoon. I hate mysteries, especially when they involve finances. I handled the store inventory and would have remembered ordering a set of such pricey mage books. Stress triggered one of my headaches, adding to my cranky mood.

Mother stepped through the old velvet curtains separating the shop from the downstairs parlor and kitchen. "Are you alright, dear?" she asked.

"I'm lovely. Did you enjoy your nap?" I replied, digging through the box for any clues to the enigmatic delivery.

"Yes, Sabine, but you shouldn't have let me sleep so long. Tell me what's wrong. You've got that quizzical look."

"Just confused," I mumbled, sitting cross-legged on the floor as I emptied the crate's packing, tossing straw everywhere but coming up empty-handed. I stacked the books neatly to keep them safe. "I never ordered these and can't find an invoice anywhere. Did Luther do this? Mother, he needs to tell me these things."

"I'll speak with him. Don't fret, I'm sure there's a reasonable explanation," she replied, brushing away bits of yellow straw and touching the elegant gold-and-blue covers of the books. "It's a shame we rarely carry such elite merchandise anymore. These are well-crafted tomes. Expensive ones."

"I hope so! It vexes me when he does things like this, even though they're gorgeous. Magic is currency in our world, but I can't profit if I can't balance the ledger." I inhaled, enjoying the scent of the books, sweet with the tangible dusting of magic woven into each page. It even softened my headache. Magic is something even a baseborn can smell. For an instant, my headache retreated. The odor depends on the type of magic, of course. Light magic has a clean scent, like fresh air and sunshine. Dark magic smells vile, or at least I've heard it does. Mages who practice the shadowcraft rarely purchase their wicked materials openly.

"You work much too hard, dear. Stop frowning. It causes wrinkles, and you have such a lovely brow."

"I'm not frowning. I'm just thinking really hard."

Mother stroked the book lovingly. "I remember now. He mentioned something a few weeks ago about ordering special volumes for someone. Father tends to be absentminded these days."

"Forgetfulness doesn't cover the bills. You know our funds are low this month after paying for a shipment of store supplies. Luther never bothers with finances except to pinch from its coffers. I had to barter with the grocer for cheap coffee and cornmeal in exchange for a batch of headache draughts I made so we could eat. I couldn't even afford sugar or a tin of milk."

"I saw Master Thomas, the grocer, on my walk this morning. He praised your headache medicine. You've become a skilled apothecary and should be proud. I remember now! I believe Sir Thomas Graven ordered the books as a birthday gift for his daughter, Marigold. I hear she's home for the spring holidays from the Academy. Wasn't she your friend at school?"

"We were never friends, Mother. She called me ghost-eye and made my life a misery. Mageborns don't play with baseborn bastards. They bully them."

"Well, you were just children then. You have such lovely pale gray eyes, dearest. They're your best feature. I'm sure it was just envy on Miss Graven's part." Mother glanced at me and whispered, "Your top buttons are undone, dear. You do not wish to send the wrong message if someone comes into the shop."

"Sorry, Mother." I fastened the top two buttons of my blouse despite sweating from my labors in the stuffy shop. Mother was always conscious of ladylike images, especially as I got older.

"Much better," she said. "I'm sure you're mistaken about Marigold. People do change when they grow up."

"Perhaps," I remarked to close the subject. I loathed Marigold, a demon in blonde ringlets who had tormented me from the age of six. She got away with it because she was rich and mageborn. I adored books with a passion, but Marigold and her circle of nasty hens killed my love of school. I left at thirteen. Mother needed me anyway.

Mother opened a mystic book only to be confronted with blank pages. "I keep forgetting I can't see the magical words anymore." Her smile vanished as she closed the book. I knew how much it pained her to know she'd never see mystical script again.

I watched her wistfully turn away, but I knew how much it hurt her. My mother, Brona, was blessed to be mageborn. Unlike most of our Fable clan, who were minor charm caste, she had possessed the power to become a true sorceress. At sixteen she was accepted by the elite Mystic Academy at Túr Solas, the capital city of the Ravenna Republic. My mother excelled at her magic studies until love ruined her.

Apparently, love is a sin when not precluded by a marriage rite. A bad affair can be forgotten, but if a girl falls pregnant out of wedlock, it disgraces her and the family. It brought my poor mother trouble— namely me. Then, as if her misfortunes weren't enough, an epidemic of mage fever struck, and the Fable clan was reduced to three—me, mother, and her father, Luther.

The doorbell chimed as Altheda Dusan entered. "Sabine and Brona Fable! I was hoping to see you two today."

Glad for the distraction, I hugged her. "Good afternoon! I haven't seen you in almost a month," I said.

"Been busy, girl," Altheda exclaimed, "People are birthing babies like feisty rabbits, and the spring colds have folks down of late. I've seen more sniffles now than in the winter."

Altheda had known me literally since my birth. She was our village healer, midwife, and a dear friend. She delivered me. And when the scarlet madness—mage fever—took hold in my mother, Altheda nursed Brona through the chills, the night terrors, and the screaming insanity. She helped keep my mother alive even though the fever stripped Brona, like every other mage it struck, of her magic.

Altheda grabbed the small footstool I kept handy. I was too small to reach the higher shelves, but I kept it for her ease since she was a dwarf. Altheda often confronted people about their narrow view of those who live on the rim of society because they are different or poor.

"What's your pleasure today?" I asked, brushing bits of straw from my blouse.

"My depleted pharmacopeia needs restocking. Here's a list. Willow bark tablets, blessed thistle, dandelion root, comfrey, nettle. The works."

She handed me a long list and began counting out coins on the counter. I was glad because it meant we would have milk and meat on the table.

"How are you faring today, Brona?" Altheda inquired. "Taking your medicine?"

"I'm quite well," Mother replied, taking the list and gathering the requested medicines with quiet efficiency. "I hope you're the same. We must have tea together soon."

"I'll be looking forward to it, love." Then Altheda leaned in and whispered to me, "Has the old wizard checked you yet?"

"Last week. I'm afraid I'm still just a regular girl," I replied softly in her ear, so Mother would not hear. These tests for my mystical awakening always occurred around my birthday, which was in a few weeks. I'm not only a bastard, but because of my mother's fever, I'm baseborn as well. "I hate these silly annual examinations, but Mother always insists. My spark of hope is always snuffed out when the old man shakes his head."

Altheda nodded." Just make your mum happy. Next year, when you turn eighteen, you won't need to go." She looked at the books on the counter. "Heavens, these are lovely tomes. I'd wish for magic just to be able to have these beauties."

"I remember how the symbols shimmered before my eyes into wondrous words of power," Mother remarked, her voice overcome with loss. "Without magic's beneficence, there's nothing but an empty page."

I worried she might get upset and bring on an attack of one of the side effects that had lingered through the years.

Altheda nudged her with a grin. "Now, Brona, don't fall into a gloom. You know how it distresses you when you dwell on the past."

"Have you had your tea, Mother?" I asked. It was my subtle way of making sure she took her medicine.

"Not yet, Sabine." She sighed and wrinkled her nose. "It tastes so bitter."

"Then add honey," I suggested, dusting off the last volume.

Mother smiled." You'd add honey to anything."

"I like sweet," I said with a shrug.

"Take your medicine, Brona," Altheda told her. "You must look after yourself." Then our friend gathered her fresh stock of medicinal herbs and potions, carefully putting them in her satchel.

I deposited Altheda's coins into my felt purse and tucked them away in my skirt pocket, calculating how much food I could buy with them.

Altheda smiled, waving as she left. "I'll be calling on you next week."

"Bring your spice cake too," I called after her.

"With or without vanilla icing?" she called back.

"With!"

The promise of iced cake almost made me feel better. Her talent at baking rivaled her skill as a healer. I shoved the crate behind the counter and grabbed a broom, sweeping up the loose straw. "It's quiet today, Mother. Why don't you go back upstairs and rest? I can manage until Luther gets back."

"I'm fine, dear," she said, dusting the potion bottles in the case. "You know I like to be useful."

The doorbell chimed, alerting me to another customer. I looked up to see Sir Thomas Graven and his daughter, Marigold Graven, enter the shop.

"Goodness! Have you been rolling in a hayloft, Sabine?" Marigold remarked idly, her pristine handkerchief fluttering in her fingers. "You should pay better attention to your appearance, but you always had a dirty face in school. Still, hard work keeps a girl from straying into sin, as our pastor says."

I wanted to cram her lacy kerchief down her throat. I took a deep breath, put down the broom, and dusted off my dress. I smiled coolly and ignored her rude comment. Nor did I bow my head in submission as she thought baseborns should before their mage betters. Her eyes narrowed like a rat's beneath her frilly pink bonnet, as though I'd challenged her to a duel.

Mother greeted them with her most brilliant smile and gracefully led them to the counter. I always envied my mother's elegance. "Welcome to Fable House. Your timing is perfect. Your books have just arrived."

"Excellent," Graven replied, sweeping back his cloak and examining one of the volumes. Tall and lean with sharp features and black hair, he seemed carved out of granite rather than flesh. In contrast, Marigold was soft and round as pudding, but with none of the sweetness.

Mother looked fondly at the books. "I've seen nothing this lovely since my days at the Academy. I hope they please you."

"Indeed they do, Mistress Brona," Graven replied. Then he and turned to his daughter. "Do you like your birthday present, sweetheart?"

"Oh, Daddy, they're so pretty!" Marigold giggled with the exuberance of a toddler offered gooey candy.

Luther arrived, reeking like an ale barrel even from a distance. "Welcome, Lord Thomas Graven!" He scurried to Graven like a penitent peasant and offered his hand. Graven did not take it, but he turned aside, tugging at his own fine leather gloves.

Luther ignored the slight but grinned broadly as he brushed his gray hair off his face. "As you see, my special order for your books arrived in time for Lady Marigold's birthday. I was honored to serve you, Lord Graven. I hope your lordship is pleased with this rare collection for your lovely daughter. Old Luther Fable still has his contacts for some superior magic items."

"They are satisfactory, Mister Fable," Lord Graven said.

Thomas Graven often did business with us, buying mystical supplies or ordering books. I once sold him a special pocket tome to keep spells handy. He was sorcerer caste and one of the richer nobles in town. I think he felt sorry for my mother. I know they attended the Academy together before her banishment and later loss of magic. His patronage was needed coin in the till.

The shiny new magic books absorbed Marigold's attention and deflected any further sarcasm directed at me.

"Our business is then concluded. Take them to our carriage," Graven ordered. "I thank you for your assistance in this acquisition."

"Happy to be of service. Fable House thanks you for your patronage." Luther nodded, taking the seven volumes of magic I envied. Mother opened the door for Luther as he stumbled past Marigold, who wrinkled her nose and fluttered her lace handkerchief as she left.

Lord Graven tipped his tall hat to us before leaving. I remembered to curtsy. I don't trust mageborns, despite my longing to be one. But Thomas Graven was always kind to my mother, which perplexed me, actually. Marigold was not so mysterious.

Luther returned, pleased with himself. "Well, Lord Graven was a satisfied customer if I must say. The mystic scribes still know old Luther Fable, and I know how to deal."

"A wonderful sale indeed!" I said, hoping to extract some information. "Such an expensive purchase will help our coffers this month. Do you have the invoice? I need it for the books."

"None of your concern, missy," Luther snapped. "This was a business exchange between gentlemen. The good word of Graven will help our business."

"Luther, I keep the accounts, and nothing was noted about this," I replied, my temper fermenting. I feared it would be an empty argument, for he had probably already spent any profit.

"Lord Graven paid me for the damned books, so stop nagging. Now get out of my way, girl," Luther mumbled. "It's what you call an investment, you ignorant little slut. I did it at cost, as a favor to Graven. It will cultivate the Fable House reputation."

The only thing Luther ever cultivated was a thirst for ale, I thought. *Maybe whiskey.* "Graven is rich," I said. "We are not! I had to barter for food this week."

"Don't pester me, you little bastard. You need to spend money to get money!" Luther shouted, bending down nose to nose with me.

His breath stank, but I stood my ground. "We've nothing to spend."

"Hold your tongue, girl!"

"Both of you stop this at once," Mother. "Father, go upstairs. Sabine and I will clean up and make supper."

"I'm not hungry, Brona!" Luther snapped.

"Don't yell at her!" I said.

Luther's eyes narrowed on me. "Why's your hand in your pocket like that? You hiding something, girl?" grabbing at my skirt pocket and seizing the precious coins. "Hiding my money now, are you? You ungrateful little thief!" Luther slapped me hard across the face. My cheek burned, as my hands and head became enflamed—which they did when I was angry or upset. I set my jaw for another blow as Mother rushed between us.

"Father, please stop! It was for a lovely sale Sabine just made with Altheda. No one is hiding anything from you. Sabine works so hard. You promised not to hit her anymore."

"We need money for food," I insisted, jerking away.

"I need it more. I've a business meeting with some important folk." Luther chuckled, clutching the money close to his chest. "This will come in handy."

"For what? Swilling beer and losing it all at cards while we starve?"

Luther unbuckled his belt. "You need a beating, girl?"

It was my own fault. He lunged at me, but I ducked and bolted for the door, hiking up my skirts as I ran. The folly of my temper and Luther's drinking always wreaked chaos. But his belt didn't have time to touch my back this time. Only his curses followed me as I fled for the nearby woods.

I'm not sure how long I ran. Only sheer exhaustion forced me to stop when I was deep in the forest. I collapsed near the stream, breathing hard. I splashed my face with the cold water, wishing for something, anything to change my life.

My frail moment of precious peace was broken by rowdy voices nearby. I followed the sounds until I came upon a pack of local boys, maybe around nine or ten years old, laughing as they brutally beat the ground with sticks and rocks. I raged when I saw their victim—a small green-and-gold pukis dragon, its poor head bashed in by the vicious human monsters. Their cruelty flared my once-spent temper. I snatched up a big stick from the ground and rushed them, shouting curses. My screams must have been intimidating, or they thought I was mad, because they ran off.

I dropped to the ground and blubbered like an idiot. Through bleary eyes, I saw that their atrocities had killed more than this poor pukis dragon. Broken eggs lay scattered in the grass. The pukis must have had a nest nearby and tried protecting her eggs from those fiends! In the glow of the afternoon sun, I glimpsed one gleaming, unbroken egg in the grass. I wiped my eyes and touched its blue-and-green shell. I felt its warmth. I gathered a thick pile of leaves and carefully laid the egg there. I found a stout branch and dug a grave for its poor mother and shattered brothers and sisters. I covered the grave with dirt, rocks, and fallen branches. I stayed in the woods until sunset, pondering my fate and the egg's.

I could not abandon this poor egg to cruel nature. I'd read pukis dragons are rather small, about the size of a house cat, but reputed to be mischievous critters. Some mages keep them as pets because they look like tiny dragons. I knew Luther might protest, but I didn't care. Mother would let me keep it.

I gently wrapped the pukis egg in my scarf to keep it warm. "No one's going to hurt you, my little dragon. I will protect you now." I walked home slowly, cradling my pukis egg in my hands.

CHAPTER 2

I had cut up a ragged, old bedspread for nesting material. I knew the egg needed to be kept warm and safe, but other than that I was clueless about pukis dragons. I tucked blanket scraps around my egg in a wicker basket and set it near the hearth.

How long do pukis incubate? What do they eat when newly hatched? I fretted like a mother hen. Or should I say mother dragon? *What if it hatched when I'm away? Worse, what if Luther tosses my dragon egg into the trash for spite, or worse, cooks it!* Reading up on pukis dragons was at the top of my list today, so I planned to visit our library after breakfast.

When I came downstairs, the sweet aroma of baking cornbread distracted me. I checked and, upon seeing the edges were dark, took the cornbread out of the oven to cool. It smelled so good, but what I desperately craved was the strong coffee percolating on the stove. I fixed a cup, mourning the lack of cream and sugar. A pallid Luther staggered into the kitchen and sat down. I put the steaming cup in front of him, which he cautiously picked up with a puzzled side-glance.

"Don't worry, it's not poison," I quipped and poured a cup for myself.

"Any sugar?" Luther mumbled, sniffing the hot coffee with closed eyes before sipping.

"We're out. The grocer wouldn't extend any more credit." I tasted the potent brew and puckered.

"This brew could use cream too. Lots of it." Luther took a handful of coins out of his jacket and laid them on the kitchen table. I knew this was the money Altheda paid me yesterday. He was almost petulant, a common behavior after one of his drinking bouts. In sober moments, Luther could even be civil to me. I wondered if we might get along if he wasn't so drunk all the time. Hard to say. Even clear-headed, he had the temperament of a cranky ogre.

The money was enough to pay the grocery bills and buy proper food. I tucked the coins in my apron pocket. Then I took the green bottle of strong headache tonic from the shelf and placed it on the table. "For your head woes. Better eat something too."

He uncorked it and swallowed a generous dose. "Make sure you buy sugar, and tell that penny-pinching grocer to shove his credit threats. Fable House pays for its goods." In his stupor, he finally noticed the basket with the colorful egg nestled in it on the hearth. "What's this? Breakfast?"

"Don't you dare," I warned, protectively swooping to the basket. "It's a pukis dragon egg. I rescued it from a pack of evil boys yesterday. The vicious thugs killed its mother and smashed her eggs, except for this one. I chased them off with a big stick. Bloody cowards."

"Well, you inherited the Fable temper, for sure." He stared at the egg with bloodshot eyes. "A stupid pukis egg. Dwarfish little dragons with a bad attitude. Haven't seen one of them in years. They normally don't nest this far north. Damned hard to housetrain too." Luther shrugged. "Not very bright either."

"I'm keeping him," I declared, tucking soft, wooly strips around my egg. "He's got no one else now but me. Mother said I could keep him."

"He?" Luther snorted. "So sure it's a boy?"

"Well, no, but I can't always call the egg it. And don't get any ideas about selling my egg or making him a snack."

"Don't get flustered, Missy. I wouldn't eat pukis no matter how poor we are. Mages used to keep them as pets, but they've gone out of fashion now. Probably won't hatch, so don't get too attached." He moaned and rubbed his temples.

I poured more coffee into his cup. "I made cornbread if you want some."

"Just a small morsel, to offset the coffee's bitterness."

"I'll buy sugar and a tin of cream, and let's see … Butter, bread, cheese, and eggs. I'll make omelets for supper."

"With fried potatoes?"

"Yes, with fried potatoes." I nodded, cutting a slice of warm cornbread, thinking how butter would make everything taste better.

"Just don't eat the eggs in front of junior," Luther snickered.

I narrowed my eyes, but Mother walked into the kitchen, so I kept my sharp reply to myself. With Luther, there was always an opportunity to fight later. I just relished a bit of peace now.

I watched Mother as she moved through the kitchen, I envied mother's golden tresses and gentle blue eyes, especially when I looked in a mirror. My wild dark hair and odd gray eyes made me feel like the homely ghost-eye Marigold had taunted me with at school.

"Coffee?" I asked her.

"Not this morning, dear. I think mint tea would be better."

"I'll make your tea. I already heated up the kettle for you. How are you this morning? Do you have a headache?"

"I'm fine, darling. Just tired, that's all. There's no need to worry. How is your little friend this morning?" she asked, stroking the egg with her fingertips.

"Still in one piece," I said, scooping mint tea into the pot and pouring in the hot water. "Mother, I'm going to the market and then the library. Would you watch over my egg while I'm gone?" I fetched her favorite teacup and the last of the honey, then set them on the table.

"What's the bloody thing gonna do? Fly away?" Luther scoffed , holding out his cup for another refill.

"Of course, I'll look after it," she said. "The shell is a lovely blend of blue and green. I do know their shells match their coloring when hatched. Why are you going to the library?"

I poured more coffee for Luther and refilled my cup too. "I wanted to find something more definitive on the care of pukis dragons."

"The town library is rubbish," Luther said, biting into his cornbread. "We've some old books in the attic. I know there's at least one good volume on the pukis dragon. Nothing but tiny winged hooligans if you ask me."

"Misery," I countered, downing my coffee in one gulp, bitter but reviving. Grabbing my shopping basket and cloak, I dashed out the door.

"Don't forget the sugar!" Luther shouted.

# # #

The brisk, sunny morning brightened my mood as I rushed down the wooden walk to the general store. After paying our debt, I bought cream, cheese, butter, bacon, a few red potatoes, sugar, eggs, and a bag of good coffee beans. I even bought a loaf of fresh-baked bread from the bakery on the way home. Mother liked toast in the morning. We hadn't had bread for three days. The bakery goods were better than mine, and I wanted Mother to have a treat. Eager to get home, I looked forward to finding the pukis book in the attic and looking after my precious egg.

"Oh, Sabine! Sabine, wait! Over here!"

I flinched at Marigold's high-pitched voice. My cheery mood vanished.

Marigold Graven sat like a queen in an open carriage, garbed in a lavender dress and bonnet dripping with lace, impatiently waving me over. A driver patiently held the reins of the horses, his expression glum.

"Goodness, have you fallen deaf?" Marigold remarked. "I called and called you."

"Sorry, Marigold. What do you want?"

Marigold sighed, fluttering her fan. "What could be so pressing you could not even acknowledge me?"

"I do work, Marigold." *My life does not revolve around you.* "I'm just in a hurry to get back to the shop."

"I was coming to see you, so it must be fate we ran into each other. My maid just abandoned me. She's getting married and didn't even ask for my permission. I fired her on the spot for such insolence."

"I thought she abandoned you." I imagined the girl was thrilled to leave Marigold's employment at any rate.

"Well, the ungrateful wench did abandon me when she announced she was engaged. I dismissed her. Can you imagine such betrayal? Without even considering me! Such ingratitude!"

"I'm sorry you lost your maid, but what does that have to do with me?" I replied.

"Well, I need a new maid. I thought I would do you the honor of giving you the position. I noticed Fable House is very shabby these days. Working for a noble family like mine is a great honor. I mean, your prospects in life are grim, Sabine. You've no dowry, magic, or name to offer a husband. Serving me as my maid would save you from inevitable poverty."

I'm sure she would remind me of this daily.

"Thank you for your offer, but I—"

"Our pastor suggested it himself."

"He suggested me?" I asked, confused. "Do I know him?"

"Oh no, he doesn't know you. Why would he? You don't travel our social circles, but you should know of him. Do you even attend church, Sabine? The gods are ever watchful. We all have sins that need to be absolved through penance and prayer."

I want to absolve her of talking. Perhaps being forced to listen to her prattle is my penance.

"He suggested I give some poor girl a chance, so I thought of you. Of course, you would need to address me properly as Lady Marigold. A servant should not be too familiar. You understand magic better than most baseborns, though your family was mostly just charmed caste. They lost their magic in the last mage fever plague, didn't they? Our pastor did a stirring sermon last week about sin and mage fever. He believes the fever to be punishment from the gods for our sins."

"You seem rather smitten with your pastor," I remarked.

"Does it show? Oh, but you don't know. We're betrothed." Marigold beamed. "His name is Greeley Havelock. Greeley is a mage, of course. Wizard caste. Yet, he chose a humble profession. His religious devotion is just one of many signs of his goodness."

"I pray the gods grant you the happiness you deserve."

She jabbered on and on. I knew the source of her offer wasn't compassion but a desire to rub my nose in my baseborn poverty. I put up my hand until she finally fell mute. I spoke plainly. "Thank you, Marigold, for your kind offer, but I must decline. Fable House needs me, as does my mother. We are doing quite well and need no assistance. Good day."

Marigold's mouth formed a stunned little circle. As I turned away, her voice mutated from cheery-sharp to angry-shrill. "Ingrate! How dare you refuse my generosity? You're just a baseborn bastard, and your mad-touched mother is a whore!"

My temper snapped. I spun around on her so fast that she cringed in her fancy leather seat. "Never ever insult my mother! She has more class and grace than you will ever possess. You best restrain your insults, Marigold. Being mageborn doesn't give you the right to insult my mother. And baseborns don't need magic to hurt someone. Remember that."

I relished the pale terror on Marigold's face for a second before I bolted. I briefly glimpsed the grin on her driver's face when I glanced back, fearful she would chase after me like she did in school. I cursed my temper! A headache flared, tormenting me. I reached the shop, breathless, and noticed a rich carriage parked in front. Now what? Could it be a customer or more trouble? I never knew anymore.

I quietly entered through the side entrance to the kitchen and found Mother sitting at the table conversing with a strange, raven-haired woman in an elegant crimson dress. She glanced up at me with black eyes.

Mother waved me over to the table. "Sabine, come meet our guest, Sorceress Veda Arcana. Veda, you remember my daughter! She was so young when you last visited. I think Sabine was only six?"

A tall woman with skin like dark honey who smelled of gardenia, a scent I recognized. Yes, I remembered now. "Welcome, Lady Arcana." I curtsied.

"Just call me Veda," she said with a smile.

The memory of Veda's visit brought no comfort. My mother became quite sick during her previous visit. Altheda had been summoned. Veda had been kind to me but sent me off to my room without explanation or soothing lies. I remember whispers behind closed doors. Mother recovered but was bedridden for several days. No one tells a child anything useful when they're scared.

"Goodness, you've grown up, Sabine!" Veda said.

"Not so much," Luther remarked. "She's almost as short as that dwarf, Altheda."

Mother frowned. "Father, such unkind words. Altheda is a devoted friend."

Luther shrugged, more interested in what I had in my shopping basket now than listening to women.

"Altheda and I are having tea together next week," Mother told Veda. "She'll be so happy to see you again."

"I look forward to seeing Altheda." Veda looked at me once more. "Come closer, Sabine. Brona tells me you are quite a good apothecary and skilled with numbers."

Mother poured more tea and offered me a cup. Then she looked over at Veda and said, "She is quite smart. She helps run the magic shop and keeps the books." Then she turned to me. "Veda's just moved to Crimson Hollow. She was also my favorite professor at the Academy."

Mother rarely spoke of her time at the Academy and even rarer with joy. They expelled her for the sin of becoming pregnant out of wedlock, which did not endear me to this mysterious lady. How could mother consider her a friend?

I pulled my dragon basket closer, uncomfortable with the stranger. "You taught at the Academy and want to move here? Why? Crimson Hollow isn't exactly cosmopolitan. It's a one-wizard town."

"A small village is a solace after living in such a large city," Veda replied. "My family once owned a tower outside the village, about ten miles from here. I just bought it."

"The crumbling old tower overlooking the river?" I asked. "I know the place. It's very rundown. When I was growing up, the other kids were scared of it. They whispered it was haunted or cursed. When I was twelve, I explored the tower and even climbed to the top. No ghosts. Just some irate owls who hated it when I trespassed on their territory."

"Sabine!" Mother cried. "That was dangerous!"

"The tower or the owls?" I jested.

Veda only laughed. "A bold venture for one so young. Did someone dare you?"

"I dared myself," I replied, sitting across from her. Despite my mistrust, I found Veda fascinating and glamorous.

"It was still foolish," Mother added. "You could've been hurt."

"The tower needs repairs and a little love," Veda said to me. "I was in town contracting workmen, so I thought I would stop in and say hello. I've retired from teaching and focus on my research now. Brona was just telling me about how you rescued this precious pukis egg. Do you know anything about these tiny, mischievous dragons?"

"I'll learn."

Mother knocked her teacup over. I thought it an accident until I saw her pupils dilate. Her body convulsed, and she began wailing. I jumped up and rushed to her. "Mother!" I cried, taking her by the arm. "Come upstairs and rest."

"Get your hands off me, you stupid bitch!" She who birthed me raged, pushing me away. She paced the kitchen tearing at her hair, weeping uncontrollably, cursing violently. I grabbed her hands, talking to her in low, soft tones. She calmed for a moment, then broke off screaming.

Luther picked her up forcibly. I hated it, but it was the only way to control her when she was like this.

"Take Brona upstairs," Veda told him. "I'll prepare something to calm her down."

I followed Luther to Mother's bedroom. She howled like a mad cat as she fought him. Suddenly Veda was in the room with a glass filled to the brim with a blue concoction. "Drink!" she commanded.

My mother paused her ravings when Veda held the glass to her lips. She obediently drank it down. After a moment, she sat on the bed, dazed and compliant. I plumped her pillow and guided her to lie down on the bed. Veda covered her with a quilt.

"I'm sorry you had to see that, Sorceress," Luther apologized.

"Nonsense," Veda said. "I'm glad I was here. Are her episodes always this violent?"

"Sometimes, but this one is not so bad," I replied. "What did you give her?"

"Just valerian to calm her until this fit passes. She'll sleep for hours. Stay with her, Luther," Veda said. Then she turned to me. "I want to know what she has been taking."

"Oh no!" I cried. "My poor egg!" I rushed downstairs to the kitchen in a panic. I didn't see any broken shells anywhere. Or my egg. Then I glanced up to see my precious pukis egg hovering in the air.

Veda suddenly materialized in a lavender mist beneath the floating egg. "I cast a levitation spell on the poor thing during the confusion." The dragon egg gently floated down to its homemade nest with a wave of her hand.

My stomach gradually unknotted as I cradled it, relieved. "Thank you, for helping Mother and for saving my little dragon egg. Levitation is a tough spell, as is teleportation."

"Hard enchantments to master," she agreed. "I was harder."

I understand that.

"Your mother told me how you rescued the pukis egg," she said. "I'm glad you did. Kindness and compassion are rare in this world. Many turn a blind eye, but you did not. Perhaps fate guided you to bring it home."

"I don't believe in fate," I replied, stroking the warm shell. "I believe in myself."

She nodded approvingly. "Good. Most people blame fate for life's tribulations."

I still didn't trust her, but she calmed my mother and saved my egg. Still, there was more to Lady Veda Arcana than just a retired professor. I sensed secrets in this sorceress.

CHAPTER 3

I struck a match and lit the lamp. The glow barely brightened the bleak attic, which had only one tiny round window, which filtered thin rays of light from outside. I bumped my head on the low ceiling beams and cursed. Even being small wasn't helpful up here.

I set the lantern on the floor and rummaged through the musty space crowded with chests and crates packed with old junk and books shrouded with cobwebs. Crumbly books stacked haphazardly like doomed towers tumbled in my quest when I bumped them. I cursed Luther if he'd sent me up here on a fool's quest. I searched through books moth-eaten, moldy, or chewed by hungry mice, the decayed pages fit only for the hearth fire. I did find a few mystical volumes in a small chest, but other than the covers, I could not read the contents within. *I should ask Mother about those later,* I thought. I harbored a suspicion they might have belonged to relatives passed, hidden away to forget the magic loss the Fables suffered.

I was on my third trunk when I found the dragon manual Luther assured me would be here. It was bigger than I imagined. Over forty chapters and even bonus drawings of various pukis dragon breeds! Thankfully, the volume was unchewed and retained a solid binding. I hugged it with joy. Now I could begin learning about my little dragon egg.

I spotted a trunk draped in shabby green velvet, forgotten for gods know how long. Curious, I ripped off the velvet, waving and coughing at the dust cloud I created, but revealing a lovely cedar chest—too fine to be shoved into this grimy attic! I touched the lid, which was carved with beautiful runes and clearly custom-made. I coveted this beauty immediately. I would ask Mother first, I decided. I fretted this chest might have belonged to my namesake, Grandmother Sabine. If this were true, Luther would pitch a fit if I even touched her belongings.

Curiosity beckoned me to open it, and a faint mist of magic touched the air with fresh sweetness when I dared. Within I found a few books—common editions on magical symbols and lore, and a couple of mystic books strong with the scent of magic, their immaculate pages unreadable but untouched by the ravenous mice and moths. Expensive treasures too. Beneath the books, I found tokens of girlhood—colorful glass beads, wooden and crystal charms, and a bouquet of pink flowers bound with blue silk ribbon, still unbelievably fresh and alive. I inhaled the ripe scent of magic on them. No wonder. A mystic spell still clung to the flowers, giving them unnatural life.

Beneath the books lay a folded gray gown of fine quality, the hem and sleeves embroidered with white rune symbols. I found a few small pocket tomes, filled with runic symbols written in blue ink. Some pages were blank, perhaps because they contained the mystic language hidden from us baseborns. I thumbed through the visible writings and recognized my mother's hand.

This was my mother's dream chest. An old tradition in which girls keep their precious wishes tucked away. Girls usually collect bridal tokens, but a mageborn collects magic. It hurt to see my mother's lost dreams concealed in a musty attic. I touched the neatly folded gown, the touch velvet smooth. Students at the Mystic Academy wore such uniforms. I saw Marigold wear a similar gown when she was first accepted at the Academy. She flaunted it for days as she bragged to the whole town about her acceptance. My mother merely sighed, remarking how mystic students wore the uniform at school, not at home.

I wondered about the fragrant flowers in my hand. Were they from her deceitful lover who abandoned her and rejected me? Did she cast a spell to preserve them, or did he? The urge to crush those flowers welled up inside me until I thought I would burst. My hands and face burned hot as fiery coals. I flung the bouquet back into the chest and slammed the lid. I covered the chest with the ragged velvet like a bad memory.

My headache raged for hours, like an angry troll in my head thundering to get out.

# # #

Over the next few weeks, I focused on learning all the secrets of the pukis dragon. I carried the egg with me everywhere, even when I went to the market or for a walk. I garnered curious stares and whispers, which I ignored. I studied each chapter of the book thoroughly as I impatiently watched my colorful egg for signs of his hatching. I wasn't sure if the pukis would be a he or she, it was just a feeling. I preferred to think of it as a dragon egg too. I wanted to give him some esteem. Though, after weeks of patient care and observance, I worried he might never hatch.

I was still fretting when I started supper that night. Tired after a long day in the shop and not in the mood for much fuss, I decided to make bacon on toast. I tucked my dragon egg basket near the stove so I could keep an eye on him.

"Hatch!" I muttered as I sliced the bacon, willing the birth of my dragon through my wish alone.

Luther sat at the table, reading the paper. "Talking to your egg again? That's grounds for the asylum, missy."

"I am maintaining a positive attitude despite adversity."

Luther threw the paper down. "Damned elections. Why do folks even bother to vote? They're always rich, mageborn, or noble-blooded who rule. They don't care about us as long they have their power and gold. Nothing changes! Nothing! Damned idiots."

"You're raging at the paper again, which is also grounds for an asylum," I remarked.

"Don't get so snippy, girl. The world's a rotten place. Full of corruption and poverty, except for the few who have the money and rank, of course. Might as well bring back the monarchy."

"There's been no monarchy in the Ravenna Republic for over two hundred years. At least with an elected premier, we need only suffer seven years of their rule."

"How's that any better?" Luther sniffed.

"My point is, kings can live for decades and rule whether they deserve to or not," I replied. "The people now vote for their leader and have some kind of choice. The word on the street is Alexander Duchene will win again. Didn't you vote this week, Luther?"

"Why bother," he shrugged. "Same folks always win. And what do you know about politics?"

"I studied it in school. It's a shame I can't vote until next year. The High Elections won't come again for the premier for years." I grimaced as I turned the sizzling bacon, impatient for it to cook and for Luther to shut up. It irked me I was denied the vote because of my age and he didn't even try.

"Bah! You're just a mollycoddle. The world's harsh, missy." He returned to his crumbled newspaper. "Nothing ever goes good in this world. Might as well fry up that stupid egg too. Never gonna hatch."

"Misery," I countered, slicing the bread with vengeance as I stared at my egg.

My mother entered the kitchen and laughed. "A watched egg never hatches, dear. Though you should watch the frying pan."

Grease sputtered in the pan and I stepped back. "Damn it!"

"Language, dear," she chided.

I fixed a cup of Mother's medicine while the bacon fried. I used the new formula Veda gave me to combine with Altheda's medicinal tea regimen. Veda heartily approved of Altheda's old prescription but added a dried and finely powdered flower of a southern carnivorous plant I was not familiar with. The concoction was bright red. It even turned the tea red as blood. I poured hot water over the herbs in Mother's favorite teacup. A noxious odor issued from the new mixture. She had been calm for weeks now, so the stink was worth it. "There now, it's medicine time. I added extra sugar to cut the bitterness. So drink up."

"I'll drink, you bossy girl," she said with a sigh. I watched her sip from her cup obediently before I returned to the stove and my egg watch. "Even if the smell isn't acceptable, the taste is tolerable. Have you decided what you want for your birthday?"

"Cake and a live dragon," I quipped and turned the sizzling bacon. I paused, the truth slowly dawning. "Mother, what day is this?"

"Happy birthday, darling." She smiled and clapped her hands. "Come in, ladies, I think she finally realized it's her birthday."

Altheda and Veda entered the kitchen, showering me with hugs and kisses. I laughed, happy to see them both, and relished the hugs, glancing hopefully at Mother, who remained at the table. For a brief moment, I thought she would join in and give me a birthday hug or kiss too. She did not, and the moment died a natural death. I always wanted her physical affection, but it was the one thing she never gave me. I never understood why.

Veda handed me a slim package wrapped in blue silk. "A small token for your birthday."

"Thank you," I said, curious about her mystery gift. I was not expecting a present from Veda.

"Presents after dinner," Mother insisted, plucking the gift from my curious fingers and laying it with two other brightly wrapped packages already on the kitchen table.

I had been unsure about Veda at first, but her kindness to mother made her golden in my eyes. She became a regular visitor in our home, and even Altheda liked her. I longed to ask her questions about my mother's Academy days and find out if Veda had ever defended her when they expelled her. But I withheld my probing questions. I think I was afraid of her answer.

"Don't burn the bacon," Luther grumbled.

"Stop fussing!" I shouted. Then I put the first batch of bacon on a towel and added more strips to the frying pan. I put the bread in the oven to toast.

"I see Luther is his usual chipper self," Altheda remarked dryly.

"Come, Father. Wish Sabine a happy birthday," Mother said.

Luther sniffed, not even looking up from his paper. "Happy birthday," he mumbled.

I ignored Luther's indifference. I was more interested in Altheda's spice cake smothered in vanilla icing. Perhaps I might have cake for dinner. I hugged Altheda. "I completely forgot about my birthday. Oh, the cake is lovely. Thank you!"

Altheda laughed, cutting the cake into slices. "Your mum thought it would be a nice surprise. Come on, Luther, make yourself useful and fetch us some plates and forks."

Luther folded up his paper and obeyed, casting a sour glance at Altheda. She never tolerated his boorish attitude. Altheda's dwarf size never hindered her. He put the dishes on the table and returned to his newspaper, pretending to ignore us. I suspected his true goal was a share of my delicious-looking birthday cake. At least he wasn't drunk today. I took his soberness as a birthday blessing.

An incessant, rapid knocking on the kitchen door disrupted our little celebration. Luther threw down his paper again and stomped to the door. "You chatty hens are too busy to answer the door! Damned nuisance, I say."

My happy mood vanished when Luther opened the door. Marigold stood there on the arm of a bony-faced young man. He was a picture of grim severity in a black suit and cloak, tall with floppy brown hair and a prominent brow ridge that eclipsed dark eyes. Marigold sauntered in without invitation, her peach-and-white flounced skirts swirling.

"Sabine!" she exclaimed, embracing me and brushing each cheek with a kiss.

Dumbfounded, I fell mute. Did I die? Was I banished to a strange hell populated with Marigolds to torture me? I thought I was done with her after our last bitter encounter. Then Marigold's syrupy smile focused on Veda the way a snake spellbinds a poor mouse. As she abandoned me for better prey, I rubbed her kisses from my cheeks. I glanced at her companion, who awkwardly remained in the doorway until my mother motioned him inside. He stepped in and politely removed his hat.

"What can we do for you, Marigold?" I asked. "I'm afraid the shop is closed for the day, but I'm sure Luther would be happy to assist you."

"Would I?" Luther asked.

"Yes, you would," I hissed.

Marigold delicately removed her lace gloves. "I just thought I'd pop in and say hello to my good friend, Sabine." Then she bolted to Veda's side. "Oh heavens, I see the honored Sorceress Veda Arcana is gracing your establishment. Surely, you remember me. I'm Lady Marigold Graven, and this is my betrothed, Pastor Greeley Havelock. I had a class with you at the Academy on spell composition last year."

"How could I forget," Veda replied politely.

"My father, Sir Thomas Graven, has been anxious to invite you to our circle of friends in our quaint town." Marigold fluttered her hanky with each syllable as she directed her conversation to Veda, who listened patiently. "Goodness, I'm only home for two months before I return to the Academy, yet I feel completely bored here already in this tiny hamlet. I know you must especially feel desolate here after the thrill of living in Túr Solas, but we do have some charming things to offer our more prestigious citizens. Associating with the proper people is crucial, as you know, Veda. As leaders of our quaint local society, we wanted to welcome you personally to Crimson Hollow. Father sent messages to your tower, of course. When I was coming to see dear Sabine, I thought I recognized your carriage out front, so I knew I must invite you myself."

"Do forgive me, but I have been occupied with my research and the restoration of my tower, Lady Marigold," Veda replied.

"Oh, do call me Marigold."

"Well, Marigold, surely you want to offer good wishes to Sabine on this day," Veda said.

"For what?" Marigold replied, her tiny brows creased in confusion.

"Her birthday," Altheda piped in. "I mean, you're such a *dear friend* to Sabine."

It was all I could do to not to fall to the floor in hysterics.

"Oh, of course," Marigold muttered. She tugged at her fiancé's arm. "Aren't I here for Sabine's birthday, Greeley?"

"Indeed, my love," he nodded with confusion.

"So he does speak," I murmured to Altheda.

"A religious miracle perhaps?" Altheda whispered back. "I saw her carriage parked down the street when we arrived. I think she was lying in wait, like a lacy spider."

"I just hope they don't stay for cake," I moaned.

"I wish to invite you personally to our services, Sorceress," Greeley said as he bowed. He turned to us. "I also wish to extend the invitation to this humble house as well. I have been pastor here for only a few months, but I have not seen any of you at church yet."

"We don't attend," Luther replied bluntly.

Brona's diplomacy was subtler. "Pastor Havelock, what my father means is we're often too occupied with our business. Perhaps we shall attend soon." My mother had a nice knack for quelling Luther's snappish answers.

"You one of them reformers?" Luther asked.

"I'm a member of the Reformed Church of Unified Gods," Greeley announced proudly. "My family converted from the old religion several years ago. We see the two founding gods, Ystenia and Hadúron, as the core of the faith. The other deities serve them and are saintly representations of their powers as they serve the race of man."

"I belonged to the old faith," Luther remarked. "Never saw reason to change. Lots of fuss and bother, if you ask me. Gods don't need us anyway."

I dreaded a tirade over religion. I never went to church. I knew Luther stopped going to church when the plague took his wife and his magic. Mother never attended except on the anniversary of her mother's death. I was curious to ask Greeley how the other gods felt about being demoted to little more than saints in the Reformed Church, but as it was my birthday, I just wanted him and Marigold gone so I could have my cake.

"No matter your denomination, the gods watch over us all," Greeley replied seriously. "Religion feeds the soul better than bread."

Obviously, Pastor Greeley Havelock never missed a meal, despite being reedy thin. "I'm sure the gods will forgive us," I interrupted. "They have better things to do, after all, than wonder who is praying to them."

"Sabine!" My mother tried to appear shocked, but I noticed the faint curve of a smile.

With solemn sincerity I added, "Well, I can assure you, Pastor Havelock, I do say my prayers. In fact, I just made a most earnest prayer a moment ago," I said, staring at Marigold.

Even Luther chuckled, but my humor ended when Marigold eyed my basket with the egg near the stove. She danced over to it, tapping it with her finger. "How pretty! Is it magical? Is it for sale?"

"No!" I burst out, rushing to my precious dragon nest. "Not for sale!"

"Why not? What is it?" she demanded.

How could someone who studied at a famous mystic academy not know the world's magical creatures? My mother once told me possessing magic does not promise intelligence, I reminded myself.

"It's just a silly pukis egg," Luther sniffed. "Bloody nuisances. Won't hatch anyway."

"It will so!" I insisted.

"Oh well, no one keeps them as pets anymore," Marigold said, her tone dismissive. "I thought it might be something interesting. Why are you even caring for it? It should be discarded. No one would want it."

"I do," I snapped, hating her even more for such a cruel remark.

"I'm helping Sabine care for the dragon egg," Veda interjected coolly. "It is a special project. Research for the Mystic Circle, you know. I'm not at liberty to discuss it."

"Thank you for coming," Mother told Marigold, gently guiding her to the door. "Do have a good evening. Send my regards to your parents."

Pastor Greeley gently took Marigold's arm. Even he looked embarrassed. I almost felt sorry for him.

"We shall leave you to your supper." Greeley bowed to me. "Birthday blessings, Mistress Fable. Come, Marigold, we should return home."

Marigold frowned but allowed Greeley to lead her out the door. Then a loud cracking sound behind me alerted my attention.

"My damned bacon better not be burning!" Luther shouted.

It wasn't the bacon.

CHAPTER 4

Luther banged his fist on the table. "Curses, you silly women, my bacon's burning!"

"Shut up!" I cried. Anxious, I watched the eggshell's crack. His bacon could burn to cinders for all I cared, because my baby dragon was finally coming into the world.

"It won't breathe fire, will it?" Altheda mumbled.

"You've read too many fairy tales," I said, laughing as I watched my little dragon poking through the egg's prison. "Once he's out of the shell, we just need to keep him warm. And feed him."

"Feed him what?" Altheda asked.

"How about feeding me?" Luther suggested.

"Father, really!" Mother sighed. "This is important! You're not helpless!"

"Bacon's burning, I say!" Luther insisted. "Why are you bothering with that damned egg? It'll hatch itself. What about me?"

I sniffed something burning and jumped back. Black smoke spewing from the oven like an angry fire-breathing dragon was the problem, not the bacon. In a better humor, I would have found the fire-breathing part ironic.

"The bacon's fine, but the bread's burned!" I cried.

Grabbing an oven mitt, Mother pulled out a pan of charcoaled toast. The smoke made us cough and laugh through teary eyes. Well, except for Luther.

"Damn, the toast is a pile of smoking coal! Do I have to starve to death?" Luther grumbled. "All this muck about silly birthdays and presents. Now, this damned thing is hatching."

"Shut up, Luther!" Altheda shouted.

"Dear gods, stop your whining!" I cried. I took the sizzling bacon off the stove. "I worked all day in the shop and did the inventory to boot. You didn't even show up until noon, then you napped in the corner." I grabbed a plate, scooped slices of bacon on untoasted bread, and shoved it in front of Luther. "There! Eat your supper. If you can feed yourself, that is."

Luther bit into his bacon sandwich. "Better open a window to clear out this smoke."

"Luther, it's Sabine's birthday," Altheda chastised him. "Why be so damned difficult?"

"Keep your words to yourself, Dwarf," Luther warned.

"Make me," Altheda said. "Your balls are low enough even for me to snap off, old man." Altheda may be only a little over four feet tall, but her temper could bring down a giant.

Luther scowled and turned away from her as he chewed.

"Sabine, look!" Mother cried.

I turned to see a tiny head, a deep blue with faint green markings, poke out of the shell, miniscule wings damp and weak. He roared in a squeaky voice as he struggled to shed his shell fragments. "It's a male," I whispered, fearing I would startle my little dragon.

"How do you know?" Altheda asked.

"See the tiny crest on his head?" I said, daring to touch him. "The book says only males have those. I knew he'd be a boy dragon." Bright-green eyes gazed up at me, and my heart was lost. I was the first one he saw! I was relieved since the book did not clarify if they imprint at first sight. He didn't bite or snarl at me when I touched him, but eagerly sniffed my hand. Then he looked up at me with such trust! He mewled as he shook off the broken shells like colorful beads. Shaky and wobbly, he roared and tumbled over! Well, it was more like a chirp than a roar. I scooped him up in my hand and carefully dried him off with a dish towel. His fragile wings were thin blue membranes, and I feared I might tear them. He snorted in a funny way, and I laughed.

"He's adorable," Mother said.

"How big do they get?" Altheda whispered, passing a small plate of bacon and bread to Mother and Veda. "They don't grow to a giant size, do they?"

"The pukis breeds are usually quite small, no more than the size of a house cat or small dog. Some are even smaller," Veda said. "They all pretty much look the same at birth, and the eggshell colors denote the shades of the babies."

"And he's hungry I think," Veda said, munching on a slice of crisp bacon.

Indeed, his mouth opened wide as a baby bird's, eager for food. I grabbed a slice of bacon and crushed it, then fed him the pieces, which he gobbled up with gusto.

"He loves it!" Veda said, then she laughed.

"Who doesn't love bacon?" I replied, also laughing, feeding him more. "My, he's a hungry little fellow."

"They are omnivorous, but they do prefer meat," Veda told me. "He is a fine little fellow."

The three of us doted on the newborn dragon around the stove, eating our bacon sans toast and ignoring Luther's grumbles for more food. "Is this all I get?" he demanded. "Not enough to feed a mouse. Sod the toast, just give me more bacon."

I fed my dragon the last piece," I said, grinning. "We're all out." Then I laughed at Luther.

"I'll make some more," Mother offered. "You sit down, dear. It's your day."

"Damn it to hell, I'm going out," Luther said, grabbing his coat. "A man can't even get a decent supper in his own home."

"Father, don't be so spiteful! It's Sabine's birthday," Mother protested.

"I don't care," he snapped. "I see no point in making a fuss over your brat or that damned creature." He grabbed a huge piece of cake and marched out, slamming the door.

"Good riddance," Altheda said. "Sadly, it means he'll be drinking his supper at the tavern."

It didn't surprise me. Whenever Luther craved a bottle, he became short-tempered and took any excuse to escape to the nearest alehouse.

"I hope he doesn't come home drunk," Mother said with a sigh.

"He will," Altheda replied dryly. "You need me to stay tonight in case he gets too rowdy?"

"We'll be fine," Mother replied. "He's just in one of his moods."

"That man's always in a mood," Altheda replied.

"Oh dear, I'm so sorry he's spoiled your birthday," Mother said to me.

"Nonsense," I replied. "Luther always has these temper snits when he wants to drink. I don't care a fig about his moods, and neither should you. I have my dragon and a wonderful cake with gooey icing. It's perfect. We'll have a lovely time. Nothing can spoil this day for me."

"What will you call your little dragon?" Veda asked.

My dragon roared for more bacon with his gravely, chirpy voice. I smiled and stroked his little head. He was fiercely determined despite being so tiny and helpless. I often felt the same in the world. "His name is Rory," I announced, cradling him in my hands.

#

We all doted on Rory as we ate cake without Luther's sulky presence spoiling things. As the night wore on, I noticed Mother's anxious glances at the door. I'm sure she worried Luther would stagger in drunk, but as darkness fell, there was no sign of the old man.

Later that night, I couldn't sleep. I sat on my rumpled bed, watching over my baby dragon. After Rory stuffed himself with bacon bits, he curled up in his basket and fell asleep. His funny little snoring sounds made me smile. I thought about my life. Turning seventeen did not change things. What was my future? I was surrounded by magic every day in the shop. Magic. I could have been a sorceress, like my mother before the fever destroyed her. How could I rise up and command my own life without it? It was foolish dream-weaving, for my mother's fragile condition bound me here. It would not be so bad, if not for Luther. I was still a baseborn bastard, but when I looked at Rory, I sensed some hope in a magical future. Maybe I was a fool.

My soul-searching kept me busy for hours that night.

I looked over my birthday presents. Mother gave me a pair of blue gloves I had coveted for months in the dress shop. Veda's present intrigued me. Wrapped in exquisite blue silk was a lovely cylinder-shaped charm on a silver chain. I would keep the silk as a scarf. The charm made me feel glamorous. I'd never had any real jewelry before. A strong scent emanated from the charm. I sniffed and shook it. Veda told me the herbs inside it were for luck. I could always use luck. I put it on, finding the aroma pleasant but nothing I recognized.

Altheda gifted me a small basket of my favorite cookies with chocolate chips and walnuts. I grabbed one and munched on it, the sweetness comforting as it awakened my hunger. Almost at the same time, Rory grew fussy. I thought he needed to be fed again. "Come on, baby," I said. "Let's cook up some bacon porridge."

My eyes felt tired, and the effects of staying up all night caught up with me. Fresh hot coffee and breakfast would set me right. I put on my robe and checked on Rory, I didn't want to leave him alone, so I picked up his basket and slipped out of the room. Thinking of Rory and my rumbling stomach, I hoped we had bacon left in the larder.

Downstairs, an incessant knock on the door detoured me from my kitchen destination. Who could it be at this hour? I decided that Luther probably forgot his house keys. I went to the front door, but instead of Luther, a gray-cloaked figure leaned against the glass.

I took my hand off the doorknob and backed away. "We're closed. Come back later."

"Please," a hollow voice begged. "I mean you no trouble. I just need medicine. I've been traveling for a long time. When I rode into the village, I saw your sign. You're magic dealers. I'm a shapeshifter. I just need some wylsavan root. That's all. I can pay and then I'll go."

Hesitant to let in any stranger at such an hour, I ran and put Rory's basket behind the counter. I seized the broom for defense. Through the narrow glass window, pained eyes pleaded beneath a voluminous hood. Shifters are a mysterious lot, from what I've read, at least. They are powerful and held in high esteem among the mystic castes. They also suffer from health issues because of their shifting. He held up his left hand and cast a light spell to show me the tattoo of the shapeshifters. I'd never met a shapeshifter before in my tiny backwater town, so I was curious.

He leaned against the doorway. "Please… I just need wylsavan root. Do you sell it?"

I unlocked the door and stood back, giving him space to enter but keeping my broom ready. "Yes, but take care. This is a decent house," I warned.

"Thank you. I apologize for the wretched hour," he whispered, stepping inside the shop. "I have been traveling for some time. I have urgent business and ran out of the root."

Shapeshifters have perilous lives. Their magic can take on any human or even animal shape, making them valuable as spies and assassins also makes them a target. The sorcery they use is draining. It takes a toll on their health, leading to a number of health issues.

"It's alright," I replied, closing the door. "I was up anyway. I'll prepare it for you. Do you prefer liquid or powdered?"

"Powdered is easier to travel with, and I can add it to any drink," he replied in a hoarse voice. "Are you scared of me, girl?"

"No," I replied boldly. "Because I have this powerful broom to protect me." I grinned. Although shapeshifters are respected by the magical castes, most baseborn folk fear them as much as they fear necromancers. His face was shrouded by the gray hood. I just saw a man in pain.

"What is your name?" he asked.

"Sabine. Sabine Fable. May I ask yours?"

"Kalem Shura, Lady Fable," he answered with a slight bow.

"I'm afraid I'm just Mistress Fable. I'm neither mageborn nor noble. Just call me Sabine."

"To me, you are noble, Lady Fable."

He winced with pain, so I hurried. I wondered if he was a spy on some mission and had to spend long periods in disguise. Wylsavan is a potent drug designed to treat pain, nervous conditions, and spasms. Shapeshifters suffer from these maladies. I hurried and scooped a healthy amount of the powder into a bag and closed the tie. A cry startled me. Rory had woken up. I handed Kalem the bag.

"Is that a baby pukis crying?" Kalem asked, taking his herbs.

"Yes, he just hatched last night, on my birthday as a matter of fact." I looked under the counter, and sleepy green eyes greeted me. I picked up the basket and put it on the counter. I picked him up, scratching his head. He made odd gurgle sounds and leaned back, enjoying it. "He thinks I'm his mother. I saved his egg when his mother died," I whispered.

"I'm glad you did." He left two gold coins on the counter, far more than the powder was worth. "They are cute when small, but very mischievous."

"That makes us a good match." A ruckus from the kitchen followed by a series of vulgar curses announced Luther's return. "Thank you, Sorcerer Shura. I hope the medicine helps. Excuse me."

I rushed into the kitchen to find a drunken Luther rifling through the pantry, knocking over tins and sending cabbages rolling onto the floor. Pots and pans scattered.

"Where's my breakfast!" Luther demanded. He slammed a cupboard shut. "What are you staring at, you little bastard? I'm hungry."

I'd had an ugly hunch Luther would return drunk. Rory shivered in my arms, and I held him close. Luther's moods could be volatile, and I was scared for my newborn and frightened Rory, now wishing I had left him in my room. "Hush, you'll wake Mother. It's barely dawn. Sit down and be still! I'll make some coffee and breakfast."

"I want breakfast now!" Luther droned. Disheveled and reeking of stale beer and sweat, he dropped into a chair. "Not any porridge slop either. I want bacon and eggs."

"You'll get your breakfast. Just be quiet," I hissed.

"Why you fussy about being so quiet? Did I heard a man's voice out there? What you hiding? You behaving like a tramp? Got some illicit goings-on with some man, missy? Or should I say whore?" He sniffled and looked up at me, his red face angry. He bolted up and grabbed my arm. "Yes. Turning whore … Just like your mother. Whore!"

"My mother is no whore!" I screamed, struggling against his grip. "Let me go. You're drunk!"

"Whore!" he raged. Then he punched me in the face with a closed fist.

I stumbled back against the stove but managed to hold on to Rory, who squeaked in terror. The blow dazed me. Blood ran from my nose, and my eye throbbed. Damn.

Luther removed his leather belt and seized me by the neck. "Stop!" I gasped. As he lifted me up, choking me, I kicked at him. Rory yelped and snapped, biting Luther's finger. His little teeth were so tiny and soft that he didn't even leave a mark. Luther stumbled back more from inebriation than Rory's attack, his florid face murderous now. He shoved me to the floor and swung his belt. I turned over, holding Rory close to protect him. The familiar sting of his belt on my back struck me again and again as I struggled to get to my feet and escape.

"Let's see how pukis cooks up, shall we?" Luther threatened and grabbed at Rory. I screamed and kicked at him, cursing with fury as I kept my baby dragon out of his reach.

Suddenly Luther's body lifted off the floor, was hurled across the room, and landed in a heap in a corner. He cursed as he scrambled to his feet to fight but paused when he saw who'd thrown him.

Out of the corner of my eye, I saw Kalem Shura standing in the kitchen doorway, shimmering with magic. Luther's fury quickly dissolved into fear at the ominous sight of the gray-cloaked shapeshifter.

"Do not harm her further," Kalem said.

I looked at Luther, his terrified face a rare sight. When I looked back, the shapeshifter had gone.

Mother rushed into the kitchen, her long blonde hair wild and her face fearful. "What is going on? Father, what did you do?"

"Nothing, Mother. Please, go back to bed," I begged. "He's just drunk. It's alright."

It wasn't alright, but I didn't want my mother to panic over Luther's mad fit.

"I think my arm's broken! Your bastard daughter did this!" Luther raged.

"I did nothing!" I cried, holding a shaking Rory close to me. "You're drunk and threatened to cook Rory!"

Mother collapsed into a chair and began to cry. I shot a deathly stare at Luther, who did not look me in the eye. "See what you did!" I said.

Holding Rory in my arms, I ran to my mother and knelt before her. "Please don't cry, Mother. A customer needed treatment, so I opened the shop. I would never have opened the door, but he was a shapeshifter in need of medicine. He paid me triple its worth for my kindness. You know how Luther gets when he's drunk. The shapeshifter heard us fighting and intervened to protect me."

"Get your bastard out of my house," Luther bellowed. "Or you can both fend for yourselves in the gutter. I own this place. Do as I say or else."

Mother wept at the sight of us both—me with my bloody nose, a crying pukis dragon in my arms, and a drunken Luther glaring bitterly at me, holding his damaged arm.

CHAPTER 5

My luck flips like a bad pancake. I could not fathom why! For once things had been going so well! Mother's fits stopped, we had food on the table, Rory hatched, and even Luther stopped drinking so much. Until Luther came home drunk that night. Now my life was a nightmare.

Mother sent me to my room and summoned Altheda to examine Luther's damaged arm. I wished the shapeshifter had stayed to help smooth this mess out, but he disappeared. Now, Luther demanded I be thrown out of the house or he'd cast out Mother too. Damn it, damn it, damn it! The old man would do it too, just for spite! As head of household, he owned Fable House.

"You shouldn't provoke him," Mother whispered, gently dabbing ointment on my back. "You know how he gets when he's drunk."

"I'm sorry, Mother. He just makes me so angry."

I always promised to be silent, but that promise was always hard to keep. My back hurt like hell. Mother was not prone to displays of physical affection, like hugs or kisses goodnight, so treating my wounds was one of the rare times she touched me. Even after a clash with Luther a child, she would tend the welts and cuts with tenderness, somehow making the abuse worthwhile.

I cursed at myself, though, for my own unruly temper and stupidity. I should have fled for my beloved woods or run up to the attic to hide when he came home drunk. Stricken by his usual hangover, Luther usually forgot about the previous drunken night, and I'd escape a beating.

Grim thoughts tormented me as I fiddled nervously with my birthday charm, trying to figure out its smell. Plants could be used for healing, beauty, and magic. I knew the deadly and the healing ones, some of which are both. Mother had trained me in the apothecary arts since I could read. Her mother taught her, and my grandmother and namesake, Sabine, was quite renowned for her herbal skill. Nothing was familiar about this scent, and Veda assured me it was for luck. She was wrong. My luck stinks like troll dung.

"Is little Rory doing well?" Mother asked, covering the ointment jar as I eased the blouse over my damaged flesh.

"My baby dragon is fine, but he was scared too." Rory was curled up in my lap and had calmed down. "My birthday must be cursed. Last year, we didn't have money for extras when my birthday came, but you and Altheda made me a cake. Luther came home drunk and itching for a fight then too. My cake ended up smashed on the kitchen wall. It was chocolate too! It's always something with Luther. He hates me, but I hate him even more."

"He doesn't hate you." Mother sighed. "He hates what his life has become. He wasn't always like this."

"He never calls me by my name. It's usually "missy" or "bastard." He hates that you named me after Grandmother."

"It was her idea to name you Sabine if you were born a girl. She supported me keeping you when everyone else told me to give you up."

I wiped away a rogue tear, refusing to cry and further upset her. Mother was my whole world, and all she'd had since my birth had been misery. Luther never kept quiet his opinion about my mother raising me rather than give me up to the local church orphanage. He often needled me when Mother was out of earshot, saying, "I'd have handed you over like a hot potato."

Rory snuggled on my lap, looking up at me with innocent eyes as I lamented my situation. I knew he didn't really understand me. But it helped to have someone, even a newborn pukis, to talk to. I never had friends because I never fit in. An animal doesn't judge you, not even a magical one. They never care about silly things like status or money. They just want love. And bacon.

I gently scratched his head, much to his delight. I was amazed at the touch of his skin, which was not scaly at all but soft, like a thick, rough velvet. "I wonder if you are one of the pukis breeds that can talk. Can you talk, Rory?" Funny little grunts answered me. For a moment, things weren't so terrible, because I had Rory. I picked him up and held him high. "We share the same birthday, little dragon. How's that for fate?" I cuddled Rory and then fed him a dish of porridge with crushed bacon Mother had brought up. She had made me a cheese sandwich, but Luther's beating soured my hunger. I wondered if dragons liked cheese.

A light rap on the door was like a death knell. Altheda opened the door and stepped in. "It's just me. How's our girl."

"She has a black eye and a couple welts on her back," Mother said.

"How black and blue am I?" I asked, afraid to look in the mirror.

Mother applied a cold compress to my eye. "Time will heal it."

Nothing heals in this house. "Am I deformed now?" I asked, tenderly touching the swollen eye.

"No, don't be daft," Altheda said with a laugh.

"Is Luther's arm broken?" I asked.

"No, the old fool's arm's not broken," Altheda said. "Just a sprain. Actually, I think that man's still drunk. Tell me about this mysterious stranger who came in the night."

"He was a shapeshifter," I said. "I saw his sorcerer mark. I almost didn't let him in, but he was clearly in pain and asked only for his medicine. He told me his name was Kalem Shura. He was kind too. Most high mystics aren't kind to common folk, but he was. He liked Rory too. Luther took it into his stupid head that I was whoring myself because he was so damned crocked when he came home."

Mother took my hand and said, "Come downstairs, dear. Let's sort this out. Leave little Rory. Altheda will look after him."

My gut twinge morphed into spasms, but I followed her down to the kitchen. I did not flinch when I faced Luther. I'd done nothing wrong. He looked like a corpse after a three-day wake. Altheda was right. I thought the old coot was still drunk by the way he swayed on the chair. His arm was in a sling and he cradled it like a martyr.

Luther finally glanced up at me, squinting. "Did I do that?" he croaked, taking in my swollen and bruised face.

"Yes," I replied coolly. Maybe he forgot about threatening to throw me out of the house and cook Rory.

"Well, no real harm then," he mumbled, looking down. "Too much beer last night, I suppose. I don't remember. Why did I do that?"

"You were drunk and jumped to conclusions like a rabid jackrabbit," I answered.

He hung his head, pouting as he held his arm. "I told Brona I was sorry. Can you fetch my headache tonic? I feel poorly."

My sympathy was dry. He never told me he was sorry, ever! I glanced at Mother as frustration burned inside me. Something inside snapped. My hands and face flamed hot as I fled the kitchen.

"Come back, dear!" Mother cried. "It's alright! He doesn't even remember what he did or said last night. Have some porridge and fresh coffee. You'll both feel better."

"No, I won't!" I cried, sitting on the stairs. "We shouldn't have to live like this. That old man terrorizes us because he owns the title to this shop. You put up with it!"

"He's your grandfather and we owe him respect."

"Respect or fear? How can I respect such a waste of a man! We slave away while he gets drunk and gambles away what little money we have! He beats me when he's drunk and shrugs it off."

"He wasn't always like this," Mother whispered. "He was kind once. The fever destroyed our lives. Losing my mother devastated him. It's my fault too."

"Because you had a bastard and kept it."

"Fate is cruel to us, but we still must be kind."

"How can I be kind to a man who never misses a chance to call me bastard or hit me? It's not your fault. You didn't bring home that damn plague. It spread throughout the republic without your help. You suffered from its ravages then, and you're still suffering. I saw how upset he made you last night, and he didn't even hit you. He hit me, Mother. Look at my face! He's beaten me for years until I learned to run. I'd keep running too, if not for you. I come back because you need me. I want to protect you, but you can't protect me. It's a circle of damnation."

"I know, which brings me to what I wanted to really talk to you about. Maybe you should stay with Veda for a while."

"What? You're throwing me out?"

"Of course not. Please listen, dear. Veda and I discussed you staying with her days ago, before this dreadful mess even happened. She needs help with research and running her house. She's offered to train you. Give you a position of respect."

"As what? Her maid? I already had an offer to be a servant from Marigold. I turned her down. I will never be anyone's servant."

"No, not as a maid. As her secretary and companion. An honorable role. An assistant to manage her tomes and accounts, and help with her research. You can have a place in this world, outside Crimson Hollow. Start a new life with some security. You're so good with numbers and so smart. It's a shame you did not continue your schooling. This may be a chance for you to rise up before it's too late."

"I don't understand," I said, sitting down on the stairs, my head throbbing, and not from my black eye. "You're sending me away."

"No, I am not. I want you to have more choices than being trapped here in this house and town. I lost my options when the fever took away my magic."

"And because of me," I said.

"No, never. I never regretted having you for an instant. You are my darling girl. The world is cruel, and the weak suffer under its hand. You're tough and resilient. I know how desperate you are to make something of yourself." Mother wearily sat on the stair, shaking her head. "I'm not strong. Veda's potions have helped, but we know my health has been fragile since the fever. I thank the gods every day that you were born strong and healthy. If I die—"

"Stop it!" I cried.

"If I die and Luther is still alive, your life will be a misery if you stay."

"I'm already miserable," I said.

"You could marry one day. I've seen a few boys try to court you. Why don't you accept their affections?"

"I will never marry. Never. Such affections are false, Mother. You know this."

"Not all of them," she whispered. "Some have true hearts. Do not let my situation shadow your future. You are so pretty."

"No, I'm not." I rubbed away a hateful tear. Mother's golden beauty was something fate denied me, along with my magical birthright. My impish face, unruly dark hair, and pale eyes were too odd. I would never charm a rich man with my looks. Nor would I want to.

"You're always so hard on yourself," Mother said.

"I'm practical. I know there's no future for me with a local boy. No one from a good family or even a mageborn would ever consider a dowerless, baseborn bastard as a good match for their son. Why must I wed a poor man just to be married? A promise of poverty is feeble compensation for keeping my virtue. I want to be free. I want to live my own life."

"Then take Veda's offer."

"Why?"

"Magic," my mother whispered. "There is a small chance you could change your fate."

"I have no magic," I replied dryly. "What are you even talking about?"

"Veda researched mage fever for years. She believes the side effects of magic loss can be reversed, even cured. You would have been born with magic too, if not for the fever. Maybe she can help you."

"Then let Veda help you too!" I cried, taking her by the shoulders.

She recoiled, as she often did when touched. I let go. She never liked to be touched by anyone, but it still hurt.

"She cannot help me. When she lasted visited, when you were small, she attempted to restore my magic with an elixir she was working on. But I'm allergic to some key ingredients."

I sat back, stunned. "You never told me this."

"Because it failed. Veda used the treatment on both me and Luther. I was allergic to the formula, and it nearly killed me."

"That's why you were so sick then."

Mother nodded. "Yes. On Luther, it just didn't work. It made him more bitter. It didn't even get rid of his eye twitch. I accepted my fate long ago. Your fate is still unwritten. She could cure you."

"How, if it's so dangerous?"

"Because the treatment cured her," Mother replied.

"Veda had mage fever?"

"Five years ago. Ironic, because she was always studying the disease. Mystical diseases were a focus of her personal research. Veda contracted mage fever and lost her magic. She kept it a secret out of fear and lived in exile, but she never stopped looking. Then she found something in a book. An ancient book. She used the knowledge from it to cure herself, but the cure is volatile. It has different effects on people. She thinks the treatment is different for each person."

"Why can't she help you now?"

"Because the foundation of the cure contains both unicorn root and seeds of the dragon orchid plant. I'm allergic to both. Sabine, listen to me. You're so strong. You never suffered the maladies of mage fever. She may be able to help you. Together you could find a remedy for mage fever. You can be at her side!"

"You know you can't run the shop without me," I insisted. "You never take your medicine unless I remind you."

"You take so much upon yourself. This incident may shake up Luther to change his attitude. He may own this place, but he has forgotten how to run it. I promise to take my medicine."

"You're still sending me away," I said, turning my face away to hide my tears.

"No, I'm sending you toward an independent life," she insisted.

# # #

The next day I was packed off to the dark tower. OK, I'm being dramatic. Veda's tower is not dark, just old and crumbly. Veda sent a proper carriage with two lovely horses and a driver for me, which for a ten-mile journey would have cost a pretty coin. The vanity hidden within me wanted Marigold to see me sitting proudly in such a fancy ride.

"I know you'll never admit it, but I think you'll at least enjoy the peace at Veda's," Mother said, touching my cheek. "She likes you too, so behave and be a good girl."

"Yes, Mother," I mumbled. I focused on Rory, tucked in his little basket on my arm.

"And don't sulk so," she said with a faint smile.

I was still angry at my mother for sending me away, even if I liked Veda. I did not feel comfortable going. My wretched little home was all I had, and leaving my fragile mother in the care of Luther filled me with anxiety. Old coot didn't even show his face to say goodbye. I wasn't surprised. I never expected anything good from him.

Altheda arrived just before I left, carrying a big batch of goodies. The weight of her basket almost made me collapse, filled with brownies, cookies, fruit, sandwiches, and muffins that smelled so heavenly it almost brightened my mood. Almost.

I hugged Altheda. "Make sure Mother takes her medicine. I'll be by to visit when there's time."

"I will," Altheda promised.

The driver helped me into the carriage, like a highborn lady, to a seat with green cushioned upholstery. I was suddenly glad Mother made me wear my best dress, a midnight-blue cotton with black satin trimming on the bodice and sleeves, and fake pearl buttons. It looked nice but wasn't the most comfortable dress. I preferred a comfy tunic and trousers over any fancy dress.

Mother grasped my hand just before we drove off. When I turned to her, she seemed so sad that I almost wept. "You're a Fable, Sabine. Always remember you come from a proud house."

I barely had time to squeeze her hand before the carriage pulled away, the horses quickly gaining speed. I held Rory as we rode through the town toward the forest road. Briefly, I glimpsed Marigold coming out of the dress shop. I just barely caught the shocked look on her face as I rode past in the extravagant carriage.

CHAPTER 6

I couldn't dispel my doubts about leaving my mother alone with Luther. Guilt followed me all the way to Veda's tower, for part of me wanted to leave my home and the other wanted to protect my mother from Luther's excesses.

My thoughts and feelings fled as the carriage pulled up to Veda's home. I could not believe the dramatic change in the crumbling old tower since I scaled its dilapidated stairs as a child on a personal dare. The decrepit ruins had been reborn as Arcana Tower and looked quite nice. Over the weeks since Veda arrived in our small town, broken windows were replaced, and a new red roof fixed any leaks.

Veda welcomed me into her tower with a warm hug and her arms around my shoulders. Stiff in my best gown, I was unfamiliar with such intimacy I handed her Altheda's basket of goodies to cover my discomfort.

"Marvelous!" Veda exclaimed. "She is not only a superb healer, but her baked goods are temptation itself."

Inside the tower, the wooden floors shined like new, and all dust and cobwebs had been vanquished by clever spells. Beautiful carpets covered the floors, and exquisite tapestries hung on the walls. I especially liked one with a red dragon and a sorcerer on a mountain.

"It looks amazing," I said. Rory, exhausted by the excitement, napped in his warm basket. "Was this all regular work or did you use magic?"

"Both. The workmen in town were happy to restore this place. It was pricey but worth it. I believe in supporting local workers and guilds. The rest I enhanced or restored with a simple spell or charm. The plumbing is a bit erratic, but we'll manage. I think your owls must still live in the parapet. I consider them a good omen."

I was self-conscious about my black eye, though Veda knew what happened. She was angry, not at me, but at Luther's violent behavior. She gently touched my face, and a tingling of magic spread through it. Eager to see, I ran to the nearest mirror on the wall. "The bruising and swelling are gone!" I exclaimed.

"I just used a touch of healing magic. I'm not a mystic physician, but we all learn to handle a few scrapes and bruises through simple techniques."

"Mother told me you had mage fever and lost your magic. Then found a cure to restore your powers."

"Yes, it's true. Five years ago," she said.

"What happened? Why doesn't anyone know of this miraculous hope?"

"The Mystic Council rejected my claim. So far, it's worked only on me. I don't think they even tried my theories."

"Why?" I asked. "You think they'd be thrilled to find some hope."

"They reject baseborn medicine as any form of treatment. For them, magic must be key. And though my regimen contains many of the ingredients that are used in magic, it does not require a mage."

"That's the reason?"

"A mageborn prejudice. It has hampered our research into finding both a vaccine and a cure for the side effects. I believe everyone requires different doses of medicine and ingredients. A book I found lists several examples. At first, I thought they were tests or experiments, but my theory is they are different cures. Some ingredients can be toxic or are dangerous to those with certain allergies. Didn't your mother tell you she's deathly allergic to two main components of the cure?"

"Yes, she did," I replied. "I'd like to think we could find a substitute or way to change that for her."

"So do I," Veda said, nodding. "The council never believed I had mage fever. Partly my fault, as I kept my condition secret when it happened. But if you are willing, I will try to cure you, and in return, you can help me study and develop a treatment for all. My main goal is a vaccine to prevent the fever, but that is a different battle. I'll explain more later. This is not a one-potion cure, and I must be careful to ensure you are not allergic or in any danger. Can you be patient as we find out together?"

"Patience never blessed me, but for the chance at being mageborn, I can endure anything. Does that make me a bad person?"

Veda laughed, richly and without malice. "Of course not! You're such a strange child."

# # #

Determined to make myself useful to Veda, I dug in and worked hard putting her financial books in order, cataloged all of her thousands of boxed books before putting them into the library, dusted every corner, wrote dozens of letters at her direction, and organized her incoming correspondence.

Unlike my own flesh and blood, Veda thanked me for my efforts and praised my cooking. It made me work all the harder to please her.

After four weeks, even Veda asked me to ease up my sixteen-hour days. We politely argued but I relented. Walking through the woods was my treat to myself.

I buttoned my jacket against the brisk morning air and cloudy sky that were refusing to recognize summer. The forest floor crunched beneath my feet as Rory, clinging to my shoulder, sulked. He resented being taken from his snugly bed so early, but the pukis manual advised outdoor activities.

"Come on, Rory. Stop being so grumpy," I begged. "You need to learn about nature. Get fresh air. Chase butterflies. It takes more than magic to learn to fly." Over the intervening weeks, I sensed Rory understood me on some level, but so far, he hadn't displayed a talent for speech yet. I could tell when he was pouting based on his sullen grunts. "Come on, it's not that bad," I coaxed.

The wind kicked up, and he burrowed inside my jacket. I sighed in defeat and scratched his head, which he tolerated. I needed to get Rory used to new things, along with housetraining both outside and inside. Once he began exploring outside his basket, I added a small box filled with sand where he could relieve himself, which he finally adapted to after a struggle—a learning process I never wanted to repeat. Pukis poo is stinky. Since he'd hatched nearly a month earlier, being outside was needed not only for opportunities to develop his potty habits but for exercise to strengthen his wings.

"I know, it's chilly this morning" I told him. "Dragons despise the cold. OK, you win. Let's go back to the tower, and I'll warm up your bacon gruel." I wrapped him in my blue scarf, part of the birthday gift that had enclosed the pendent Veda gave me. I touched the pendant, the scent of the herbs inside still strong. It awakened a sense of homesickness too. I missed my mother, my room, and even my favorite coffee cup. Ironically, even a miserable home was still a home.

Mother and Altheda had visited twice in the month I'd been at Veda's. Their carriage ride to and from cost a pretty coin I am sure, for it's a ten-mile trip to the tower. Veda always paid, insisted on it even. Luther never came. A blessed relief. Mother's visits were bliss, spared of Luther's arguments, screaming, and threats of violence. We could actually enjoy a nice meal in peace.

The morning sun had come out, and Rory wiggled out of my scarf, suddenly playful. I spun around, holding him high. "You are getting so big!" He gurgled, lifting his head for a chin rub, my little buddy again. He still couldn't fly, but he fluttered fragile wings with excitement.

I walked back to Veda's tower but stopped at the sight of an unfamiliar figure banging on the front door. It wasn't the grocer. There was no cart laden with our weekly order, and this man was not pudgy and didn't carry the odor of garlic. Tied to a tree near the entrance, a nervous gryphon stamped its feet. I'd never seen one before, so the gorgeous creature fascinated me. But I shifted my focus back to the stranger. Visitors at dawn never bode well. I moved swiftly, snatching up a sturdy fallen branch from the forest floor as the man continued his relentless knocking.

I pressed the blunt end of the branch against the back of his head, and he stopped beating on the door. Good. I was nervous, since he was twice my size and looked strong. "Who are you?" I asked. "This is the tower of Veda Arcana, a great sorceress. We do not take kindly to strangers banging like barbarians at this hour!"

The man lifted his hands in surrender and slowly turned his head. "You're rather petite to be a threat."

"Try me," I challenged, shoving the stick roughly against his neck.

"Ouch, I surrender," he said with a laugh. "I'd rather not be splintered to death. I swear, I'm no stranger and mean no harm. Just tell Veda I'm here, Lady Fable."

Lady Fable? I now recognized the voice and medicated smell of the mysterious shapeshifter from my ill-fated birthday. "Kalem Shura, how did you know it was me?"

"I could never forget my kind savior. Aren't you going to invite me in? I've come a long way."

I relaxed my weapon, pitiful as it was. "You know, you pick the oddest times to show up. Veda's probably still asleep, or she's been up all night with her research."

"Sounds like Veda."

"Does she truly know you?"

"Yes, and I promise to behave, lest your ferocious dragon attack me."

Rory perched on my shoulder, fascinated by the new human. He was neither nervous nor afraid. Instead, my pet stretched out his neck to the shifter for affection.

Kalem gently stroked his head crest. "I see your little dragon is thriving."

Rory perked his head up, chirping as though he knew the conversation centered on him.

I opened the heavy wooden door. "He likes you. He doesn't like everyone. Come inside, but let me tell Veda you're here."

The night Kalem showed up at Fable House seemed so long ago. Then, I never got a good look at his face. But that morning in Veda's tower, he pushed back his hood, and I saw him clearly. A shapeshifter conjures up shadowy images of beings with piercing eyes. They're written that way in tales I read as a girl. But Kalem's face was gentle, clean-shaven with brown hair and eyes. A young man to be sure, but still older than I was. Taller too. But then, almost everyone is taller than me.

"The biggest growth spurts are in the first three months," Kalem commented. "They need to be fed every few hours."

"I know! They're demanding little critters. I've been studying their development in my pukis manual. I'm also learning things about him not listed. Bacon gruel is his favorite food, but he tends to like fruit too, which I didn't expect."

"Pukis dragons are more omnivorous than people think," Kalem said. "Just don't give him chocolate. They're allergic."

"What rude troll was beating on my door at this hour?" Veda asked, moaning as she walked down the stairs, rubbing her eyes but still elegant in her silk robe.

"Well, it's not a troll," I said. "I was just coming to get you. His name is Kalem Shura, and he says he knows you."

"Yes, I know Kalem," she remarked, glaring at him. "You keep the strangest time of any man I know."

"Sorry." He shrugged.

"Have you even slept?" I asked her. "Did you work all night again?"

"The research demanded I stay awake until a couple hours ago. I just got to sleep."

"I made some coffee. It should still be hot. I'll fetch some for us," I offered. Despite being up half the night, she looked luminous. *Must be a spell*, I thought. When I have a sleepless night, I resemble an ancient hag. "Are you hungry? I can make us all breakfast."

"Famished." Veda laughed. "I possess sorcery in all things but cooking. Have you taken your potion yet?"

I nodded, forcing down a wave of exasperation. Before I was to begin her official cure, Veda insisted on testing out the ingredients on me individually for days at a time. Her concerns about allergic reactions were maddening. So far nothing bothered me.

I tucked Rory into his downstairs bed, which was a basket with strips of soft cloth. He had several basket beds throughout the tower, since he was too small to be left alone. More mobile now, at night he'd often slip out of his bed and fall asleep on the pillow above my head.

"Kalem!" Veda exclaimed. "Why are you here at such a rude hour?"

"Veda," he said, grinning and bowing his head. "I apologize for the surprise visit."

She sighed and glanced at me. "Kalem Shura was on his way to see me the night of your birthday," Veda said. "He was tasked to deliver a message to me. He endured a long journey from Túr Solas. I'm glad you were kind and helped my friend. Still, opening the door to any stranger at such an hour was risky."

"There's no good answer to that, is there?" I sighed.

"Veda told me about your grandfather and his foul temper. I don't like men who beat up women, but I feel responsible for any trouble I caused you that night. Forgive me."

"It's not your fault about Luther or his drunken behavior," I replied.

"I notice you don't call him grandfather," Kalem remarked.

"Relation by blood doesn't always mean family."

"A sad fact of life. But my temper got the better of me, and I caused you trouble. For your sake, I hope he wasn't too badly injured."

"He's fine," I answered. "He just sprained his shoulder, but Altheda says he's all recovered now." Rory's cry distracted me and I rushed to his basket. "Sorry, he must be hungry again."

Veda crossed her arms and faced Kalem. "Now, why are you here?"

"A personal message from Alexander Duchene. He requests your return to Túr Solas."

Veda frowned, actually frowned at this! Alexander Duchene was the premier of the Ravenna Republic, newly reelected to office—the most powerful man in the republic!

"I am far too busy with my research," she replied, going to the parlor and sitting in her favorite chair. Kalem followed her there, and I followed him.

"Veda, don't be difficult. You must come back," he said.

"Why?" she snapped. "He let them banish me."

"Two people died," Kalem whispered. "The court blamed you."

My ears latched onto their conversation, stunned by the revelation. *Two people died? Banished? Who banished her? Who would dare?*

"I know!" Veda replied. "They were under my care for weeks and displayed no dangerous symptoms. They tolerated the treatment well. I was careful. Then suddenly they both die on the same day? I find it suspicious. The Mystic Council just assumed my treatment killed them. Instead of letting me help with the investigation, Alexander allowed Lord Mystic Baruti to take over and banish me from Túr Solas after years of service to the Academy and the state. And Albertus Crimm supported Baruti's judgment without evidence."

I felt like an intruder as I watched them argue back and forth until Rory's whimper for food drove my pet and me to the kitchen. It was best to let them fight this out in private. I fed Rory warmed bacon gruel and nervously ate two pecan rolls. Our little province of Shedir is just a meager scrap of land in the Ravenna Republic, and Crimson Hollow an insignificant little village. What quest drove Kalem Shura to travel all the way from the capital to this place?

Now they wanted Veda back. I burned to know what happened. I could never imagine Veda doing anything in such matters without care and caution. Maybe this was why she was being so overly cautious with me. But maybe she had been treating them for something else. Upset and feeling a headache coming on, I ate the last pecan roll, sharing a few flaky crumbs with Rory, who remained calm in my lap while I waited. I petted him, and my headache abated.

Veda marched into the kitchen like a warrior marching to battle. "Come, dear. We need to pack."

"What? We're both going to Túr Solas?" I asked.

Veda took me by the shoulders. "Yes, of course. But only if you want to. I will not force you. It's a long story and I will explain."

I nodded, filled with fresh excitement, and then realized I must leave Mother behind. Here I was just ten miles away. If I accepted, I would be leaving to go to another city much farther away. "What about my mother?" I said. "I can't just leave without saying goodbye. And how will I know she'll be safe? We'll be so far away."

"Altheda has instructions to let me know if Luther even steps out of line. Do not worry on that account. But the decision is yours. Talk to your mother and return with an answer." Veda nodded. "I cannot transport you magically to your home because ten miles is too dangerous a leap. Kalem will fly you to town. Have you ever been on a gryphon?" she asked with a grin.

I shook my head, afraid and excited.

Veda laughed warmly. "It will be fine. I'll start packing, and Kalem can hire a carriage to drive us to Gray Moon Bay when you return. It's only about thirty miles from here. From there, we board a ship for Túr Solas. River travel is faster. You may stay here in my tower or come with me. I know it's sudden. If you wish to stay, I will understand. Talk to Brona."

A hundred questions burned inside me. Being polite can be highly frustrating. The terrifying and exciting fact was she offered to take me with her! I was too upended to realize I was going to travel as I always dreamed, but a shroud of fear threatened to mar my old dream.

I scooped Rory up and followed Kalem to the front yard. I'd heard of gryphons, of course, but never seen one until today. They were expensive and high-strung, and only the rich could afford such magical creatures.

In the front yard, a majestic gray-and-red gryphon stood, wings folded in. Its high-pitched cry filled the air, and the creature turned to look at me as I approached a little too eagerly.

"So beautiful," I whispered.

"She is, and like many females, she's got a temper," Kalem warned.

"Is she yours? What's her name?"

"Mathilda, and not mine per se. She belongs to the state gryphon stables in Túr Solas."

"I think she might challenge any human owning her." I hugged Rory and whispered in his ear, "See Rory, one day you'll learn to fly too." He could not understand me, but some pukis dragons have a degree of intelligence and can learn to understand and even speak. I knew my Rory was special, so I wanted to encourage him.

I gingerly reached out my hand to touch the gryphon.

"Stop," Kalem warned. "Their beaks are sharp! These creatures have a brutal bite."

At first, the gryphon recoiled its head, blinking at me suspiciously. Rory chirped nervously, crawling up my arm to perch on my shoulder. The gryphon did not bite me as Kalem feared, but sniffed my offered hand and then lowered her feathered head for an affectionate scratch.

"You do have a way with animals, even volatile gryphons. And, you take dangerous risks for such a little girl," Kalem said, coming up beside me. "You should take better care."

"I'm little only on the outside," I replied. Rory clung to my shoulder, cheeping eagerly at the gryphon, who was unimpressed by my heroic pukis dragon. "Animals like me. I was often able to befriend the forest creatures. But they're better company than humans. She is gorgeous, aren't you girl?" The gryphon nuzzled my hand and allowed me to stroke her feathered neck.

"She does like you," he said, laughing. "Much more than me."

I looked up at Kalem. "How fast can she fly?"

CHAPTER 7

The gryphon ride back to town on Mathilda was thrilling. Is there anything better than flying? I'd decided to leave Rory with Veda, fearing the excitement might be too much for my pukis dragon. I clung to Kalem, and wind gusts beat my face as we soared high above the trees. I loved it. We reached the town in no time, and he guided Mathilda back to earth in front of Fable House, drawing a bit of a crowd with our arrival.

Mother rushed outside to greet me. "My heavens, a gryphon! I haven't seen one since, well, years ago in Túr Solas."

Kalem dismounted first and then helped me off Mathilda's back. "Thank you, girl," I whispered to her before I ran to Mother.

"Mother, we need to talk. Oh, and this is Kalem Shura. He's a friend of Veda's and he's the shapeshifter who came the night of my birthday."

She turned to Kalem. "Welcome to Fable House, Lord Shura."

Kalem bowed deeply. "Forgive the intrusion," he said, "but Veda asked me to bring Sabine."

"Do stay for tea," Mother replied.

I nervously glanced at her, wondering if Luther was about and if he was sober.

"A generous invitation, but first I must make travel arrangements. I also want to add my heartfelt apologies for what happened here a few weeks ago. My presence caused trouble for Sabine. I swear I was here only for medicine. I never intended violence," Kalem explained to my gentle mother, who listened patiently.

"You sought only to protect my daughter. The situation is one we all regret, but I know your intentions were noble. There is nothing to forgive."

"Thank you, Lady Brona. I'll return soon after I've made my arrangements. May I keep the gryphon here while I'm in town? It will be for only a short while. Would you mind watering her, Sabine? She gets cranky when she's thirsty."

I appreciated that he called my mother by the term *lady*, which she had not been called since she lost her magic. "I'll take care of her," I said, patting Mathilda's head.

Kalem bowed to us and left, mingling in with the crowd that gathered around Mathilda. The gryphon merely sat and groomed herself, disdainful of human eyes.

"That was only slightly awkward," I remarked. "He is very nice, Mother. Turns out he is friends with Veda."

Mother nodded but looked worried. "Come inside, dear, and tell me what's going on."

I followed her into the shop, feeling odd. It felt strange now. I hadn't set foot inside this place since I went to live with Veda. "Where's Luther?"

She busied herself with making tea. "Upstairs, sleeping it off. Don't fret, dear. Things have been calm. I run the shop and hide the main cashbox in my room. I leave just enough in the old cashbox for him to drink a little. It's deceitful, but it's worked so far. Now, what is so urgent it required a sorcerer with a gryphon to deliver you to my door?"

"Veda's been summoned back to Túr Solas. She wants me to go with her. I won't go if you need me. It's so far, and what if something happens?"

She smiled and touched my cheek, a rare connection. "Dearest daughter, you must go."

"But what if—"

"There is no what if, there is only now. Follow your path, Sabine. Go with Veda and truly begin a new life. I will be fine. Wait here. Watch the kettle," she said.

She left the kitchen, leaving me to watch the kettle heat. A headache loomed as my hands warmed uncomfortably. She returned smiling and offered me a bouquet of flowers. I shrank at first, seeing the pink flowers tied with blue silk—the same ones I had found hidden in her dream chest in the attic.

"I know you found my dream chest, sweetheart. I hid it away because my dreams were lost. But I could not bear to discard it. The chest is yours now, in the hope your dreams will come true."

"I found those flowers when I was looking for the pukis dragon book. For now, I will leave the chest in your keeping, Mother. I wondered why you kept the flowers, but I could not ask." *Nor could I confess my fear they were from your faithless lover.*

"My mother—your namesake, Sabine—charmed them for me when

I went to the Mystic Academy in Túr Solas. I give them to you now with a mother's blessing. May they bring you magic and hope."

My headache, along with my fear, vanished. I could breathe again. I accepted them and smelled their fragrance. The bitterness I suspected about the poor blossoms melted into joy. I cherished them now. "Thank you, Mother."

"Now, go water that poor gryphon," she said, laughing. "I'll fix our tea."

I carefully placed the bouquet on the kitchen table. I fetched a bucket and filled it with water for Mathilda. Outside, the crowd gathered around her as she remained proud and disdainful, though she eagerly drank the water I brought her. My mood was bright until a shrill laugh grated the air.

"I thought you were sent to be Lady Veda's servant. Are you a gryphon keeper now?" Marigold asked, gowned in yellow with white lace and a matching umbrella against the sun.

"Yes, I train them to attack people who annoy me. Best beware." I grinned. "I think she's hungry."

Marigold frowned and stepped back, holding her frilly parasol in front of her. "Seriously, does Lady Veda Arcana know her servant is shirking her duties and mucking about with smelly gryphons?"

"I'm not anybody's servant, and it's none of your business."

Marigold stomped her foot. "How dare you speak to me like that?" The gryphon twisted her head and took a huge bite out of the elegant sunshade. Marigold shrieked in terror, but the small crowd bubbled with laughter. Marigold hiked up her skirt and fled in terror, leaving her broken parasol behind.

I stroked Mathilda's beak. "Good girl."

# # #

Altheda was able to join us, which made me happy. I missed her company. While sharing a quick round of tea and oatmeal cookies, Kalem was pelted with questions by Altheda about that night of my birthday and what he did as a shapeshifter. If medicine had not called Altheda to its path, she would have made an excellent interrogator.

Mother looked calm and even happy as we prepared to leave. Then she called upstairs, "Father, come down and say goodbye to Sabine before she embarks on her adventure."

"Mother, no!" I whispered. "Just leave it."

"I know, but family should try to get along. We don't know when you're coming back," Mother said.

Damn it, damn it, damn it.

Luther shuffled down the stairs, grumpy as a troll. "Now what, Brona? What's all this fuss for now? He paused on the stairs when he saw me. "What's she doing here?"

"Our Sabine is going to Túr Solas with Veda. She may be gone a long time. I want you to say goodbye. Properly."

Luther's brow knotted and he scratched his armpits. "You woke me from my nap for this? Who is this strange man? Is he a customer?"

"He brought Sabine to say goodbye. He's a friend of Veda's," Mother said. Then she looked at him in frustration. "Never mind. Go back to bed and finish your nap."

Luther shrugged and went back upstairs, moving slowly and grumbling with each step.

I breathed again. The farther Luther moved away, the more the threat of argument faded. Mother often made an effort to create a familial circle, but it always failed. I felt sad for her because she wanted it so much. "Don't worry, Mother. I just wanted to see you and Altheda before I left."

Kalem nodded to my mother. "Forgive us, but we need to leave. Mathilda is getting restless."

"Of course," my mother said, nodding.

My final goodbyes to Altheda and Mother were filled with tears. I longed for my mother's embrace, but her only touch was her hand caressing my cheek. "I will write loads of letters," I said.

"You better," Altheda said, hugging me hard—I think to make up for Mother's distance. "And don't you worry about us."

As we left Fable House, I clutched the sweet blossoms Mother gave me. I felt odd, like a stranger in my old home, and could not understand why.

Kalem untied a petulant Mathilda from the fence. "Are you alright?" he asked me.

I glanced back at the house I grew up in, the white paint cracked and the Fable House sign above the door faded. I realized this wasn't my home anymore.

# # #

We reached Gray Moon Bay and boarded a riverboat bound for Túr Solas. I had my own cabin, which I had not expected. It had a clean, narrow bed with soft blankets and pillows, and a low wooden chest. Behind a folding door, there was a discreet toilet.

"As my official companion and secretary, your position gives you the rank to have your own room," Veda explained. "You're entering a new world, Sabine. You have much to learn about the court in a short span. I hoped to have more time, but you're smart enough to observe and learn the high etiquette when rubbing shoulders with the ministers and premier."

"I've a keen memory. If you give me a list, I promise to absorb it on our journey. It will help pass the time."

"Good," Veda said, nodding and smiling. "I know we've not had much of a chance to talk about the cure for mage fever's side effects. And since you have had no ill effects from the tests, we will start the treatment when we arrive in the city."

"Truly?" I said, my heart thumping.

"Yes." She smiled and cupped my chin with her hand. "But remember, nothing is certain. So far it has truly worked only on me. There must be a reason for this. A logical reason based in science and magical principles. I just do not know what it is. Now rest and enjoy the trip. You'll have little opportunity for leisure when we reach the city."

At first, I loved being on the water because it was so soothing, but the novelty of river travel faded fast. I became bored and restless. I walked the deck with Rory for fresh air and talked to him, confessing all of my secrets and dreams about becoming a powerful sorceress as he sucked on a piece of bacon and stared at me with bright-green eyes. I visited Mathilda in the lower hold, where they kept animals. To my surprise, Kalem decided not to take the faster route and fly her back to Túr Solas for some reason he wouldn't state. Matilda was not happy but was appeased by my gifts of apples and dried meat when Kalem groomed her.

After several days of dull passage, we finally reached the city. I rushed eagerly to see my first glimpse of Túr Solas! I took in the beauty of great buildings and towers several stories high even from our distance on the river. The gleaming spires and colorful turrets of this metropolis mesmerized me. The tallest buildings in Crimson Hollow were only three stories.

When we disembarked the ship, a private carriage awaited us. Veda wore an elegant gray gown with red trim and elbow-length black silk gloves. I changed back into my best dress, which seemed rather drab now compared to the city. I kept smoothing out the wrinkles on the skirt and sleeves.

"You look lovely," Veda said, and with a pass of her shimmering hand, all the creases and rumples vanished. She pinned an oval brooch of white pearl to my high-necked collar. "This will dress it up."

Kalem joined us, wearing his hooded gray coat and leading Mathilda. "I will see you soon, ladies."

"Aren't you coming with us?" I asked, making sure Rory was tucked in his basket.

"I need to get Mathilda back to the stables, but I will meet you at the palace. My duty was to escort you to Túr Solas, and now I must return Mathilda to the gryphon stables. For a creature of flight, she hates travel."

"Has she forgiven you yet?" I asked with a laugh.

"Never," Kalem said. Then he sighed.

# # #

The state palace—a beautiful structure of golden stone surrounded by lush, fragrant gardens—shone as a magnificent relic from the old days of the monarchy but served as the official residence of the premier and the government. Roses scented the air at every step and bloomed everywhere. Even in the grand corridor, there were great vases with huge bouquets of them.

Kalem met us at the main entrance and led us through the halls. Enormous paintings and tapestries of historical or legendary figures hung floor to ceiling, and I longed to examine them. People in fine dress milled about with an air of importance. Even court servants dressed with elegance! Guards in dark-blue uniforms with shiny buttons and silver trim were everywhere, their faces unreadable as their gloved hands rested on the pommels of their polished swords.

All around me, the subtle aroma of magic infused the air. Then something shifted, and I sensed an odd, fiery essence—not foul, but strange and unknown to me. From a distance, a tall, skeletal man with sparse gray hair hobbled toward us. He was weighed down by heavy black velvet robes. A large gold medallion swayed from his neck, and a black wooden staff crowned with a glittering red crystal clutched in his bony hand.

"Who is he?" I whispered to Veda. "He looks grim as a ghoul!"

"Lord Albertus Crimm, the chief chancellor of the Ravenna Republic," Veda whispered back. "He's a necromancer."

Necromancers are an odd lot, even among the mage castes. Their mystic power is based in the realm of death and spirits. Crimm's scraggly eyebrows curled above deep-set, faded blue eyes, which darted to Kalem first. "You, sir, took your sweet time. Where have you been dawdling?" he old man asked.

Kalem bowed, unshaken by his vinegary tone. "I beg your pardon, Lord Crimm. You gave specific order to fetch Lady Veda and bring her to court, which I have done."

Albertus Crimm stopped before Veda and inclined his head. "Welcome, Lady Arcana. You are expected, though you should know I do not approve of this." Crimm then cast his icy stare on me like a bad spell. "You, however, are neither expected nor invited. Who is this small, homely child in the shabby dress? She is not known to me, nor did I summon her."

"It's my best gown!" I piped up, but Veda's sharp glance closed my mouth. I clenched my jaw to prevent another flash of temper from escaping my lips.

"This is Sabine Fable, and she's not a child," Veda calmly replied. "She is my secretary and personal companion. Sabine comes from a good family and is well-educated."

"I know nothing of this Sabine Fable or her family," Crimm remarked.

I fumed inwardly. He spoke of me as though I were nothing but a blot of dust. I straightened up as tall as I could muster and stared right back. "My family is from a small village in the north, Lord Crimm. I doubt you would know it."

"And what is your caste, Sabine Fable? Witch? Sorceress? Or are you some minor mystic caste with miniscule powers? If you serve Lady Arcana, you surely must possess something of value."

"My mind is my value, Lord Crimm. I'm baseborn, but I understand magic," I replied. "The house of Fable was one of the mystic castes until mage fever destroyed our magic, including mine."

"You're baseborn then," Crimm grumbled. "Not surprising."

I long to snatch his staff and bash him over the head with it. Would he find that surprising? I wondered.

"And what vermin do you carry in your basket?" Crimm demanded.

"He's not vermin!" I cried, holding the basket protectively. "His name is Rory and he's my pukis dragon. He's only a month old."

Crimm made a sour face. "Bah! Pukis dragons are vermin."

Veda interjected, her tone firm. "She is of value to me, Albertus. Your taunting is ill-timed. Am I here to spar with you, or was I summoned for a reason?"

"Come with me," Crimm snapped, turning on his heels and marching ahead with surprising speed for his age.

We followed until we reached a gilded hallway lined with many armed guards. Upon seeing Lord Crimm, two sentries standing watch by a set of double doors swiftly opened them to an elegant suite. I rushed past them at a fast clip to keep up.

The doors closed behind us, and we were in a large suite, rich with stylish furniture, silken couches, and exquisite art. Standing with his back to us, a tall, broad-shouldered man in a black suit turned his head to acknowledge us. "I have been waiting for your arrival," he remarked, his voice rich and deep.

"I have come as you commanded, Premier Alexander Duchene," Veda said formally.

He turned, and a faint smile brightened his expression briefly. He was mature but still masculine and vibrant. Older, but not ancient, and closer to Luther's age, I thought. He was certainly in better shape than Luther, whose only exercise was pulling the cork from a beer bottle.

"Come, Veda, let's drop the formalities," Alexander said. "You know I didn't want to banish you."

"Yet I was," Veda replied softly.

Albertus Crimm lifted his staff, releasing a wave of strong magic. My skin tingled and my ears rang. Poor Rory stirred in his sleep and whined.

"Albertus, is it secure?" Alexander asked.

"My spell has sealed the room. No one can hear us outside this room, nor can anyone infiltrate it with magic," Crimm said. "Veda, however, has acquired a pet. A *baseborn* assistant. She is a stranger, and I do not trust strangers—especially in dealing with a matter of state. We should send her away now."

Crimm made *baseborn* sound like a dirty word.

"No," Veda protested. "Sabine's my companion and secretary. I trust her explicitly."

"Can the girl keep a secret?" Alexander asked, looking at me. He was not mean like Crimm but offered a smile as he slyly winked.

I glared at Crimm, who was smirking over his fancy staff. I turned to Alexander and curtsied deeply. "I am Sabine Fable, and I swear I shall never reveal anything I hear or witness in this room, Your Excellency." I bowed my head.

"Can your little friend promise the same?" Alexander asked.

In my nervousness, it took me a moment to realize he was talking about Rory. "Oh, you can trust him, sir. He is a very devoted dragon. He keeps all of my secrets very well."

"Unless you bribe him with bacon," Kalem said with a grin.

"Enough delays, Alexander," Veda said. "I trust her, so please trust me now. What is wrong? Why have I been summoned with such urgency?"

Alexander spread his hands in a helpless manner, contrasting with his powerful presence. "I need your help, Veda. My sorcery is gone. Someone or something has stolen my magic."

CHAPTER 8

Alexander Duchene's startling confession riveted me, but I feared they would send me away because of the secrecy. After a few moments, I realized they were too busy arguing to remember I was even there, though Crimm's pallid eyes often glanced my way suspiciously.

"Are you sure?" Veda asked Crimm, drawing his focus away from me. "His magic could be bound instead."

"I tested him myself," Crimm said. "But Lord Mystic Baruti Tabor believes it could be an unknown strain of mage fever. When you said you had the fever, you claimed to have a headache and feel ill the day before. That is why we are afraid, Lady Arcana. There is no trace of binding spells or any magi in his system. What else could it be? Mage fever leaves nothing behind."

"Illness did not take my magic," Alexander insisted. "And Baruti did not find any evidence of the plague, else the whole palace would have been evacuated."

"Mage fever doesn't manifest like that anyway," Veda remarked, her brow wrinkled as she thought. "It's a virulent and terrible disease. I've seen its suffering and endured it myself."

"So you claim, Veda," Crimm said.

"It is truth," Veda protested. "I do know you simply do not wake up one day without magic without symptoms."

"I believe you, Veda," Alexander said. "You miraculously regained your sorcery after mage fever through a treatment you developed. That is why I sent for you. Even if this is not an unknown strain of the dreaded red plague, I have faith you will discover what this is."

"Magic is what will restore your power, not science," Crimm insisted.

"Baruti's mystical potions have done nothing," Alexander said. "I think we need to broaden our field of research to include traditional science."

"Baseborn methods are a waste of time," Crimm argued.

Kalem leaned against the wall, arms crossed over his chest, obviously bored with the discussion. I, on the other hand, was fascinated. I'd never heard of anyone stealing someone's magic before. Who or what could touch such an influential man without detection?

"The premier is a powerful man, and powerful men may have enemies close at court." I said this out loud, then regretted it when all eyes fell upon me. I wanted to shrink into the wallpaper.

"Sabine has a point," Veda remarked as she paced the room, her crimson skirt sweeping the floor as she rubbed her temples in frustration. She suddenly turned her attention to Kalem. "Did you know about this when you showed up at my tower?"

"No, Veda. I swear I knew nothing about Alexander's condition. Crimm sent me an urgent message to bring you back to court." Kalem's sharp eyes fixed on Crimm. "He refused to say why, of course. Though he did specify I come with you in case you resisted."

"Keeping this secret was imperative," Crimm insisted. "You're told what you need to know and no more." Then he turned on Veda. "Lady Arcana, you were banished from court, so this wasn't your concern at the time."

"Enough, Albertus," Alexander interrupted. "You know we only wanted things to quiet down after what happened. Veda did nothing wrong. She was neither tried nor convicted. The subjects of her tests knew there were risks."

Tension crackled and, feeling like an awkward voyeur, I decided to make myself useful. "Would anyone like some refreshment? I see there is some wine on the side table. I am happy to serve."

Veda sighed and nodded. "Yes, a wonderful idea. Thank you, Sabine."

Alexander glanced up at me and nodded. "Some wine, please. Thank you."

"I think we could all use some," Kalem agreed, grinning.

I put Rory's basket on the table. He poked his head up, swishing his tail. "No, it's not playtime. Stay put!" I whispered. He just looked at me with innocent eyes.

I quickly went to work, choosing crystal glasses and a crystal decanter of red wine from the ample selection on the sideboard. *Pray gods, please don't let me shatter one,* I thought. I served the wine, even to rude Albertus Crimm. I was tempted to spit into his glass, but there were too many witnesses about.

Crimm took the offered glass and remarked, "Has anyone told you, Mistress Fable, you have unusual eyes?"

I swear if he calls me ghost-eye, I'll smack him over the head with this expensive silver tray. "No, sir," I lied in a neutral tone, then turned away. I put the empty tray on the table. I gathered up Rory and poured myself some water.

"You do not appreciate our fine wine, Mistress Fable?" Crimm inquired.

"I'm sure it is an excellent vintage, but I never drink alcohol," I replied. "I prefer to keep my wits clear." I refrained from mentioning Luther's drunken sprees. I'll never drink alcohol as a result of those violent memories.

"We must protect the state," Crimm insisted, going back to the original topic. "Alexander's position is vulnerable now."

Veda put up her hand, shaking her head. "I know. Your domain is political, whereas mine is science and its relationship to the mystical arts."

Kalem helped himself to more wine. "Draining another's magic is tricky and deadly. Those spells are not only illegal but damned hard to conjure."

"Those spells leave mystical markers, too, which are absent from Alexander. So we wisely decided to keep this secret," Crimm added.

"May the gods save me from wise men," Veda remarked dryly. She sat next to Alexander, her voice gentle as she took his hand. "When did this happen?"

Their intimacy surprised me. It bore the mark of an old, familiar relationship.

"Just a handful of days ago, but it feels like a century. Thank you for coming."

"How do you feel?" Veda asked. "Weak? Any pain? Headaches?"

"Strangely, I feel perfectly well, just emotionally bereft without my magic. I just woke up and it was gone. All my life I walked in privilege. Blessed with sorcerous ability, I achieved a high place in the Mystic Circle as a young man. Now without my powers, I feel hollow."

I felt sympathy for him, which surprised me. The arrogance of mageborns had vexed me my whole life. Yet, I experienced compassion for his loss. "You're still a great leader," I blurted out. "I would have voted for you whether you were mageborn or baseborn."

"A baseborn would say that," Crimm mumbled under his breath.

"I appreciate your kind words, Mistress Fable," Alexander replied graciously.

"Do you suspect anyone?" Veda asked, trying to put the conversation back on track.

Crimm shrugged, his gaunt face pinched with thought. "Everyone is suspect. Alexander had just won reelection as premier, but it was a heated race. He has enemies everywhere, as any true leader does."

I pointed out the same thought earlier, and Crimm looked at me as though I turned idiot, I thought.

Rory crawled out of his basket, so I placed him on my shoulder. "Be good," I whispered, but he responded with only a grunt and flutter of wings as he settled.

"Mind your winged vermin," Crimm warned, rapping his staff on the floor. "Or I'll feed it to the dogs."

"Albertus, stop!" Veda snapped.

"Surely, such an important state official has better things to do than torment an innocent girl," Kalem added.

I protectively held Rory close to me. If I had power for one fleeting moment, I would have turned ghoulish Crimm into a warty toad. A smelly, warty toad. This amusing image sustained me as they conversed.

"From this moment, I will need all information you've gathered," Veda demanded. "Nothing must be hidden from me from this moment on. I prefer to work from my own laboratory in my home as well as an apartment at court. I assume I still have my house in town?"

"Of course," Crimm replied. "Your banishment was temporary. The state did not confiscate your personal property."

"Good, because working from home will keep speculation down. I'll send you a list of any supplies I need. It will be a very long list, Albertus. I'll report any updates I find. I agree this must remain a secret; however, I must have access to all evidence and information. I assume my banishment is officially lifted? I just want to be sure, Lord Crimm."

The bite in Veda's tone did not faze Crimm.

"Yes," he said, scowling and waving his staff. "I assume this child will assist you."

"Yes, Sabine will assist me," Veda replied. "As I explained, this will also be part of her higher education."

"Educating a baseborn in the ways of magic and advanced science? Better to give her a broom or a cooking pot where she can at least be useful, but I will not interfere with your choice of servant," Crimm snickered.

"Sabine has a keen mind and will do quite well," Veda countered.

"Of course, she will do fine," Alexander agreed. "Veda would not choose just anyone as her secretary."

I did not expect Alexander's defense. When I dared to look at him, I saw kindness in his eyes.

"Albertus is rather acerbic to everyone, Mistress Fable. Do not take it so personally. I should remind him of his manners more often." The premier glanced at Crimm with a slight scowl. "Then I would not have to keep apologizing for him."

Veda rose and took me by the hand, her voice soft. "Our debate may go on for several more hours. You look tired, dear. I'll have supper sent to your room. Get some rest. We have much work before us." She leaned in and whispered in my ear, "I feel your patience has suffered enough challenge with Crimm."

I was so relieved I thought I would cry. Crimm's nastiness had tapped all my reserves. I also had a miserable headache, and my hands were hot.

"I have arranged for a suite for you," Alexander said to Veda. "It will remain at your disposal whenever you visit the palace." Then he turned to me. "I'll have one of the guards show you to your room, Mistress Fable."

I curtsied with as much grace as I could muster and tucked Rory in his basket. He was getting skittish. My baby dragon needed to be fed, plus I was relieved to leave withered old Crimm's baleful stare.

My escort was a young soldier with an earnest face. He smiled kindly as he guided me through the long halls and up a set of stairs to an exquisite suite of rooms. It was beautiful and quite large, with two bedrooms, a sitting room, an enormous bathroom with a huge tub, and a standing washbasin, all in green-and-cream décor with gold taps—even on the toilet! A hot bath would be heaven, I decided. A collection of colorful light orbs were scattered around for brightness, along with traditional candles and lamps. The entire kitchen of Fable House would have fit into the wardrobe chests. My meager pile of clothes would not fill one shelf.

"Are you sure this is the right room?" I asked.

"Yes, Lady Fable," the soldier replied. "They call it the Gryphon Suite. Is it not to your liking?"

I restrained a smile and looked up at him, for he was quite tall. "Oh, I like it just fine. I am just accustomed to more scholarly quarters. But I like gryphons. I know one named Mathilda. And just call me Sabine," I corrected. "I'm sorry, but what is your name?"

"Corporal Braden Griffin," he replied with a broad grin.

"Really?" I laughed. "Then it's a good thing I like gryphons!"

"Indeed, though my name's spelled differently than the creatures who fly, I'm pleased you're fond of gryphons. You must be one of Lady Veda's students from the Academy."

"I wish that were true, but I'm baseborn. I have the honor of being Lady Veda's secretary and companion."

"No shame in that," he replied, smiling as though relieved. "I'm just a baseborn soldier myself, hoping to make my way in the world."

"Good luck to you."

"Thank you, Mistress Fable."

"Thank you, Corporal Griffin," I replied.

He bowed, rewarding me with a shy smile, and left the chamber.

Alone, I eagerly explored the opulent suite. The bedrooms were the same size and equally rich, just different in color scheme—one done in red and the other blue. I chose the blue room, as I knew Veda was fond of red.

Plump pillows and a blue silk coverlet of such exquisite design and softness that I longed to wrap it around me like a cocoon topped my enormous bed. Its height wasn't designed for short people like me. I searched the rooms until I found a velvet footstool. I placed it by the bedpost to boost me. I crawled up onto the airy surface and collapsed.

Even in the comfort of this quiet room, I couldn't relax. My head pained me. Rory, however, scampered around the bed, exploring the newness until he settled above my head on a green silk pillow. He obviously loved luxury too. I removed the brooch Veda gave me and opened my top three buttons so I could breathe. *Sleep, if only I could just sleep,* I thought. But its solace eluded me cruelly.

Restless, I quietly climbed down from the bed as Rory snored, curled up on the pillow. A knock on the door startled me. I chastised myself for being so silly. I opened the door to a maid delivering my dinner and another servant carrying some of our bags. Our bigger pieces of luggage floated in the air behind them. *Must be charm caste,* I thought as the servant brought in our bags without burden. The maid left my dinner on the table. I thanked them both as they left.

The food smelled wonderful, but I had a task first. I opened my bag and removed a small wooden box. I opened the lid to check on Mother's charmed bouquet of pink flowers. Satisfied they were safe, I put it back.

Rory's waking chirps from the next room meant he would soon demand dinner too. I fetched him and placed him on the table. "Well, Rory, let's see how the rich folk eat." His ears perked up, and he sniffed the platter eagerly. I lifted the large silver lid to find a feast of baked chicken, salad, roasted potatoes, strawberries with cream, and freshly baked bread with a crock of butter. A small pot of coffee and a glass decanter of water with real ice accompanied the meal. "Let's enjoy the bounty," I said with a laugh.

I diced some chicken and gave it to Rory on a fine gold-trimmed saucer. We both feasted with gusto, and I felt better with each bite. As my head pain abated, I thought maybe I was just hungry—until a chill shrouded me. I sensed something. My head throbbed again. Rory sensed something too because he whimpered and nervously flapped his tiny wings.

On the wall opposite me hung a large round mirror framed in ornate gold. I saw my reflection. Gods, I looked haggard as an old crone. Then a shadow misted over the mirror, dulling its gleam. My stomach knotted, and my nostrils burned from the odor of dark magic emitting from the mirror. I shivered from a growing chill. A dark shape formed in the glass, but I could not distinguish anything more.

I stepped back, my heart beating rapidly. The image swirled within the gold frame, becoming a violent storm cloud. *Call for the guard,* I told myself, but my voice didn't work. Damn it! I could not speak!

I grabbed Rory and ran for the door. A dark phantom emerged from the mirror and barred my way. Reflex took command as I raised my hand in defense. The dark cloud brushed against my hand and the shock that surged through me knocked me to the floor, leaving me dazed and numb.

I scrambled away as the darkness stalked me. A furious face loomed above me, full of pain and fury. Rory howled and whimpered, clinging to me. The strange, hellish phantom stopped and howled, like a woman's wail, then retreated back into the mirror.

Relief swept over me as it vanished. Holding on to Rory, I fled the room in terror. My headache pounded and my hands seared as they always did when I was upset, but they burned more painfully than usual.

I realized my hand was scorched. I stood in the hallway alone, heaving for breath, afraid to return to the room. Where the creature touched me, my skin burned hot pink. Rory whined, and I tried to calm him down. "Someone help!" I shouted, unsure of what else to do.

"Mistress Fable!" Braden shouted, running toward me. "What's wrong?" He reached me and gently took me by the shoulders. "Are you alright? You're shaking."

"I was just attacked," I whispered, my voice restored.

"Who?" Braden asked, drawing his sword. "Where are they?"

"Not who, but what. Some sort of wraith or phantom thing just attacked me."

"Damn. I'll summon the palace wizards. Are you hurt?" he asked.

"I'm fine," I said, raising my burned hand. "But the damned creature left this nasty mark."

CHAPTER 9

"Do stop fidgeting," Veda warned, studying my hand intensely as she worked her magic.

"Sorry, but your enchantment's making my hand vibrate. It feels weird. Is it part of the healing spell?" I asked.

"I'm taking samples for examination." She took a small vial and whispered a spell. My hand glowed, and the magic extracted wispy bits of shadows from my wound that floated into the vial.

"I'm disgusted now," I said. "Those dark things were inside me?"

"Nothing to worry about," Veda assured me. "But the creature left a marker of itself when it attacked you. It's all gone now. Now let's finish healing you." She cast green shimmers over my seared skin, and the burn vanished. "Does it hurt now? Sting? Itch?"

"No," I said, shaking my head. "The pain is gone. It just tingles now. Are you sure nothing of the phantom creature remains?"

"Of course, Sabine. It's all gone now."

I still washed my hands a dozen times in the bathroom with very hot water. The soap smelled like lilac, which soothed me a bit. When I returned to the sitting room, I checked on Rory. The terrifying experience had caused him to throw up his dinner all over the posh carpet. Thankfully, this was rectified by one of Veda's simple spells. I wished I could do magic like Veda. All I could do now was wrap Rory up in my blue scarf for comfort, his and mine. He slept uneasily, little legs twitching. Something told me I would also be twitchy in my sleep after this.

Veda turned to Braden Griffin, who stood near the door at quiet attention. He had sent guards to fetch Veda and Kalem and summon the palace wizards. Then he had stayed with me through the chaos. "Thank you for looking after Sabine," Veda said to him. "It pleases me, as it will Premier Duchene, that you are valiant and can think on your feet."

"Thank you, Sorceress Arcana," Braden replied, his face stoic. But his eyes gleamed with pride.

"Please ensure our apartments are well guarded, Corporal Griffin. If the guards have any questions or issues, refer them to me."

"Yes, Sorceress. I will speak to the captain of the guard at once." He bowed and turned to go.

"Thank you, Braden," I said. He rewarded me with a quick wink before he closed the door.

"He is a most pleasant young man," Veda remarked.

"Braden is baseborn, like me, trying to make something of his life." I flexed my hand, marveling at my once-again smooth skin. The memory of touching the phantom made me flinch. "Do you know what attacked me exactly?"

Veda shook her head. "The creature you described isn't familiar. Many phantom creatures have similarities, but they also carry distinctive markers. Shades, ghosts, goblins, phantoms, banshees, and specters are mystical beings of another realm, but their origins and purposes differ."

"Its purpose felt bitter, but such phantoms normally don't shock people."

"They do not," Veda agreed. "Tell me again and do not leave out a single detail."

I shrugged. "I had just eaten dinner. It emerged from the mirror like a storm. The room became cold. Oh, and I couldn't speak."

"Hard to imagine," she said with a grin.

"It wasn't fear. I'm sure my voice was muted by some spell."

"That is unusual." Veda nodded. "Did you try to touch it?"

"No, it attacked." I glanced at the magnificent mirror, the beauty of it ruined for me now. "Can the mirror be removed? It makes me nervous."

Veda's brow furrowed in thought. "Yes, they're coming to take it now. What concerns me is the palace employs a team of wizards to keep the palace free of ghosts, shades, ghouls, and all manners of shadow beings. It surprises me that such a creature penetrated palace security. The wizards receive a fine compensation for their services, so this attack should never have happened."

"Could this apparition have anything to do with Alexander's loss of magic?"

"I never discount anything when it comes to magic or politics."

"How can you trust anyone at court?" I asked. "I mean, after what they did to you. They banished you."

"I know, but there are some genuine people. Alexander is an old friend. I do not abandon my friends."

"Friends are fragile concepts to me. I don't trust people. Animals are different. They don't betray once they know you. They do not turn their backs on you or lie, but people do."

"You are a stern little porcupine. What about school? Didn't you have friends growing up? How about Marigold Graven?" Veda asked.

"Going to school with Marigold was never friendly."

"I sensed you two were never friends when she dropped in on your birthday."

"You mean barged in like a nosy gnome with ringlets." I laughed. "Did you really remember Marigold Graven taking your class?"

"Not at first. Not until she laughed." Veda sighed. "The reason I didn't remember Marigold was because spell composition is an entry-level course, often with more than a hundred students. I sense Marigold puts great emphasis on social standing."

"She's a snot."

Veda suppressed a laugh. "Well, I cannot speak to her character. I know her father, Sir Thomas Graven. He's a fine man. Do you know he went to the Academy when your mother was there? He was an advanced student a couple years ahead of Brona. They were friends, bonded I think by being from the same hometown."

"Sir Thomas has always treated my mother with respect, but he dislikes Luther."

"Luther cultivates animosity," Veda remarked. "He thrives on anger and bitterness, but his choices are his own."

Kalem returned, followed by two men in severe dark suits and tall back hats. "These wizards are here to earn their keep," he said. "They're taking the mirror for examination."

"Good riddance," I said, wincing. "I may never gaze in a looking glass again. It's strange because I had a relative who was a mirror mage. One of the few Fables who rose above charm caste. My mother was another who would have been a sorceress. I used to imagine being a mirror mage when I was little. Now I'm uneasy when I see a mirror."

"It's just your association with the attack," Veda said.

The two wizards silently summoned the cursed mirror off the wall. This made me happy. Rory had awoken when the mages arrived. Now he poked his head over the basket, growling low in his throat as the mirror floated in a sphere of shimmering magic out the door. The wizards bowed and left the room behind it. Kalem waved his hand and the door closed after them.

"Did you detect anything from Sabine's injury?" Kalem asked, plucking an apple from the fruit bowl.

"I took a sample. There's a faint mystical marker I don't recognize," Veda replied. "I'll know more after some tests. There's much work ahead of us now. The mystery of Alexander's missing magic and now a strange phantom. Make sure the wizards notify me of what they discover from the mirror."

"I will. Now, both of you need to get some rest," Kalem said. Then he left.

Sensing Rory's distress, I picked him up and sat in a stuffed velvet chair, stroking his head, which was as soft and crinkly as beaded velvet. He burrowed into the thick folds of my skirt and curled up in a ball.

"How do you really feel?" Veda asked. "In times of stress, you suffer terrible headaches and your hands become fevered. Did that happen during the attack?"

"Yes, it did. My emotions run hot and so do my hands, I guess. I'm used to it. I'm better now. Doubt if I'll sleep tonight though."

"Perhaps your magic was trying to escape" She laughed. "Child, the emotions on your face are worth a thousand words."

I carried Rory to his basket and tucked him in to hide my face. "Well, I'm confused. I have no magic, so what do you mean my magic is trying to escape? I thought you were trying to restore my lost magic."

"It's only a theory, but I believe those who suffered mage fever still have their powers. Their magic is not destroyed by the disease. It becomes trapped and somehow undetectable. I believe magic is not destroyed by mage fever but altered or imprisoned in some way."

"But it is only a theory," I said. It was disturbing to realize I might have been mageborn since birth. "Theories are easy. Reality is harder."

"Welcome to my world." Veda smiled. "Tell me, what does the local wizard do when he checks you every year for magic?"

"The old coot waves a crystal over me and pronounces me magic free. Then he demands his damned fee. If what you say is true, my mother's powers are also trapped."

"Tragically, yes. But she's deathly allergic to key elements of the treatment. It made her so ill that I could not continue the therapy. Luther's reaction was minor, but the treatment did not restore his mystical ability. Do you recall when your headaches and burning hands first began?"

"I think I was seven or so. It was at school, which I enjoyed at first. I was thrilled to be away from Luther's moods and my mother's sadness. I loved to read and learn. Crimson Hollow is a small town, so mageborn and baseborn attend the primary levels together during the elementary levels. Unless they have a private tutor, of course."

"And Marigold went to your school? Thomas is a kind and honest man, but he is also aware of social standing and rank. I find it unusual he sent Marigold to a local school."

"Well, when Marigold arrived, the students and teachers all fawned over her because of her high status. She quickly formed a circle of followers to wait upon her like she was a queen. They even did her homework. I called them her cackling hens because they doted on her as she handed them chocolate clusters from her fancy lunch tin. One day Marigold demanded I do her math assignment. I refused. I'm good with numbers and always got high marks, but why should I do her homework? She barely acknowledged me before, but she despised me after I refused her. She became my enemy and called me ghost-eye, which other students soon imitated. She even commanded I curtsy to her, being she's mageborn and I was nothing. I told her to piss off."

"Children can be the cruelest enemy. You should have told your teacher about the abuse and the cheating," Veda said.

"And add tattletale to my list of names? Never. One day during lunch, a boy threw clumps of mud at me and ruined my new dress. He called me a ghost-eyed bastard. I was mortified because my dress was Mother's birthday gift to me. It was sky blue cotton with a white collar and little fake pearl buttons. I loved my birthday dress."

"Marigold instigated it," Veda said, nodding.

"Yes. Marigold enjoyed the spectacle from behind a tree, her hens laughing with her. She giggled at my filthy state. This emboldened her toady boy even further to call my mother a filthy whore. Huge mistake. I chased him down and pummeled him with my fists until his nose bled. That was the first time it happened. My headache swelled and my hands burned like they were on fire! The next thing I remember is the headmistress dragging me away."

"No one came to your defense."

"No. Unlike the fairy tales I read, the wicked are not always punished.

The teacher's golden child, Marigold, couldn't possibly be in the wrong. In truth, she's dumb as a village idiot and evil to boot. Marigold tearfully claimed I started the fight. During the whole thing, she would not look me in the eye. That's how you tell a liar. Until then, school had been my escape. I thought the other children liked me. But they didn't. I realized at that moment I didn't have a single friend at school. I could never trust any of them again either. The teacher punished me in front of the class as an example. I suffered the blow of the wooden ruler on my hands a dozen times, but I refused to cry or confess. My hands continued to burn hot, and my head pained me even after the beating stopped. Headmistress had a note delivered to the shop too, so when I got home, I received another beating from Luther. Mother protested, but he never listened. Since then, whenever I'm in a rage or upset, my hands burn like hot irons and my head hurts like an anvil dropped on it."

"I'm so sorry."

"Don't be. I learned a lesson about people. I kept to myself afterward."

"Not everyone is cruel or faithless," Veda said.

"I left school at thirteen to help my mother. I would have left sooner, but the law required school until then. After I left, I learned more studying under Mother's tutelage in the magic shop than I ever did at school. She also taught me apothecary wisdom." I witnessed a glimpse of pity in Veda's eyes. "Don't feel sorry for me."

"I never would," she whispered gently.

I was anxious to change the subject from my past. I sat before Veda, as calmly as I could muster. "Now, what about my magic? When do I start the real treatment? For weeks we've mucked about with little tests and vials of herbs. If I have a chance to be mageborn, now would be the time. It'd be a relief to be able to defend myself with a spell when a mysterious wraith pops out of a mirror."

"Fair enough," she said with a laugh. "You have been taking tiny doses of the therapy's ingredients for weeks, and there has been no reaction. We can continue."

"So I am not allergic like my mother?"

"No, but we must continue with care. I'm sorry I couldn't help restore Brona's magic, but perhaps I can help you. I believe the burning sensation in your hands may be symptomatic of your magic trying to escape." Veda grasped my shoulders firmly. "Understand, Sabine. The first sign of trouble and we stop. Clear?"

I nodded sullenly. I'd walk through fire to get magic.

Veda went to the sofa and rummaged through her bag. She returned with a red vial full of shimmering potion. She removed the cork and handed it to me.

I was eager to snatch it from her and drink it all down, but a wisp of fear froze me. "Is this the actual treatment?"

"Yes, one of many. As I told you, it's not a one-potion cure."

"You're scared though," I said, taking the vial.

"Yes, as you know, my last round of test subjects suffered more than side effects or lack of efficacy. I worked with only four people during that medicine trial. Two of them died. The tragedy is the reactions did not occur early in the trial. The test subjects seemed fine. Their families knew there was a possibility of failure, or worse. The other two subjects had only minor reactions but didn't improve or show evidence of magic. The families did not press charges, but others were against my research and punished me. Lord Mystic Baruti Tabor and Albertus Crimm are two peas in a pod on their views about mage fever and my research. They banished me from court, and my tenure as professor at the Mystic Academy was terminated."

"But you still believe your treatment can work. You cured yourself without any of their help. That never happens, yet you did it. Didn't that count for anything with Baruti or Crimm? The Mystic Circle?"

"Most of them never believed I suffered mage fever and lost my magic. I also believe more happened than what I was told about my patients' deaths. Sabine, I want the truth, more than you know. I believe my therapy can work."

I swallowed the potion and handed her the empty bottle. "Then let's prove them wrong."

CHAPTER 10

A dull week progressed with nothing exciting or beneficial to report. Despite faithfully taking doses of Veda's medicine, no hint of my magic blossomed. I was still a baseborn bastard. Oh well. Nothing new there.

The malevolent wraith, or whatever it was, remained a mystery despite the efforts of Veda, Kalem, and a team of palace wizards investigating how it got past mystical wards and even what type of creature it was.

Alexander Duchene remained a top priority, of course. He was the key to Veda's restored status among the mage castes. She wanted to prove her innocence. She grew more stressed each day under Crimm's commands to resolve Alexander's condition. Personally, I think Crimm enjoyed tormenting Veda. The old coot tried my patience daily. He demanded results but was just as clueless about Alexander's condition as the rest of us. Each day, I struggled to keep my temper caged, like an angry troll in my mind, but it was becoming more difficult.

I stretched in my chair, loosening the kinks in my back. I was happy to be away from the palace. Rory snored in his basket next to me, wrapped in his favorite blanket. Pukis dragons need warmth. Over this short interval, he had sprouted like an eager weed, his growth matching his increasing appetite. His color had deepened to a darker blue, contrasting with his green eyes. The faint green stripes on his face were more defined, and beneath his chin, a tiny smudge of gold was visible. I doted on my baby dragon and talked to him all the time, hoping he would answer me. So far he just stared at me with those precious eyes and made nonsense sounds.

My morning ticked on and my inner troll howled for my own cure. Veda monitored my medicinal dosage each day, and I submitted to her list of questions, blood tests, and mystical scans. Each day I prayed my power would surface, just a little. But so far, nothing. Cue my inner troll throwing a tantrum. Trolls need results, not medicine.

I poured another cup of strong, hot coffee as I reviewed our inventory of items received for our research. Veda had requested a lengthy list from

Crimm, and I suspected vengeance fueled some of her more extravagant demands. There was a bitter rift between those two, so I was relieved when we moved to Veda's townhouse in the city yesterday. It not only allowed me to avoid grim old Crimm, but I didn't feel safe after the strange wraith attacked me. I was still wary of mirrors. Hence my unruly hair, as had Veda commented the day before.

Rory, curled up in the basket next to me, stirred and opened his eyes. I grinned. "Morning, sleepyhead," I said, petting him.

Rory's little grunts and tail swish meant he wanted breakfast.

"I know, baby. I'll get your bacon porridge in a minute. Just checking the list of items Veda requested from Crimm Snot-Face against what we got in yesterday."

Rory's gurgles answered me. I scooped him up with one hand and put him on the table. He sniffed my coffee but puckered when he tasted it.

"See? Coffee is human fuel. Silly dragon," I said with a laugh. I leaned back and rubbed my dry eyes. I added a dollop of cream to my coffee and grabbed a cinnamon roll. I'd had trouble sleeping, so I baked that morning. Rory's sad grunts reminded me he needed breakfast. I fetched the bowl of bacon porridge and set it down before him. He happily lapped up his breakfast as I looked on like an adoring idiot.

Veda entered the dining room carrying a massive pile of dresses so large it eclipsed her face. "Drop whatever you're doing and help me!"

I rushed over and grabbed an armful of fabric, and we laid the dresses on the couch. Veda brushed her skirt. She was stunning in a violet suit with black trim. Not a hair strayed from her perfect chignon, but wild curls often strayed from my hairpins. I looked down at my plain gray skirt and white cotton blouse, seeing a coffee stain on my sleeve. I never could wear white without spilling upon it.

I gasped. "They're beautiful," I said, feeling the luxurious, colorful fabrics. "Do you want them cleaned or mended?"

"They're for you. A young lady should have a proper wardrobe fit for her station as my companion and secretary."

"Me?" I admit I felt like a ragamuffin when we visited the palace, but I didn't expect this. "These gowns are fit for a princess to wear!"

She smiled wistfully., "Now you will wear them. These were mine when I was your age. They're still fashionable with some minor modifications and accessories. There are matching shoes stored upstairs, but we'll bring those down later. I used special charms to keep them clean and fresh. A few magical alterations, and you will be all set. I promise we'll find you new clothes of your own as well. I'm sorry we haven't had time to shop."

"Who needs to shop with all this bounty? They are gorgeous! Are you sure you want to give them to me?" I cried, fingering the sumptuous wardrobe she offered me. At least a dozen dresses, from elegant morning gowns to formal evening dresses, were for me! I'd never had such amazing clothes. "Thank you so much." I longed to hug her but feared she might push me away like my mother did.

"I don't want anyone mistaking you for a servant," she said, sensing my insecurity. She gently cupped my chin. "You're also too young to dress like a crone. I take it you want your medicine before we start?"

I grinned. "Yes, please." My inner troll calmed.

She took the tiny bottle from her pocket and handed it to me. "Any changes at all?"

"Still void of magic, but also nothing bad either."

"Be patient. I know it's hard. I don't want to take any chances."

"You're afraid I might die. I know." I fingered the soft material of a blue velvet gown, one of the many luscious dresses. "Were you afraid the treatment might kill you? When you did this by yourself. How did you do it?"

"Sit. Let's have some coffee while I explain. Things have been so hectic, I've only given you fragments. You should understand everything, since you are part of this journey. About five years ago, I was traveling during the Solstice holidays in a small province far from here. The outbreak of mage fever in the town was sudden and brutal. Small pocket outbreaks happen, and this was a remote area. The fever remained localized. It was there I contracted mage fever. The local physician did the best she could. She was baseborn but very skilled. I survived but lost my magic, and myself."

"Didn't you have any family or friends to help you? You're a powerful and revered sorceress."

"Both my parents were dead by then, and I never married or had children. I have no regrets. I loved my independence too much. I loved my academics, research, and magic. I was content and happy with my life. Then it disappeared because of a disease. I slowly recovered my strength and dealt with the side effects. I was determined to keep my condition a secret."

I heard Rory's chirps and grunts but did not see him on the table where I left him. I looked around and found him burrowing into the pile of gowns, face smudged with bacon porridge. "Rory! How did you even get off the table? Come here." I picked him up, wiping his face with my sleeve. "How did you keep your condition hidden?" I asked Veda. "Did anyone suspect?"

"I was entitled to academic leave, so I took a lengthy sabbatical from the Academy. Coming back to Túr Solas was out of the question. If they found out about my condition, my place at the Academy and in the Mystic Circle would have ended. I rented a house in a small town in the mountains and researched mage fever day and night."

"I'm sorry. To have had magic and then lose it must be bitter. I know my mother feels the loss, though she never speaks of it."

"Your lovely mother is an example to us all, for, despite her seeming frailty, she's strong inside. I endured the wretched side effects—terrible nervous shakes, recurrent fevers, and headaches. I was spared the mad fits though. I don't regret keeping it secret. People judge you when you lose your magic." Veda shook her head, pouring another cup of coffee. "Without my sorcery, I would have no place in my world. Friends and colleagues would have distanced themselves after a sincere but brief expression of sympathy. I'd seen it happen to others. I chose isolation. Then I found this."

Veda went to a large oak cupboard next to the dining table. She wrote magical symbols in the air, the runes shimmering as they revealed an ornate locked chest I had not seen before. She carefully removed a dark wooden box carved with magical symbols, then set it in the middle of the dining table. She whispered a spell, and the lid unlocked and opened. She gingerly took a tattered large book from the box.

"This isn't the same book you showed me," I said. "It's older. And odd."

"Yes, it is, because the text I gave you to study was a copy of this one. The original is too precious and fragile to risk. It is written in a common Ravenna language too, not mystical script."

"Explains why I can read it," I said, nodding. "But not who wrote this—mageborn or baseborn."

"I visited libraries, colleges, and temples all over Ravenna. I read every text and publication I could find. I interviewed mystic healers and baseborn physicians. I did all I could do but still feared a fellow mage might discover my secret. I even changed my name for a time."

My own eager wonder drew me to the original tome, even more than the copy Veda first showed me. Rory perched on my shoulder. He sniffed loudly, for even he sensed the magic around this tome, which reeked of spells, most likely wards to protect it. The original book felt mystical despite my ability to access its knowledge, a sensation I did not have reading the copy.

Veda opened the mysterious book. "During my many travels, while hunting for a cure, I visited a library far north of here. By sheer serendipity, I found this book alone on a shelf. I don't know why, but I was drawn to it. It was dusty and edged with cobwebs in the lower basement of the library. I was only down there looking for the water closet!"

I touched the book's cover, feeling the texture of the worn leather cover, and sensed something else. "It's not regular leather, but feels … Leafy?"

Veda grinned with pride. "Yes, Sabine. The cover is not leather. It's made from plants. It is an ancient technique I read about when I was younger. It's called green leather. Your copy is exact, but the original is, well, I can't pin it down. When I first read it, I noted any references to experiments and treatments for survivors of mage fever. Its chapters refer to using a combination of magic and science. It goes into detail about various prescriptions for treatments of mage fever and for survivors of the disease, written in common language."

I picked up the book and could still smell something like grass from the cover. "It makes sense if you are a mage and lose your powers. How can you read mystical script? It's invisible to baseborn."

"Exactly. The base cure was a combination of charmed plants and objects I could purchase from any magic dealer, along with basic herbs and ingredients you could acquire from any apothecary. There are scribbles in another language on the pages. I am not sure whether they are another language or the author's personal shorthand. It does not work the same for everyone, and the book points that out."

I noticed there were gaps in the volume, where clearly some pages had been ripped out or even decayed and fallen away. Seeing my inspection, Veda said, "It's not evident in your copy, but there are chunks of pages missing in the original. And that's the reason the cure has so many complications, and can even pose a danger to patients. My own cure was a fluke of luck. The formula I conceived for myself has not worked on anyone else."

"Never tell Crimm that!" I said, laughing.

She nodded vigorously. "His refusal to accept any cure for mage fever or its aftermath is well known. He insists if magic cannot restore the mage, then the mage is lost forever. I disagree. It's clear the medicines must be formulated differently depending on the patient. There are many theories. Is it the type of magic they had? Age? Sex? Previous conditions? I do not know. I'd sell my soul to find those missing pages, but in their absence, we can only research and experiment, with extreme care. I do not want any more deaths on my conscience."

More curiosity about this strange, tattered text, piqued my brain. "Why was it rotting in a library in some backwoods town?"

"I don't know, but it had been long forgotten. It wasn't even listed in the library catalog. I could not leave without it. Fate guided me to this book."

"So you took it?" I smiled.

Veda grinned broadly. "I took it. I never stole anything in my life, but I just walked out with it. After my sorcery was restored, I ran a series of tests on the paper and bindings of the manuscript. Mystic dating placed the book at nearly nine hundred years! The ink had faded and the pages were discolored and brittle, but it was still laced with enchantments. After that time, though, the spells preserving the book were deteriorating. It's possible a mage and a baseborn created this book together, but we will never know."

"A mage and a baseborn working together? That would be unusual."

"It would, but I believe this book could forge such a union. I feared for the loss of this book. That it would crumble to dust before long. Even though the tome is incomplete, I had enough to begin my research anew to help others."

She closed the book and placed it back in its magical cabinet. "Now, try on the blue velvet dress and stand in the light by the window so I can fit you properly. The party tonight demands a special gown."

I put Rory down and stripped off my skirt and blouse. Rory snuggled in the fresh pile of silks and velvets. I slipped on the soft gown, swimming in its vast length, but then Veda was quite tall. I felt like a five-year-old again playing dress-up in my mother's gowns. A pang of worry for my mother infected the gaiety of the moment.

Veda's magical fingers made the gown glow with golden light. "Hold still," she said. "You fidget like a toddler."

I felt the material tuck and nip in around my body. The very strange sensation of her wisps of magic made my skin tingle. "Am I done yet?" I asked through clenched teeth.

"Hold still. I just need to raise the hem one more inch." Her eyes scrutinized the fit down to the last detail. The vibrant sapphire blue was the most colorful gown I ever wore. "Blue is your best color," she said. "A pair of simple pearl earrings is all this ensemble needs. Sweep back your hair simply, but leave it down in back. Use the silver combs and hair oil I gave you to smooth the flyaway curls."

She made it all sound so simple.

"Well, go look at your reflection and see," she said. When I hesitated, she gently pushed me toward the looking glass. "There's no monster in the mirror, Sabine. What happened to you was not because of a mirror."

I hate logic sometimes. I turned to the looking glass on the wall and dared to look. Even I had to admire the fit of the dress. The exquisite color brightened my pasty complexion and highlighted my pale gray eyes and dark brown hair. "If I had your mystical skill for altering clothes," I told her, "I'd never have to sew for hours or prick my fingers on a vengeful needle."

Veda stirred her coffee, and her tone was conspiratorial. "Now remember, I require your keen eyes to observe the guests tonight. I doubt Alexander's condition is due to illness, but the result of treachery on some mystical level that I've yet to pinpoint. If you hear or see anything suspicious, I need to know."

"So I'm a spy? I rather like that."

"But be careful," Veda insisted. "We are just observing. You look lovely, my dear. Despite your duty, please have a good time tonight."

"What about Rory? I can't leave him alone for hours. I won't put him in a cage."

"I agree. Young pukis dragons require constant care. Bring him with you. Many a young society lady has a pet, so it's not without precedent. Just make sure he's leashed and stays with you. Yesterday, I found him sleeping with my silk scarves. I'm not even sure how he got into my drawer!"

"I think he was guarding them for you," I said, stroking Rory's head. "Weren't you, my little guardian dragon?"

Rory looked up at me, and his jaws began to work, struggling for a moment. "Like head rubs," he piped. "Sabi, feed me more bacon?"

"Oh my gods, he talked!" I cried.

"Marvelous!" Veda said, coming over to us. "Oh, this was unexpected. He's a very special pukis!"

I laughed. "Of course he's special! My Rory has always been special. He called me Sabi! I never thought he would just talk. I thought I would have to teach him."

"The perk of the pukis," Veda said with a smile. "Magic is in his blood too, as it's in yours, I am sure of it."

Excited for Rory, I hugged him, spinning around the room! But I froze in my spin when I glanced at the large mirror on the wall. Did a shadow just pass the glimmered glass? I turned away from the reflection, not trusting what was within, my inner troll afraid.

CHAPTER 11

I wasn't prepared for the pompous state reception or a petulant pukis dragon. His speech shocked me. At first I was overjoyed, but the problem was he would not stop talking. He also wanted to stay home in his comfy bed, but I dared not leave him alone.

The crowded ballroom teeming with posh guests made maneuvering difficult. It was hot and stuffy too. I longed for something to drink as I tried to keep Rory calm.

"Don't like this place," he complained, pulling against his pink ribbon leash. "Hate ribbon. Want my blanket. Too loud here."

"It's only for a short time," I whispered. "I'm sorry, baby."

His newfound speech ability wasn't helpful when a stout, heavily jeweled lady strolled by, reeking of strong perfume.

Rory's nostrils flared. "Stinky."

The irate woman spun around in a swish of lilac silk, scanning the room for the rude culprit. I cringed, bowing my head as I pretended to look at the carpet. *Don't notice me,* I prayed repeatedly, hiding a wiggly Rory beneath my lace shawl. The woman scowled and finally moved on. I breathed a sigh of relief. Being short does sometimes come in handy.

Rory gnawed furiously at his leash in protest.

"Stop that! People will stare," I said. "We're supposed to be inconspicuous."

"Sabi mean. Too tight! Hurting!"

"No it's not! Please behave!" I scratched his favorite spot on the bridge of his nose, hoping to calm him down. "I promise I'll take it off as soon as we leave. I didn't want to lock you in a cage or leave you alone tonight. I would never leave you unprotected. Now we must help Veda. Please be good!"

Rory pouted, ears flattened in annoyance. Finally, he gazed up at me. "OK. For you! Still hate nasty ribbon."

I cuddled him, which he tolerated in his martyred state. "Thank you! I know it's awful, baby. I'll make it up to you." I suspected a pound of bacon would be part of the penance. Rory sulked in my arms as I stroked his head to comfort him.

I observed the party guests, not sure what to look for. Despite the opulence, the gathering proved rather dull. A quartet of somber violinists played as the prominent guests danced and gaily greeted each other. My guess was the attendees were silently calculating how much magic, title, or gold each possessed. I wondered how they'd act instead if they were poor and had to calculate how much food they could afford.

I glimpsed Veda in a circle with Alexander Duchene and his wife, Lady Corene, whom I'd met briefly that day when I arrived. Corene, with her enviably beautiful, luminous dark skin and perfect, high cheekbones, had been kind to me when Veda introduced us. But I could see that her queenly composure was taxed as I watched her greet their guests with a stiff smile on her face. The stress of Alexander's condition stressed her too, despite her stoic bearing.

I finally noticed Corporal Braden Griffin among the guards lining the room. On duty, of course, he stood at attention in his dress uniform, a large white plume in his hat. He briefly nodded to me as I walked past.

Rory chewed furiously at his ribbon again. "Stop that!" I whispered.

"Sabi promised!" he cried, gazing at me with accusing eyes.

"I know, but not now!" I struggled for a solution until I spied the sumptuous banquet table at the end of the hall. "How about some treats?"

He stopped gnawing, pondering meaty snacks in exchange for his suffering. I took his silence as a hopeful sign and rushed to the buffet table. So much rich food! I frowned, remembering how often we scraped by because of Luther's bad habits. Despite the large throng attending this celebration, few guests were sampling the decadent menu. Such wastefulness! A silver platter of tiny meatballs caught my eye. "These would be easy for you to manage," I told Rory.

Rory slipped from my grip, diving into the delicious bounty. He emerged clutching a meatball in his jaws like a proud hunter. "Bad dragon!" I muttered through clenched teeth, snatching him away from the platter of meatballs. Rory ignored my disapproval as he devoured his treat and licked his jaws.

"Yummy balls," he said. Then he burped.

"You're going to be the death of me!" I sighed, grabbing a napkin and wiping his paws, careful of my velvet gown. I prayed no one had noticed his leap into the cuisine.

"I hope your scaly pest doesn't contaminate the food," a raspy voice said from behind.

I spun around, clutching Rory close as Albertus Crimm hovered over me, gripping his ornate staff.

"Mistress Fable, why did you bring your irksome pet to a state function?"

Rory grunted and lifted his gravy-stained face. "Crimm Snot-Face."

I'm going to die of embarrassment!

"Your pest talks now!" Crimm croaked, more startled by my dragon's talent than the insult.

I wiped Rory's face with a napkin, avoiding the old man's ghoulish stare. "Rory's very talented, isn't he? Try the meatballs. They are yummy. I have it on the highest authority." I scooped a large spoonful of meatballs onto a linen napkin and hurried away.

I fled to a quiet corner of the room, feeding Rory treats as I hid from Crimm. I would have to explain to Rory that some things should never be repeated.

From my corner, I focused on observing the guests until my eyes fell on an annoying sight—Marigold Graven.

My nemesis swanned around the chamber with disdain. Frothy lace festooned her blush-pink taffeta gown, and her plump arms were adorned with elbow-length white gloves. Every blonde ringlet coiled perfectly on her head. Her bright image contrasted with her father, Lord Graven, solemn as ever in a black suit and gray silk tie. Despite the elegant gown Veda gifted me, when I was near Marigold, I was still the poor baseborn schoolgirl she tormented. I prayed to every god above that Marigold wouldn't notice me.

"You look distressed."

I recognized the deep voice as a friend, not foe, but when I turned around, an older man with a thick head of gray hair and sad brown eyes stared down at me.

"Kalem? Is that you?" I whispered.

"Yes," he said, nodding with a wicked grin.

The old-man image was quite startling. "If not for your voice, I wouldn't have recognized you." I did recognize a familiar odor on his breath when he leaned in. "Except I detect a whiff of wylsavan root. Are your joints bothering you again?"

"Just a bit. The root tea does help. I'll make sure I use a croaky tone when I speak to the others. And eat some mint candies. I do intend to enjoy some fine wine and gourmet food tonight."

"Try the meatballs. Rory loves them."

He leaned in conspiratorially and whispered, "Have you noticed anything strange?"

"A great deal of pomposity, but nothing suspicious. To be honest, I'm not even sure what I'm looking for."

"Just use your common sense. That's what Veda's counting on." He looked down and scratched Rory's head. "I see little Rory is enjoying the food."

"Kalem nice," Rory mumbled between chews.

"He's speaking now!" Kalem exclaimed. "That's rare! You must be thrilled."

"I was until he called Lord Crimm a snot-face."

Kalem burst out laughing. "I wish I could have seen Crimm's face!"

"Stop laughing! It's not funny! Crimm already thinks he's vermin and hates me. I was mortified."

"Don't worry. His bark is worse than his bite. Your gown is lovely, by the way," Kalem said. "Blue is your color."

"Thank you." I felt awkward but smiled.

"I'm going to circulate among these fine, wealthy nobles and mages. I may die of boredom before midnight. Pity me."

I smiled broadly. "I do. Go forth and spy!"

Adopting the slow stride of an aged man, he disappeared into the crowd. I liked Kalem because, unlike many mageborns, he was decent. He had been away of late, and I was glad to see him, even if he was in shapeshift mode.

My smile faded when I saw Lord Thomas Graven and Marigold coming toward me. Damn. Do the gods ever listen? Were they daring me to become an abject atheist?

"Good evening, Mistress Fable," Lord Graven said, nodding, Marigold on his arm.

"Good evening, Lord Graven, Marigold," I replied with a curtsy.

Marigold pointed her pink lace fan at Rory, who perched on my shoulder. "Is that creature the product of the silly egg you guarded so zealously?"

Rory snorted and belched loudly.

Good dragon.

Offended, Marigold frowned and opened her fan wide, as though it were a shield, glaring at Rory with disdain.

"Goodness!" I laughed. "Rory just had some rich snacks. So sorry."

"Your mother told me Lady Arcana gave you a post in her household," Graven said. "Congratulations."

"Thank you, Lord Graven," I replied graciously.

"So you're Veda's maid now?" Marigold remarked sweetly as she fanned herself, though her eyes had the warmth of a snake's. "I recall offering you the same honor, which you refused."

I ached to snatch her frilly fan and smack her with it. "I'm her companion and private secretary," I answered lightly. "Are you returning to the Mystic Academy?" I asked in an effort to be polite.

"Perhaps. Since I'm betrothed to Pastor Havelock, I may not. I do have an exciting future to plan as his wife, after all. Anyway, my witch skills hardly need additional instruction. I am a Graven, after all. Why are you here?"

"I was invited."

"I don't mean that. I meant here in the city. We're here for the inauguration, of course," Marigold continued in a bored tone. "My poor mama was not up to traveling, but she insisted I attend in her place. It's stimulating to be back in Túr Solas again. Living in such a tiny hamlet like Crimson Hollow can stagnate the intellect. You must be dumbfounded by such a bustling metropolis."

Marigold shrugged before I could reply and continued on her favorite subject: herself. "Well, the inauguration ceremony will be boring, but the gala following will be thrilling. We're attending all the functions. I had to have so many new dresses made, else I could not attend them all. I can't wait for everyone to see my ball gown. I'm going to be officially presented to the premier and his wife tonight. A great honor."

"Premier Duchene is a kind man. He likes Rory too! He told me stories about his pukis pet when he was a boy," I remarked absently.

Her eyes narrowed into slits. The fact that I met Alexander before her rankled Marigold.

"Rory is a fine-looking pukis," Graven interceded with a rare smile. "Such a pet can be a handful, but I think you'll manage, Mistress Fable." He turned to his daughter. "Marigold, I see Lady Duchene speaking with Veda on the couch. Go introduce yourself and be charming."

Good luck with that, I thought.

"But Papa," Marigold protested.

"Be a good girl and do as I say. I'll join you shortly. I just have a private message from Mistress Brona for Sabine," he whispered, patting her hand patiently, his tone brooking no refusal. "It's just about business. Nothing as interesting as Lady Duchene's elegant gown. You must ask her where she acquired it."

"Her gown is exquisite," Marigold said wistfully. "Very well, Papa." She departed, her lace fan beating like an incensed butterfly.

"Is anything wrong?" I asked, my heart thumping in my chest.

"No, but I was asked to give you these." Letters tied with blue twine magically appeared in his hand with a soft burst of golden light. I recognized the stationary and my mother's perfume. The scent made me ache for her. "Your mother entreated me to deliver these from her and Altheda, since I was coming to Túr Solas. I planned to visit Lady Veda's house tomorrow, but since you're here, I thought you would like to have them now."

I accepted them gratefully. "Thank you. Is my mother well?"

"She is," Graven said, nodding.

"And Luther?"

"He's been drinking and gambling heavily again, I'm afraid."

"He promised to change, but I knew those were empty words," I said.

"We both know Luther's failings, but Brona is managing quite well. I think your position with Veda freed her to stand up to Luther and take control of the business. Brona instructed me to tell you to ignore Luther's antics and stay with Veda. She can offer you a future. This alone will make your mother happy."

"You're very kind, especially when it comes to my mother. May I ask why?"

"There is no great secret, Sabine. We were friends as children, and as young mages we attended the Academy until tragedy struck her. She's a fine lady who suffered more than she should have."

I'll admit, I felt a bit ashamed for prying, but his answer brought a sense of relief. "I'll write to Mother right away. Thank you, Lord Graven. You've always been kind to us. I want you to know I appreciate it."

"Remember, your mother wishes only for your happiness." He bowed his head and walked away. I tucked the letters into my sleeve. I longed to read them, but it would have to wait until later when I was alone.

Luther's failed promises did not surprise me, but I'd always been there to help my mother. I never imagined her having the courage to leave.

I noticed the earthy odor of wylsavan root and looked around, but neither Kalem nor his old man persona was anywhere to be seen. A young man in a black top hat and maroon coat bumped into me, forcing me out of my reverie "Hey! That's rude!" I called out.

The strange man glanced back without apology and then disappeared into the crowd as though I were a doormat. Bloody cheek!

Damn it! Where did he go? Why was he rushing? I wondered. Holding on to Rory, I tailed the maroon-coated stranger. If anything was suspicious, that man was! The heat of the room began to take its toll. I began to sweat, and the hall became a stifling prison. I found the double-glass doors leading to the gardens, wondering if the rude, fancy young man had come through this way.

Once outside, I saw nothing but peaceful green lawns and trees in the moonlight. *I should tell Veda about him,* I thought. The garden patio was a lovely refuge from the party and my past, filled with lovely, fragrant flowers and trees decorated with golden light crystals. The three sister moons were high and bright, breaking night's gloom. I was about to go back inside when I heard voices.

"No one need find out," Crimm said.

I jumped and looked around, but I couldn't see him! I spun around, frantic. Nothing! Where was he? I sensed the familiar smell of magic in the air. Then I heard another man's voice, one I did not know.

"It's not my fault," the stranger's voice insisted. "I have my own problems."

"I suggest you face this problem," Crimm snapped.

Rory's ears perked up, and he growled. Their voices muted. I backed away in a panic to retreat back inside. Suddenly, Crimm emerged from a patch of shadow as a demon steps from hell. The dark veil behind him vanished, revealing another man hovering in the dark.

Crimm grabbed my wrist with the strength of a vital man instead of an aged one. I struggled, but his grip tightened so hard I feared he would snap my bones. His withered face close and his breath hot on my face, musty and ancient as a gravestone. "What are you doing, Fable? Spying?"

Rory growled and snapped at Crimm. The aging necromancer released my arm, scowling.

"Albertus, we better leave," mumbled the stranger.

I didn't see his face. As he retreated out of sight, I could only tell that he was a short man wearing a long dark cloak. He wasn't the man I'd followed, but I found this one more suspicious.

"Keep your wretched dragon under control or else, Fable!"

I held Rory protectively. "How dare you lay hands on me! Don't threaten me or my baby dragon, Lord Crimm! You assaulted me! He just defended me."

I held Rory close, comforted somehow. The threat of my headache abated, despite Crimm's belligerent accusations.

"What were you doing?" Crimm demanded.

"Nothing! I just needed some damned air! Why are you skulking about in a shadow bubble and whispering with some stranger? If you're so damn blameless, why are you so afraid?" My hands heated and my headache grew worse, but I took deep breaths, stroking Rory's head as he growled at Crimm.

"Fable! What's wrong with you?" Crimm demanded as he seized my arm again.

I threw off his grip, defiant. "If you touch me again, I'll punch you!"

He released me, his face a thundercloud of anger. "How dare you!"

I untied the stupid pink ribbon around Rory's neck and tossed it to the ground. I would not keep my baby dragon tied up like a possession for their fancy party. "Come on, baby. Let's get away from here."

Suddenly, screams filled the night air. Not just one person, but many crying out in panic. We both stopped in our tracks.

"What's happening?" Crimm said.

Corporal Griffin burst through the double doors. "Mistress Fable! Lady Arcana needs you. Come quickly."

I rushed into the room to find people, even palace guards, fleeing the hall with terror in their eyes. I understood when I saw Alexander Duchene thrashing on the floor in a delirium, his nose and eyes bleeding. Veda and Lady Duchene knelt over him.

"Stay back, you foolish girl!" Crimm ordered, blocking my path. "Can't you see? He has mage fever!"

"I'm baseborn and immune, Crimm. I survived the disease in my mother's womb. Step aside so I can help."

CHAPTER 12

Scowling, Crimm moved aside, but I glimpsed fear in his eyes. I pushed through the terrified crowd, holding Rory tight. People shoved past me, all nobility and manners forgotten as they fled. Mage fever terrified all mageborns, even a crusty old coot like Albertus Crimm. Some powerful mages simply vanished in a magical puff or flew away.

"Everyone remain calm! Stop running!" Crimm shouted, rapping his staff on the marble floor.

No one heeded his words. Everyone fled, even nobles who were not even mageborn. Mage fever was not the only threat in the world. Other deadly plagues existed, dangerous to both castes, and mage fever was just the first suspect based on the symptoms Alexander exhibited.

My eyes watered from the odor of mystical terror singeing the air, and bumped into Lord Graven carrying Marigold, a puffy pink meringue in his arms. Marigold must have fainted from the shock. I could never figure her out.

"I'm so sorry," I mumbled to Lord Graven. "I'm trying to reach Veda."

"It's turned into a madhouse," he remarked, frowning at his fellow mages who stumbled over themselves to escape. "Manners vanished along with good sense."

"Bloody panic," I muttered.

"Do you and Veda need help?" Graven asked. "I can return after Marigold is safe."

"No, it's best to take Marigold to safety and wait in your rooms until we know more."

Graven nodded and shifted Marigold in his arms as he calmly walked away.

At least he departed with some dignity. The rest of the highborn noble and mage lot just ran screaming like banshees. Rory folded blue and green wings over his face, shivering. All this nonsense upset him.

When I finally reached Veda, she was kneeling next to Lady Corene over Alexander's shaking body. Corene held a cloth to his face to stopper the bleeding. Corene didn't abandon her husband despite the risk of infection and possible death.

Veda conjured swirls of green sorcery in her hands, murmuring magic words I did not understand. I dropped to my knees next to her, waiting until her incantation was complete before I spoke. "What the hell happened?"

"I don't know. He was fine, and then this!" Alexander's body glowed like an emerald as Veda worked her sorcery. "Hold him still! The spell should stop the bleeding in a moment."

I grabbed his wrists. I'm stronger than most people realize, and managed to still his quaking body with effort.

Corene, hands and gown bloodstained, held her husband's head in her lap. "It's not working, Veda! The bleeding won't stop!" She threw the blood-soaked cloth aside and magically summoned a fresh towel. She held it to his face to staunch the bleeding, whispering prayers.

"Give the spell time to work!" Veda cautioned.

After a tense span of seconds, Veda's green magic shimmered brightly and faded. Alexander's bleeding and convulsions finally stopped. I breathed a sigh of relief. It was only then I realized the hall was eerily silent and empty now.

"Praise be to the gods," Corene muttered with relief.

"Good. Now we can move him," Veda said. "Quickly!"

"I'll carry him," Braden Griffin offered.

Veda and Corene both looked at him with respect and gratitude. He hadn't fled like the others. True, he was baseborn and immune to the mage fever, but what if Alexander's attack wasn't that malady? Braden's actions spoke of a true noble character as he lifted Alexander in his arms as though he weighed no more than a basket of feathers.

"This way," Corene beckoned Braden, swiftly leading them out of the reception hall.

I jumped up to go follow, trying to keep pace with Veda.

"Did you see or sense anything suspicious before this happened?" Veda asked, slowing down long enough to grab my arm and pull me up to her speed.

I glanced back at Crimm, who followed with a swift stride for his age but kept a safe distance. "A few moments before, a foppish young man raised my suspicions, but mostly he annoyed me because he was rude. I'm not sure why. I just sensed something was odd about him. I trailed him outside to the garden, where I stumbled upon Crimm talking to a stranger. I didn't see them at first because they were hidden by a shadowy spell."

"That's strange," Veda remarked.

"I know! Crimm accused me of spying on him. He grabbed me so hard I think he left bruises. But he crossed a line when he threatened Rory. I swore to punch him if he ever touched me or threatened my baby dragon again. I know this might disappoint you, but what Crimm did was more wrong."

"Calm down. I'm not disappointed. Did you see the stranger he was speaking to? Was it the rude dandy you followed?" Veda asked.

"No. It wasn't him, but I didn't see the other man's face because he scuttled off into the night like a cockroach. He was shorter too and wearing a dark coat. The one I followed wore a fancy deep red coat and was taller." Panic assailed me. Crimm was the chancellor of Ravenna, and powerful men sometimes abuse power. "Will I go to prison for threatening to hit Crimm?"

Veda shook her head. "Don't fret about that, dear. You won't be punished. We'll talk later, but now we must attend Alexander."

I had no idea why Crimm hated me unless he despised all baseborn bastards on prejudice. In a perverse way, I understood Luther's contempt for me. His beloved wife, Sabine, my namesake and grandmother, perished from mage fever. I had the bad manners to survive. But Crimm's animosity remained a mystery.

Kalem joined us in the hallway, looking disheveled and still wearing his old-man face.

"Where the hell have you been?" Veda asked with a sharp look.

"Lost in the chaos of hysteria and bad manners, Lady Arcana. My wards went off all over the palace. I was checking them outside when all this happened," Kalem answered as he rushed to keep up with us.

"Wards?" I asked. "For what?"

"Remember the dark spectral essence that attacked you your first night here?"

I shivered. "How could I forget? It left a scorch mark on my hand when it touched me." Then I remembered the odor of wylsavan root. "Have you worn the same face all night?"

"Yes," Kalem replied. "Why?"

I stepped up my pace to keep up, glancing back at Crimm, who followed me like a curse. "I smelled wylsavan root right before the strange man rudely bumped me and vanished into the crowd. I didn't see you nearby."

"We could be dealing with another shapeshifter," Kalem said. "What about Alexander?"

Veda shook her head. "I don't believe it's mage fever, so drop the panicked expression, Kalem. I stopped both his bleeding and convulsions with a spell."

"Of course," I said. "Mage fever doesn't respond to direct magic. If he was infected, no spell would have worked."

We reached the premier's private apartments. Veda opened the double doors with a wave of her hand. Braden carefully laid Alexander on the bed. A worried Corene held her husband's hand. Braden stayed in the background as he awaited future commands.

Kalem leaned in and whispered to me, "Are you alright? You look flustered. Poor Rory looks upset too."

"Crimm Snot-Face mean," Rory grumbled.

I stroked Rory's head, wincing. "Please stop saying that!"

"Sabi mad?" Rory sniffed.

"No, of course not," I said with a sigh.

Rory calmed in my arms, away from all the manic people. "Alexander just had a very public collapse and people scattered like frightened bunnies. I had a nasty fight with Crimm right before this blew up. I'm waiting for the axe to fall."

Kalem's face was sympathetic. "What the hell happened?"

"Bad timing. I'll explain later. I can't think just now." I realized Albertus Crimm still waited in the hall. I figured he was afraid to follow us in. *Good,* I thought. *He can stay out there.* Obviously, his anger with me did not overpower his dread of the disease.

"Sabine, come see this," Veda called to me, examining Alexander's hands. "What do you see?"

Rory crawled to my shoulder as I approached Alexander's prone body. I looked carefully and remarked, "His fingernails are green. Mage fever doesn't cause that. It may be poison or even an allergic reaction of some kind."

"Exactly." Veda smiled slightly.

"What?" Corene gasped. "Poison! Will he die?"

"No," Veda assured her. "I believe the cause of symptoms is due to skalvich poisoning." Waves of magic poured from Veda's hands over Alexander. "Yes, it is skalvich poisoning. The symptoms resembled mage fever to everyone because of the bleeding and convulsions the leaves produce in high doses."

"But not green fingers," I said with a grin.

"At least it's not the scarlet madness. The last thing we need is another mage fever epidemic. Will he recover?" Corene asked.

"Yes. I believe he must have ingested only a small dose. Otherwise, he would have died by now," Veda said. "Skalvich plants make you sick, but it takes a massive amount to kill you in one dose. Only two days ago, my mystical and blood tests showed no toxic essence in his system. This is new. This was a scare tactic, designed to show him as weak before the whole court."

"This reeks of conspiracy," I said. "They wanted to shame Alexander in public. Why?"

"A traitor wants to weaken his position as the leader of our republic," Corene remarked. "My husband has many enemies. He's a good man. Good men have more enemies than wicked ones. How did this even happen? His food and drink are tested with care. His clothes are meticulously cleansed with mystical enchantment."

Veda nodded. "Skalvich is tasteless and odorless. It had to be a high dose to render this reaction. Usually, people get a rash and fever, and that's it. It's like poison ivy, just more virulent."

I gasped. "What about his clothes?" I asked. "Skalvich oil is toxic if the skin absorbs the poison through the pores. It could have been on his clothes or even in his toiletries."

Veda nodded. "We need to investigate all avenues. Strip him and carefully put every garment and even his jewelry into a clean sheet. I will personally test it and use magic to purify it later." She turned to us, misting us with a dose of light blue magic. It smelled like flowers. Rory tried to lick the air. "This should purify all of us. Still, take care. Kalem, I will need you to assist me. Make sure you wear gloves as a precaution. Take everything to my mage lab in the palace. And Kalem, please drop the old-man face."

"What must I do?" Corene asked.

"Stay with your husband," Veda said, smiling. "Help watch over him until we figure this out."

Kalem shimmered, and in a blink his stooped, elderly image with gray hair and wrinkles vanished, replaced by his true youthful face and proud posture.

Braden watched, fascinated. "Impressive, Sorcerer. Tell me, does it hurt to shapeshift?"

"Oddly, my friend, you are one of the few to ever ask," Kalem remarked, grinning at Braden. "It puts a strain on any shapeshifter."

Veda looked at Corene. "We have no idea how Alexander was infected. I'll brew up an antidote and make sure everyone has a good dose for protection."

Crimm banged on the door with his cane. "Well, is it the red fever? Answer me, Veda!"

Veda sighed and opened the door. "No, but there are conspirators in our midst nearly as deadly. Come in. Just don't touch anything."

Crimm leaned on his cane as he entered, grimacing as he looked down on Alexander's body. "There's no disease? Are you certain?"

"He was poisoned," Veda said. "He'll recover though. The poison was not fatal, nor meant to be, I think. It would take a fairly large dose to cause this. I am sure it was done using magic. His reaction was too severe for casual contact with the plant."

"It would need to be condensed," I said, thinking. "No apothecary would even have this plant in their stores. It serves no purpose."

"Except to cause harm or misdirect," Veda said.

"Damn it. I will handle security and summon the wizards to investigate," Crimm said. He nodded and beckoned Veda closer with his boney hand. "I'll speak with you privately first." Crimm and Veda stepped into the hall. I couldn't hear anything, which pricked at my nerves. Then Veda returned.

"What did he tell you?" I asked, knowing that, despite all the current trauma, the old man would not let this dispute die.

"Nothing, but he asks to speak with you tomorrow morning. He didn't say why, but he assures me you are not in trouble. He knows you have a duty to help me and Alexander now."

Damn, damn, damn! "And you believe him? Should I escape tonight before he locks me up?"

"Don't worry," Veda replied, touching my cheek. "You're not in danger of being tossed into a dungeon."

"We have laws against unlawful imprisonment," Alexander croaked, looking around in confusion. "What the hell happened?" He looked down at himself. "I'm a mess!"

"The bad news is you were poisoned, but the good news is you will live," Veda replied.

"But who did this to him?" Corene demanded, her face flushed with anger.

"Probably the same traitor who did something to his magic," I said.

Too many mysteries fogged my brain: unknown poisoners, strange spectral creatures, and whatever Crimm was hiding. I didn't trust him. I certainly didn't want to see the old crank alone. I wanted to shut out the world and go to bed, but it was going to be a long night.

I looked down at my beautiful velvet gown, realizing it was spattered with bloodstains.

"Don't worry, I'll restore your gown," Veda assured me, and with a motion of her hand, my new dress and person were free of bloodstains. "We must remain at the palace for now, for security and practicality. We'll stay in the same suite, of course. I know you're tired, but go back to the townhouse and pack some clothes, my notes, whatever you think we'll need."

"Of course," I said with a nod.

"Good," Veda offered with a smile. "Braden can escort you."

"And when you return, I request Corporal Braden to protect us. I want a brave soldier we can trust to join his personal guard," Lady Corene commanded.

"Hurry and be safe, my dear," Veda softly said, brushing a lock of unruly curls from my face.

"I will, Veda," I replied.

Braden beamed with pride at Corene's praise. I do not think he stopped smiling our entire drive back to our townhouse. Despite Veda's assurance, I wasn't in a smiling mood. Crimm stressed my thoughts. I did not want to meet him tomorrow. Braden did not seem bothered by my silence, nor did he attempt small talk. He just drove the carriage, patient and comfortable next to me. Rory, calmed by the cool night air and away from loud strangers, fell asleep in my lap.

When we arrived at the townhouse, I unlocked the door and gently handed Rory to Braden when we reached the stairs. "Please hold him while I get our things, please? I'll only be a few minutes."

"No problem, Sabine. I like the little fellow." Rory settled happily in

Braden's large hands, purring contently as he began to stroke his head.

I rushed upstairs and packed two bags for us, along with some toiletries. I gathered up Veda's research journal and notes, stuffing them in another satchel. We could come back for the rest later.

"That's quite a haul. I'll swap you for this tiny dragon," Braden said with a laugh when he saw me lugging my bounty downstairs.

"Thank you," I said. I set the heavy bags down and took Rory. "It's a shame. I was just beginning to feel at home here."

"It won't be for long," Braden said. "I know you and Lady Arcana will unravel this mystery."

"I hope so. You were truly brave tonight."

"Thank you, Sabine."

"Oh, wait!" I rushed to the kitchen and grabbed a basket of my cinnamon rolls. I returned and offered them. "It's not a medal for courage, but they taste good. Don't know about you, but I'm starving."

"Happy to share, Miss Sabine."

On the way back to the palace, we ate gooey sweet rolls. When we arrived, he escorted me to my suite laden with Veda's and my luggage. I watched him leave, eating the last of my rolls and giving me a final grin before he took the stairs.

Once inside the safe haven of our room, I put Rory on the bed, where he snuggled on a very plush velvet pillow.

"Braden nice," Rory said.

I stroked his head. "He is nice. It's good to have a friend here so far from home."

"Crimm Snot-Face is mean," Rory grumbled.

I shook my head, trying not to encourage his naughty side. "I know, but you mustn't say bad things in front of Crimm, even if he is a snot-face."

I carefully laid my precious letters from my mother and Altheda on the table. I longed to read them, but I had my duties first. I needed to change from my posh gown into something more practical. My hands were sticky from the icing. I washed them off and slipped off my velvet dress. Then I changed into a blue blouse and black skirt I pulled from my bag.

Growling in agitation, Rory went around in circles on the bed as I buttoned my blouse. "What's wrong, baby?" A sudden rush of cold made me gasp.

The chill was all too familiar, sinister, and dark. I looked around the room, but not a mirror in sight. The candles in the chamber flickered red, and a howl pierced my ears. A black ghostly mist swirled around me like a storm, lifting me up as I struggled in the shadow's hold, screaming.

CHAPTER 13

The phantom seized me by the neck, burning my skin. Its piercing wails paused for a heartbeat as I thrashed in its hold. I forced myself to look at my destroyer.

A she-creature molded by fury and shrouded in shadow. Her essence stained the light, for I could see only darkness in her grasp. Red eyes stared into my soul, sniffing out my buried sins. Long misty hair, black shimmers of death, swirled around me.

I am going to die. Damn it, I am going to die.

Light burst around me, stunning the wraith. A gleaming mystical knife sliced through the swirling black, freeing me from the creature's grip. I dropped to the floor, trembling, and pushed myself up on my elbows. Swirling with black mist, she lurched at me again. I scooted away in mute panic until strong hands dragged me away from the apparition. I was confused until Braden lifted me in his arms.

"Get her out of here!" Kalem shouted as the furious wraith pitched for him.

Braden bolted for the door. The creature shifted from Kalem and darted through the air, blocking our exit. Braden didn't flinch but held on to me as he evaded her touch.

Kalem forced the shadow back with beams of light. The demonic specter howled in defiance. Kalem continued attacking, but his quarry swirled around the room, evading his assault with mystical speed. Crimson eyes flared, framed by streams of ashy mist as she howled. I sensed her rage, fighting down nausea and fear when she cast her eyes on me again.

"Get down!" Kalem shouted, and his sorcery forced a bubble of light around my attacker. She shrieked in defiance. Suddenly, with a final scream, she vanished. The sudden silence provided a blessing overcast with fear. Sickened by the charred air and terror, faint wisps of ash dusted the carpet where she'd disappeared.

For a moment, we all just stopped, feeling fear and exhausted by it. I was too stunned to even protest Braden still held me in his arms. I felt like a helpless maiden for the moment, so I allowed it.

"What the hell was that thing?" Braden asked tightly.

"I don't know," Kalem replied. "It should not have penetrated the new wards or escaped my shield."

I looked around, reality sinking back in. "Rory!" I didn't see my baby dragon anywhere. "Oh gods! Rory!" I patted Braden on the shoulder to put me down. I swayed on my feet but refused to buckle in front of my comrades. I used Braden's arm to stabilize me. "Where's Rory! Baby! Come to mama!"

A scared cry from under the bed sparked hope. I stumbled to the bed and looked underneath to find Rory curled into a ball, shaking. "Come here, baby! It's alright."

He lifted his head and scrambled into my arms. I stroked his head and cuddled him. "How did you even know I was in trouble?" I asked the two men.

"My new wards activated," Kalem said. "I followed the trail here. I ran into Braden along the way and recruited him. The creature should not have been able to bypass the new wards protecting the whole palace. This angers me. I don't look forward to telling Crimm this." Kalem took a glass specimen bottle from his pocket, summoned the ashy remains into the bottle, and corked it. "I'm not sure what I just faced. But I'm damned sure going to find out."

"I'm not sure I want to know," I said. Then I shuddered, touching my newly scorched neck.

# # #

The next day my stomach was still queasy. Veda had tended my wounds when she'd arrived the night before and healed the phantom's burns. She insisted I stay in bed to recover, but Albertus Crimm's demands would have haunted me. I prefer all of my pain to be over with quickly.

So Veda asked Alexander to allow Braden to accompany me to Crimm's office to ensure my safety. I agreed because, frankly, being alone in the palace was deadly.

"Where's your little dragon?" Braden asked.

"I thought it best that Veda look after Rory during my audience with Lord Crimm. I fear what he might say to the old coot."

"Are you sure you're well enough for this? You look awfully pale."

"I'm always pale," I said, laughing. I put my hand over my stomach, hoping it would remain calm. After the initial shock of the creature's attack, I'd vomited several times. "I'm fine, really! Veda gave me a potion, which helped. I'm just a bit hollowed out after last night. I'm sorry you had to witness that."

Braden grinned broadly. "Don't be embarrassed. If I were tossed around by a monstrous entity, I'd be sick too. I grew up on a farm with nine brothers and sisters. I've seen my fair share of things, but I think I'll leave this adventure out of my next letter home. My mum might fret more than usual."

"Good choice."

We reached Crimm's official suite, and I stood a moment, staring at the ominous double doors. "I better go in alone," I said, as though convincing myself.

"I'll be right outside the door," Braden promised. Then he leaned in to whisper. "After all, you faced a monster last night. Crimm is just a cranky old man."

I nodded, took a deep breath, and opened the doors.

A thin, dour-faced secretary in a severe black suit sat at a desk with stacks of scrolls and papers. He greeted me with bored indifference. "Please state your business."

"I'm here to see Lord Crimm. My name is Sabine Fable."

"Why are you requesting an audience with Chancellor Crimm? He has no time for silly requests, you know."

"I'm not requesting but was in fact summoned by Lord Crimm himself. If he's too busy, I'm quite happy to go."

Mr. Dour-Face gestured for me to wait and rose from his spotless desk. "Wait here."

I stood in the outer office, feigning patience. The austere décor was as grim as I'd imagined—dark wooden furniture and neutral wallpaper with little color to brighten the room.

The secretary emerged from Albertus Crimm's sanctorum. "The chancellor will see you now."

"How gracious of you," I remarked dryly. I expected him to demand I wipe my feet before entering the holy office of Crimm. I stepped inside the private chamber, and the secretary closed the door behind me.

The mageborn finally acknowledged me after an eternity of seconds, busily writing in a ledger. "Mistress Fable." He brusquely gestured for me to sit in the chair opposite him.

I obeyed, hoping this would be brief.

"Veda informed me of the assault you suffered yesterday from the unidentified wraith or phantom. No one knows what it is. Which displeases me." He glanced up. "You do look ghastly. Are you well enough to continue, or do you wish to be excused?"

Such gracious manners. "I'm fine," I replied evenly.

"The report on this creature is disturbing. Veda has requested a change of suite and I granted it. You are lucky, Mistress Fable. It attacked two other people last night."

"I didn't know that. Was anyone hurt?"

"They are dead. One minor nobleman and a palace guard. Both were mageborn. So far you are the only baseborn it has hunted. Veda wanted to spare you the news after your attack last night."

But you didn't want to spare me, did you? I thought. But in reply, I coolly said, "I trust Veda and Kalem will find a way to solve this mystery."

"You are baseborn and barely have an education. What would you know of such things?"

I clenched my jaw at his tone. "Magic is no guarantee of intellect and poverty is not a surety of stupidity."

He frowned and leaned forward. "We must discuss what you saw in the garden." Crimm picked up a looking glass of silver from his desk. He handed me the mirror. "Look, and tell me what you see."

I took it, perplexed, but I also sensed the magic of the mirror. My reflection confirmed I looked awful after a night of terror and vomiting. The glass misted over, revealing a pleasant scene of a man playing with two children in a garden. I assumed the man and the two boys were rich, based on their elegant clothes and the lush garden. The vision shifted into a montage of family scenes, the people moving and talking within the looking glass. Such magic mirrors are pricy toys for the rich.

"I don't understand. What's this about?" I asked, confused.

"Keeping looking."

I obeyed, irritated by his silly game. I finally saw a close-up of the man in the mirror. I didn't recognize the man, in his thirties maybe, clean-shaven with dark curly hair. Then I noticed his eyes. They were light silver, like mine. *Ghost eyes.* Marigold's words mocked me all the way from childhood. My stomach knotted and my head ached. "Why are you showing me this? Who is this man?"

"He's the gentleman I was speaking to last night when you interrupted us. He is concerned, and rightly so. Your presence at court is an issue we must resolve now."

"I still don't understand what you are talking about. From what I see, his eyes are like mine. Other than that, I know nothing of this person."

"Rare silver eyes, Mistress Fable. Some believe eyes like yours are descended from ancient fey bloodlines, long since extinct in our world. I doubt a baseborn bastard like you would be descended from such an illustrious ancestry. The old legends are rubbish, of course. But your eyes are rare and have been noticed."

"Fascinating, but this conversation isn't about mythology."

"It is about bloodlines though. Your mother was Brona Fable, dismissed in disgrace from the Academy. What did she tell you about your father?"

"My mother has never been a disgrace in her life, Lord Crimm!"

"Lord Remus Runecroft, the mage from the mirror, is a respected wizard. A husband and devoted father with two sons. I've known him since he graduated from the Mystic Academy. He apprenticed with me in law. Remus Runecroft was born of an ancient noble family. You are nothing. Now, what do you want from him? Why are you here?"

"Because I work for Veda as her companion and secretary."

"Do you expect me to believe those are your only motives? What do you know about your mother's time at the Academy and why she was expelled?"

Foggy after a wretched night of vomiting, my mind finally woke to his accusation. That toady little man must be my father—the fiend who abandoned my mother. "I know only what my mother told me." *Which was nothing, but he does not know that.* "If this is my father by blood, I want nothing from him." My stomach curdled again and my headache returned.

"Yes, he is your father by blood. He's wealthy, titled, and mageborn. Remus is concerned you'll drudge up the past and extort money. Now promise to say nothing about your connection to him. A bastard has no rights, after all. And you would only bring shame upon yourself."

"Shame? The shame is his." I slammed the mirror on the desk and the glass shattered. I felt it like a shiver through my body. "Please tell your cowardly friend Runecroft he needn't worry. You call Remus Runecroft a devoted father! A devoted father cares for all of his children, not just the convenient ones. As far as I'm concerned, he's just a coward who took advantage of my mother. I wear my mother's name with pride. I am a Fable. And never insult my mother again, Lord Crimm, or I'll show you just how baseborn I am."

Crimm stared at me, shocked anyone would talk back to him. "Mistress Fable, you cannot speak—"

"Go to hell!" I jumped up and fled his office. On my way out, I bumped into Remus Runecroft, who was waiting in the reception area. The dour secretary looked down, fumbling with papers. I tried to move past Runecroft, but he stopped me.

"Please, my apologies, Mistress Fable," he said. "I see my timing is a bit off. I am Lord Remus Runecroft."

It was disconcerting seeing my silver eyes reflecting back at me. "Bully for you."

Crimm, who had followed me out the door, stepped between us. "Remus, you're early."

"I just wanted to ensure Mistress Fable's cooperation. If you would give me a moment, Albertus, I would speak with her alone. She seems a trifle upset. Young girls are so frail."

Frail? I'll show him frail.

"I will leave you two in private." Crimm brusquely summoned his secretary. "Come along, Frederick. I think you should take an early lunch."

They vacated the room in haste.

Except for his silver eyes and rich clothing, Runecroft was ordinary and short. I was aghast to realize my lack of height and curly dark hair were inherited from him. This man ruined my mother's reputation. Hatred, abandonment, spite, and judgment flared into one violent emotion burning to explode.

Runecroft sighed and smiled broadly. "Albertus told me you had my eyes, but sadly, not my magic. My sons both possess magic but did not inherit my silver gaze of the fairy born. Strange you did."

"Why? Because I am a bastard?"

"No, of course not. It just seems odd a baseborn would inherit such fey eyes."

"What do you want?"

Remus Runecroft dropped his false smile. "Just a promise you will say nothing about any connection to me."

"Fine. Now get out of my way."

He stepped aside. "Excellent. After all, I paid compensation for what happened. The law was on my side."

My hand was on the doorknob, but stiffened at his words. *Compensation. Law on his side?* He was hiding something. "What do you mean, paid compensation? Law?"

"To keep things in the past, that's all. I should not have to suffer for a youthful mistake."

I stepped back as the terrible truth dawned on me. "My mother told me what you did." Mother told me nothing, but he did not know that.

He grabbed my arm, angry now. "Mistress Fable, I'm not a cruel man, but I will not tolerate threats to my reputation. I never intended harm to your mother. Brona was a lovely girl. So talented at magic too, until she lost her powers."

"She told me what you did."

He grew flustered, tightening his grip. "Do not believe everything she says. It's only her opinion. I was only being affectionate. It was late and I had too much wine. Then Brona began to scream, drawing unwanted attention. It was all a misunderstanding. Then a fellow student interfered and threatened me. Me! A Runecroft! Your mother made quite a fuss for such a little indiscretion. My family took offense at her accusations, so they took care of it."

I jerked my arm away. I always thought my mother had a tragic romance born of youth. Never this! I backed away. "She wasn't sent away because she was pregnant. You raped her and you covered it up!"

"No, it wasn't rape!" he cried, waving his hands in desperation. "Nothing so crude."

"Did she refuse you? Did she say no? Did she struggle?" I shouted.

"Yes, but silly girls always say no. They don't really mean it. I said I was sorry. My family made sure all charges against me were dropped. She was shamed and expelled for her troubles too, so don't think you have grounds after so many years. Why should I suffer for one night of folly? You can do nothing. But if you threaten me, I will not hesitate to make your life difficult, Mistress Fable."

"Like you did to my mother? You abused your privilege to bury the truth of your crime and ruin my mother."

"We paid your family money in good faith for no further legal threats. If your mother hadn't become pregnant, it would never have been an issue. My family even offered to give you our blessed name and take you if you had been born a boy with the gift of magic. You had neither."

"Thank the gods," I said. "I would rather be given to a family of trolls than you!"

"Well, her greedy father was obliging enough to take our gold. Luther Fable accepted the fee in exchange for silence. So you must abide."

"I abide by nothing I had no say in!" Damn Luther! He took money from this wretch after what he did to my poor mother! Then he drank and gambled it away rather than use his ill-gotten gains to care for his family! The pain Remus inflicted on my mother damaged her in ways I'd never understood until this moment. Mother was so gentle and loving but hated to be touched. All those years of shrinking from even my touch made sense in this dreadful moment of truth.

I balled up my fist and punched Runecroft so hard he fell on his ass. I ran, but he followed me into the corridor, where Crimm waited.

"Come back," Remus demanded, holding his spurting nose. "You do not understand!'

I spun around, trembling. The agony of my head nearly blinded me. My hands felt like they were on fire. "You raped her! That's what I understand. My mother was outcast and shamed for *your* crime! I've been called bastard since I was born, but you're the fucking bastard! You raped my mother!"

A thunderous jolt erupted from my body. Fiery waves of red magic flared from my hands, and the force struck Remus so powerfully that it tossed him several feet down the hallway. I stumbled back, sorcerous beams gushing from my hands, wildly striking the walls and floor. The guards and even Crimm jumped out of the path of my mystical rage. I vaguely heard Braden's voice calling to me. Struggling to his feet, Remus fled down the hall, howling like a banshee.

Weeping, I crumbled against the wall, my hands bleeding magic.

CHAPTER 14

I curled up in bed, squinting against the harsh sunlight streaming through the window. I covered my face against the brightness. *What the hell happened to me?*

"Welcome back," Kalem said, entering the room.

"From where?" I moaned, rubbing my eyes. "Hell?"

"You've been unconscious for almost a day. How are you feeling?"

"Like crap." I looked around, sitting up. "Where am I?"

"You're in a palace suite. A new one, untouched by any strange spectral creatures. We didn't want to move you too far," Kalem said, sitting by the bed.

"Where's Veda?"

"She just stepped out to check on Alexander. We've taken turns looking after you. Do you recall anything?"

"I remember feeling queasy after the wraith attack." I winced as more memories surfaced. "Sorry I threw up on you."

Kalem grinned and shook his head. "I'd have been surprised if you hadn't, the way you were being tossed around by that damned apparition. Take your time."

My muddled brain was slow to process. "I had an appointment with crabby old Crimm. I just wanted it over with. And … Runecroft!" Memories flooded in with cruel clarity. "Damn Albertus Crimm! Do you know what that shifty old necromancer scum was up to?"

Kalem poured a glass of water and handed it to me. "Calm down. Drink this and tell me."

I opened my mouth to protest, but I was so thirsty. I gulped the cool water in a single swallow. Another panic set in when I didn't see Rory. "Where's my dragon? Rory!" I called, kicking off the sheets. Rory's startled squeak surprised me. I looked under the blanket. "There you are! Come out now."

Rory scurried out from beneath the covers and curled in my lap. "Sabi better?" he asked.

"Yes, baby." I sighed with relief, patting his head.

"Sabi snores." Rory sniffed and preened his little wings.

"How did I even get here?"

"Braden carried you here after Veda sealed off the magic streaming from your hands. You'd lost consciousness by then."

"You mean I fainted like some pathetic swooning maiden!" I was mortified. Then the word *magic* penetrated my foggy mind. "My magic?" I whispered, stunned. "How could I forget?" The memory of sorcerous energy pouring from my hands in my anger bloomed in my memory. The sensation of fiery water coursed through my body.

"Sabi magic everywhere," Rory chirped, sniffing my hands. "Magic smell nice."

"Is it why my hands feel numb?"

"Most likely. What else do you remember?" Kalem asked gently. "Take your time."

"I thought Crimm was going to chastise me because I threatened to punch him. Instead, he tricked me! His summons was about a man named Remus Runecroft. Apparently, he's my father by blood. Crimm warned me to stay quiet about the noble Runecroft being my father. Crimm's tricks and what Runecroft did to my mother break any promise I made to stay silent!"

"Damn. Did you even know Runecroft was your father? How did Crimm even know?"

"I didn't know until Crimm told me. My rare silver eyes apparently tipped him off. Runecroft is also a friend of Crimm's. But I think there's more to it. Runecroft has my eyes, but he also knew about me being at court. But how? Did Crimm tell him?"

Kalem refilled my water glass, which I eagerly downed. My mouth was a wad of dry cotton. "Crimm is Runecroft's friend. Mentor even," he said. "'Your eyes are rare."

"I always hated my eyes. Kids mocked me when I was little. They called me ghost eye. Explains why Crimm loathed me on sight. He adores Runecroft. I told Crimm I didn't care. Here's the thing, until that moment, I never knew my father's name. Mother always refused to tell me. I was sometimes curious to know who he was. Then I would get over that. Why should I care about someone who rejected my mother? Now I wish I'd never heard of him."

"I'm so sorry, Sabine," Kalem said. "Albertus shouldn't have done that. It's neither his concern nor his jurisdiction."

"Not the way he tells it. But that's not the worst of it. I was so angry, I told Crimm off and tried to leave. Then I bumped into Remus waiting outside his office. It's like he was lurking. Why was this powerful wizard so anxious about me? So I played my own trick. I pretended to know more than I did. Why was he so desperate to cover up a youthful affair unless there was a darker truth? Then I learned why. My poor mother never had an ill-fated romance. Remus Runecroft raped my mother."

"What? Damn them both!" Kalem snapped, jumping to his feet.

"Yes. I was too clever and received more truth than I wanted. Gods, you should have heard Runecroft! He thinks he's the victim. She wasn't expelled because of an affair, but because she was raped and must have filed charges or something. He bragged about how they believed him and not her. That's why the Academy dismissed her. There was no justice for my mother. He made sure of it."

Kalem muttered, shaking his head. "He should never have put you through this. He had no right to hurt you."

"I lost my temper. Big surprise. My temper always wins. I just couldn't take any more. I balled up my fist and hit Remus so hard I must have broken his nose. He dropped like a bag of overstuffed velvet. I ran out of the room, my head throbbing and hands burning. He chased after me, begging me to be silent. How dare he! I thought I'd die from my own rage. Then the magic burst."

Years of jealous yearning for mage powers have been granted, at a price, I thought. *My angry inner troll must find this amusing.*

"Those petty men are nothing, Sabine," Kalem whispered. "Listen to me. Know who you truly are and they can never hurt you. Your magic is restored. Now you control your destiny—not them. I'm going to have words with Crimm."

"I would prefer you turn him into a warty toad. Or dung beetle. Your choice."

Veda entered carrying a tray laden with food and a pitcher of milk. "Thank heavens you are awake! We've been so worried. How are you feeling, dear?"

"She remembers about Runecroft," Kalem said, taking the tray from her and putting it on the side table.

"Did my magic really manifest?" I asked, afraid to believe the treatment finally worked and wanting to banish Runecroft from my mind.

Smells of food made me dizzy as my barren stomach rumbled. Rory's nose twitched and his wings flapped in anticipation. "Is that roast beef?"

"Yes," Veda said softly, stroking my cheek. "Now hold still a moment." Her fingers shimmered with blue magic as she examined me. "I must admit, I never expected such an impressive display of power. I detect no ill effects, but you need rest. Your body was drained. The repressed magic in your system must have exploded. Imagine a broken dam, flooding sorcery wild and uncontrolled. I managed to stop it. Your body couldn't cope and you passed out."

"We put you to bed and looked after you. Rory wouldn't even eat while you were unconscious," Kalem said with a grin. "Despite the temptation of bacon I offered him."

"Kalem nice," Rory said.

"Poor baby," I whispered, scratching his ears. "Does this prove your theory now?" I asked Veda. "About the disease not destroying magic, but blocking it?"

"That is another tale, but not the most important now," Veda replied.

"The truth is out. I mean about Runecroft being my ... I cannot say 'father.'"

"Braden told us everything," Veda said, nodding. "Runecroft fled the scene, apparently with his britches smoking."

Good. "Where's Braden? I didn't hurt him when I—"

"No. He's fine. He's also officially assigned to Alexander's personal guard. Otherwise, he would be here."

"Good. He deserves the promotion." I nodded, feeling the kinship of a fellow baseborn making it in the mage-driven society. But now I was a mage too. *Does that change us?* I wondered.

"The boy's been asking about you. He's been so worried. It was quite a scene. Even Crimm stayed with you until we got there."

"I doubt his intentions were good."

"I know you're furious and upset. You have a right to be," Veda replied. "Crimm must deal with the truth about Runecroft. It's his burden, not yours. He must also deal with me."

I tried to get out of bed, but dizziness overwhelmed me. I lay back down, angry and helpless. Anger I can deal with, but I despise being helpless.

"Careful, you're still weak," Veda said. "That's why I brought food. I experienced something similar when my sorcery was restored, though not on such a grand scale. My magic wasn't locked away for seventeen years. Yours was. In a strange way, I believe your strong emotions may have helped release your magic."

I lay back, drained and frustrated. "Odd, since my passions have been my bane since childhood. People always told me I was too emotional, like they have the right to judge me."

Veda took my hand. "Focus on your recovery and healing. Your life is different now, Sabine. Now you are mageborn."

"I'm mageborn," I whispered, feeling strange. "How is Alexander?" I asked, hoping to change the subject from myself.

"Much better," Veda replied. "He sends you his personal good wishes and welcomes you to the caste of mages. You're a mystical miracle." Veda gently brushed back a lock of my frizzy hair and turned to Kalem. "Give us a moment."

"I need to take care of something anyway," Kalem said with a nod.

After he left, Veda sat by my bed. "Talk to me, Sabine. I know that look. You're seething with fury."

"My feelings may be transparent, but at least they're honest!" I cried. "I hate all of it. Crimm, Runecroft, the string of foul lies and injustice. My mother suffered. Her reputation was lost! How could she even bear to look at me? And Luther … Luther knew too! They paid him to keep silent."

"It may not be the right time, but I must tell you something now," Veda said.

I turned over and looked at her. "You knew, didn't you?"

"Yes, I knew from the beginning. Brona came to me after it happened, with another friend who cared about her too. We tried to get her justice."

A friend? A realization hit me. "Was it Thomas Graven?"

Veda nodded. "Yes. How did you know?"

"He's always been kind to my mother and me. I was always suspicious of him, mostly because he's a rich mageborn and his daughter's a brat."

"Thomas Graven is a good man. He was willing to testify as witness for your mother. He came upon them by accident when he heard Brona screaming. He pulled Remus off her and brought her to me. We demanded Remus be charged, but we were blocked at every step. The filth denied everything, of course. The Runecrofts are powerful. Remus's father was on the Board of Academy Regents then. Any hope of justice was crushed."

"It's wrong!"

"Yes, it was wrong. They expelled her for speaking the truth. Later, when she was pregnant, it complicated matters. Luther was the one who told the Runecroft family that Brona was pregnant."

"Explains why Luther got a settlement and why they offered to take me if I turned out to be mageborn and a boy."

"It's an ancient tradition to offer adoption, especially for male babies. It does not have the stain of rape, so they looked noble for it. For them, it was just another maneuver. Brona wanted nothing to do with it." Veda took me by my shoulders. "Even if Runecroft confessed today, it wouldn't matter. There's a five-year statute of limitations on filing criminal charges for sexual assault. It's bitter, I know, but you must put this behind you."

"You should have told me!" I cried. "I was in the same room as my mother's rapist."

"I know. I am so sorry. I'll never forgive myself. Brona made me promise to keep what happened secret," Veda replied gently. "Runecroft is often away from court, preferring his family estate. I never thought you would cross paths, or that he even knew about you. Once you were born, they forgot about you and your mother. I'm not sure how Remus knew you were Brona's daughter. Remus using Albertus to draw you in was duplicitous, but he was a coward then and he is a coward now."

"Remus is a worm hiding behind the robes of power."

"If I had known what Albertus was up to, I'd never have let you go alone. I plan to have some choice words with that old necromancer. It's unforgivable what he did."

"Get in line. Before you came back, I told Kalem about some of this. He said he was going to have words with Crimm."

Veda laughed. "I best intervene before there is another violent episode at the palace. Kalem's demeanor may appear calm and stoic, but he has a temper—especially when someone helpless is hurt."

"Few folk would ever refer to me as helpless." I recalled Kalem was swift to come to my defense when drunken and violent Luther struck me. I only hoped Kalem wouldn't get himself into trouble over me. I looked at my hands, still numb. The memory of dazzling sorcery magic burning Runecroft's ass as he fled down the hall almost made me smile. I was still angry but realized something. "Veda, my head doesn't hurt and my hands aren't hot. I'm really furious now too, but there is no pain or burning!"

"Because your sorcery is finally free. You're not just a witch or charmer. You possess your mother's gift. Do not waste it, Sabine. Life gives few blessings."

"I understand little of blessings, only curses, Veda. I became mageborn the same day I learned who and what my father was. I'm not just a bastard, but a rape child."

"Never speak of yourself that way," Veda said. "Your mother loves you. Never doubt that." She put the tray on the bed. "Now eat and grow strong. I need a healthy mage to assist me."

After she left, my only desire was to fill my hollow stomach. I hadn't eaten in over a day and was ravenous. The tray was filled with a delectable assortment of meat, fresh sliced bread, butter, cheeses, fruits, and sweets!

"Come on, Rory, let's feast!" I diced roast beef and mixed it with gravy in a fancy silver dish. He devoured it quickly and begged for more. His little wings wiggled when he ate. I indulged him, knowing he must be as hungry as I was. I ate two large roast beef and cheese sandwiches, two apples, a bowl of strawberries with cream, and a plate of oatmeal cookies. I downed it all with frothy chilled milk. I could not believe how much I stuffed myself and was not even sick. But then, I had not eaten in over a day. The drain of energy on my body must have been catastrophic.

I licked my fingers, belly sated, strength returning to body and mind. I went to the bath chamber and dared to look in the mirror. Mirrors no longer frightened me, but my reflection did. I looked like a hag over easy. I ran a bath and soaked in steaming, soapy water. Rory perched on the rim of the tub, fascinated by the bubbles. I remembered the letters! In all the chaos I had almost forgotten. I got out of the tub and changed into a fresh nightgown.

I gathered them up, a little afraid at first. My fears evaporated as I read them. Mother was fine. Altheda's letters, tucked in with Mother's, confirmed the same. Mother took care of the magic shop and kept the real cashbox hidden from Luther, for fear his gambling and drinking would drain our precious funds. I was relieved my mother was well, thriving even. I decided that I must write to them at once. Oh, I could tell Mother Veda's treatment worked! I only wished I could be there to see her face! I pushed the rest of what happened to me into oblivion.

Then a thought struck me as I gathered paper and pen to write home. *The mage script!* The mystical script only a mage could see. Could I read the mystical script previously invisible to my baseborn eyes?

I scooped up Rory. He squeaked in surprise but didn't struggle. Veda's stack of magic books on the table loomed like a forbidden mountain. Eager and hesitant, I grabbed a book from the top and laid it before me. The book covers always had common print so anyone could sell them, but the writing on the pages inside could be seen only by a mage.

I put Rory on the table, and he eagerly sniffed the mystical books, his wings twitching. "Sparkly," he said with a grunt. Then he licked the cover.

I closed my eyes, took a deep breath, and opened the book. My heart thudding, I finally opened my eyes and looked down. At first, the page remained blank, and I despaired. Then the sheet shimmered like stardust and the mage script emerged across it like a dance in dark golden ink. To my surprise, I was able to read and understand the strange letters as easily as I could common language.

I fell to my knees and wept, grateful only my dragon could see.

CHAPTER 15

Frustrated after thirty-one failures, I closed the book and rested my head on the table.

"Oh Rory, I wish we could find a clue to Alexander's condition, but I've found nothing. I'd give up and go back to our room, but the imperious master librarian refused to allow most of the books on my list outside his library." I rubbed the back of my neck. "Damn, this tomb of a library makes me cranky, not to mention stiff and sore."

"Maybe we should visit the gryphon stables?" Braden suggested. "You know Mathilda gets fussy when you don't visit her with a few apples and some head scratches."

"I'll take her some treats later," I said. "Kalem promised to teach me how to ride a gryphon good and proper."

"They're magnificent creatures," Braden agreed, "but your pukis is not so magnificent drooling all over that book. The master librarian will have a fit."

Rory, was captivated by the book I'd just rejected. He rolled over on his back, nuzzling his face against the manuscript like a cat in heat. The shimmering golden cover design enticed my dragon.

I snatched the book away. "No, no, no! Stop! You're drooling all over it. Bad dragon."

"Shiny," he replied all in wide-eyed innocence. "Gold smell good. Gold feel good."

"Please tell me the cover's not embossed with real gold!" Such extravagance annoyed me.

The master librarian, a middle-aged man stark as the gray velvet tunic of his office, approached with another rare manuscript and placed it before me. "I found one of the books you requested from Lady Arcana's list. Please handle with care. Are you done with the other book?"

"Yes, thank you."

He frowned when he touched the book Rory so recently coveted. "Is this dragon drool, Lady Fable?" he asked, gingerly picking up the book with ivory silk gloves stained by Rory's offensive dribble.

I winced and nodded. "I'm so sorry. I'll be more careful."

"In the future, properly train your pukis or leave him in your chambers," he commented as he wiped the book with a silk towel. "Useless beasts. I best not find toothmarks," he added, frowning at Rory before walking away.

I stuck my tongue out at his back. I patted Rory's head and whispered, "Don't you listen to the mean man."

I cracked my neck and opened the newest book. I frowned despite the book's beauty—gold-leaf trim on fine paper. The cover sported a cluster of semiprecious gems on soft white leather. All a fancy facade with no substance. "This index doesn't even look enticing. Ugh. The title, *Rare and Forgotten Rituals and Enchantments*, is misleading on this one." I was tempted to let Rory lick this one out of spite.

"Shiny," Rory chirped, sniffing the golden pages. "Want."

"Why don't you play with your new toy," I coaxed, shaking the little cloth bag filled with beads. Rory ignored me, his gaze locked on the forbidden book's cover. The chew toy I'd painstakingly made from bright-yellow cloth was no longer worthy of dragon play.

Braden, my tolerant beast of burden for the day, brought me another stack of books from the less important volumes mortals like us were allowed to touch. "Still wearing those silk gloves the librarian demanded?" he asked.

I wiggled my fingers. "I might just keep them. They're soft and comfy." I thumbed through the new stack of books. "At least this batch has no sparkly decoration to tempt Rory. Best take this one away before he eats it," I said, handing the fancy edition to Braden. "This place is so empty. Does anyone even come here to read?"

Braden laughed, shelving the tempting shiny book on the higher shelf, out of Rory's reach. My dragon gazed up at his lost treasure, fluttering his delicate blue wings. I was thankful he couldn't fly yet. "I don't think anyone comes here," Braden said. "It's mostly a depository of rare books for show."

"Do you like to read?" I asked.

"As a boy, I was too wild to read much outside school. I never could sit still long enough to read a book for pleasure."

"I've always been the solitary owl, so reading was an escape for me. I enjoyed walks in the nearby woods with a good book." I left out how my escape usually followed Luther shaking his belt. Some things were best left unsaid. "I'm afraid this isn't very exciting work for the new personal guard to Premier Alexander Duchene."

He shrugged. "It's my afternoon off, actually. Thought you'd like the company."

"Thanks. I think Veda hoped this project would dust the cobwebs off me. I've been cooped up in my room too long. All I did for a week was sleep and eat like a lazy old cat." I glanced at Rory. "Or a baby pukis dragon."

Rory lifted his head with pride, "Dragons fierce. Not lazy. Grow big. Breathe fire."

"You'll have to indulge him," I told Braden. "I've been reading him dragon tales from a children's book. He's obsessed with dragon lore now."

"Well, he's a brave little dragon," Braden commented, scratching Rory's chin. In response, my dragon sat on his hind legs and puffed out his chest, swishing his tail with joy. "Why are you reading him children's books?"

"It's complicated," I answered, feeling embarrassed. "They're not just for Rory. Most mages learn to control their talents as their magic grows from childhood. I'm new to the mage world. Veda suggested I start with the educational manuals outlined in *The Young Mage Golden Moon Books*."

Braden grinned broadly. "You mean …"

"Yes, I'm basically learning magic basics from toddler books. The books are short with pretty illustrations and simple exercises for mage training. If you tell anyone, I'll never forgive you. And stop laughing!"

Braden put his boots on the table and leaned back in his chair. "Sorry. You'll have to learn some pretty powerful spells from your toddler books before you intimidate me."

I laughed, punching him in the arm. I paused for a moment, curious but hesitant. "So, you aren't scared of me? I mean, after what happened?"

He sat up straight and took his feet off the table when his holiness the librarian walked by. "Hardly. Why?"

"I mean … You never told me how you felt about what happened the day my magic went crazy."

Braden shrugged. "You don't scare me, Miss Sabine. I was more upset by how Lord Crimm and that Runecroft fellow treated you. I heard enough to know what he'd done to your poor mum. If I found out someone hurt my mum like that, there'd be blood on the walls, not magic burns."

"Thanks, Braden." The back of my neck prickled, and I glanced around, unsettled.

"You feeling alright?" he asked.

"I'm fine," I said, shaking my head. But my prickle of unease remained. Rory noticed something too and growled nervously. It was odd, but I sensed someone close. "Something is here," I whispered to Braden, "Act casual and be ready."

Braden's hand gripped the hilt of his sword and he nodded. I stood, taking a couple books as cover. When I approached the first bookcase, I detected a strange distortion, like a warped image in a mirror. I dropped the books and swung my fist at what looked like empty air. But I struck something solid. There was a cry and the thud of someone hitting the floor.

Braden stepped in front of me as Rory spread his wings, hissing and spitting from Braden's shoulder. Then Braden drew his sword and commanded, "Show yourself!"

Pink magic shimmered and fell away to reveal Marigold Graven sprawled on the floor, blubbering with plump cheeks flushed like raspberry jam.

"You!" I cried. "What the hell are you up to?"

She just continued to cry.

Braden lowered his sword and looked at me helplessly. "You know her?"

"Sadly, yes. Her name's Marigold Graven."

"You didn't have to hit me!" she wept into a lacy handkerchief.

"Well, I didn't know it was you, did I? Why are you sneaking about using nasty spells to spy on me?"

"It's an invisibility charm!" she cried. "And it's very challenging to conjure."

Finally, I held out my hand. "Get up before you wrinkle your gown."

Marigold pouted but took my hand and stood up, smoothing her frilly skirt and straightening her bonnet.

"Well? Why are you stalking me?" I demanded.

She shook he head. "I wasn't stalking you. I had to speak to you alone, but you're never alone. Either Veda or the mysterious shapeshifter is with you. Or this tall brute—"

"Hey!" Braden protested. "I'm no brute."

"Let's go," I told Braden.

"Please wait," Marigold begged. She glanced up at Braden, who was hovering over me like a big protective bear, and whispered, "Can't he step out and guard something?"

"Braden, would you please give us a moment?" I asked softly.

He nodded. "Very well. I'll be right outside the main door, *guarding something.*"

After a moment, Marigold finally spoke in hesitant beats, each word a struggle. "I had to see you because I needed to apologize. I'm sorry about how I treated you, but I had good reason!"

I could think of a thousand things she should apologize for going back to grammar school. "You're not making sense."

"You're mageborn now. Your new status makes it more acceptable for us to be friends."

Gods save me from throttling her. "So, when I had no magic, I was beneath you and beyond your precious friendship?"

"Let me explain," she said, stamping her foot. "Father always said to be kind to you and your mother."

"How awful for you." Rory snorted loudly at that, and I scratched his ears. *Good dragon.*

She twisted her hanky in her hands, eyes downcast. "I never understood Father's generosity toward a fallen woman and her bastard."

"Tread carefully," I warned.

"Your family may have had some magic once, but they were mostly charm caste and common. Never part of our inner circle of society. I mean, Luther's a crude and drunken gambler. And your mother had a chance but was cast out of the Academy for losing her virtue and lying."

"How dare you! You could never possess the grace and virtue of my mother! And she never lied about anything in her life."

True, I hated Luther. He could be eaten by a troll tomorrow and I wouldn't care, but he was still my blood and not Marigold's to judge. Knowledge of what my mother suffered was still raw. "You know nothing about anyone who isn't rich and mageborn," I said. "You must think the rest of us are just baseborn trash!"

"You're right. I know nothing about people outside my caste. Even my dear Greeley says I should be less narrow and be more … Inclusive. Yes, that's the word he used."

"Inclusive? Do you even know what it means?"

"Yes, I think so," she said with a nod. "It's true your mother has always been gracious. Father wanted Mother to be friends with Brona.

She didn't understand why he asked such a terrible sacrifice of us. One afternoon, I heard them arguing in their bedroom, so I listened at the door. Mother accused my father of having an affair with Brona and thought he was your father too."

"Lord Graven isn't my father."

"Well, I know that now! Father always denied it, of course. I hated you because I believed it was true. I wanted to punish you for making my mama unhappy."

"You succeeded." I turned away, but she grabbed my hand.

"Please stop. I'm sorry. About everything. I heard about what really happened to your mother. I know Lord Runecroft is your father. Everyone knows it now. I also know he hurt your mother."

"*Hurt* is a pale word for rape."

"I was hateful to you because I was jealous of Father's attention to someone beneath us. Can you forgive me?"

Only Marigold could distort an apology into a long-winded insult. My anger bubbled, but a sharp scent tinged the air, and screams in the hallway distracted me.

Marigold's face puckered, and she put her lacy hanky to her nose. "What is that burning smell? It's horrid. What is that?"

Rory's little paws nervously tugged at my hair, and I held him close. "Something dangerously familiar."

I ran for the door, Marigold's heels tapping behind me. People were running in the hall and all in the same direction, obviously away from something. I dodged colliding with the panicked crowd to reach Braden, who stood confused with sword drawn.

"What the hell is going on?" I asked.

"Damned if I know. Best go back inside!" he shouted.

A swirl of dark energy appeared at the far end of the hallway.

The wraith! The red-eyed specter of my nightmares rampaged, hurling people against the walls. Braden pulled me toward the library and was blocked by the master librarian peeking through the door.

"Step aside," Braden commanded.

The librarian only screamed at the sight of the creature and slammed the door in our faces. Braden tried to open it, but the asshole locked it! Braden kicked at the door, angry. Marigold stood unresponsive with terror as the wraith raced toward us. My childhood nemesis picked the damnedest times to be silent.

"We need to go," I cried, seeing the wraith fly toward us.

Braden grabbed my hand. "Run!"

I pulled Marigold behind me as we fled in the panic. A wash of magic passed through us as we turned a corner. Several palace wizards marched toward us, ominous figures in black suits, brandishing staves topped with crystals radiating magic. We stood aside as they passed. I tucked Rory into my skirt pocket for safety. "Stay there, baby. I'll protect you." Marigold worried me, so I shook her by the shoulders. "Snap out of it. I don't have time to coddle you."

"Let's go and let the wizards do their job," Braden said. "We need to find shelter. Can you do a spell to raise a shield or something?"

"*Golden Moon* magic books, remember! I can barely float a pencil."

We ran down another hall, emptied of people, and skidded to a stop when the dark specter appeared before us, swirling with black energy. Her howl shattered my ears. Marigold screamed, her hand flying to her forehead as she started to swoon. I grabbed her by the arm, pulling her behind me as I ran, following Braden. "Don't you dare faint!" I warned Marigold.

A haze of sorcerous mist and several wizards appeared in front of us, blocking the wraith's path. They conjured a shield to stop her in her path.

"Look, they defeated it!" Marigold pointed.

"We can't stay to watch," I said, following Braden toward another staircase, dragging Marigold behind me.

I thought we were safe. Then the wraith materialized before us, pulling us both into her violent orbit. We screamed, helpless in her hold. I focused on light, bright light, and willed it to be. A brilliant flash drove the creature back, and she dropped us to the floor.

The dark entity stared down at me. Braden, dazed, moved to protect me, though there was nothing he could do. My heart thudded in my chest as I scooted away. Marigold lay where she had fallen, a pale image of pink ruffles. I thought this time she had truly fainted.

The wraith's howl thundered, and I threw up my hands, feeling another jolt of energy burst from my body. Streams of green magic gushed forth from my hands, transforming into viny leaves. It formed a dome that covered us. It was like lacework around us, but I could see through the gaps. Rory fell out of my pocket but clung to my skirt. The beast attacked, but the leafy dome shielded us from her wrath.

Braden gasped. "What'd you do?" he asked.

"I've no idea," I mumbled, shaking. "But it's working."

A burst of red magic danced over our heads and encased the creature, stopping her in her tracks. I craned my neck to see Kalem and Veda trapping the wraith creature. The palace wizards surrounded her, their staves bright with magic as they conjured a mystical cage to hold her.

With the wraith finally captive, Kalem knelt down by us and laughed. "Well, that's one way to shield yourself from a spectral beast."

I tugged at the vines. They proved to be tough as iron despite the leafy texture. "I can't break through," I said.

"What do you mean you can't break it?" Braden asked. "It's your spell."

"It protected us, in case you didn't notice."

"Great, but we still need to get out," Braden said, punching at the crisscross design of steely leaves holding us in.

Rory scampered up my arm and settled on my shoulder. "Magic smell good," he said.

I tried to focus on dispelling the enchantment, but nothing happened. I had no idea what to do.

Braden leaned back on his elbows, laughing. "Do you need one of your *Golden Moon* books?"

"Stop that! It's not funny."

"I find it hilarious," Braden said.

"Enough, you two," Veda said, but despite the terror caged nearby, she laughed too. "Are you both alright?"

"I'm fine," I said, punching at my leafy dome. "But I can't undo this."

"No more conjuring for you," Braden said through a grin.

After a few moments, Veda guided me through a spell to undo my odd magic. The palace wizards finally lifted the viny green dome above our heads so we could move.

Marigold opened her eyes and screamed.

Veda calmed her down. "It's all over now. Come, dear, I'll take you to your father." Marigold glanced back once at the bound apparition and burst into tears before Veda guided her away.

I stood, wobbly kneed and dazed. Kalem and Braden flanked me protectively as I stared at the terrible phantom beating against its prison.

"I can't believe you actually caught her," I whispered to Kalem. I cuddled Rory in my arms as I perceived more than anger and hatred coming from this strange specter.

I sensed pain.

CHAPTER 16

I followed Veda down the winding stone stairway, Rory bouncing under one arm and my free hand lifting my skirt to keep from tripping. "Is there a reason the steps are so narrow and there's no rail to hold?" I asked.

Veda gracefully walked down as though on air, whereas I feared tumbling to my death down the steep stairs. "This is an old palace. The architect's original design was to impede an adversary or a prisoner's escape."

"Archaic designs are always quirky," Kalem added, leading the way.

"I'd settle for safe," I said. I've never been known for my grace. I'd even trip running up the stairs at home. "Why are we going to the dungeon anyway?"

"Where better to keep the captive wraith than a dungeon?" Veda replied.

My stomach knotted with fear as I asked, "You mean the rampaging creature from hell is down there?" Rory squeaked and tried to wiggle up my sleeve. I pulled him back, calming him by scratching his head. "Why are we going near that thing?"

"To witness a mirror master at work," Veda replied. "Come along now."

We reached the lower level, and I followed them at a swift pace through the narrow passage. "How can a mirror master help with the creature?"

"By conjuring an unbreakable glass prison," Veda replied. "You once told me you were fascinated by mirror magic. As a newborn mage, I thought this would be an excellent educational experience for you as well, since you're a newborn mage. Richard Nightshade is a renowned mirror master. Exposure to magic in the making is crucial to your growth."

A mirror master. Eager curiosity superseded my panic, though only a little. I followed them to a well-lit area in the underbelly of the palace.

"Alexander and I agree this creature must have a secure prison," Kalem said. "Especially since no one yet has found a way to destroy or banish it."

This perplexed me. Even as a baseborn, I thought anything could be banished. "Could it be a lost race of dark fairy? Legends say they were immune to human magic."

Kalem shrugged. "Legends make poor facts. No one knows. There are many myths about the ancient fairy races. Some scholars believe they never existed."

I always believed in the fairy races—the ancient race that lived before humans came into existence. But most folk just think them a myth now.

"Are the current shields holding?" Veda asked.

Kalem shook his head. "They don't hold for long. If this doesn't work, I'm not sure what our options are. The wizards reinforced their shields several times in the last twenty-four hours, and they keep watch over the thing." Kalem glanced back at me with a quizzical look. "The only magical threads still binding the creature since yesterday are the leafy vines you conjured in a panic. The wizards are dying to know what you did."

"I don't even know what I did," I said.

"If you want to go back, there's no shame," Veda whispered. "I understand how frightened you must be. The creature attacked you more than once."

"No, I want to witness this," I insisted. "And I am not scared." It was a blatant lie to cover my terror, but I had to see this! I hugged Rory close to comfort him and myself as we followed Kalem to a large chamber. I noted that this dungeon was clean—downright immaculate even—with no trace of moldy damp or rank smell one associates with such dismal places. The walls were lined with sconces that glowed with light orbs instead of fire. Of course, my image of dungeons was formed from reading old fairy tales, legends, and novels—the bleak darkness, creepy cold chills, bloodstained stones, chains, curses, ghosts, the echo of screams! My childhood imagination hadn't been marred by this, as some warned. I suffered no nightmares or fears from it, though Luther often called me a macabre little bastard for enjoying those stories. Of course, today dungeons are no longer used for torture. At least, that's what we're taught in school. Still, I wondered if the ancient spirits of tormented victims still lingered here.

"Will he mind us watching?" I whispered as we joined the group of wizards preparing the area.

"Nightshade is an old friend," Kalem said. "He invited us specifically to watch."

I felt better until we passed from the corridors into a vast chamber. Sorcery's glow drew my attention toward the raging creature trapped in a bubble of red magic. My inner terror swelled again, and Rory buried his face in my hand. The wraith's fury abated briefly when she saw me. She even looked at me! I turned away for a second, then returned her stare. She possessed aspects of the feminine mixed with her darkness. I noticed remnants of my mystical vines still twined around her.

"Come, Sabine," Veda said, gesturing for me to approach. "We can watch safely from here. The mages created a shield of protection for us, just to be safe."

I looked down and saw Veda and Kalem standing back several feet in a circle charged with magic. Runes blazed with purple energy of protection. I stepped inside the circle to wait, placing Rory on my shoulder. His tiny claws dug into my jacket. I winced but endured it, knowing my baby was anxious.

Like businessmen in severe black suits with somber faces, the palace wizards formed a circle. Grim as undertakers, they invoked incantations. Keyed up by the wizards' invocations, Rory bounced on my shoulder, worries forgotten for a moment within our charmed circle.

A tall, mature man in his gray years entered the chamber. He moved with the agility of a young man. His silver hair and neatly trimmed beard retained a touch of their former red color. The wizards bowed to him as he entered the center of their circle. I decided this must be Richard Nightshade. The other mages shrank in his presence as though they were lowly acolytes. He wore power with grace. His long black coat billowed as he walked around the captive wraith without a glint of fear in his eyes.

Silence fell, and I watched in anticipation as Nightshade's incantations filled the air. His deep voice spoke in the mystic tongue I now understood, but he spoke so fast I could not follow! Sorcery charged the room, and my skin tingled with it.

One wizard stepped forward and placed a base of pure silver etched with runes in the middle of the circle at Nightshade's feet. Nightshade spoke a single word, and the carved runes blazed bright as stars. He took a small pouch from his pocket and opened it, pouring white sand into his gloved hand. The sand swirled in his palm, shimmering as it spread over the silver base.

Breathless, I witnessed a handful of sand spin into a cylinder of mystical glass. The glass bubbled and expanded as he tossed more sand into the small cyclone whirling before him. It glowed so brightly that I shielded my eyes. Then it dimmed. The glass dome floated fully formed, clear and shimmering with magic. It was quite large, over ten feet high. The brilliant half-bubble levitated high above the silver foundation etched with runes. Nightshade circled the base, touching each rune with a wand, lighting them again.

The heated enchantments warmed the chamber. I began to sweat but didn't care. Rory loved the warmth as much as the magic. Unafraid now, he hummed in his throat with each spell cast.

Then the wizards circled the creature. Panic surged in my gut again. How would they move her to the new prison? The wizards summoned shimmering golden rope, coiling it around the red shields containing her. Then they drew her toward the silver base. As she thrashed against the crimson bubble, I could see the shields weakening around her! They moved fast now and bound her over the rune-charged silver. She raged, and even though her cries were muffled by her prison, I felt them. Bind her quickly, I prayed.

The mystical prison confining the wraith split like seams in cloth as she ripped away the last of the shields. I held my breath as Nightshade shouted the final enchantment as the glass dome lowered over her. Newly bound, she beat against the glass. The silver base clicked, like a lock. The old mage continued summoning, each word flashing into a beam of light that circled the cylinder.

Then Nightshade stopped. He stepped back to examine his work. Bound by swift spellbinding, the creature beat against her glass prison like a violent moth. Spells woven into the glass muted her howls, but I sensed them deep in my chest. The mirror magic and dark creature held captive by it mesmerized me. Despite her mystical jail, I feared her. I watched the wraith, a living storm in a bottle.

"You can still see remnants of your vines," Kalem whispered to me. "Odd. All the other wards and spells did not hold. Are you sure you don't remember what you did?"

I shook my head. "It was instinct. I wish I could tell you. It's hard to know what you're doing when facing the stuff of nightmares."

Tendrils of inky hair floated about the dark shape, fluid like a maiden under water. She swirled in her small glass coffin, scarlet eyes staring down at us. I stared at the captive and flinched, feeling an anguish I couldn't understand.

"You're awfully quiet," Kalem whispered. "That usually means trouble."

I feigned calm. "I'm just enthralled by what Nightshade did. It was fascinating to watch."

Despite Kalem's bravado, he kept a safe distance. "We were lucky he was in town. There are a few other mirror masters, but he's the best. I wonder where Crimm is. He would find this wraith-demon fascinating."

Yes, creepy and deathlike. Just like him. "Where is Crimm? One would think he'd be here for this."

"I don't know," Kalem replied. "It's odd he's not here. I told his secretary, Frederick, we would be here. You know, it's strange. I haven't seen Crimm in days, not since the day you woke up after your magic was freed."

"I hope you didn't argue with him on my account," I said.

"Sometimes that's the only way to get through to the old man. After I ranted, he dismissed me like a schoolboy, and Frederick escorted me from his office."

I laughed. "That sounds like Crimm," I said.

"When I tried to see him when this she-beast was caught a week later, Frederick informed me Crimm retreated to his country house for a few days." Kalem frowned and shook his head. "It's not like him to leave the city, not with so much strife going on at the palace."

Veda joined me. "What did you think of Nightshade's magic?"

"A true wonder, thank you." Rory, tired out, was curled in the crook of my arm, sleeping. "Will it truly hold?" I asked her.

"The wizards will maintain the glass cage. Nightshade has precise guidelines."

A thud against the glass made me jump. I swear our mysterious wraith captive looked right at me. Rory wiggled in my arms, whining. Her red-eyed stare knotted my stomach. "The glass looks so fragile. Are you sure this contraption will hold her?"

"I hope so, else my reputation would be ruined," answered the mirror master, stepping away from the circle. "Forgive me. I'm being rude. I'm Duke Richard Nightshade. You must be Sabine Fable, the newly born mage I've heard so much about. I congratulate you, Lady Fable, on your rise to the mage class. The court is abuzz about you."

"I prefer not to be buzzed about," I said with a sigh.

"I didn't know you followed court news," Kalem remarked to Nightshade.

"I keep abreast of what is crucial. My visit was solely to attend Alexander's inauguration. I despise the superficial gloss of court politics. I prefer the country and its peace. Any sane person would."

"I am simply glad you could help us," Veda said. "Alexander extends his thanks."

Nightshade kissed Veda's hand. "I congratulate you for your success, Lady Arcana. I always had faith you would someday find a way to prove your research."

Veda looked at me with pride. "Sabine is more than a theory. She's a bright young woman who has a better future now, though I shall selfishly keep her as my secretary and companion if she wishes. We are in the early stages of her mystic training to determine her mage caste."

"Are you ready to publish your research?" Nightshade asked her.

"Not yet, but I hope to publish my findings after more successful outcomes. There is so much more that needs to be done. I've had much opposition, as you know."

"I do, Veda," Nightshade said. "It is a shame you have been ostracized for your theories. But truth will reveal all." He turned toward me and gently kissed my hand, as though I were a proper lady. "Lady Fable, I heard you helped stop this strange creature. You're rather tiny to be so bold."

"I confess I didn't know what I was doing. It was instinct … Instinct based entirely in terror."

"Don't let her small size fool you. Sabine's tougher than she looks," Kalem remarked.

"Still, I'm honored to meet you, Duke Nightshade," I said. I hoped my etiquette was correct.

"And I you, Lady Fable. As a mage, you've the right to be addressed as *lady*. Never forget that."

"Thank you. I had a great-uncle who was a mirror master. Long since passed, of course. Magic and mirrors always fascinated me."

"Glass of all origins and makes can be charmed by a mirror master," Duke Richard explained. "Elements of glass provide unique elements for magic. For this, I wove my own. Our talents are unique. As unique as this creature. We can charm a looking glass and create mirrors to spy, shields to resist dragon fire, and potion bottles to preserve enchanted elixirs. Or we can spin a glass prison like this one." His eyes rested briefly on Kalem. "We're a sorcerer caste but possess special talents, much like a shapeshifter. It is good to see you, my boy. It has been years. I am glad you found your path. A shapeshifter no less. Your mother would be proud."

Kalem's face softened, and he looked a little sad. "Thank you. I have been lucky to find my way." He paused, uncertain and downcast. "May I ask after Abigail?"

"My granddaughter is well. She is staying with me in town. She would welcome a visit from you. I plan to be in town on business for several weeks. I am staying at my townhouse, which is preferable to my palace apartments. When Alexander sent me an urgent message, I could hardly ignore it. A unique creature required a unique prison. I relished the challenge."

The buzz grew louder among the cluster of wizards. They were arguing over a scroll someone delivered. Veda went to see what was happening. We all joined her, beneath the dark gaze of the captive in glass.

"They have finally found her mystical marker," Veda said, looking at the scroll. "It's a taman shade."

"Impossible," Nightshade said. "They were wiped out centuries ago."

"Magic doesn't lie," Veda said, handing Nightshade the lengthy document. "Read the results yourself in this report."

Duke Richard inclined his head, opened the document, and read it. "Alexander must be informed at once."

"I remember reading something in one of my books on mythological creatures," I said. "Taman shades were a race of spirit fey merged with ghouls or revenants by dark sorcery."

"We cannot rely on legend," Veda said. "We need facts and proof."

Nightshade nodded to me. "Legend or not, a taman shade is deadly. Take care until you have learned your magic and understand its strength. I would be saddened if such magical potential was vanquished. Magic doesn't always shield one from death. Remember that. Good day, Lady Fable."

When Nightshade turned to go, Veda leaned in and whispered, "We still have the task of helping Alexander regain his magic. Go back to our suite and order some dinner. We still need to solve this before his inauguration."

"Do you think Alexander's enemies might want to expose him to the mage castes on his big day?"

"Anything is possible," Veda said, nodding. "Go on, and I'll meet you there shortly."

"I'll get everything ready. I have more research to organize anyway."

I left the chamber, relieved to be away from the taman shade. I walked up the innumerable steps to the main floor. When I got there, I paused in the doorway, breathless from so many stairs—and confused to see there weren't any guards in the hallway. Rory stirred awake and appeared distressed. The corridor was quite empty of people, unlike before.

"This is odd,"

"Not good," Rory replied.

Several men in dark gray robes stepped from the shadows, surrounding me. I raised my hand, flashing what little magic I could summon. A fleeting flash of green fizzled in my palm. *Damn it, damn it, damn it.*

One of them stepped forward. "Come with us, Sabine Fable."

"What do you want?" I demanded. "I'm not budging until you say who you are!"

Two men grabbed me, and I jerked away. "Don't touch me or I'll hit you harder than any spell!" I screamed, but no sound came out. Dirty magic tricks.

One of the men tossed red dust in my face. Instead of sneezing, I just stopped. I could not move! I could not speak! My mind remained awake, but my body went limp as a rag doll. They snatched Rory from my arms and stuffed him into a large sack. Helpless, I cursed internally as the cloaked strangers carried me away into darkness.

CHAPTER 17

My captors' spells caused my flesh to tingle, and the enchantment wrapped me like a blanket. It wasn't warm and cozy, but cold as a grave. Mute and paralyzed, and my vision clouded, I couldn't fight back or even scream. That got my blood up. My eyes and nose watered from the red dust. It was embarrassing because I couldn't even wipe my own nose.

Silent as thieves, they carried my body at a swift pace. My gut knotted each time I heard Rory's muffled cries. Then I sensed an unsettling mystical shift, and they stopped moving.

My abductors laid me on a cold floor. A whispered spell cleared my vision. I stared up at my captors, faces hidden in black hoods, flanking me on all sides. I refused to cry or beg, but my heart thumped with rising panic. *Did they bring me here for murder? Where am I? This doesn't make sense. None of this makes sense.*

"Release her from the enchantment," ordered the man who had tossed magic dust in my face. I recognized his nasal voice.

My arms and legs could move again! I rolled over and raised myself on my elbows, assessing my enemies. Dizziness prevented me from standing, but anger sustained me. "Where's Rory! Give me my baby dragon now! If he's hurt, magic won't save you."

"Be quiet," taunted red-dust man. "Unless you want to lose your voice again."

"You'll lose your balls if you try!"

Angry, he pushed back his hood. His face exposed, I saw a middle-aged man with beady eyes and thin lips. "Silence, girl! I am a keeper of the Mystic Temple. You must obey me."

"I don't obey spineless men who abuse magic to kidnap women." When dealing with bullies, you must hunt for a weakness, any weakness. Then you can forge a weapon from it. I learned that from being tormented at school. This measly man was nothing but an underling, despite his posh title. I heard Rory crying and spotted one of the men clutching a wiggling burlap bag. "Give me my dragon, or you'll be the last of your line. Now!"

A booming voice intervened. "Give the girl her pet."

The man dropped the bag on the floor and stepped back. Rory burst out of the sack and jumped into my arms. He gurgled and growled, rubbing his head anxiously against my face. I stroked his head gently, cooing soft sounds to calm him down.

The room brightened like the dawn. Despite my fury, the visual beauty around me stunned me. Exquisite art and wall murals surrounded me. High above, a domed ceiling of brilliant stained glass filtered the moonlight.

A tall man strode into the room and sat in an ornate wooden chair carved with runes. Robed in rich scarlet, a staff of polished ebony in his hand, I knew this man was no underling.

"Do you know why you've been brought here, child?" he asked.

"Brought here? Seriously, are you mad? I wasn't *brought* here. Those men used ghastly spells to subdue me. The bitter taste of the dust they used still clings to my mouth! Do you condone abducting a defenseless woman?" My legs wobbled like pudding, but I managed to stand.

"Insolent girl! Show some respect!" the keeper shouted, shrill as a fishwife. "You stand before Lord Baruti Tabor. You must bow, Mistress Fable."

I recalled Richard Nightshade's words. I lifted my chin and squared my shoulders. "You may address me as Lady Fable. I am mageborn and it's my right."

He gasped. "You dare contradict me, a keeper of the Mystic Temple?"

Damn. He does like to repeat himself.

Baruti raised his hand and grinned. "She does indeed, Rupert."

"Your name is Rupert?" I laughed.

Rupert's anger bubbled. "You dare—" but Baruti's gesture silenced him. He took his place with the rest of the black-robed flock.

Of course I knew who Baruti Tabor was. He was one of the most powerful men in the realm. Lord High Mystic of all the mage castes.

"Why take me in such a criminal manner?" I asked Baruti, ignoring my *keeper.*

"I only desired to interview you," he said, his deep voice soft. "I apologize for what happened, though I'd not attribute defenseless to your character."

"They restrained me with magic. I don't find that enchanting."

Baruti turned to Rupert. "I didn't authorize the use of spells or ask you to abduct her. Did you even ask her? Answer me!"

"Yes, *Rupert*, answer him," I said with a smile.

"Lord Tabor, I only used red fairy dust and a binding spell to keep her from escaping."

"Sounds exactly like kidnapping to me," I remarked. "You admit your guilt. Good. When I press charges, there will be no doubt."

Rupert squirmed like a rat. "It's not my fault! She's never alone, my lord! She's either with Veda, or the shapeshifter, or feeding a gryphon in the stables…—who bites, by the way—or cavorting with that baseborn officer, Braden.

"I do not cavort!" I protested.

Rupert scowled at me, wringing his hands in fear. "We couldn't risk an argument. You didn't want Veda's interference, so I judged it best to act when she was finally away from the others. You commanded we bring Fable to you, and I have done so!"

What does Veda have to do with this? And how long were they watching me?"

"I didn't say abduct the girl," Baruti said. Rupert's prideful look crumbled, and Baruti turned his attention to me. "I apologize for their dreadful actions. I promise they will be punished."

I doubt that. "Well, I am here now. What do you want, sir?"

"Only to ask a few questions," Baruti said. "Have you visited the Mystic Temple before? Its beauty is renowned. For many, this temple is not only a center of mageborn law but a sacred pilgrimage site."

I'd wondered where they'd brought me. They must have used some high sorcery to transport me the few miles to the temple, away from Veda's protection and the palace. "I had planned to visit when my duties allowed. Why am I here, Lord Tabor?"

Baruti glanced at his flock of black-robed keepers. "Leave us."

They dispersed like distressed crows.

"You have a pukis dragon. Is he your familiar?" he asked.

"He's my friend," I replied, holding Rory close.

"He's quite young. The green and blue markings are lovely. I heard he talks too. You're lucky. Why is he so silent now?"

Rory's look of fear when he glanced up at me was not a good omen. If my dragon didn't trust him, then I didn't either.

"He's just shy," I said. "And he's been traumatized by your keepers." *I am suspicious of his casual conversation,* I thought. *He wants something.* "But I'm not here to discuss my pukis dragon, am I?"

"Indeed," he said, nodding. "Your circumstances are more than just unique. From baseborn to mageborn is an impossibility."

"Ask Veda. Her genius freed my magic bound by the side effects of mage fever. Her research should be supported, not shunned."

"She has only herself to blame. Do you know your mage caste?"

"Not yet." *I really don't like him. He brought me to his place of power to intimidate me. I won't bow so easily. He's hiding something too.* "Veda wanted to wait until I learned to control my powers first. My magic is still unstable."

"Lady Arcana is the unstable one. She muddles with science and magic as a child plays with marbles. Her theories about mage fever are unsupported, even with your so-called case as an example. Your magic may have just been latent. It happens more often than you think. The truth is, no one can be born without magic and then suddenly possess it. If any mageborn survives mage fever, their magic is lost forever. Did Veda explain why she was banished?"

"Yes. Two people died during one of her trials for the treatment. She was blamed, but the inquiry was never completed."

"The investigation is ongoing," Tabor replied. "Only two deaths, you say?"

"I don't understand."

"Never mind. What matters now is you're a key witness to another investigation." He leaned forward, as though expecting something.

"I am confused. What are you asking, Lord Tabor?"

"Let me be succinct. I know your mother is Brona Fable. Recently, however, it was revealed your father is Lord Remus Runecroft. A powerful and ancient house. What did you think of your noble father?"

"I met Runecroft once, and that was enough. He's not honorable despite his grand lineage. If you know so much, you must know Runecroft raped my mother. His powerful family had her banished from the Academy to hide his crime. Where's the justice for my mother?"

"Brona Fable's case was judged long ago and dismissed. It's no longer a concern. Your case is yet to be judged. Have you seen Remus Runecroft since the day you met?"

"No." *My inner troll is growing more nervous.*

"Are you sure? Lady Fable, please understand I'm not accusing you. But I do understand the temptation. The threat of old secrets. Your family is poor, born of common stock, at best meager charm caste before mage fever took even that. Your grandfather, Luther Fable, has a problem with drink and gambling. The family business is on shaky ground and your mother is often ill. Perhaps you realized an opportunity to extort money from Runecroft by threatening to expose his unfortunate past. Greed knows no caste."

"I'll never be that greedy. I want nothing from Runecroft. And he is not innocent."

"He was judged innocent by those of higher rank than you."

"Judgment formed by privilege, not fact. Runecroft hurt my mother, and I hate him."

"Enough to kill him?"

Kill him? What does he mean? "What? Is he dead?"

"You tell me, Lady Fable."

"I have nothing to tell! What's happened?"

"Remus Runecroft has been missing for some days. In fact, he's not been seen since the day you two met. I understand the exchange was memorable."

"I barely remember anything after my magic exploded. I was unconscious for over a day."

"I find your role in this mystery intriguing. Did you argue? Did tempers get out of hand? You did wake up, and from reports, you were not helpless."

"But I was weak and recovering from something no one could explain. Ask the palace kitchen. All I did for a week was eat and sleep."

"But no one was watching you all the time, were they?"

"It's obvious your keepers kept watch. This has devolved into more threats than questions. You're trying to trip me up and draw out a confession. Truth does not matter to you. You've accused me of blackmail, and now murder! Is there a body? The law requires proof of a corpse."

"Don't be clever with me, girl," Baruti snapped.

"I'm only being honest. I never lie. A habit that has brought me more trouble than reward. All you've done is try to manipulate me with word twists and assumptions. You know nothing of me or my family! Now I want to leave."

"If you confess, I will be merciful. You're just a young girl with no background or education. You've been thrust into a world you know nothing about. Meeting your father unleashed anger because of how your mother suffered. Just tell me if Runecroft is still alive."

"I know nothing! I swear it."

"You have a motive and now the magic. And friends. Perhaps that shapeshifter, Kalem, or Veda helped you."

My inner troll is howling with worry now. "Ask your keepers! Even Rupert confirmed I'm never alone. During the same meeting with Runecroft and Crimm, my magic exploded, and I was unconscious for a day. There are many who witnessed that fact. I left magic burns on the wallpaper. It's hard to miss. What does Lord Crimm say?"

"Frederick informed me Albertus Crimm has been out of town. Lord Crimm was upset by this incident between you and his friend. Frederick promised to send me word once he returns."

I find it hard to fathom Crimm being so sensitive. "I know nothing. Now let me go!"

"Enough!" Red mystical energy flowed from Baruti's staff, cascading over me and Rory. I was bound again and could not move. "You refuse to confess, so I must extract the truth from you."

Extract. That worries me.

A middle-aged woman wearing an exquisite gray velvet gown entered the chamber. She looked to Baruti, who pointed to me and nodded. She walked toward me, removing her white gloves.

"What the hell is she going to do to me?"

"If you're innocent, you have nothing to fear, my child. This lady is a truthsayer and in service to the temple. The process will be painful, I'm afraid, but you've left me no choice."

Screw sorry. I read about truthsayers, and not just in a novel. Truthsayers are often used to interrogate prisoners. She touched my temples with her bare hands. I looked into her eyes, seeing only dark pupils dilating as her fingers pressed against my skin. She invaded my thoughts. It hurt, like squiggly worms crawling through my mind. Probing, she hunted for my dark, criminal secrets. Pain seared my brain as she kept burrowing until I couldn't hold back anymore and screamed.

The truthsayer's hands jerked away. Baruti's magic dissolved as I dropped to the floor. My agony gave way to useless tears.

"The girl is innocent, Lord Tabor. No lies, no subterfuge, no secrets," the truthsayer pronounced. "She knows nothing about Runecroft or his fate. Her resilience is quite strong for an untrained mage."

The truthsayer left the chamber, untouched by the pain she caused.

Baruti looked disappointed as he dropped into his chair. "It appears you are innocent, Lady Fable."

"Damn you," I croaked. Too weak move, I curled up on the cold marble, holding Rory.

A swirl of purple mist bloomed, and Veda appeared between us. "What's going on?" Veda gasped when she saw me, then took me in her arms. I was too drained to refuse. "What have you done to her? Answer me, Baruti!"

"She was summoned for questioning," Baruti replied coldly. "You were not invited."

"You abducted her," Veda countered. "It is unlawful."

"An unfortunate mistake," Baruti said with a shrug, "for which I apologized already. My mages misunderstood my directives. But Sabine was under suspicion for a serious crime, so I interrogated her."

"You had me kidnapped and tortured!" I croaked. "Runecroft is missing." I pushed my hair off my face and stood on wobbly legs. "He claimed I was involved in his disappearance and ordered some truthsayer bitch to probe my mind when I did not tell him what he wanted to hear."

"You had no right to treat Sabine like a common criminal." I swayed, but Veda held me up. "It's against the law to subject anyone to a truthsayer without consent."

"I overruled consent. Runecroft is missing. It turns out she knows nothing, so be glad, Veda. She is returned to you. Now leave."

"Alexander will hear of this," Veda promised.

"Tell me, Veda, have you restored his lost sorcery yet?" Baruti needled. "Yes, I know what is happening and why you were summoned back to court. Do you think you can keep secrets from me? I know everything in this kingdom."

"Except where Runecroft is," I shot back.

"Don't taunt me about secrets, child!" Baruti shouted, his voice full of fury. "Veda has many secrets."

"What are you talking about?" Veda cried.

"My son, Desta. He is dead! Don't look so surprised, Veda! For you, it's just another failed experiment! I forbade you to treat him with your untried cures and potions. Now he's dead because of you."

Veda looked visibly surprised. "True, he begged me to help him," she said. "He hated being away from you, but you insisted on hiding him when he lost his magic to mage fever all those years ago. But I swear, I never treated your son, as you commanded."

"Why do you think you were banished?" Baruti asked. "Do you think the loss of two insignificant people in a voluntary experiment would have moved me? Only the intercession of Alexander Duchene protected you then. Death follows you, Veda. Beware. I follow you now."

"I never touched him," Veda insisted. "I am sorry he is dead. I kept the secret of his condition, as you asked. What evidence do you have?"

"Desta wrote me a letter before he died. You went behind my back and gave him the experimental treatment. Well, he died from it. I will never forgive you."

"It wasn't me," Veda insisted. "Maybe you should look deeper before casting blame. You abused Sabine to get back at me, which I will never forgive. Send a truthsayer to me if you must, for I have nothing to hide." She took my hand, and a rush of sorcery swept us away into a mystical tunnel. The magic was clean and bright, like fresh air.

We appeared in our suite at the palace as though we'd just walked in. She guided me to the sofa. "Sit down, dear. I'll fix you something for the pain."

I collapsed on the sofa. Rory licked my cheek, wagging his tail. "Sabi head hurt. Make better."

I patted his head and rested my head on the sofa cushions. "How did you find me?"

"I used your blue scarf to scry for you," Veda said. "The one I gave you for your birthday."

"Ah, my birthday! When all I had to worry about was a drunken Luther and a newly hatched pukis dragon. Good times." She gave me a potion, which I drank down. It was sweet, but the taste of the foul red dust lingered. "You know, this is the first headache I've had since my magic was released."

"Truthsayers are not known for their gentleness. I'll send word to Kalem and Braden that you're safe. They've been out looking for you. Baruti should never have touched you. This is maddening. First Alexander loses his sorcery, then Runecroft goes missing. Now Baruti thinks I killed his son."

"Don't forget the taman shade," I said with a laugh.

Veda sighed. "How could I forget the taman shade."

"What do we do?"

"Be watchful and trust no one."

There are times I wish I drank. This is one of them.

CHAPTER 18

"Are you sure Crimm returns today?" I asked, following Braden and Kalem at a swift pace.

"His secretary, Frederick, confirmed it last night when I spoke to him," Kalem replied. "Crimm needs to answer for his unexplained absence in a time of crisis."

"Crimm dotes on Runecroft," I said. "Surely he'd want to know what happened to him." I looked around. "Is it just me, or are the halls unusually empty of people for peak afternoon times?"

"It is strange," Braden commented. "It's usually crowded this time of day."

"People are nervous, I think," Kalem said. "Too many strange things have been happening. I want to interview Frederick too. He's been giving excuses about Crimm's whereabouts for days."

"Has anyone reported Crimm missing, or are we just suspicious?" Braden asked.

Kalem frowned and stepped up his speed. "Suspicious. According to Frederick, he's not missing. However, Crimm didn't retreat to his country house. I checked. Nor has anyone seen him at the palace in days."

"I wonder, who first noticed Runecroft was even missing?" I asked. "How did Baruti Tabor even know?"

Kalem shook his head. "This concerned me too. When I asked Baruti how he learned Runecroft was missing, he admitted Frederick told him, not Crimm."

"But who told Frederick?" I asked.

"Baruti didn't know," Kalem confirmed. "Frederick's supposed to be waiting with Crimm in his office now. I want answers."

"I just wish I could have witnessed the meeting with Baruti," Braden commented. "I never heard a thing even though I stood guard outside Alexander's office. Neither did Sabine."

"Veda was mad too but banished us both before things got interesting," I said.

Kalem laughed. "Well, Rory did threaten Baruti with dragon fire," he said. "You couldn't hear anything because I cast a silent spell protecting the room. Standard procedure for such meetings."

"Can a pukis breathe fire?" Braden asked.

I shook my head. "No, but Rory can dream." I thought about home, and how I often used to want a wall of silence. I decided that I might have to learn that enchantment if I went home again. If I could ever cast a spell properly.

Braden looked at me, concerned. "Are you sure returning to Crimm's office won't upset you? I mean, considering the last time you were there."

"Don't worry, I'll be just fine. It doesn't upset me now. I despise Runecroft, but he cannot hurt me anymore, or my mother. I saw what a coward he is. I promise not to singe the wallpaper again," I said, moving faster to keep up. "What about Baruti Tabor? What's his fate?"

"This might anger you," Kalem warned.

"Go ahead," I said. "It cannot get any worse."

Kalem paused, turned around, and gently took me by the shoulders. "The official story is you were abducted yesterday by some religious cult. Baruti Tabor's explanation is all the interest in how a baseborn rose to mageborn. You became a target for some fanatical baseborn group who think mageborns have too much power. They abducted you yesterday here at the palace, but you managed to escape unharmed."

My inner troll is boiling. "Cult? Fanatical baseborns? There was no cult. Baruti Tabor ordered his keepers to take me."

"I know! Baruti Tabor's retribution would be far worse if we accused him openly. His power has strong currency here," Kalem cautioned. "I hate it too. I'm sorry, Sabine."

"No justice for the wicked." I wasn't surprised. Baruti Tabor was too powerful to be charged with a crime, and I was not powerful enough to influence justice.

"I don't understand how Baruti could defend his actions," Braden said. "What he did was criminal."

"In the meantime, Alexander opened his own inquiry outside the Mystic Circle about Runecroft's disappearance. He put me in charge. He also informed Baruti that criminal investigations are outside his jurisdiction," Kalem pointed out. "Baruti didn't like it, but I don't care. I just want the damned truth. Thankfully, you're not a suspect now. I'm sorry you suffered a truthsayer interrogation, but it clears you of any suspicion."

"What Lord Tabor did to you was rotten," Braden complained. "He should answer for his crimes. Potions and spells can't cure that kind of rottenness."

"Magic has currency in our world, and Baruti is rich with it," I said.

"Baruti bad man," Rory grumbled. "Mean magic. Hurt Sabi. Someday my fire breath burn him."

"We'll keep you safe now," Kalem promised me. "Until we solve this, Alexander assigned us as your bodyguards. Veda insisted on it. The cover story for your kidnapping gives us a reason to stay close. Baruti's keepers will have to face me if they come for you again."

"And my sword," Braden added.

"Be it sword or sorcery, they'll regret it," Kalem said. "And I'll enjoy it."

"Thanks," I said. "It's just frustrating. I should be able to defend myself with magic. I am a mage now."

Rory scampered down to my arm and gazed up at me. "You have me. I am fierce."

"Yes, I have a dragon!" I said, scratching his ear.

"A teacup-sized pukis who gets fussy without his nap," Kalem said, grinning.

Rory scowled at Kalem, indignant. "Dragons do not nap. We recharge."

"You're also learning from the *Golden Moon* children's tomes," Braden added. "I don't think there are any deadly spells there."

"Fine, I get your point," I said, feeling a little defeated by logic. "When they took me, all I could manage was a green flash and some insults. Sadly, my insults had more potency."

"It'll take time and patience," Kalem cautioned. "Veda and I will make it a priority to teach you." He was pensive for a moment. "There are too many threats to the security of the republic now. Too many odd things happening. We need to keep together as we investigate this. I feel it's all connected—Alexander's condition, the taman shade, the bizarre poisoning of Alexander at the ball, Runecroft's disappearance, Baruti Tabor. All of it."

We reached Crimm's private office. The doors were closed and locked. Kalem knocked on the door, but no one answered.

"Now what?" I asked. "Do we break in? Or politely wait?"

"Sabine!" a sharp voice cried behind me. "There you are!"

Oh no! Not now! I turned around as Marigold and her fiancé, Greeley Havelock, walked toward us. Startled, Rory crawled up my arm. His claws pressed sharply into my shoulder as her high-pitched voice pierced my ears. Braden and Kalem fell back, as though a dangerous enemy charged.

Marigold's blonde ringlets bounced as she rushed at me, brushing my cheek with a brief kiss, her perfume fog stinging my nostrils. "Dear me, where have you been? I just heard the inauguration ceremony is postponed! I hope it's not for too long. My betrothed came all this way too! My new gown is scrumptious, and I can't wait to show it off. It's the most delectable shade of pink." She stepped back, waving her fan gently. "I was so relieved they captured the dreadful wraith or whatever the dreadful thing was. Greeley, tell them how relieved I was."

Greeley Havelock stood by with a helpless look on his boney face, a tall thin guardian holding her parasol. "You were most relieved, my love."

"I've been telling Greeley about all our adventures here," Marigold chittered.

"Our adventures?" I asked, confused.

"Marigold detailed her terrifying encounter with the wraith you captured," Greeley remarked. "She told me how you bravely defended her against the beast, for which I am grateful. Still, a helpless maiden should not risk herself so boldly. It is not seemly."

"It was so frightening!" Marigold cried. "The wraith had me in its grasp! I thought I would perish in that instant."

"Do not torment yourself, sweetheart," Greeley comforted her.

"Just thinking about it makes me faint." She whipped out a lacey handkerchief and dabbed her forehead.

"I was scared too," I admitted. "But now the wizards have it confined in a glass prison."

"Is it true they summoned Richard Nightshade? I know he is renowned as a mirror master," Greeley inquired.

"Yes, and Nightshade's mirror magic worked wonders," I confirmed. "The prison he conjured is strong. He made sure of it."

"Do they know what the creature was?" Greeley asked.

I was about to tell them it was a taman shade, but Kalem's expression warned me off. "The wizards are still studying it," I said instead.

Marigold dabbed her face with her delicate kerchief, expressing her distress. "I appreciated the flowers and chocolates you sent when I was so ill after our encounter with that dark horrible creature!"

Flowers? Chocolates? I suspected Lady Veda had a hand in that but allowed me to be credited for it.

"There, there, my dear," Greeley soothed Marigold, and then he bowed to me. "I'm delighted to see you're safe, Lady Fable. Marigold informed me that you are now mageborn, thanks to the treatment of Lady Arcana. I'm astounded this miracle occurred. A wondrous event. I'd be keen to hear more about your holy experience. A true miracle. I'm planning a sermon about it."

Religious people usually make me twitchy, mostly because I put little stock in gods or the men who serve them. My perplexity with Pastor Havelock wasn't his faith but his affection for Marigold Graven. They could not be more opposite. Despite this, I sensed his earnest meaning.

"Thank you. It's a combination of magic and science, as Veda says."

"How are you so strong, Sabine?" Marigold asked. "But you are born of the hearty peasant stock. This morning I heard some dreadful cult abducted you! How horrid! But you were fortunate to escape. How did you do it? Have they been arrested?" She turned to her tall and stoic fiancé. "Isn't it dreadful, Greeley? Oh, do tell me what happened, Sabine! I must know."

"I'm afraid Sabine is prohibited from sharing her tale. It's classified information for now, for Sabine's safety," Kalem answered.

Marigold looked up at Kalem, an imposing figure with his hooded red coat and brooding expression. "Who is this grim mage? He's so mysterious and tall."

I forced a smile. "This is Lord Kalem Shura. Kalem, this is Marigold Graven and her fiancé Greeley Havelock." I pointed to Braden, irked that she'd dismissed him without a glance. "And you remember Braden Griffin. He protected you during the wraith attack."

Greeley bowed politely to them both. "I am honored, gentleman."

"Are you a member of the court?" she asked Kalem. "What is your caste? I must know."

"I am many things, Lady Graven," Kalem replied, ignoring the rudeness of her question. "Most of which I cannot talk about."

"Goodness," Marigold tittered, fanning herself.

Rory sniffed at Marigold, swishing his tail. "Smell strong. Stinky."

"Rory! Bad dragon," I scolded.

Marigold frowned and whisked out her fan. "It talks?"

"He is Rory, and he talks now. Sometimes too much."

Greeley laughed. "Ah, such a silly little pukis. It must be my cologne, dear. You are right, I should always let you choose my scent when we are wed, of course. It would not be proper otherwise. We men do not understand such things."

"We never do," Kalem agreed with a sympathetic look.

Rory grunted loudly, but he didn't shrink from Greeley as he patted his head. I could almost hug Greeley for distracting Marigold from my dragon's blunt words.

"Now be a good dragon," I whispered to Rory.

Rory gave me a sidelong look. "You were thinking it."

"Not the point!"

Marigold recovered her aplomb. "Have you been before the Mystic Circle yet? Do you know what your caste is? Witch? Sorceress? Or are you charm caste like most of your family before mage fever? Anyway, it's so thrilling. I was so nervous at my ceremony, I got the hiccups. The Lord Mystic Baruti Tabor himself proclaimed me a true witch. Mother and Father were so proud."

"A happy day indeed," Greeley said.

"Oh wait!" she cried, rummaging through her silk purse. She pulled out a letter. "The reason I was trying to find you! I almost forgot. This is from your mother. The silly postal detail delivered it to our room by mistake."

My mother's immaculate script in green ink and the Fable House seal on the buff-toned paper were unmistakable. A balm to a stressful day. I could use a little good news from home. "Thank you," I said with genuine gratitude.

Marigold sighed. "Well, we must be off! We're meeting Papa in the gardens."

They strolled down the hall. When they finally disappeared around the corner, Kalem said, "Dear gods, that lady was exhausting."

"Welcome to my world," I said.

We returned our focus to Albertus Crimm's office. I looked around the hallway. There was no longer any physical evidence of my magical explosion. "They must have swiftly repaired the damage I did."

"They did, but the scene caused quite a stir. And no one felt bad about Runecroft getting singed in the pants," Braden said. "I felt bad I couldn't help."

"It's alright," I said. "Veda told me Crimm stayed with me until she arrived. Is that true?"

Braden nodded. "He did, but I kept an eye on him. It was strange he never went after his precious friend."

"I'm done waiting," Kalem said.

"Maybe Frederick Dour-Face is just running late," I suggested.

"I doubt it. Crimm is a firm taskmaster." Kalem waved his hand over the door handle, unlocking it. "And a little magic won't hurt a thing."

We stepped inside the drab interior of Albertus Crimm's outer office. No one was there. Frederick's desk was tidy, with neat stacks of scrolls and papers in a wooden inbox, a pen, inkpot, and blotter in their places. I felt unsettled being back there, remembering what happened. But I kept it to myself.

Braden's hand on my shoulder steadied me. "Are you alright? You look upset."

So much for my bravado, but I never could keep my face neutral. "Don't fret. I'm fine. It's just weird being back here after what happened."

Kalem looked unhappy. "Frederick should be here." He tried the door to Crimm's private office, but it was locked too. "No wards. Just simply locked like the outer doors. No spells."

"Is that unusual?" Braden asked. "That's what most folks do."

"For Crimm it is. He keeps important papers here and always used wards on his private office." Kalem murmured a spell and the door opened.

Inside Crimm's private office, everything was neat, orderly, and boring. "There's nothing here," I said. A large wooden trunk against the wall caught my eye. "Odd, I don't remember that chest when I was here before."

Kalem looked at it. "No, I don't remember it either. Crimm dislikes clutter."

I sniffed the air, noticing a familiar odor. "Kalem, did you drink wylsavan root tea today?"

He shook his head. "No, I've been feeling fine lately. I smell it too."

Rory became anxious, crawling around my shoulder, whining. "What's wrong, baby?" I asked.

"He's nervous about something," Braden said.

"The chest is unlocked," Kalem said. He moved his hands over the wood. "Strange. I smell magic inside the chest." He opened the lid and stepped back when he saw what was stuffed inside.

I'm not the weak, fainting maiden type, but my stomach turned when I saw Crimm's secretary, Frederick, coiled inside the chest, lifeless eyes open and mouth agape. "I feel bad now."

"Why?" Braden asked, his face pale.

"Because I called him Frederick Dour-Face behind his back. Now he's dead."

Upset, Rory burrowed his face in my hair, whining.

Braden looked at Kalem. "Didn't you say you spoke with Frederick only yesterday?"

Kalem closed the lid, but not the image in my mind. "I did speak to a Frederick, just not the real one."

"That body's been dead for at least a week," Braden commented.

"I know," Kalem said, nodding. "Spells on the body are masking the stench of a decomposing corpse, else we'd all be retching at this point. This means a shapeshifter used Frederick's shape."

"And murdered him," I said.

CHAPTER 19

Veda handed me a cup of chamomile tea and sat next to me on the sofa. "Sabine, I'm sorry you witnessed such horror. Talk to me."

I felt dazed, oddly. I took a deep breath and looked at her. "I'm sorry, what did you say?" I looked around. "Where's Braden and Kalem? The last I saw of them was when they led me away from the corpse."

"Drink your tea, dear," she said. "Braden is just outside the door, guarding our suite. Kalem will be back shortly. He's been closeted with Alexander. How are you feeling?"

"I'm not happy about finding a dead body, but other than that, I'm quite well. I didn't like him when I met him. Now he's dead. I feel bad and a bit guilty. The image of Frederick's rotting dead body in the chest unsettled me." Veda looked at me strangely. "Really. I'm not going to crumble and cry. I've been through worse lately." I sipped the tea but tasted nothing but its heat.

"I know, and I'm worried about you because you have been through too much of late."

I fretted about Rory as I tucked my scarf around him. "Poor baby was so distressed when we discovered the body. Now he's sleeping on my lap, swaddled in my blue scarf. He seems so content now."

"The scarf has your scent, so it comforts him."

"I'm not broken. It was just an ugly scene." A thought occurred to me. "I wonder if the Frederick I met in Crimm's office was the shapeshifter or the real person."

"I don't know. Excellent question. It's hard to say how long this was going on. I think the imposter was waiting to make his exposure count the most. We've had so much to worry about, and now there is murder. But you need to relax."

"What do we do now? We haven't even done what we came here for. Alexander is still unable to use his magic."

"I'm not concerned about that now. I'm concerned about you. You're not safe here."

"What are you saying? You're not sending me home!" I put down the empty cup, balancing Rory in my lap. He stirred with my distress. I believed he could sense my emotions. I was sure of it. I held him close, drawing comfort.

"No, but I want you protected. Lord Nightshade extended an invitation for you to stay at his house. It is proper, don't worry. His granddaughter and housekeeper are there too. I contacted him earlier, and he has agreed. Braden will go with you."

"When did you do that?"

"About an hour ago, when you were sitting catatonic on the couch. Do you even remember Braden and Kalem bringing you to our suite?"

I shook my head. "No. Where have I been?"

She took my hand. "In shock. It is common after such an experience. You've suffered too many grueling experiences since we arrived here. I think it caught up with you."

I covered my face with my hands, embarrassed. "Gods, just tell me I didn't swoon."

Veda laughed softly. "Your stony reputation is intact, my dear. Your mind just needed time to digest such a grisly scene. Dangers here are mounting, and I'll be damned if I can figure out why all this is happening. But I do want you out of danger, just for a bit."

"You need me here!"

"I need you safe." Her expression brooked no refusal. "If you will not do it for me, do it for your mother's sake."

"That's not fair!"

"I know," Veda said, smiling. "But I promised her I would keep you safe."

"I keep Sabi safe," Rory said.

"I know you will." Veda said, scratching his chin. "You're a brave little dragon."

"Why Nightshade?" I asked.

"He's an old friend, and I trust him. I treated his granddaughter, Abigail."

"Did she suffer the fever?"

"Yes, at the same time as your mother. She was just a child then. Over the years I've tried to formulate treatments to ease her symptoms, as I did for your mother. I even tried my cure."

"Was she allergic too?"

"No, it just did not work, though I have not given up hope on her or your mother." Veda stood and poured us more tea. "Abigail's parents died from it, as did Richard's wife. All he has left is Abigail. She suffers much like your mother. I do have a new treatment for her to ease her symptoms. You could deliver it for me, which makes an excellent cover for your visit. It would be kind if she had someone to visit with too. She's very isolated."

"You're playing on my better nature," I accused her. "I really don't have one."

"Your mother disagrees."

Veda played the mother card again. I relented. "When do I leave?"

"Within the hour. Braden and Kalem will escort you."

"I'm not afraid, you know."

"I know, dear. That's what worries me."

# # #

I was out of sorts during the carriage ride. Kalem and Braden sat across from me like two guardian statues. They kept watching me but didn't attempt conversation. The silence was oppressive, but I was just too tired to respond. At least Rory enjoyed the ride, sticking his head out the window, tongue hanging out like a dog. Yes, my dragon is weird. His silliness eased my stress as I stroked his head. I missed my long walks in the old woods back home. I missed Mother too and hoped she was alright. *My letter!* There had been so much going on that I'd forgotten about Mother's letter. I checked my jacket pocket and was relieved it was still there.

"You OK, Miss Sabine?" Braden asked abruptly.

"Don't worry so. I just checked to see if I had my mother's letter. I haven't even had time to read it. What with the dead body and all."

"Point taken."

They both relaxed, a little. The crowded bustle of the city calmed when we entered a richer neighborhood with paved streets. Nightshade's sophisticated brick townhouse sat at the heart of an elegant neighborhood housing a pristine section of rich nobility and mageborn. It was easy to tell because the streets were clean without a speck of horse or gryphon dung. Nice trick if you can afford the magic.

We left the carriage and approached the house. I felt out of place in such a grand district, even more so than the palace. I was sure Marigold would delight in such fancy surroundings. Rory enjoyed the new smells.

"Are you sure this is the house?" I asked Kalem, standing before a townhouse that resembled a small castle. "I wasn't expecting anything this grand."

"Yes," Kalem confirmed. "It's been in the Nightshade family for generations."

"Too rich for my taste," Braden said. "I prefer a homey place, like my family's farm."

I put Rory on my shoulder and walked toward the door. "I think my legacy is just a wooden shop with bad plumbing." I touched the large brass doorknocker, and it shimmered. The metallic knocker transformed into a human-style face with a long bulbous nose and piercing golden eyes. It glared down at me and announced in a high-pitched voice, "No solicitors allowed. Go away."

I wasn't expecting a silly door fixture to speak. "I'm Sabine Fable. I'm here to see Duke Richard Nightshade. He's expecting me."

"He's busy," the doorknocker answered tartly. "Go away."

I wasn't in the mood for dealing with a mealy-mouthed metal charm. As I craned my neck to glare back at the cold metallic face, it withered under my dark stare. I said, "Unless you can detach yourself from this door to check personally, shut up. I need to speak to a living person. This is urgent."

"No! Go away!" it sneered.

My damned curse of a temper snapped like a dead twig. I kicked repeatedly at the door to solidify my point. "Summon Lord Nightshade or I will rip your face off!"

"Best send for your master," Kalem added casually. "She might just melt you with her magic. She's new to her powers, so it's hard to say what she'll do to you."

"Sabine is quite a dangerous sorceress," Braden remarked with a grin.

The brass face protested vehemently. "Help! I'm being assaulted! Stop it!"

I kept pounding and taunted back, "Make me."

Excited by the commotion, Rory licked the brassy face. The doorknocker screamed. "Oh, gods! I've been slobbered by a deadly, disgusting reptile. Someone please wash me! It is still licking me! I'm covered in reptilian dribble. Ah, the humiliation!"

"Door thingy tastes funny," Rory complained. His little face screwed up as he brushed his tongue with his paw.

I kicked the door again. "Rory is a dragon, you metallic moron." I stepped back, feeling oddly released and centered again.

"Feel better?" Kalem asked.

"Yes, I think I do," I answered, tugging my jacket.

The door abruptly opened, and I stumbled back. An irate middle-aged woman with tuffs of curling gray hair peeking from her lacy cap glared down at us. "Great gods, what's the commotion? We want no strangers here. This is a noble house, and the master won't tolerate such nonsense. Leave immediately or I'll call the constable."

I spoke fast, tucking Rory under my arm. "Please wait! We're here to see Duke Nightshade. Lady Veda Arcana sent me. I'm Sabine Fable. He's expecting me."

"Ah, yes, I almost forgot. Sorry about the knocker. He's a bit rude to strangers. I'm the duke's housekeeper, Mrs. Doran."

"Wash me," the brass face begged.

She whipped a small hand towel from her pocket and wiped the metal visage. "You pipe down, or you'll find yourself locked away in an iron box." She turned her eyes on Braden and Kalem. "Who are these two ruffians flanking you?" She looked at them like they were boys with dirty faces and muddy feet despite Braden's sharp uniform.

"Sorcerer Kalem Shura and Sergeant Braden Griffin," I said.

Stout and proud in her starched gray dress and spotless white apron, she sized us up. I've known women like her—scrupulous and stalwart women who take their positions seriously. I kept my tone respectful, knowing this.

I heard angry voices, and Mrs. Doran's mouth tightened as she glanced over her shoulder. The shouts escalated as they loomed closer and closer, words undecipherable due to heated anger. I recognized Nightshade's voice, but not the other. Suddenly a young man shoved Mrs. Doran out of the way and knocked me down as he charged out the door. Rory squeaked and clung to my hair as my butt landed on the hard cobblestone path.

Braden and Kalem rushed to my aid, but I waved them away. I shouted curses at the fleeing man's back. "Hey, troll-face! Knocking people down is rude, you know!"

The mysterious rude man in his fine maroon coat and black top hat jumped into a waiting carriage and sped off without even a glance.

"I guess you told him." Kalem smiled as he helped me to my feet. He scooped up a confused Rory and handed him to me. "Glad you're feeling better. We were getting worried. You went silent after, well, you know."

I brushed off my skirt. "I know. Veda told me I went into shock. I'm better now."

"I guess screaming is good medicine for you. Who knew?" Braden said.

Something bothered me about the rude stranger, but I couldn't decipher what it was. I turned around to see Mrs. Doran and Duke Richard Nightshade standing at the doorway.

"Lady Fable, your gentle presence was expected. Do come in," Nightshade invited.

Mrs. Doran bestowed a sliver of a smile as she opened the door for me. She stopped Kalem and Braden from following. "You two wait outside for now. I'll fetch you when Lord Nightshade says so."

I followed Nightshade to a richly decorated parlor. He motioned for me to sit down. "As for the dispute you just witnessed, I would be grateful if you kept it to yourself."

"Of course. I will say nothing. I'm sorry you witnessed my outburst. I've such a temper."

"I would never have guessed," he said with a smile. "Still, I must apologize. There is no excuse for his mistreatment of a lady. Forgive me."

"There's nothing to forgive, sir." Of course, I ached to ask who the stranger was. Manners are so damned difficult.

An anguished scream startled me. Nightshade tensed as a young woman burst into the room, weeping. Nightshade took her in his arms as she cried. She pushed him away. She paced as she tore at her hair, spewing insults and crying. My mother's flare-ups had often been like this before Veda's new medicine helped her.

Mrs. Doran ran into the room, distraught as she begged, "Come away, Miss Abigail. You're just upset again. Please take your medicine. It'll make you feel better!"

"Get away from me!" Abigail screamed. She crumbled to the carpet, crying uncontrollably.

In the confusion, they had forgotten about me. I felt for Abigail. I'd been through this with my poor mother. I got up and knelt by her side. "Hush now. It's alright. Just breathe slowly. Breathe."

Her tearstained face suddenly calmed down when I touched her shoulder. I was not expecting that. "Who are you?" she asked softly, taking my hand.

The sudden shift surprised me, but I was relieved. I smiled, brushing the hair off her face. "I'm Sabine." Then, Rory did something unexpected. He crawled into her lap, trilling in his adorable way and rubbing his head against her hand.

"Oh, how sweet. Is this a pukis dragon?" she asked, gently stroking his back.

"Yes, his name is Rory. He's still a baby."

Rory rewarded us with his squeaky growl, and she laughed. Mesmerized by my little dragon, she wiped her eyes and sat cross-legged on the floor next to me. "He is so friendly and his coloring so lovely. He feels like rough velvet."

"I think he likes you," I said.

"Grandfather, look!" Abigail said with a laugh. "Have you ever seen such a sweet little dragon? I just adore him." As she petted Rory, the dark cloud of her madness lifted. Rory lapped up the affection, of course.

I dared to glance up at Richard Nightshade, fearing anger at my intrusion in his personal pain and privacy. I saw only relief in his face. He touched Abigail's hair gently.

"There now, Abigail," Nightshade said softly. "Mrs. Doran made you some nice tea and biscuits. Will you take your medicine now?"

"Yes, Grandfather," she said wistfully as she played with Rory. Then she turned to me. "I'm so ashamed, and you are a guest. Please forgive me. Share my tea. Grandfather said we would be expecting a houseguest. Mrs. Doran always makes oodles of biscuits."

Mrs. Doran left to fetch tea and biscuits. Abigail looked embarrassed, glancing at me shyly. "I'm sorry for my outburst," she whispered. "I hope I didn't say anything too dreadful."

"It's alright. My mother has them too. She had mage fever many years ago."

"Then you understand! She lost her magic too?"

"Yes," I said. "Most of my family perished in the last great epidemic."

"It is a cruel disease," she whispered. "It's like it never leaves you."

She was quite pretty, with long dark hair and big brown eyes. She continued to hold my hand. "Grandfather doesn't like to talk about it. I was only six years old when I caught it. It killed my parents. My grandmother too. You're lucky you still have your mother. Does she live with you?"

"No, she's back home. I'm from a small town called Crimson Hollow. I miss her though. I write when I can."

"We usually live in the country. It's very peaceful there, but a little lonely. Morgan Ashstone used to visit, but Grandfather is very angry with him." She leaned in and whispered, "He was just here. Did you see him? He's a young mage with many prospects."

The idiot who knocked me over, I thought but kept that to myself. "Perhaps. Tall young man in a maroon coat? Handsome?" That was just a guess, as I hadn't seen his face. Pretty girls have handsome beaus. It's the rule.

"Yes! Morgan and Grandfather were arguing. I hate it when they fight. Then I felt ill and strange. They were fighting because of me. Morgan wants to marry me. Grandfather refused him again. Grandfather is very protective. He knows people can be cruel. Having mage fever is a stigma, and he's just trying to protect me."

"You're lucky to have someone who cares so much," I said. "Do you want to marry Morgan?"

"Once I did," she said wistfully. "But my heart feels differently now." She giggled like a girl, scratching Rory's tummy. "What does Rory like to play with?"

I laughed. "Anything shiny," I said. "And if you give him bacon, he's your friend for life."

"Abigail?" Kalem said, uncertain as he stood in the doorway.

Abigail turned, and her face softened with affection. "Kalem, it's been so long. I've missed you."

I realized at a glance Kalem loved Abigail, and she felt the same.

CHAPTER 20

Mrs. Doran carried a tray of shortbread biscuits, sandwiches, and hot tea to the low table. "There now, we have some lovely refreshments." She frowned when she saw Kalem. "I told you to wait outside."

"It's alright, Mrs. Doran," Nightshade intervened. "Kalem is an old friend of the family. He turned to the rest of us and said, "Mrs. Doran is an excellent housekeeper, but she has been with us for only two years. She does not know Kalem was once my ward."

"Alright then." Mrs. Doran nodded. "I'll bring another cup for the gentleman. Sorry, sir."

"It's quite alright," Kalem said.

Kalem sat close to Abigail. They were as shy with each other as adolescents, talking of small things, while Mrs. Doran fussed over Abigail. Duke Nightshade chose the velvet stuffed chair facing us. He seemed content to see the two together. As our tea progressed, I felt like an intruder and ate too much shortbread.

When Doran measured out Abigail's medicine, I remembered the bottle Veda sent along. "Oh wait, Veda formulated a new treatment for Abigail. She prescribes a spoonful twice a day. And she should eat something with it. But it's in my satchel, which is still in the carriage. I'll go get it."

Kalem put down his teacup. "We forgot about Braden! He's still waiting outside!"

"So did I," Nightshade said. "Mrs. Doran, Braden Griffin will also be a guest. He's assigned to Sabine as one of her protectors."

"I'll bring him inside," I said.

Nightshade laughed. "Yes, don't leave the poor fellow outside. Apologize to Sergeant Griffin for me. I fear we forgot all about him in the excitement."

"Well, bring him in, and take some biscuits to the boy," Mrs. Doran offered. "I'll see to it he has a room prepared. Will Kalem be staying as well?"

"I'm needed at the palace, but I will visit again if the duke and Abigail are amenable," Kalem said.

Nightshade nodded, and Abigail's face beamed.

"Thank you. I know he'll understand," I said, gathering some shortbread in a napkin. "Things have been crazy for us all. I'll be right back." I scratched Rory's head. "Behave!"

He grunted lazily in response, content to snuggle in Abigail's lap. I opened the front door and was surprised to find Braden standing right there in the doorway, looking a bit sheepish.

"I thought you'd forgotten about me," he said. "I was going to knock and risk the wrath of Mrs. Doran."

"I'm so sorry," I said, handing him the treats. "You can come inside. Mrs. Doran knows the duke invited you too."

"Thank you." He accepted the napkin of cookies, then he leaned down and kissed me on the mouth.

Surprised, I jumped back. My reaction was not what he expected either. He looked away. "Sorry. I did not mean to offend, Lady Fable."

"No, of course not! You didn't offend me. I was just surprised." It was also my first kiss, which I would never confess to anyone.

"You're mageborn now. Maybe I'm not good enough anymore?"

"No! How could you think such a thing?"

"I'll wait outside," he said with not a little vehemence and left the doorway. "Maybe I'm more useful if I'm guarding something."

When the door closed behind him, I felt he was closed to me forever. Braden was my friend. One of the few I'd ever had. Did I just muck that up? He had never acted like that before!

When I entered the parlor again, Rory sensed my distress. When I joined Abigail on the couch, he crawled back into my lap, trilling softly in his throat and rubbing his head against my arm.

Worry about Braden stressed my stomach. All I could think about was his hurt look, followed by his angry one. *Damn it, damn it, damn it! What did my face look like when he kissed me? Appalled, terrified, or disgusted? I was taken by surprise. Now he hates me! What's wrong with me? Now I've mucked it all up. Damn it!*

Abigail doted on Rory, composed as if her fit had never happened. Richard Nightshade seemed to be studying her and Rory. Mrs. Doran handed me another plate of goodies, which I accepted with a forced smile. Rory sniffed the bounty, begging with eager eyes. I let him try a little sandwich with cucumbers and soft cheese. He thanked me with little grunts as he chewed.

Nightshade and Kalem excused themselves for a brief "business talk," which I knew was code for all the murder and mayhem going on at the palace. My suspicion was they did not want to upset Abigail with such gruesome things. I was in agony, wondering if I should go outside and talk to Braden.

"Grandfather's very impressed with you," Abigail said, stirring her tea.

"Me? Why?" I asked, bewildered by her statement.

"You're unique. He told me about you. Grandfather usually doesn't like people, but you made an impression. You suffered mage fever's cruel theft of magic as a baby. You only recently acquired mystical power. It's a miracle. This has never happened before, except for Lady Veda Arcana. Many dispute her claim she ever had mage fever, but I always believed her. You're also independent and hold a position of respect with Veda. All this without the sponsorship of a wealthy family or noble name."

I sipped tea, hoping to settle my stomach. "You're too kind. I'm blunt and opinionated, and I have a dreadful temper. Veda has been generous to me. Her treatment restored my magic. Now I hope to make a brighter future, for myself and my mother."

"A treatment that is hopeful but doesn't cure everyone. Including me."

"When did you try her cure?"

"Two years ago. Grandfather had such hopes. It's not just about the magic. My attacks worry him so."

"My mother suffered similar side effects to the fever. Veda tried to cure her, though it was several years ago. The medicine almost killed her, but she didn't regain her powers. Her new medicine has eased her extreme symptoms. I think it's like the formula you are taking now. I hope it helps."

"My reaction to Veda's cure was not so deadly as your poor mother's. I became a little feverish and developed a rash, but nothing so life-threatening. It just did not work for me. I do hope the new medicine helps. I always worry about what I say or do when I have an attack."

"You must never fret about what you say or do when you're sick, Miss Abigail," Mrs. Doran said.

"Veda asked me to tell you not to give up hope. What she did for me could change things for others. The formula for her cure is tricky. It is not the same for everyone. We are discovering new things all the time."

"I will hope then," Abigail said brightly, hope in her eyes. She leaned in closer, her voice barely a whisper. "If only I could banish this madness and pain, I'd endure a life without magic with contentment. Sabine, before your magic was restored, did you also suffer from fits like me? If it pains you to talk about it, please forgive my curiosity. You need not answer."

"No, it doesn't upset me. I suffered blinding headaches but was spared the horrific episodes my mother endured. My hands would burn so hot it felt like they were on fire. It usually happened when I was angry or upset. Like I said, I've a nasty temper. Sadly, I always remember what I've said or done. At the time, I never connected my symptoms to anything to do with mage fever or my magic being still inside. Once my magic was freed, those symptoms vanished. Except for my temper, of course. Nothing can cure that."

Abigail laughed, taking my hand. "You are a delight. I must confess I endure the same. Before my madness drowns out all reason, my own hands burn like hot coals and my headache is agony itself. Oh, you do understand!"

I nodded with the shared memory. I decided it must be her magic trying to get out like mine had. It was a shame the treatment did not work for her. I wished I could help her.

Abigail poured me more tea. "Now tell me about the mysterious wraith you captured almost single-handedly. Grandfather says it's a taman shade."

"Miss Abigail, it's a frightening tale," Mrs. Doran interjected.

"Nonsense!" Abigail insisted. "I'm not a frail female who curdles at the sight of a mouse. Just because I'm ill does not mean my heart and spirit are any less hardy."

"It happened so fast," I said. "I didn't catch it. I mostly remember running from it in terror. My sorcery is still so raw and new that I can barely recall what I did. In a fit of panic, I created a strange rope of green vines, which helped bind the creature. But Kalem was the real hero in catching it—and the palace wizards who helped hold it."

"Do any of them ever smile?" she whispered with a grin.

"I don't think so," I said.

Abigail fed Rory shortbread as she listened. Who knew dragons liked sugar? I just hoped he wouldn't get sick. Mrs. Doran would be miffed if he barfed on the fancy carpet.

"What was Kalem like when he was younger? He never talks about his childhood," I said.

"We've known Kalem since he was a boy. But I'm not surprised he doesn't talk about the past. It's a tragic story. I'm not sure if I should tell you all, but I will say this. Kalem is a noble and true man. His father was cruel beyond imagining. There was a scandal, and he banished Kalem and his mother. Grandfather took them in. Kalem loved his mother dearly, but she died not long after her husband divorced her."

I felt for Kalem and understood his distance. Despite my troubled childhood, I still had my mother. "How old was Kalem?"

"Fourteen. Grandfather made him his ward and even talked about adopting him. But Kalem was proud then and lived on his pain. He wanted to make his own way in the world. He left, changed his name, and traveled. He was born Faelan Anteros. I didn't see him for years, until today. Kalem sometimes wrote to me over the years. I had faith he would make a mark for himself among the mage castes. Grandfather and I were so proud when he became a shapeshifter. Now he works for the republic, as Kalem Shura. I kept all his letters, even though Morgan asked me to burn them once. I realized in that moment Morgan had deep flaws in his character. How could I destroy letters from a dear friend?"

"I'm glad your grandfather tried to help him."

"So am I," Abigail said. "But, on to more intriguing and less sad subjects. What's the taman shade like? I wanted to see it, but Grandfather thinks it's too disturbing. It must be terrifying to look at. He says they're supposed to be extinct."

"Everyone is baffled. When the creature was finally trapped in the glass prison the duke conjured, I sensed pain and sorrow. I felt sorry for her."

"You believe the taman shade is female?" Abigail asked, stunned.

"I believe so. It did not speak, but I sensed it was trying to communicate with me."

Abigail looked down at her cup, stirring purposely. "I pity it now. Nothing should suffer."

We passed the time playing with Rory, who wrapped himself in Abigail's green silk scarf. It complemented his own mottled dragon hue of blue and green. It amused her so much she insisted I keep it. Duke

Nightshade and Kalem returned to the parlor, finding us doting on a dragon tangled in green silk with cookie crumbs on his face.

"Where's Braden?" Kalem asked. "I thought he was allowed in?"

I fumed impotently as I kept a smile pasted on my face. "He did come in for a moment, but he went back outside. I think he's guarding the house." I hated lying to Kalem.

"What nonsense," Nightshade said. "Mrs. Doran, bring the boy back in. I think you intimidated him a bit too much."

"I'll be right back," Mrs. Doran mumbled. "I swear, young men don't have a brain in their heads."

She was gone for less than a minute when she rushed back to the parlor. "I need help."

"Braden? Is he hurt?" I asked, panic rising.

"You need to see for yourselves," she said.

We all jumped up to follow her.

Braden was standing by the front steps. He was not moving, but I saw a glimmer of panic in his eyes.

"The boy's been hexed," Nightshade said, opening the front door wide. "We best get him inside. The neighbors love to gossip."

Kalem cast a spell, and Braden floated into the house. I followed, feeling terrible. If I had not overreacted to his kiss, then he would not have been spelled like that. *What's wrong with me?* I wondered.

Inside the parlor, Kalem lowered Braden to the floor. Nightshade and Kalem examined him, mumbling to each other. *If I were a better mage, I could be helping,* I thought.

"I think it's a simple stasis charm," Nightshade remarked, his hands glowing as he moved them over Braden. "That's good, because I think I can remove it."

"Yes, remove it!" I cried.

After a quick flurry of mystical words, Braden's face softened, and he fell back to the couch. "That was unpleasant," he managed to whisper. He winced when he touched his forehead. "What the bloody hell happened?"

"Someone immobilized you with a nasty enchantment," Kalem replied. "Do you remember seeing anything? Did someone approach you?"

Braden shook his head and accepted a glass of brandy from Nightshade. "Thank you, sir." He drank it down and shook his head again. "All I remember is that one moment I could move and the next I couldn't. It was misery. I knew someone magicked me. I saw no one, but with mage folk, that's not unusual. Begging your pardon, sir."

"No worry, my boy," Nightshade said.

"Did you at least get to eat your shortbread cookies?" I asked. I laughed, hoping he was no longer cross with me.

He glanced up, confused. "What cookies? I never came inside the house. What's wrong? You look pale, Miss Sabine."

My mouth went dry. "You didn't come into the house before this? I gave you shortbread and …" I did not want to go into the rest of it. *It wasn't Braden who kissed me! That makes me feel even worse somehow.*

"What is it, Sabine?" Kalem asked.

"The imposter was in the house. I gave him that nice shortbread, and then he left. I thought Braden was upset with me, which is why I didn't say anything." *And the false Braden kissed me. Not Braden, but a damned, evil shapeshifter.*

"Why would I be upset with you?" Braden asked, confused.

"Never mind, it's nothing." I turned to Nightshade. "Our enemies know we are here. I should leave." *I am not going to mention the damned kiss.*

"This shapeshifter is pissing me off," Kalem remarked.

"Language," Mrs. Doran warned.

"I'm afraid language is the least of our troubles," Nightshade said. "How do we know this Braden is the real one?"

I looked at Braden and asked, "How many brothers and sisters do you have and where did you grow up?" A simple question, but would a short-term imposter know this?

"Nine. We grew up on a farm."

"Why was I embarrassed after the wraith attacked me?"

"You threw up. A lot."

"It's Braden. But, we can't stay here now. It's too much of a risk for the duke and Abigail."

"Nonsense," Abigail said. "This scoundrel will not chase away my new friend. Kalem and Grandfather are powerful sorcerers. Our guard was down before, that's all. And Mrs. Doran is a charmer too."

"She is?" I asked.

"I made the doorknocker," Mrs. Doran said. "Dear me, I best check on it. He should have given us a warning."

Kalem looked at me strangely. "What else happened?" he asked quietly. "You're not telling us everything."

I clenched my jaw. "Nothing."

"Your face is red," Kalem noted gently. "Something is troubling you."

"Shapeshifter Braden took more than cookies," I whispered to him. "He stole a kiss. It surprised me and we quarreled. Then false Braden stormed out, but I didn't think he was an imposter. I was upset, but it wasn't Braden who kissed me, which upsets me more. Stop looking at me like that," I hissed. "What's odd is why this imposter would want to kiss me. It was not Braden. It's weird. Very weird."

"What are you two whispering about?" Braden asked.

"Nothing," we answered simultaneously.

Kalem's face was pensive. "You're too hard on yourself," he said to me softly. "Not that you're not worthy of a kiss, but I agree. Why did this imposter go to such extremes to kiss you? And then leave?"

Mrs. Doran rushed in, angry. "My charmed doorknocker is smashed. It's like someone took a hammer to it."

I sat on the couch, and Rory crawled into my lap, still tangled in Abigail's green scarf. "Sabi sad?"

"Not sad, just confused." Despite the terror and mystery propelling my life, all I could wonder about was why Braden had never kissed me. *What's wrong with me?* I wondered.

My morose musings was disrupted when Rory threw up on the sofa.

CHAPTER 21

Later that night, Mrs. Doran showed me my room. It was fancy but cozy, with a large bed topped by a yellow silk bedspread embroidered with blue flowers and a mountain of fluffy pillows. Despite feeling drained, I brushed out my frizzy hair, cleaned my teeth, and scrubbed my face—especially my lips, because the shapeshifter kissed me. But it didn't wash away feelings of violation or my confusion about the real Braden.

I changed into my nightgown and curled up on the bed with Rory to read my mother's letter. Rory sniffed every inch of the soft bedcover before he settled next to me. I opened the letter, hoping for mundane news, and was rewarded for once. Mother wrote she was well, Luther stopped drinking (though she was not holding her breath about his sobriety), and the shop was almost solvent. She sent her love and affection.

I pressed the letter to my chest, relieved. I was sad, too, because I missed the comfort of my mother's presence.

"Mama Fable well?" Rory asked.

"Yes, Mother's well and seems to be thriving." I smiled and folded the letter.

"Sabi want to play now?" Rory asked, headbutting my knee.

"You're perky for being so sick a few hours ago. Did you have to throw up on the sofa? I never want to experience Mrs. Doran's icy glare again."

Rory's innocent gaze crumbled my resistance. "Magic fixed things. Sofa all clean now. Smells like magic too." He rolled on his back, snorting.

I laughed, scratching his ears. "OK, but I'd be a better pukis mom if I kept you away from sugar. Want to practice flying?"

"No," Rory grumbled, curling up on a plush pillow.

"Just to exercise your wings. Come on. We'll make a game of it."

"No! Sleepy now." He tucked his face between his paws and closed his eyes.

It worried me he had become so reluctant about learning to fly, but I decided not to press it. "OK, let's go to bed."

Over the next three days, I kept Abigail company and supervised her medicine, noting any reaction, no matter how minor. She was genuinely nice, but a little sad and isolated from the world. I suspected Duke Nightshade of being overprotective of her but knew she was all he had in the world. I had those same feelings about my mother. Luther didn't count.

Still, I sensed a steely inner strength in Abigail. We talked about books and played games with Rory. I felt an empathy for her despite our caste differences. I never thought someone so highborn could be so nice. I decided that Marigold should take a few lessons from her. In many ways, Abigail reminded me of my mother: kind, gentle, and soft-spoken.

Braden stayed by my side most of the time, but it felt awkward now. *Why does this bother me? Do I want to kiss Braden? What's wrong with me?*

I needed to work, to solve something. My connection with the outside world was limited to brief contact with Kalem. He would come to the house to bring me letters from Veda, which was my lifeline to her and what was happening at the palace. It was too dangerous to communicate any other way. Apparently, the baseborn way of courier notes was safer than magical means. I also made myself scarce when Kalem and Abigail talked, to give them a private moment.

I tried to keep Rory out of trouble and away from Mrs. Doran's sharp eyes. Flying lessons were a failure so far. He would exercise his fragile wings only when coaxed with treats.

"You spoil him too much," Mrs. Doran remarked when she saw us in the parlor. "Stop coddling your dragon. He will never do for himself otherwise."

Abigail was fascinated by Rory and had begun to study my pukis manual. One morning she said, "Let me see if I can charm him into flight."

"Very well, but keep a close eye on him. He can get distracted very easily," I said with a laugh. Rory actually wiggled his wings for her. Of course, she had bacon to offer, but still. I let them alone to play together, feeling like a failure. How could a pukis not be interested in flying?

I decided to take out my frustrations over being kissed by a shapeshifter, Rory's stubbornness, and my conflicted feelings about Braden by pounding bread dough. I had to punch something. Braden sat at the wooden kitchen table, sharpening his sword and dagger as I worked.

"What's wrong? he asked bluntly, looking at me intently.

"Nothing's wrong," I said, kneading the bread dough in a frenzy.

"You sure things are good? You've been acting strange the last few days."

After twenty sweaty minutes, I molded my doughy victim into a loaf and set it out to rise. I washed my hands in the sink, wiped down the counters, and washed the bowls. Then I put on a fresh pot of coffee. Anything to keep busy.

"Sabine, what's wrong?"

I shrugged, keeping my eyes downcast. "Nothing. I'm fine."

Braden leaned back in his chair, frowning. "My mum warned me, if a lady says she's fine, it usually means trouble. Stop running from me and talk to me."

I paused my frenzy, wiping my hands with a kitchen towel. "I'm sorry, Braden. It's not your fault. I've just been so worried about … said. "Well, everything. Murders, scary shades, dead bodies, and missing people. I can't teach my dragon to fly. And the shapeshifter pissed me off."

"So, you're not mad at me? Because the last three days you've hardly said a word to me."

I'm mad at myself. "Of course not."

"Then why won't you look me in the eye? Because the shapeshifter looked like me? And he kissed you?"

He knows! Damn it, damn it, damn it.

I sat down at the kitchen table across from him. "I don't know why it bugs me so much. It confused me." I wanted to scream that my first kiss wasn't from him but from a murderous shapeshifter. But I couldn't. I was lying to my friend because I was afraid of the truth. *What's wrong with me?* I wondered. *I can't have a romance anyway. I'm busy.*

Mrs. Doran's entrance into the kitchen silenced us like naughty children. "Coffee smells welcoming," she said. "Has Miss Abigail taken her medicine this morning?"

"Yes, and the good news is that there've been no reactions or episodes for the last three days. But Veda said we must be vigilant observing her reactions, just in case."

"Where's your hell dragon hiding?" she asked, taking the coffee pot off the stove.

"Rory's playing with Abigail in her room. I'm hoping he will try to impress her with flying lessons. His flying development concerns me.

The pukis manual said he should be doing short flights at around five or six weeks."

"Well, you know my thoughts on it, but the funny little creature does calm her down," Mrs. Doran noted, setting out a silver service on the kitchen table for polishing. She looked at me quizzically. "Even Duke Nightshade remarked on it."

"Rory does have a soothing effect on Abigail," I said.

Mrs. Doran fetched cups and plates, as well as the small pitcher of cream from the icebox. "Not on me, he doesn't. Nosy little dragon pilfered one of my blue crystal earrings from my dresser and a silver buckle from Nightshade's wardrobe! I found them in his basket."

"Rory took one of the silver buttons from my uniform yesterday," Braden said. "Found him nesting with it, the button threads still dangling from his mouth where he bit it off. Mrs. Doran was nice enough to sew it back on."

"I'm sorry, but pukis dragons do like shiny things." I sighed.

"Your tiny dragon gets into things somehow," Doran said. "I doubt it's because he's a slow learner. Spoiled yes, but not slow."

The front doorbell sounded—one of Mrs. Doran's new additions to replace the smashed knocker. She took the pot off the stove and wiped her hands on her apron. "You pour us some coffee, and I'll see who it is."

After she left the kitchen, Braden got up and gently took me by the shoulders. "Don't shut me out. I'm your friend. We've only each other to depend on during this insane time."

I wanted to lean my head against his chest but held back. I looked up at him instead and took his hand. "I'm sorry. You are my friend. I never want to lose that."

"You never will, Sabine. You try to be the big bad wolf, but you scare only yourself," he whispered. "You're too hard on yourself."

Loud voices distracted us. Braden and I looked at each and followed the shouting to the front door to find a flustered Mrs. Doran pushing a man away.

"I demand to see Abigail!" the man shouted.

"Duke Nightshade forbade you to come here again!"

Braden marched toward the door. "Mrs. Doran, shall I remove this gentleman from the premises?"

"Yes, Braden, please do," she said. "He's not welcome here."

Upon closer view, I recognized the rude visitor who knocked me on my ass when I arrived three days earlier. Morgan Ashstone! Ugh. He was the maroon-coated gentleman with the arrogant look. But something else gnawed at me about him, but I could not fathom the reason.

"Abigail!" he shouted, pushing past Mrs. Doran.

"Leave now," Braden commanded, taking him by the arm.

Ashstone jerked away, as though Braden's touch fouled him. "Baseborn scum! How dare you lay hands on a mageborn lord!"

"Morgan, please stop!" Abigail cried from the stairs. "Just leave."

Braden forcibly shoved Morgan out of the house, taking him by surprise. Morgan spun around and threw a punch, which Braden easily avoided. Braden hit Morgan in the gut, and the mageborn bent over in pain. He straightened and punched Braden in the jaw, but it did not even phase my friend.

Braden's fist struck Morgan's face this time. He stumbled back, his visage red with rage and blood. Morgan flicked his hand, and a surge of gray sorcery knocked Braden several feet back into the house. Then glimmering ropes of energy bound Braden against the wall by the staircase.

I rushed to Braden, unsure of how to disentangle him from the mystical bindings. Abigail cried, begging Morgan to go as Mrs. Doran held her.

"Come to me, Abigail," Morgan pleaded. "You love me! Leave this house and come away now!"

Nightshade rushed down the stairs, furious. "Morgan, I told you to stay away!" With a wave, his sorcery freed Braden from the wall. Then the duke wrapped his arm around Abigail and glared at Morgan. "See what you've done! You've upset her! Leave now. Do not come back."

"But she loves me!" Morgan insisted. "None of you understand." He rushed toward Abigail, but Nightshade summoned a shield, barring him from touching her.

Morgan Ashstone had gone beyond pissing me off. Distressing Abigail and assaulting Braden infuriated me. I marched toward him, balling my fists. "Get out, you bully! Now!"

He laughed and shoved me aside.

I shoved back. "You have a bad habit of assaulting women. I'll fight back. Bet you're not used to that!"

"You dwarfish, baseborn slut," he threatened. "I'll show you." He drew back his arm to strike me.

Suddenly Rory appeared, growling as he latched onto Morgan's ankle. The scum kicked my Rory across the room. My heart and breath paused as my temper bubbled over. Green magic surged from my hands, throwing the intruder out the door on the mystical wave. With a swing of my hand, the door slammed. An upsurge of green shimmering vines streamed from my fingers, sealing the front door shut.

I paused when I saw what I had done. "Did I do that?" My knees went wobbly. Braden caught me before I hit the floor. I struggled to stand, but my body was numb. "Rory! Is he hurt?"

Abigail wiped her face and ran to Rory, gently scooping him up. I heard faint squeaks as she cradled him. "I think he's fine. Just shaken up, poor thing." She carried him to me and laid him in my hands.

He curled up in my arms, shaking. "It's OK, baby," I whispered, stroking his head crest.

"My dear, you took a dreadful chance confronting Ashstone," Nightshade said, kneeling next to me. He looked at the green vines covering his front door. "But your handiwork is most unique." He turned to Braden. "I'm sorry. Are you hurt, my boy?"

"Just my pride," Braden answered.

"Morgan behaved in a most dishonorable fashion," Nightshade said. "He couldn't stand against you as a man, so he cheated, using sorcerous tricks. You should take pride in your actions, Braden. You behaved with nobility and honor. Morgan broke the law using magic to assault someone. I will personally file charges against him. He has gone too far this time."

Braden's shoulders straightened, and he held his head high. "Thank you, Duke."

Mrs. Doran could not open the door. She went to a window and said, "He's getting in his carriage and riding away. Good riddance."

"I am ashamed to have known him now," Abigail said. "I am appalled he tried to hit a lady. It is unforgivable."

Abigail and Braden helped me to my feet. I still felt dizzy, but I was calmer.

"What do you call such green magic?" Abigail asked me. "It was amazing."

"I have no idea. It's what happened when we trapped the taman shade. I don't know how it works."

Mrs. Doran tugged at the vines, but they wouldn't budge. "Blasted things are tough."

"I think you'll need a strong blade to cut those. Sorry," I said. They helped me to the sofa with Rory. I sat down, feeling shaky. Abigail brought my blue scarf to comfort Rory.

"Is the little fella hurt?" Mrs. Doran asked. "Shall I bring him a bit of bacon?"

Rory's ears perked up, and I smiled. If he was hungry, he must be OK. "Yes, thank you."

"I'll bring us all some refreshments," Mrs. Doran said. "It may be morning, but I think we could all do with a spot of brandy."

"How did Rory appear so quickly to attack Ashstone?" I asked.

"He flew down to you," Abigail said. "He saw you were in danger and wanted to protect you."

"I fly fast," Rory said, bobbing his head. "Bite nasty man's leg."

I would not cry in front of everyone.

"Oh, Grandfather, I am so sorry," Abigail said. "You were right about Morgan. He's full of so much anger and hatred. How could I have been so foolish?"

"He's an ass," I mumbled and then winced. "Sorry."

"No need to apologize," Nightshade replied. "Morgan is an ass."

Something strange about Morgan Ashstone lingered in my mind like a nasty shadow. I felt it when he knocked me down that first time. But that was when I realized it wasn't the first time. I'd seen Morgan Ashstone before …. At the fancy party! He rudely pushed me aside then too. I had trailed him to the gardens and ended up being confronted by Crimm. The relevance of this eluded me, but there had to be something to it.

"I was easily swayed by his romantic gestures," Abigail said.

"I wish now I had never taken him as an apprentice," Nightshade said. "It's rare to find someone blessed with the way of the mirror. Morgan had a genuine talent for it, but he became difficult. His temper became erratic. Then he became obsessed with Abigail." He turned to me, looking at me with great interest. "Sabine, the magic you manifested is unusual, especially since it was more of an instinct than a constructed spell."

"She did it once before," Braden said. "When the taman shade attacked us at the palace. She made a shield of those vines, then roped the evil creature with them. It was something to see. Palace wizards still are scratching their heads over that one."

I glanced at Braden, narrowing my eyes. "I recall you couldn't stop laughing when I was unable to remove them."

Braden shrugged. "Well, it was funny."

Nightshade nodded and leaned forward. "I remember seeing the remnants of those green vines still woven around the taman shade when the bindings of the powerful wizards had already vanished. Yet fragments of your magic still clung to the creature. And your eyes are silver, not just gray," Nightshade remarked.

"My eyes are my bane. As is my temper."

"In ancient legends, the fey people had such eyes," Nightshade explained. "Your green magic is reminiscent of some of those stories. Now, people believe their race a myth, but myths often hold old truths. And older magic."

"I doubt my ancestry includes the fey," I said, laughing.

"The past is full of mystery." Nightshade smiled. "Who knows?"

A wall mirror in the parlor shimmered, and Kalem's image appeared. "Richard, are you there?"

Abigail's face brightened when she saw Kalem's face in the mirror. I noted the strain in Kalem's voice. Something was terribly wrong.

Nightshade rose and walked to the mirror. "Yes, I'm here. The glass charm I gave you for emergencies works much better than I imagined. What's happened?"

"The taman shade is gone."

Nightshade's expression darkened. "Impossible. The shade couldn't have broken free from my glass prison."

"Nothing was broken," Kalem replied. "The glass prison and its captive are gone."

"What about all the wizards guarding it? Alexander himself ordered more than a dozen wizards as security to guard the taman shade."

"The wizards are dead."

CHAPTER 22

Nightshade's sorcery accelerated the horse's speed, so we arrived at the palace quicker than I imagined. Kalem ordered the gates opened when he saw us. The horses slowed and the carriage rolled to stop.

"Could the horses be harmed by his spell?" I asked, worried about them.

"No, my dear," Nightshade said. "They rather enjoy it, I think. Their hooves don't even strike the ground. It's like they are flying."

"They're quite well," Abigail assured me. "Grandfather would never harm an animal."

Kalem, who was waiting for us, briefly clasped hands with Nightshade when he stepped from the coach. "You made good time," the shapeshifter said. "Thanks for coming so quickly."

"I'm glad you came to meet us, Kalem," Abigail said. She departed the carriage with grace, taking delicate steps.

I just jumped to the ground, my dragon tucked under my arm.

"They shouldn't be here," Kalem exclaimed, nodding toward us. "It's not safe for Abigail, or Sabine."

"Duke Nightshade's orders," Braden replied, climbing down from the driver's seat.

"Why?" Kalem asked. "What's happened?"

"Morgan Ashstone trespassed into my home this morning," Nightshade explained. "He went mad. He assaulted Mrs. Doran, Sergeant Griffin, and Sabine. I may be a mage, but I'm only one man, and I could not risk leaving Abigail alone with that madman stalking her. The brute presented no hesitation when it comes to harming a woman."

"Abigail, did he hurt you?" Kalem asked, concerned.

"No, silly, it was me," I said, relishing Kalem's awkwardness for a second. I would have been miffed, but he was so clearly besotted with Abigail's welfare that I forgave him. "To be fair, I'm the one who foolishly picked a fight with the mad mage."

"Morgan nasty man. Hurt Sabi. Kicked me. I bit him hard," Rory added proudly. "Then Sabi got mad and made door green. Won't open now. But it smells nice."

"The green vines again?" Kalem asked, raising an eyebrow.

"Don't ask me how," I said.

"I was supposed to protect you, my dear," Nightshade countered. Weary, he leaned on his cane. "Lady Fable is most formidable when angered. But I could not leave Abigail there, even with the feisty Sabine and her brave little dragon as defense."

"I'm bravest dragon," Rory said, puffing his chest.

Nightshade revealed a rare smile and scratched Rory's head. "Indeed. I locked up the house with wards and sent Mrs. Doran to my neighbor for her safety. Morgan will be dealt with lawfully, but until then I'm taking no chances."

Abigail took her grandfather's arm, concerned. "This has been a great strain on Grandfather."

"Apparently nothing is secure now," Kalem said, his face grim. "The theft of the taman shade still in its glass prison has perplexed everyone. Someone knew how to break your wards, Richard. But worse is the murder of the dozen wizards who guarded it."

"How did those poor men perish?" Braden asked him in a low voice. "By blade or magic?"

Kalem motioned us to follow him into the palace. "No one knows yet. A physician will perform the autopsies."

"Such macabre work," Abigail remarked. "Those poor men, murdered."

"We shouldn't speak of such things," Kalem said.

"Kalem. I'm not so frail, despite my illness. It's easy for me to be brave. I have you, Grandfather, Doran, and my new friends who protect me so well. There are more pressing matters now that demand our care."

"I'll be glad to see Veda," I said. "I've missed her."

"She missed you too. Veda's waiting with Alexander and Corene in the reception hall," Kalem said.

The journey through the halls was bleak. I sensed the fear in the air. We arrived at the reception hall, and sentries opened the double doors to admit us at Kalem's signal. Inside the large formal chamber, Alexander Duchene waited in his official state chair with his wife, Lady Corene, sitting by his side.

"Welcome, my friends," Alexander said warmly. "I appreciate all of you coming."

Veda greeted me warmly and kissed my cheek. "My dear, how was your stay with Duke Nightshade?"

"Most pleasant, but Morgan Ashstone caused a bit of trouble."

"I remember him," Veda whispered. "Nightshade's former apprentice. He tried to court Abigail, but I understand things went badly. How is she doing?"

"Heartier than we give her credit for."

"I'm glad to hear it," Veda said.

"The duke's very kind," I said. "I like Abigail too. I hope the new medicine helps her. I assume there have been some developments since I have been away. What's happened?"

"If I am right, at least one piece of our troubles will be solved," Veda said. "One more guest is arriving. I pray my intuition is right."

We didn't have to wait long for our mystery guest to arrive. Lord Mystic Baruti Tabor was admitted by the guards and strode through the chamber like a king, his staff striking the carpet with each step. "Why am I summoned here?" he demanded. "How dare you command me like some baseborn servant. I am the Lord Mystic of the Mages!"

"You're also a citizen of this republic, Baruti," Alexander replied coldly. "You are not above its laws. I invited you to attend us privately out of deference to your office." Alexander stood and fixed his resolute gaze on Baruti. "But I will not defer to treason."

Baruti's superior attitude unshaken, he paused before Alexander. "How dare you accuse me of treason! Where is your proof? I am a loyal citizen, Alexander. I would never betray you."

"Liar!" Lady Corene spat, looking directly at Baruti.

"You wanted to punish Alexander," Veda added. "I know a rift developed between you, because of me. Only recently did I understand why."

"You understand nothing, Veda," Baruti said.

Veda held her ground and faced him. "You and Alexander were friends once. Lately, your friendship turned bitter. Then I learned of Desta's death. You said nothing to anyone about your son's demise. Why? It's only when you abducted my apprentice, Sabine, we learned of your sad loss, and you blamed me for Desta's death."

"Apprentice? How is it your lowborn secretary is your apprentice?" Baruti asked.

"When my science restored her magic," Veda smoothly replied.

Kalem stepped in and said, "We suspect you became vindictive when Alexander didn't severely punish Veda for the deaths of her patients who were testing her cure. But it was not about them at all. You wanted vengeance for your son's death."

Baruti deflected Kalem's remark with a wave of his hand. "Do you think you have the right to interrogate me! I know you, Faelan Anteros. You changed your name to Kalem Shura after your father proclaimed you a bastard and tossed you out. Your whore mother took her own life out of shame."

Baruti's taunting pained Kalem. I saw it in his eyes. Nightshade and Abigail looked worried, but Kalem quelled his rising anger and evenly demanded, "You must answer the question, Lord Tabor. It's not a choice."

"Charge me or let me go," Baruti taunted.

"I charge you with treason," Alexander replied.

"You're all mad as Veda is," Baruti said. "I've done nothing."

"You stole his magic," Veda remarked coolly. "Very childish thing to do, but you did use a charm reserved for young children with unruly magic. When mageborn children develop their powers too soon, this charm prevents them from harming anyone. I discovered it in Sabine's golden mage training manuals. It's included with the parental guides."

My damned toddler books! Who knew they had a purpose besides my embarrassment?

"It was developed because binding a child's magic can harm their development," Veda continued. "The unique thing about this charm is the child tests as mageborn, but they cannot use magic."

"Your prattling is boring now," Baruti said.

"I'm also fascinated by the fact you knew Alexander had lost his magic yet did nothing to help," Kalem said. "You revealed yourself when you stole Sabine and tortured her."

"I revealed nothing. Lack of empathy is not a crime."

"We shall learn the truth soon enough," Alexander said, gesturing to the back of the room.

A truthsayer came forward, the same one who had probed my mind. I didn't even see her until now! My head ached in memory of her touch. Rory shivered in my arms, growling, and I stroked his head to calm him. "It's alright. She's not here for us."

"This lady serves the Mystic Temple," Baruti protested.

"She's a citizen and obeying a request to aid a criminal investigation,"

Alexander replied. "I recall you employed the same tactics when you unlawfully abducted Lady Fable. You ordered the truthsayer to probe her mind without her permission and without evidence."

"I refuse to submit to the truthsayer. I am the Lord Mystic!"

"Denied," Alexander said. "Over a dozen palace wizards dead! Members of my court dead or injured by an extinct taman shade suddenly terrorizing the palace. Crimm's secretary, Frederick, found murdered and stuffed in a trunk. Crimm and Runecroft both vanished. The taman shade is gone, despite being confined in a glass prison conjured by a mirror master of the highest ability. This goes beyond my personal problems. I am sorry, Baruti. This ends now. If you are innocent, this act will clear you of blame. Truthsayer, you may examine the suspect."

The lady in gray approached Baruti with the same distant calm she used on me, removing her gloves, her face neutral. Several wizards, grim-faced in black suits, surrounded Baruti in case he resisted.

"Wait! You can't restore your magic without me," Baruti cried when the truthsayer reached for him. "Stop this!"

If that wasn't an admission of guilt, I don't know what is.

Alexander summoned a shimmering ball of light in his hand. "Your confession comes too late. My sorcery is restored, thanks to Veda. She created a potion and removed your spell an hour ago. Continue your examination, Lady."

"But I just admitted I tricked you into thinking you lost your magic," Baruti protested. "You cannot do this now!" he shouted as the truthsayer's hands reached for his temples.

I hated the man, but I recoiled at the memory of her touch. Braden squeezed my hand, sensing my discomfort. In a moment, Baruti's face twisted with agony as he cried out.

The truthsayer stepped back and calmly put on her gloves. "Premier Duchene, Lord Tabor is guilty of implanting the charm to restrain your sorcery. He also instructed his temple keeper, Rupert, to contaminate your clothing with the skalvich poisoning. It was a spiteful act of retribution. He wanted to shame you before the state as a weak and incompetent leader. He did this because his son, Desta, died. He blamed Veda's treatment. He used her dead test subjects as an excuse to prosecute her. When she was only banished from the city, he felt betrayed."

Ashen with pain, Baruti squared his shoulders and resumed his proud posture. "Now that you have exposed me, sentence me. I regret nothing. I have nothing to do with the rest of your troubles. Yes, I wanted to punish you! I wanted you to feel helpless, and stealing your magic was all I knew. I had no idea you would recall Veda!"

He cast bitter eyes on Veda. "I had plans for you too. A clever death, but then all this other chaos happened. I decided to watch and see you fumble. You're still fumbling like the fools you are."

"Did Baruti kill my patients or anyone else?" Veda asked the truthsayer pointedly.

"No, but the court physicians tasked to review your case submitted their report. They concluded there was no evidence your treatment caused their deaths. Lord Tabor concealed most of their findings and told the premier the evidence was inconclusive. His crime there was an abuse of his sacred office. Using magic to impair Alexander's Duchene's magic, however, is a treasonous one."

"Do you even recall the names of my patients?" Veda challenged Baruti. "Do you?"

Baruti mutely turned his head in disdain.

"They were Albus and Helen Wickham!" Veda cried. "They lost their powers in the last epidemic and suffered severe side effects for years. I wanted to help them. Instead, they died in my care. I wanted to know if I was truly responsible, but you denied me the truth."

"I wanted justice for my son, but you denied me. You murdered Desta!" Baruti yelled.

"Lady Arcana voluntarily submitted to my examination an hour ago. She is innocent," the truthsayer interjected. "She never treated your son. Your blame is ill-placed."

"And the rest, Truthsayer?" Alexander inquired.

"Lord Tabor is not guilty of any disappearance, Frederick's murder, or the deaths of the palace wizards. He is also innocent of any knowledge about the taman shade. Its existence was a surprise and mystery to him as well, but one he hoped to use to cause you shame."

"How could you do this to me?" Baruti exclaimed to the truthsayer. "I gave you a position of respect in the temple. Your loyalty is to me."

"I am a truthsayer," she replied without emotion. "It is my duty. You taught me that, Lord Tabor. Duty before emotion. Truth before lies."

"If Veda did not kill my son, then who did?" Baruti cried. The powerful man bent over, raging his grief. "I spent my life ashamed of him. I kept him hidden away to save my own pride. Now I am punished."

Alexander's tone was sympathetic but firm. "Lord Tabor, I give you a choice. Submit to having your powers bound and stand trial for treason, or sign a confession and I will commute your sentence to exile. You will relinquish your position as Lord Mystic, and your property is forfeit to the state. You will be confined to your chambers until you leave the city. Perhaps you might choose the monastery where you banished your son. Oh, and all your temple keepers will be summoned for investigation. If they are wise, the guilty will confess or face the truthsayer."

Embittered, Baruti bowed stiffly to Alexander. "I accept my exile."

One of the wizards bound his wrists with metal rings covered with runes and snapped them closed. Then the wizards slowly turned and escorted Baruti out of the hall.

"What are those metal bracelets for?" I whispered to Veda.

"They're enchanted. They will bind his magic for now, until he has gone and is in his chosen place of exile."

Abigail ran to Kalem and embraced him for a moment. I understood her love and concern for him after what Baruti cruelly said about him and his mother. I admired her gentleness. Me, I just wanted to pound Baruti with my fists until he begged for mercy.

"Alexander is letting Baruti just walk out of here! He'll keep his sorcery too! That's not fair!" I complained.

"Alexander dare not do more," Kalem replied. "Baruti's lost his position and wealth. For him, that holds more bitterness than any prison. Annoyingly, he wasn't guilty of the rest, which means our investigation is not finished." He turned to Veda. "It's clear an enemy is actively working to ruin you."

"But who? If Baruti is not behind the rest of this trauma, who is?" Veda asked.

It bothered me too. Then a dark idea occurred to me. "Veda, the two patients who died. What if they were murdered to frame you?"

CHAPTER 23

My words gave everyone pause as they exchanged looks.

"Hear me out," I said. "Consider how odd things have been, and I'm new here. There's been many attacks on both me and Veda."

"In fairness, you received the most assaults," Veda added. "And we have no idea who was controlling the taman shade. The creature is a mystery."

"Who would want to control such a thing?" Kalem asked. "None of this makes sense."

"Yet it is all connected," Veda said, pacing the room. "This supposedly extinct creature didn't just appear out of nowhere to attack Sabine without direction. Granted, it attacked others later on, but I think its goal was Sabine."

"You have a point," Kalem said, nodding. "A lot of bizarre things have happened since your return."

"But a portion of the darkness was directed at Alexander," Veda countered.

"Perhaps to get you back in the city?" Kalem suggested. "Alexander would summon you, as you are one of his oldest friends he can trust. But also, I think Alexander may have been attacked because he did not punish you enough. That's why Baruti looks suspect to me. This was a separate case, I believe. I fear the assaults on Sabine were because of her close connection to you, Veda."

"Are you saying the taman shade attacked me because I work for Veda?" I asked.

"Am I a curse to all my friends?" Veda exclaimed.

"Of course not," Alexander insisted. "At least we can proceed to investigate what is really happening now that my most embarrassing magical issue is resolved. I appoint Kalem and Veda as chief investigators to the missing mages and deaths." He kissed Veda's hand. "I also thank you for your sacrifice in exposing Baruti's part in these troubles. I know enduring the truthsayer was painful." He turned to the truthsayer. "No offense, we are grateful for your loyalty to the state, Lady. You helped resolve a serious threat today."

She bowed to Alexander. "I am not offended. I live to serve, Premier Duchene." She turned and gracefully exited the chamber.

"The woman still gives me the creeps," I whispered to Braden.

"You're not alone."

"How are you feeling?" I asked Abigail.

"I'm feeling quite well. I'm most intrigued by all of this mystery. Does that make me a terrible person? I mean, so much tragedy has transpired."

"I think you are just happy to experience a little excitement," I answered.

Lady Corene embraced her husband. "My love, I know you still have many burdens now, but I'm glad you are restored. Know I would love you no matter what." She hugged Veda, "Your idea was genius."

"How could you be sure it was Baruti Tabor?" I asked Veda.

"Honestly, I wasn't sure until recently," she admitted. "However, I had a nagging suspicion after he abducted you. He treated you so brutally over Runecroft, and it didn't make any sense. He never really cared about Runecroft. He loathed the man. I think he abducted you to get to me, which confused me until his outburst about his son's death. It exposed his principal error, combined with admitting he knew Alexander lost his sorcery. These revelations concerned me."

"But submitting to the truthsayer!" I shivered. "I would never have such courage, knowing what it feels like. My head aches if I even remember her touch."

"Unpleasant, but worth the price to absolve me once and for all," Veda said. "Now Baruti knows I'm innocent. His payment was losing his eminence as Lord Mystic of the Mage Castes. The rest is his burden."

"Now the difficult work truly begins," Kalem said. "Missing mages, taman shades, and murders."

Alexander shook Kalem's hand. "I also apologize for Baruti's cruel words about your mother."

Kalem's neutral expression fell away, revealing a sad smile. "My mother was a gentle and kind soul. Nothing can tarnish my memories of her."

Abigail stood next to Kalem, holding his hand, joy evident on her face. Nightshade looked at the couple with contentment and a little sadness too.

I whispered to Rory, "I think Duke Nightshade is happy Abigail and Kalem have found each other again."

"Keep me informed of your progress in the investigation," Alexander told Kalem. "I trust your unique talents will solve these terrible crimes. I must summon my council now. I have an inauguration to reschedule and much to inform them of. Good luck. If you need anything, just ask, and it shall be granted."

After Alexander and Corene departed, I was concerned about Abigail's condition. The morning had been exhausting on an emotional level. My mother would seem fine one moment, then would instantly shift when her fits came.

"I will order a suite prepared for you and Lady Abigail," Kalem said to Nightshade.

"Thank you," he replied. "Abigail should rest, but I don't want to leave her alone."

"I'll stay with her," I offered. I saw disappointment on her face. I suspected she wanted to be useful and out of the house. "But perhaps Abigail can help us for a bit if she's up to it. It will keep her distracted, and I can continue to monitor the treatment in a more natural environment."

"Abigail, you should rest," Kalem insisted.

Abigail lifted her chin, resolved to not be removed from the drama. "No! You surely need help with this urgent investigation. Please don't banish me to a corner. I can take notes, organize the files, and help with your research. I can serve tea and sandwiches. I just don't want to feel useless. I promise to take care and not overexert myself."

"Abigail is right. I think we also need to stay together as much as possible," I added. "There are too many bloody mysteries roaming these halls."

"Agreed," Nightshade said. "I don't want Abigail to be left vulnerable. The taman shade's theft disturbs me. Men died because of this, and we must rectify these horrors." His worried face softened. He brushed a lock of hair from Abigail's cheek and sighed again. "Very well, you may help. But at the first signs of stress, you must rest."

"Thank you, Grandfather," she said, smiling brightly.

"Wonderful," Veda said. "Kalem and I will order all documentation on our cases sent to my research room. That will be our headquarters. We have a lot of work to do."

Ready to work?" I said to Abigail.

She nodded, eager. I handed her Rory. "First duty is keeping Rory out of trouble while we set up our investigation chamber."

"Oh, that should be no work at all!" She beamed, cuddling him.

"He looks innocent, but he's a mischievous pukis," Veda remarked. "I'm still missing a bracelet and a silk scarf."

"Me no mischievous," Rory said. "Play and nest. Crunchy bacon rolls would help calm me."

"That sounded like a bribe," Braden whispered.

I sighed. "Just don't overfeed him."

# # #

Braden helped fetch and carry for us as we set up our investigation room. No one was left alone, for safety. The rest of us formed a collective using chalkboards for ideas and detailing each crime—Frederick's murder, Crimm's and Runecroft's disappearances, the shapeshifter who kissed me, the murdered palace wizards, and the taman shade. Some clues might have seemed insignificant, but everything mattered.

We designated a board for each case and had a central blackboard where we made connections. Braden stood guard just inside the door, but I suspect it was Veda's idea to keep him close after what happened. He would sometimes grin at me, though he did strike a commanding pose.

I felt like a student in school again, except this was more interesting. I bemoaned the chaotic notes Kalem handed me. "Your handwriting is atrocious," I said. "It looks like a drunken troll composed these."

"His script was always rushed when he was a boy," Abigail said, shaking her head. "Give them to me. I can translate his scribbles." She took a fresh sheet of parchment and a pen. "My handwriting is faultless because I had the patience to practice." She busily worked as Rory's paws darted for her pen feather now and then.

But languishing on the table, Rory finally became bored as we focused on our research and ideas. He chewed up Abigail's writing quill and knocked over a box of paper.

"Naughty pukis," Abigail said. "Be good for Abigail."

"Abi, Sabi, Abi, Sabi," Rory muttered over and over, grabbing a quill in his paws and rolling back and forth.

"What are you going on about," I asked with a laugh as I picked him up.

"Poem," Rory replied. "Names rhymes. So made a poem."

Kalem and Nightshade returned after being gone for several hours. Happily, Kalem was carrying a tray of coffee and sandwiches.

"Wonderful! I'm starving," I cried.

"Food?" Rory perked up, his feather quill quest now forgotten.

Kalem grinned and gave Rory a bacon sandwich. Abigail joined Kalem, pouring coffee for us. Rory grunted happily as he devoured his treat.

I set him on the desk with his meaty treasure. "There you go, boy."

"What did you learn?" Veda asked.

Nightshade removed his long coat and hat. "My mystical glass prison was indeed taken, taman shade and all, like they said. There are strong mystical markers that indicate the work of another mirror mage. There is also the residue of a portal spell on the wall."

"Can you open it?" Veda asked.

"It's blocked by wards, but I will see what I can do to reverse it."

Veda put down her coffee and said, "Sabine told me Morgan Ashstone caused trouble. I hate to bring up a sensitive topic, but I remember he was your apprentice when I was treating Abigail. He studied mirror magic under you."

"Yes, he did," Nightshade said. "Morgan showed promise in the beginning, but his mage ability with glass began to falter. His obsession with Abigail broke all ties. Do you think he could be involved in this?"

"Would it really surprise you?" I asked. "His presence is too convenient. I think Morgan Ashstone has been lurking about for a long time. I'm almost positive I saw him at the gala when Alexander collapsed. I wasn't sure at first. I knew him but I couldn't place him. He bumped into me and was rude, just like when I came to your house."

Braden laughed. "So, rudeness is why he is suspect?"

"No, but his presence coincides with specific events."

"We can't connect him to what happened to Alexander," Kalem pointed out. "Still, I'll summon him by state order to come in for questioning. Maybe even summon the truthsayer. I'm happy to add Morgan Ashstone to my suspect list."

"What else have we learned?" Veda asked. "What about the monastery where Desta lived?"

"I enabled a proper meeting with the monks about Desta without the burden of travel. A charmed glass ball does wonders in a pinch," Nightshade said.

Kalem shared what they learned. "We just contacted the local mage first, and he summoned a few of the monks. The head abbot confirmed Desta lived there until he died and admitted he was Baruti's son. We asked for a meeting with those who knew Desta and his situation at the monastery. They were compliant, especially when they learned Baruti Tabor is now a traitor. Desta arrived at the monastery as a teenager, bitter over his loss of magic after surviving mage fever. It was all a big secret."

"According to the abbot, Desta never suffered any real side effects and was in generally good health," Nightshade remarked. "He was never friendly with the other monks. But they tolerated it because Baruti Tabor generously donated to them every year for their silence. Desta's living quarters were not the sparse monk chambers with a low straw bed and wooden chest. He lived quite luxuriously in their compound in one of the guest quarters."

"What about his death? Did anyone ever visit him?" Veda asked. "His demise and its connection to me are disturbing."

"This is where it gets interesting," Kalem said. "For years, no one visited Desta, not even his father. The monks confirmed Baruti Tabor wrote his son letters, but Desta never replied. He openly hated his father. The head monk kept Baruti informed about his son's life and health. Then about two years ago they had a new novice. For the first time, Desta made a friend."

"Who was this charmer?" I asked, feeding Rory some of my cheese sandwich when he gazed at me like a martyr.

"Someone named Thomas White, but now they think his name was false," Kalem said. "Thomas White stayed for a few weeks, and then one day he just left. No notice, no note, or saying 'Sorry, the religious life is not my path.' He was just gone as if had never been there. But that's not the interesting part. Three days later, they found Desta dead in his room. Beside his bed was the letter that caused Baruti's vendetta against you, Veda."

Veda rested her head in her hands. "Well, at least that explains the whole tale of my supposedly treating Desta. But it still does not make sense. I never visited that monastery. So how could I treat him? Veda rubbed her eyes and poured another cup of coffee. "Much less enough details that it would be accepted by Baruti."

"I don't think Baruti cared," Kalem said. "Perhaps the letter noted you sent him the potions? Desta often received packages and gifts from his father. Baruti must have been so guilt-ridden about Desta's death that he wanted to blame someone, and Desta's letter gave him someone to blame."

"What about when you were being investigated for your patients' deaths?" Kalem asked.

"I never parted with the original book," Veda said. She paused then said, "Baruti asked for my research as part of the investigation, and I complied. I gave him copies of my all research, formulas, and records. Including a copy of that book. But never the original."

My own distrustful nature rose to the occasion. "Did you get them back?"

"Not for many weeks."

"Then someone had time to make copies of your work," I said. "And the copy of your special book that was the source of your treatment."

"I never hid what happened to my patients, even after their deaths. I worked hard with hope for their recovery," Veda said. "Things had been going well. Before those deaths, my formula was never lethal. Yet Baruti's son supposedly died from my cure even though I never treated him. Did anyone perform an autopsy on Desta?"

"Desta's will requested a private burial and no embalming," Kalem said. "The monk admits he received this request only a few weeks before he died. The convenience of the will would be an optimum cover for a faked death. The abbot also admitted to his shame that there was a desecration of Desta's grave they never told Baruti about."

"What kind of desecration?" Veda asked.

"That's where things go from interesting to suspicious," Kalem said. "After Desta died, he was buried in the monastery's cemetery. They gave him a rich funeral according to Desta's last requests in his will for a rich burial, for which the monks received a lot of gold. They supplied an exquisite cedar coffin, carved headstone, blessings, and incense. They buried Desta in expensive silk robes. The next day, the grave was desecrated and his body burned. They thought grave robbers were responsible."

"You don't believe that, do you?" I asked, taking another sandwich.

"You think Desta is alive? And his death an elaborate ruse?" Veda asked Kalem.

"It's possible. And Desta's mystery friend, Thomas White, is also suspect in this, I believe," he said. "Desta's official death was almost two years ago. But it would be hard to track him without more information."

Abigail put down her quill. She'd been quite interested until I noticed her distress. "I think you are due for your medicine," I said, reaching for my satchel and going to her. Rory pounced on the fluffy quill pen and rolled on the desk with it in his teeth. His antics made her smile as I measured out her dose. She opened her mouth like a baby bird for the spoonful of medicine.

She sipped her coffee and her mouth puckered. "Ugh, it's gone cold and bitter. Is there more cream?"

"Perhaps you could take Abigail to our chamber," Nightshade suggested.

Braden nodded. "I've arranged everything."

"Excellent." Then Nightshade turned to Abigail. "Sabine can stay with you until I return. I've already sent for Mrs. Doran to stay with you while we're here. Remember your promise, Abigail. You are tired, so now you must rest."

"I'll take her," I said, scooping Rory under my arm. He scowled at me, as he could not continue battle with the offensive feather quill.

"I'm fine," Abigail insisted.

I could tell how tired she was. "You shouldn't overdo it," I advised. "Let's go to your suite. We can order desserts. We've oodles to do, and it won't be done in one day."

"Is that the tone of patience I hear?" Veda asked, grinning.

I laughed. "Don't get used to it."

"Very well," Abigail relented with a sigh. "But I'm coming back tomorrow."

"I think you've had enough excitement today," Nightshade said to her. "Sabine and Braden will take you to our suite. I will join you later." He kissed Abigail's forehead. "Now do as Sabine asks."

"I will check on you later," Kalem promised. "And don't forget our code words to make sure you're not talking to a shapeshifter who is not me."

"I won't forget," she said, nodding.

We had a merry if tense walk to Nightshade's suite, Braden leading the way. Guards were everywhere. The palace seemed void of the mill of colorful people who usually made the place lively and loud.

"How do you like having magic? Abigail asked. "It must seem like a dream come true for you."

"I dreamed of magic all my life," I admitted, patting Rory's head. "I was obsessed with it. Magic would give me status and security. But I also know some folk will remember only that I was a baseborn bastard. My hometown is small but has a long memory. It's my curse."

"People are cruel," Abigail said. "I've always been protected, but my rank as a noble affords me respect. You had to earn yours."

"Now my magical new life has devolved into hunting murderers and traitors. Instead of learning spells and how to control my magic, I live in fear of strange shades and conspiracies."

"These corridors are so empty," Abigail remarked.

"People are afraid," Braden said. "But don't you worry, Lady Abigail. They'll fill up again when things go back to normal."

I saw a familiar outline rushing toward us.

"Who is that?" Abigail asked, pausing her step.

"Sabine!" called Marigold as she ran down the hall. I cringed inwardly as I stopped. She ran toward me as her father, Thomas Graven, pursued her. Damn, the girl could run despite wearing layers of petticoats.

"Goodness, who is that?" Abigail asked.

"Our curse," Rory grumbled.

CHAPTER 24

Marigold's perfumed arms locked me in a flowery noose. My eyes teared up from her potent fragrance haze. When she finally let go, I stepped back.

"Gracious, Sabine! I haven't seen you in days. Where have you been? Oh, I see your giant sentinel is still following you."

"His name is Braden Griffin," I reminded her.

"No matter," Marigold dismissed my words with a wave of her fan. "Can you believe the murder of the palace wizards? That terrifying wraith that chased us all over the palace is apparently gone too! No one is admitting it, of course. I'm just so terrified. Papa and I are going home. So?"

"So what?" I asked, confused.

Poor Rory's little claws dug painfully into my shoulder. "Don't like Marigold," he mumbled in my ear.

"It's not my fault," I whispered to him.

"What?" Marigold asked.

"Nothing," I said quickly. "We just need to be somewhere. I'm sorry, but we need to be on our way."

"Where have you been all this time?" Marigold asked. Rory grunted and she frowned. "Does your little vermin always have to tag along too? Doesn't he have a cage?"

Rory snorted angrily, swishing his tail. "I'm a dragon, fierce. Breathe fire. Not vermin. Not stinky."

"Does he really breathe fire?" Marigold asked.

I wish. "No, but you did just offend my little dragon."

"Lady Fable has been staying with me," Abigail responded. "As a guest of my grandfather, Duke Nightshade."

Marigold's eyes flared with happy surprise, and she moved closer to us. "Goodness! You must be Lady Abigail. Your grandfather is Duke Richard Nightshade, the mirror mage who created the creature's glass prison."

"Yes, he is," Abigail said.

"Then how did the wretched creature escape?" Marigold asked eagerly.

"Permit us to introduce ourselves, Lady Nightshade," Thomas Graven interjected with grace. He presented himself and Marigold with practiced eloquence. "I am acquainted with your most honored grandfather, Duke Nightshade. I hope you're well despite the rather dark turn of events."

"Yes, my grandfather has mentioned you, Lord Graven. I'm pleased to meet you. We are quite well. I was just retiring to my suite," Abigail said and curtsied as a signal the exchange was over. Clever.

"Yes, my sentinel and I must be going," I added with a brief curtsy. I was tense, not just because it was Marigold, but because she might be the shapeshifter pretending to be Marigold. I glanced up at Braden, whose own grim face was reflecting my suspicion.

"Please, Papa! I don't need to go with you to the stables, do I?" Marigold begged. "May I visit with them instead while you make arrangements for our journey home? The stables are so smelly."

"I am sorry, but Abigail isn't well and needs to rest," I said. In truth, I doubted anyone could truly pass as Marigold. It would be exhausting. But my suspicions lingered.

"Then we shall be on our way," Graven said, bowing to us. "Come along, Marigold."

"But Papa!" she cried. Then she curtsied again to Abigail and followed her father.

"That was close," I whispered.

"Do you think we might have been a touch rude," Abigail asked, concerned.

"We must be cautious," I reminded her. "And shapeshifters can look like anyone."

"Here's the apartment I arranged," Braden said when we reached a pair of white double doors. "It's called the swan suite. It's close to our research room and I've also requested additional guards to protect the halls."

"There's even a small gold swan on the door above the knocker," Abigail said, delighted. Elegant and soft-spoken, she was the essence of graciousness when we entered. She became a gentle hostess as she showed us to the plush couch.

Braden politely declined to sit. "I'm on duty, Lady Nightshade."

Abigail looked around the lavish chamber, nodding her approval. "My compliments, Braden. This is quite comfortable. Are you sure you will not sit?"

"I am sure, my lady."

"Please just call me Abigail," she insisted. "No need to stand on ceremony."

A large tea tray on the low table in front of the couch awaited pouring. After hours of downing coffee, tea sounded lovely.

Braden took charge and even poured for us, arranging cups and saucers. "I arranged the tea myself, to make sure there was no tampering." He tossed a ginger cookie to Rory. "Sorry, boy. No bacon at the moment." Rory caught it in his mouth and munched his goodie loudly, scattering crumbs all over the cushion.

"You serve tea like a proper gentleman," Abigail remarked when he handed her a cup.

"My mum raised ten children on a farm. Mostly barley and oats. Manners were instilled at an early age. We behaved if we didn't want a whipping. Don't look too shocked, Lady Abigail. It was just a long-handled old wooden spoon, and Mum rarely had to use it. All she had to do was wave it in our direction, and we minded her."

"Goodness," Abigail said with a laugh. "Sounds like she was queen of the farm."

"That she is." Braden nodded with a broad smile. He fixed me a cup with milk and three heaping spoons of sugar that way I like it and passed it to me. "What's wrong, Sabine? You've got that anxious look in your eyes."

"Sorry. It's just my inner troll shadowing my thoughts," I said, sighing.

"Troll?" Abigail asked. "Goodness, what do you mean?"

"I guess you might call it suspicions or worries haunting me. Impatience. My anger. Things that have been a potent source in my life. I call them my inner troll. I just find it too convenient that we bumped into Marigold." Rory, face full of crumbs, settled in my lap as I wrapped him in my blue scarf. It always calmed him down. "If Marigold knew about the murders of the wizards and missing taman shade, she wouldn't leave her room without a platoon of guards and a magical shield to protect her."

"Her father was with her," Abigail said. "Perhaps she just didn't want to be alone in her room while he made arrangements."

"I know. Maybe my suspicion is overactive with all the horrid muck happening," I said.

"No, you're not considering what we are dealing with," Braden said. "Your inner troll is your instinct warning you to beware. We all need to take care."

"My grandfather would agree," Abigail added. "I was thrilled to come to the city for the inauguration. But frankly, my only desire now is to retire to the country again, just like Grandfather." Abigail sipped her tea with delicate grace and put down her cup. "Do you miss your homes? I understand you're both from small towns."

Braden shrugged. "I miss my family sometimes, but I don't miss working on a farm. I like it here, except when we have mysterious murders and strange creatures rampaging about."

I looked into my empty teacup, swirling the leaves. "The city is amazing, but I miss my mother and my friend, Altheda. Altheda makes the best spice cake. She always baked a cake every year for my birthday. My mother is gracious, beautiful, blonde, and blue-eyed. I'm the opposite of her in every way. I always felt like a dark changeling left by the fairies. The epidemic and my birth damaged her future. Now with my magic restored, I hope to make her proud and take care of her."

"Why do you say you damaged her future?" Abigail asked.

"I'm a bastard. Mother had to raise me alone. Long story. Well, a short story. But it was bleak for her."

"The aristocracy is filled with bastards," Abigail said, nibbling a ginger cookie. "Birth does not measure a person's worth. Our society puts too much stock in caste and wealth. And you could never ruin your mother's life. You are full of heart and kindness, whereas Morgan Ashstone is an example of an arrogant mageborn who is cruel."

"Did you ever really love him?" I asked.

"I was fond of him at first, but love? No. I was just so lonely. Grandfather was his mentor for a time, and I became attached. Then he became difficult. But on to happier topics. Sabine, are you going to apply to the Academy?"

I hadn't even thought about it, actually. With everything going on, I never thought about going back to school, even to learn magecraft. "I don't know."

"You should consider your future," Abigail said. "If your skills are above charm caste, which I think they are, it would give you impressive credentials. You should broach it to Veda. She would be supportive of your studies."

"I know, but I also want to help with Veda's research," I said. "Magic was the most important thing to me for so long. It meant everything to become mageborn. I would have done anything. I want to help my mother. Her health is so frail. She's better now, thanks to Veda's medicine. I believed being mageborn was a way for Mother and me to move out of poverty. I may still be rubbish at using my newly found magic, but I want to use it to help those who suffered the fever and its brutal aftermath. The Academy may be a logical way to pursue this. I just thought Veda would teach me, but it would make my mother so proud if I attended the Academy."

And no one would ever look down on me again, my inner troll crowed, dancing.

"What are you thinking now?" Abigail asked Braden, who was frowning at the door, arms crossed over his chest.

"Sabine's suspicions about Marigold," he mumbled.

I laughed. "Sounds like my inner troll made a friend."

"Marigold smelled funny," Rory complained.

"Yes, her perfume was so strong," I said.

"Not perfume. Her," Rory said, then he burrowed into my scarf.

A knock on the door raised suspicions all around. I motioned Abigail toward one of the bedrooms and stood against the wall nearby so I could hear.

"Sabine! It's Marigold!"

Braden glowered and opened the door, cautious, hand resting on the dagger in his belt.

"I need to speak Sabine," Marigold demanded.

I swear she is haunting me! Why won't she stay away?

"She is occupied with Lady Nightshade," Braden informed her. "If you have a message, I am happy to deliver it."

"Oh no, I'm sure she will want this," she said. "Wait. I put it in my handbag. The servants delivered a letter for her to our room again by mistake. The baseborns never seem to do anything right."

I cringed for Braden! "Is everything well?" I asked, stepping into view.

"Oh, goodie!" Marigold giggled. "I have a letter from your mother. I thought you would want it."

She held it out to me. I stepped forward and took it from her hand. "Thank you, Marigold. Now I must attend Lady Nightshade, if you'll excuse me."

"Do not stand on ceremony. Please read your letter. I too am anxious to hear about our hometown," she said, looking around the corner into the chamber. "Is Lady Abigail ill?

"I'm sorry, but this is not a good time," I told her. "Perhaps later."

Braden looked out over her head. "Where are the damned guards I ordered?"

My stomach knotted. I looked at the letter. The stationary was the same, and the words were written in the green ink my mother favored for her personal notes. But something was odd. Then I realized the source. Rory's words, *Marigold smelled funny.* I held the envelope to my nose. Mother's letter smelled like wylsavan root.

"You're the shapeshifter," I said. My inner troll raged at my stupidity.

"Took you a while to notice," the shifter smirked. She lifted a gloved hand and made a pushing gesture, sending Braden and me flying across the room. I hit something sharp and fell face down on the plush carpet. Desperate, I pushed myself up and tried summoning my power. My hands glowed green, but nothing happened. *Damn it, damn it, damn it.*

Abigail rushed into the room and gasped when she saw us sprawled on the floor with a frilly-dressed shapeshifter gloating over us.

"Magic not cooperating?" the shifter said with a smile. Then she yelped in pain when a glass vase struck her head from behind, dispersing shattered glass, water, and orphaned flowers to the floor. It knocked the shifter off balance. Abigail looked pleased with herself.

The shifter grabbed her wrist. "Be grateful you are a prize not to be harmed, Abigail." The voice became masculine, though he still wore the female form. "Come with me, and you will be glad you did. Please."

"No! I'll do no such thing!" Abigail cried, struggling against his hold.

Dazed, I rolled to my side. Blood streamed into my left eye. I touched my forehead and winced. *Damn.* "Let her go," I said.

"He sent me to take you, Abigail," the shifter said softly. "Just come with me now."

"Let me go!" she screamed.

I scrambled to my feet, facing the enemy with nothing but reluctant magic and my attitude. Braden rolled, leaped to his feet, and charged the shifter, punching the false Marigold in the face several times until blood poured. The shifter knocked Abigail to the floor. I grabbed her hand, pulled her up, and pushed her out of harm's way.

Then a burst of sorcery pitched Braden off the shifter.

"Who the hell are you?" I demanded, buying a moment to gain my balance.

The intruding shifter paused, and the image of Marigold's blonde ringlets and lacy clothes vanished. A tall man with dark skin and angry eyes stood before us.

"I am Desta Tabor."

"You look chipper for a dead man," I replied.

"Clever," Desta said. "Not clever enough. I am a mage now. I know you looked into my past. Isn't my shifting impressive? I would have fooled you too. Shame my perfume was not enough to hide the wylsavan root, but no matter. Now get out of my way, you common little slut."

Mrs. Doran appeared in the doorway and marched toward Desta. "Rude, wretched man! Stay away from Abigail."

"You stupid old sow. How dare you, a meager charm caste servant, order me?" Desta slapped her across the face, but Mrs. Doran remained rooted where she stood, then shimmered into Kalem!

Desta was nonplussed long enough for Kalem to punch him in the face. Desta stumbled back, and Braden jumped him from behind, spun him around, and knocked him out with a solid punch. My giant sentinel may not have had magic, but he possessed impressive fighting skills and a brutal right hook.

"Excellent work," Kalem remarked. "Magic is wonderful, but sometimes you just need to hit someone."

"I heartily agree," Braden said.

"Nightshade was watching the room using a charmed hand mirror," Kalem told me. "We were worried. Spying may be rude, but it was necessary to make sure you were safe." He cupped my chin and examined my cut. "Looks nasty, but it appears worse than it is. Trust me, my work has brought me many scrapes and bruises." He held his palm over my eye. A soothing coolness eased my pain.

Abigail handed me her lace hanky, and I dabbed away the blood. "There now. All healed," she said.

"Thank you," I replied.

Kalem tossed Braden a roll of thin blue ropes. "Tie him up with these. These bindings are laced with heavy wards to prevent him from using magic or shapeshifting his way out of this." Abigail rushed to Kalem's arms, and they held each other.

I looked around. "Rory? Where are you?"

"Sabi!" he cried out from the curtains he was clinging to. Then he flew to my shoulder. "See! Smelled funny."

"You were right, baby," I said, scratching his head.

"I'm sorry to shatter this lovely moment, but we need to find out what Desta Tabor knows," Kalem said.

"And we need a new suite," I moaned, observing the broken furniture and glass.

"Agreed. This investigation is far from solved," Braden remarked. "This evil man is only part of the problem. I thought if anyone showed up, it would be foppish Morgan Ashstone."

"So did I," Kalem said. "But finding Desta might be the key to this."

"Where is the real Marigold?" I wondered aloud. "Was the man with her earlier really Thomas Graven? Do you think she's dead?" I inwardly shrank at the thought. I loathed Marigold, but I never really wished her dead.

"Don't worry, Sabine. We'll find out," Kalem replied.

"Can you convince Desta to betray his partner in crime?" I asked.

"He won't have a choice," Kalem said harshly.

CHAPTER 25

Finally, we returned to Veda's townhouse! Exhausted and relieved, we stepped through the door into the dark and musty house, bags in hand, dragon bouncing on my shoulder.

"You know, Veda, palace life is fancy, but also red with blood and chock-full of terror and conspiracies."

Veda dropped her bag and flung off her velvet coat. With a wave of her hand, the light globes illuminated the house. She collapsed on the couch. "I know there is more work to be done, but I'm so glad to be home. For one night, I want my mind free of murder and abductions to solve."

"At least they found Marigold and her father unconscious in their rooms. They had been drugged, but they are recovering. Marigold is not my favorite person, but I don't wish her dead. We know Desta pretended to be Marigold, but who pretended to be Thomas Graven?" I asked.

"We believe unless another shapeshifter was involved, it could have been a high glamour spell. Morgan Ashstone is still suspect. Shapeshifters are rare and prized for their magic. They truly change form."

"Which causes physical side effects over time. Kalem will sometimes drink a tea from wylsavan root for his joint pain."

"A glamour enchantment is most likely," Veda said. "It is a complex enchantment but presents only the image. It's also not as debilitating as shapeshifting. The wylsavan root Desta used must have been in high doses for you to notice it. It also explains his use of heavy perfume when pretending to be Marigold."

"I wish her strong scent tipped me off sooner. Marigold loves her perfume, but even she would have shown a teeny bit of restraint. Do you think they'll summon the truthsayer to interrogate Desta Tabor?"

Veda nodded. "Unless he cooperates, yes. Alexander will override any refusal, as the case involves murder and abduction."

"Good," I said, almost too eagerly. "I know I sound evil at the moment, but we need answers. The truthsayer scares me. But if anyone can find the truth, it's her. Now, all I want is to sleep in a bed safe from shades, shifters, and creepy temple keepers."

"Yes, we both need rest. You go on upstairs. I'll bring up a pot of chamomile tea to help us relax. We deserve an early night."

"Thanks," I said, chasing after Rory. He was excited and just would not settle down. He was flying all over the place, the strong wings I once prayed for now vexing me as I chased him up the stairs, "Please, Rory, I want to sleep!" I cried.

He swirled above the landing, gurgling and laughing. "I'm a dragon! Fear me!"

"Baby, it's not a game." I leaned against the wall. "Please come down. Mother dragon needs to sleep with a hoard of pillows. I will need a guardian to protect my fluffy stash."

He made another spin above my head, then swooped down and landed on my shoulder. "Very well, I will guard your pillow hoard," he huffed.

His needle-like talons pinched through my jacket. I would definitely need to sew in some padding to stave off those sharp claws. "That's my good boy," I gasped.

"This nest is better," Rory said as I wearily walked to my room.

"I agree. We weren't here long, but I like this place much better."

He jumped off my shoulder as I collapsed in my bed and pulled off my shoes, throwing them aside, and just breathed. "I'm relieved they are moving the research to Veda's townhouse. I don't like the palace anymore. Alexander is cured, Baruti is exposed and in custody, and Desta is captured at least. I feel safer here."

"I'll miss the yummy meatballs in gravy," Rory said, settling on the bedpost.

I laughed. "I knew you would focus on the important things."

"I do like this home better, but what I miss most is our tower in the woods," Rory said.

"Me too. I miss Mother and Altheda too. Would you like to go back?"

"Yes," he said, bouncing. "And can Braden come with us? I like soldier Braden. He's nice and brings me bacon treats."

I closed my eyes. I would miss Braden too.

Rory fluttered down to settle next to me, wings beating. "Sabi tired? Sleep? Not feel good?" He turned up his head for a chin rub, his throat's gravelly hum filling the room.

I turned on my side. "Just tired," I whispered. "I'm still worried."

"Mama Brona's letter?" Rory asked.

"Yes, it worried me. Your speech is really improving fast."

"Dragons hear things, and once we hear, we remember. But you have fears?"

"The letter with my mother's handwriting disturbs me. I can't stop thinking about Mother. I'm going to write her a new letter tonight before I go to bed. I'm even worried about Luther and Altheda."

Rory snuggled against my arm and folded his wings in. My inner anxiety relaxed a bit. "You do make me feel better. Your presence calms Abigail too. I need to investigate this talent as opposed to thieving bits of jewelry and shiny things. I wonder if other pukis dragons can help people like Abigail. Even Nightshade commented on your effect."

"I'm a special dragon" he touted with pride.

Veda softly knocked on my door. "Sabine, may I come in?"

"Yes," I said, propping myself up on my elbows. Didn't have the energy to do much else.

She entered, her skirts softly rustling. "How are you feeling?" she asked, sitting on the edge of the bed and handing me a cup of steaming chamomile tea.

"I'm fine, but I'm worried about Mother. What about the letter Desta used? It looked like my mother's handwriting. How did he get his hands on it?"

"We don't know, but he could have taken a letter from your room, copied it, and then returned it. As a mage, it wouldn't have been difficult. Such simple magic requires only rudimentary spell skills. We have no idea how long Desta had been spying on us all. He could even have been posing as a servant and rifled through your room. Were any of your letters missing when you checked?"

"No, all my mother's letters were there."

"Most likely it was just a clever enchantment. Not hard to do," she assured me.

"It is for me." I looked at Veda. "Abigail asked me if I plan to attend the Mystic Academy. But I don't know. My mage skills are shaky. I've no idea what my mage caste will be. I want to control my mage powers, and I just can't do that now."

"The Academy would be good for you. An excellent place to train and learn. What do you want? I will be happy with whatever you decide."

"Depends." I laughed and looked at Rory. "Do they allow pets?"

She chuckled herself. "I don't know. What is really bothering you about the Academy?"

I sat up, holding Rory in my lap. "It all sounds amazing, but I can only think how unjustly my mother was treated there. At the same time, it would make her proud of me, and gall old Luther," I said with a laugh. "And there are some people here I would miss. I like Abigail, and—" My voice faltered.

Veda took my hand and whispered, "You would miss Braden. There is no shame in admitting that."

I could not speak of my feelings, even to Veda. They were too strange to me. "I have the magic I dreamed of all my life, and I cannot even do a simple spell." Veda's forehead furrowed in thought. I knew something bugged her. "What's wrong?" I asked.

"Desta's sudden appearance and easy capture. I just find it mystifying."

"You think he wanted to get caught?"

Veda stood and paced the room. "I do. I believe it's all part of some deception. But I was going to wait until tomorrow to fret about it. All I have done is fret since coming here. Kalem and Alexander also share my concerns. All this time, Desta and Morgan eluded detection and capture. Now Desta lands in our laps with ease? No, I don't like it. Too much horror has transpired. When Kalem was questioning him, Desta was unconcerned. He smiled at Kalem and shrugged. He's up to something."

"Does Baruti know his son is alive?"

"Yes. Alexander allowed Baruti to see him."

"Was that smart? What happened?" I asked.

"Baruti pleaded with his son for forgiveness. Desta remained silent in his prison cell, looking away in a daze. Some things can't be healed, I guess."

A tiny part of me understood resentment. My childhood was a series of resentments against Marigold, school, Luther, and my bastard life. But I never plotted murder or mayhem on anyone because of it. "You're not going to be able to sleep either, are you?"

Veda threw her hands up in the air. "I'm exasperated. I just wish I could banish all this from my mind. If I had a potion for it, I would drink it without hesitation."

"I understand," I said, laughing. "I know desperation and wanting to banish something or someone. When I was seven, I tried to make a magic potion to banish Luther."

Veda chuckled. "Very impressive. What for, or dare I ask?"

"I just wanted Luther to disappear," I replied casually. "One night he came home drunk and angry, which wasn't unusual. He screamed about his woes for hours, blaming us for his miserable poverty. If old toad-face hadn't gambled or drank our profits, we'd not be so poor. I told him that."

"I'm sorry," Veda said. "I know Luther made your lives hard."

"It's alright. Luther's temper was a common part of life. I numbed myself to most of it, but Mother's nerves could never cope. That night Luther was especially vile to Mother. He never physically hit her, but he called her horrible names until she fled to her room in tears. He cast a vicious look at me, and I knew his wrath meant the belt, not words. I wasn't dumb. I ran. I'm very fast when motivated. He couldn't catch me. I rushed all over the shop like a crazed squirrel. Drunks make poor runners. I eventually fled upstairs and hid in the attic. I knew he'd be too lazy to climb up there. He cursed and threatened for a time. I hid in the attic for hours, until I knew he must have fallen asleep. I decided to banish Luther from our lives forever."

"Oh dear. What did you do?" Veda asked with a small smile.

"I couldn't read an actual spell book because I was baseborn, so I decided to make up my own curse. I was too naïve to understand that wishing for magic and having it are not the same. When it was quiet, I snuck downstairs. I tiptoed around until I found Luther passed out in the kitchen. I picked the ugliest roots and foulest herbs in the apothecary section. I pulverized them and mixed in vinegar. Then I lit a black candle and wrote my own incantation with my stubby lead pencil on paper I snatched from the tomes shelf. I thought spell paper would make my hex real. My curse was simple: 'I banish nasty Luther Fable forever and ever into a dark, smelly hole.'"

"Very precise," Veda said.

"I thought it should be specific and did not want him banished anywhere nice. I poured the revolting concoction that I'd brewed with my seven-year-old spite into a black potion bottle. The dark glass made it more curse-like. It smelled rancid! I crept into the kitchen. Luther was passed out on the table, snoring like an ogre, clutching his wine bottle. I poured my foul potion into the half-empty bottle and fled back to my hiding place in the attic. I knew it'd be the first thing he drank when he finally roused from his stupor.

"What happened?"

"He drank it the next morning. Luther didn't vanish, except to the water closet with stomach cramps. So much for the curses of an angry girl." I laughed. "Well, he did suffer in there for hours."

Veda smiled. "I'd say your concoction provided its own curse. I have a feeling you might excel at potions now that your magic is released."

"You're not happy here in the capital either, are you?" I asked bluntly.

"Does it show so much," she asked with a sigh. "At first I thought Alexander's summons would redeem me. Vindicate my research and the good it could do. But I'm done with court policies and politics. Except for Alexander and Corene's company, I haven't missed it. They are old friends, but even their lives are changed by state protocols. I think I preferred being a banished sorceress."

"That makes us a compatible force. The banished sorceress and the bastard sorceress. We could solve mysteries and brew potions from the red tower in the woods, guarded by a fierce dragon. Granted, he will only get to be the size of a cat or small dog, but a dragon always demands respect. Toll shall be paid in bacon if our patrons wish entry."

She burst out laughing, lighting candles in the room with a touch of her finger as the sun's fall darkened the sky outside my window. "You are mad, you know? But do you want to stay in Túr Solas?"

"I'm not sure. It's not been as exciting as it's been terrifying." I grinned.

"I've grown disillusioned with this city and the court. Every breath we've taken since coming to Túr Solas has dragged us down with shades, conspiracies, and death. I want to go back home to our tower in the woods. Once this madness is solved, we will return home if you want. There we can properly hone your magical skills in peace. Remember when our biggest worry was our grocery delivery from town and the petulant owls on the roof? I would like to go home. And if you choose not to go to the Academy, I will train you to be a proper mage."

"Really? I want to go home too. And I would prefer you to be my teacher. I miss our tower and Mother. Luther, I can deal with as long as we don't share the same roof."

"That's the most magnanimous thing you have ever said about Luther!"

"Don't put too much faith in my words. I'm so tired, I think I'm a bit delirious."

"Speaking of tired," Veda whispered, then she glanced down at my sleeping dragon. I tucked my blue scarf around Rory as he snored.

The doorbell chimed downstairs, loudly. Veda shook her head and stood up. "I must adjust the volume on my house bell. It's far too loud. I'll see who it is. You rest now."

I could not rest as easy as my dragon as the murmur of voices filtered up to my room. I crept out of the room in stocking feet so I would not disturb Rory. On my way down, I saw Kalem and Braden standing with Veda in the foyer.

"I thought we at least had the night off," I said. "What's happened? Did Desta offer to confess?" Their sudden silence and furtive glances pricked my spine. My tension returned. "What the hell is going on?"

Veda and Kalem stepped aside, and Altheda stepped forward. Pale, with shadows under her eyes, she looked fraught. My initial joy at seeing my old friend turned my heart to grave dust.

"Has something happened to Mother?" I asked.

Altheda burst into tears. "Oh, Sabine, no one knows where your mother is, or if she's alive. Fable House burned. No one knows how it happened. It's gone. Nothing but ashes on the ground."

"Mother's dead," I choked.

Altheda rushed to me. "No, dear. We don't know her fate yet. No one can find Brona or Luther. The local watch and even that old wizard are investigating the tragedy. I sent a message to you via a wizard post. It should have reached you two weeks ago."

"I received nothing."

"When I didn't hear from you, I decided to come here. I arranged the fastest passage I could. I went to the palace and found Kalem first. He cast a load of spells on me to make sure I wasn't some sort of imposter before they brought me here. What's been going on?"

"Have they found any clues to what happened?" Veda asked.

"No one knows what happened. Some folks say Luther burned down his shop, but as mad as the old codger is, he'd never give up Fable House. Some talk is he got into trouble over his gambling debts. I'm worried about both of them. I'm so sorry. Sabine? Can you hear me?"

My arms and legs went numb as I stumbled to the stairs. I vaguely sensed Rory as he nestled close on my shoulder. I struggled to breathe.

"Mother can't be dead," I whispered.

CHAPTER 26

Silence.

I'm not sure how long silence enveloped me, blocking out emotional agony. Then a soft drone vibrated in my hands. It was Rory, coiled in my lap, his rhythmic breathing penetrating my silent shell.

I sensed distant blurred images around me. Not important. *My mother can't be dead.* The thought repeated in my mind. *My mother can't be dead.* I closed my eyes, and my lungs breathed air again. A cruel mystery beckoned now. *Where is my mother? I must find her.* I blinked until my vision cleared to a stark reality.

"Sabine," Veda whispered brushing a stray lock of hair away. "Can you hear me?"

Faces came into focus—Veda, Kalem, Braden, and Altheda all staring at me. I realized I was sitting on the sofa in the parlor. I had no memory of moving there.

"I hear you. I hear everything," I replied. "What happened to them?"

"You're in shock, love," Altheda said. "I'll fix something to calm you."

"No," I refused, shaking my head. "I need my pain. I need my anger." Only Rory's closeness eased my anguish. "Explain everything, Altheda. I need to know what happened."

"Sabine, you're not in a fit state," Braden cautioned.

"Good. Then more grief will not be so shocking. Why feel better if the world is about to make you miserable again? I need to know what happened."

Altheda sat on a stool next to me, nervously patting my hand. "Truth is, we don't know what happened to them."

"Just tell me what you do know," I begged. "Please."

Altheda nodded, patting my hand like she did when I was small. "Brona and I had mint tea together that morning as usual. She planned to open the shop at nine. She told me she had to check the books later, so she might be home late. She left for the shop then. An hour later I got the message from Becky's husband she was in labor. I was out delivering

Becky Farley's baby. You remember the Farleys. They live on that old farm north of the town. I was gone all day."

"So, you saw her that morning?" Veda asked. "Brona was on her way to the shop."

I was disappointed. The chain of events meant she could have been in the shop when the fire came. "What about Luther?" I asked. "Has he been drinking?"

"No, the old man had been good of late, but Brona and I both know being sober is a fragile state for him. But things had been quiet. Luther was probably home in the shop. He tended to sleep in more, especially when he was off the drink. But I don't know. It was just a normal day." Altheda shrugged. "The delivery went well. A baby boy. An easy birth, which was a relief. Poor girl had a difficult pregnancy. Come evening, I left Becky well in hand with her mother and husband looking after her. Old Man Farley drove me back into town in his wagon. We were almost home when I saw the fire like a beacon against the night sky. We rode hard into town, and that's when I saw Fable House in flames. I cried out for Brona and Luther over and over, but I didn't see them anywhere. Neither did anyone else. The town was in a frenzy. The local watch and volunteers were busy carrying buckets to douse the fire and keep it from spreading. I knew Fable House was lost when I saw the mass of flames shooting through the roof. I'm so sorry."

"But were they inside? Did anyone see them?" I asked.

"Who could tell? The blaze engulfed the whole building. Folks were scared it would spread, but it didn't, thank heavens. It took hours to douse it. They even dragged the old wizard out of bed to help. Useless old fool lives on the edge of town, but you had to be blind and deaf not to know what was happening. He cast some barrier spells to contain the fire, then shouted some incantations until it finally subsided enough to be drowned. Brona and Luther weren't anywhere to be seen. Folks think they perished."

"But they don't know," I said.

"Do they even know how the fire started?" Veda asked.

"No, but there's going to be an investigation," Altheda replied. "Some folk were already gossiping old Luther might have done it. You know, came home drunk and left a candle burning to catch the curtains or something. One year he burned a hole in the sofa, remember? And there's been gossip about his gambling debts. But that's all it is. Just talk,

Sabine. A lot of gibber jabber. And Brona was running the shop now, not Luther. She's become so strong."

Altheda angrily wiped a tear from her eye. Kalem handed her a small glass of sherry. She drank it down in a single gulp. "When the flames finally burned out, nothing was left of Fable House. Just smoking ash and charred chunks of broken wood."

The thought of my gentle mother possibly burning to death choked me. Fire. Such a terrible way to die. My chest tightened again and my eyes burned. I wouldn't wish such a terrible end on Luther either, the drunken sod. No. I would not believe it. I refused.

Altheda wiped her eyes again and took a deep breath. "Well, after the fire was finally put out, they began searching for the bodies. After some hours, the constable told me they hadn't found anything. I took that as a speck of hope. Then he told me there was no point in looking anymore. He said they're probably dead and just burned to ashes. I told him he was wrong. I'm a healer and know a few things. There'd be something left, but no one's looking. So I began asking anyone who crossed my path if they'd seen Brona or Luther before the fire. No one had, not all day. One bit of information I gleaned was the shop never opened that day. I found this out when I was waiting for my coach to come here. Mrs. Witchborn caught me and told me she went to the shop that very afternoon for a set of potion bottles, but the door was closed and all locked up. She said she even banged but got no answer. Makes no sense, since Brona opened the shop as normal in the morning. I told the constable this, but I don't think he took me seriously. Had the nerve to give me a sympathetic look and pat my shoulder. Nonsense! It would never be closed in the middle of the week."

"Not even in his most drunken, rabid state would Luther shutter the shop for a day, except on holidays. Mother wouldn't either," I said. Braden sat next to me, but he did not touch me or speak. I tried to focus, but all I could think about was my mother and even damned old Luther.

"This is very strange," Veda agreed. "And too convenient."

"What do you mean?" Altheda asked.

"I'm sorry, Altheda," Kalem said. "Suspicious and deadly events have threatened all of us. I'm afraid you walked into the middle of it all."

Kalem knelt next to me, his tone soft and even. "Sabine, I swear we'll get to the bottom of this. If your family is still alive, we will find them."

I understood his kindness, but at the same time, I longed to shirk his tenderness and rage instead. I held Rory close for comfort. "If my mother has perished, nothing will matter. But Altheda says the shop was closed that day, which never happens. If someone started the fire to cover up something else, they must be alive somewhere."

"That's why I came all this way," Altheda said. "This is all wrong. I wanted you to know firsthand from me. I believe something happened to them too, and it has nothing to do with the fire. No one in town believes they are alive."

My volatile thoughts seized on this fragile evidence. "Fable House is gone. My family is missing. Even a baseborn would be able to locate remains in the ashes, no matter how bad the fire. They were taken, like the others! How else would you explain this? I think I know by whom, and you all know it too."

"I agree," Veda said, nodding. "Desta is a key player, but why let himself be captured so easily? He is working with someone. There is too much for one man to pull off alone. I want to caution you against hoping too much, Sabine."

"Not wise advice," I said. "This wisp of fragile hope is all I have. Chaos and death have plagued us since we arrived in this damned city. Morgan Ashstone is still at large, but we have Desta Tabor in custody."

"I'm trying to fathom why this madness has extended to Brona and Luther," Veda said.

"Why not?" I cried. "Everything else has gone to hell. Damn it, damn it, damn it! I thought we'd have a moment of peace, and now Altheda arrives with this terrible news. Desta is sitting in a prison cell with a smile on his face from all reports. You know he won't talk willingly. What about the truthsayer? Can you override his refusal?"

"When Altheda arrived at the palace, I had just received permission from Alexander. I summoned the truthsayer. I agree. Desta Tabor knows more than he is revealing."

I managed to stand and looked at Kalem. "I want to be there."

"I won't stop you," he said. "I wouldn't dare."

#

I hate waiting. My inner troll stomped its feet, raving in my head. Good thing the truthsayer was staying out of my mind today. "What's taking so long?" I asked Braden. "We've been standing here forever. And this room is cold."

"It's barely been five minutes, Sabine," he whispered.

Rory began to fuss, then wiggled out of my arms and onto my shoulder. "I want good look," he told me.

Finally, two guards escorted Desta Tabor into the interrogation room, followed by a pair of wizards for added security. After the recent murderous episode, I was surprised there were any palace wizards left. Desta's previous blue bindings had been replaced by metal rings around his wrists, which I assumed bound his magic. But I assumed nothing anymore.

The truthsayer waited next to Kalem and Veda, dressed in elegant gray gown with matching hat and gloves, as though she were attending a high tea.

"Have you ever been in this wing of the palace before?" I asked Braden.

"No. It's a special section."

"*Special* is code for *restricted*, isn't it?" I whispered.

"Yes. It's warded from top to bottom and for special mageborn prisoners," Braden said. "The security is tight and very secretive. Being just a baseborn, I've never guarded this section. Only mageborns are allowed to work in this area."

"This room is drafty," Altheda whispered, "despite there being no windows."

I barely noticed the chill or lack of windows. My rage kept me warm. I studied my environment—a stark chamber bleak as death, with a few light globes for necessary light. Walls and ceiling were constructed from charcoal-hued tiles. No windows. The only way out was the steel door, which I hoped was just as charmed. But the room was peculiar. "What are the walls and ceiling made of?" I asked Braden.

"One of the wizards told me it is a special warded tile, forged by a high sorcerer. Magic is infused through every inch of the material. Very rare, very expensive. They told me the tiles can never be broken by force or sorcery. The chamber is constructed to feel barren," Braden said. "I suppose it's meant to intimidate people. Prey on their fears. I know I'd be praying in a place like this."

I studied Desta Tabor's smug expression. Kalem read a long list of charges, but Desta was not in the least concerned. "Desta Tabor may have lived in a monastery most of his life," I said, "but I doubt he ever prayed."

"I don't like the look of him," Braden noted. "He isn't afraid. He looks downright smug. Are you sure you want to watch this?"

"What I want is to beat the truth out of him until he is a bloody pulp." My inner troll grinned at the idea. "I'd feel better if we had more muscle. It would be hard for him to cast spells if he's being punched hard in the face."

"My girl, you're a feral little thing at times," Altheda remarked, smiling up at me.

"Sabi needs to be feral," Rory said. "Bad mage is nasty."

Nothing like the support of your dragon. "See, even a baby pukis knows this man is evil," I said.

The truthsayer approached the captive shapeshifter, removing her gloves as she reached him. Desta did not resist but smiled as she reached up to touch his forehead. The memory of her hands on my face disturbed me, but I refused to look away.

"Is it working?" Altheda whispered. "He looks so calm."

I watched on, impatient, my inner troll demanding justice. Then he finally reacted! His face contorted with pain, but he laughed. *What the hell is going on,* I wondered.

The truthsayer's cool demeanor broke. She actually looked confused. Then she let go and stumbled back.

"What's happened?" I demanded.

Even Veda's usually calm exterior shattered. "Why did you stop?"

"I want to know as well, Lady," Kalem said. "Why did your probe terminate so early?"

"Damn the reason why! Where's my mother! Where's Luther!" I shouted, running toward them. "What's happened?" I turned on the truthsayer. My anger startled even her icy calm. "Well? You scrambled my brain without mercy or authority. What about him? Even if my mother's fate were not at stake, he is a suspect in murder, abduction, and who the hell knows what? And Morgan Ashstone? What about him?"

Altheda pulled me back, her strong hands firm on my arms. "Easy, girl. Let the poor woman answer."

I longed to let Altheda hold me in her arms like she did when I was young, but her comfort would be transitory. Veda was at my side as well. I wasn't sure if they were supporting me or prepared to hold back me if my angry troll escaped.

"I will speak with Kalem and Veda first," the truthsayer whispered.

"No, now!" I demanded.

"Sabine, hush now," Veda begged, holding my hand. Then she turned to the truthsayer and said, "Please tell us what is happening."

"He's clever," the truthsayer replied, shaking. "Much of his own memory has been magically wiped. Only fragments of information remain to clarify certain facts."

"Which are?" I asked, breathing heavily.

"Your mother and grandfather still live," she told me quickly. "They are being held prisoner with the other missing mages, Remus Runecroft and Albertus Crimm. But only for as long as deemed convenient."

"But you don't know where?" I asked, shaking.

"No. And something else as well." She turned to Kalem. "In his mind, Lady Abigail and her grandfather have already been taken."

Kalem grabbed Desta by the throat. The prisoner did not even flinch, though Kalem's grip tightened, making the despicable man's words raspy as he said, "Take care, shapeshifter, if you want to see your precious Abigail again."

"Braden, go check on Duke Nightshade and Abigail," Kalem commanded, keeping a tight hold on Desta's neck.

"Stop it, Kalem," Veda commanded. "We need him alive. For now."

Kalem let go and stepped back. I understood the murderous rage he was probably feeling, and the pain feeding it.

"They were taken about fifteen minutes ago," Desta said. "My friend Morgan Ashstone is grateful all of you were so preoccupied with me. It gave him the opportunity to deal with old Nightshade and rescue Abigail."

"Morgan Ashstone is involved," Kalem said darkly.

The truthsayer put on her gloves. "The magic used on Desta left a sting of its own. His mind is damaged. I saw him help with the murders and abductions. But everything else is gone. Removed using powerful magic."

"It was a failsafe move," Desta said with a grin. "I suggested it myself in case I was captured. You can probe me all you want, bitch. I openly confess to killing poor old Frederick. I confess to kissing Lady Fable disguised as baseborn Braden. I even admit to those murders of those pesky wizards guarding the taman shade. We needed our precious shade back, you understand. The knowledge you need is gone. You will never find them alive unless you let me go."

"You wanted to be caught. Why?" Veda asked.

Desta tilted his head and sighed. "Veda, so vain and sure of herself. The science mage. You will understand soon enough."

Braden returned, heaving for breath. His grim expression alone confirmed Abigail was gone. *Damn it!*

"Where is she?" Kalem raged.

"Kill me. Enjoy the moment, but she will be lost to you forever if you do," Desta said.

"One last thing. They are not finished," the truthsayer warned. "They need one more."

I looked at the truthsayer, confused. "What do you mean one more?"

The truthsayer replied, "They want you, Lady Fable."

"Want me for what?"

CHAPTER 27

Despite Veda's insistence that I get some rest, I couldn't manage a wink of sleep. I alternated between pacing in circles like a madwoman, and tossing and turning in my bed and kicking off my covers. Rory was not happy with me. I swear if my dragon were bigger, he'd have kicked me to the floor. Despite his annoyance, he refused sleep too. He patiently listened to my rants and mumblings.

"Maybe I should just give myself up to Desta. If they want me, for whatever bizarre reason, then they'd take me to Mother and the others. Maybe Veda and Kalem could track me via a spell or charm me in some way."

Rory frowned and sighed. "No, Sabi. Desta's a bad mage full of lies. Everyone told you so last night. There's too much risk. Wicked mages would expect you to be enchanted. And if Kalem and Veda can't track the others, you would be lost too. Can't lose my Sabi."

"Nothing else shows any promise of helping them! Poor Mother and Abigail. They're the ones I worry for the most. They need their medicine. We brainstormed for hours last night to no effect," I complained. "We scried for everyone individually, and we could not find one soul, one hint, in the scrying bowl to locate them. We burned through so much magic and coffee hunting for them, with nothing to show for it." I raked through my hair and glanced at Rory. "But you're right. Morgan and Desta would expect us to use tracking spells. They'd be prepared for any trick."

"See, Morgan and Desta are bad mages!" Rory emphasized. "Last night everyone was tired and cranky. That's why Veda and Altheda ordered you to bed."

"Yes, like I was still five years old," I complained. "Like I could embrace sleep with all this insanity going on." The sky lightened outside my window, and I closed the curtains. I wasn't hopeful enough to watch a sunrise. "Damn Desta Tabor and his sly threats. Why do they want me? Why?"

Rory curled up on the bed, green eyes bright in the shadows. "Truthsayer didn't know. She said Desta's memory has holes. Maybe your powers are special and they're magic thieves. Steal from you. Bad mages, like I said." Rory rolled over and stretched his blue body. "Sabi needs sleep. Thoughts make sense when you sleep."

"I can't sleep, Rory."

"Then drink your brown potion," he suggested, glaring at me.

"Veda cut me off. Braden and Altheda brewed so many pots of coffee last night. I think I drank most of it. I can't think of a way out. Damn it, damn it, damn it. Mother is a prisoner of mad, crazy mages, and there's not a damn thing I can do about it. I'm stuck here."

"Are we locked in? Like a silly princess in a tower?"

"No, of course not. Well … My brain is, I think. And I'm no princess. I don't have the manners to pull it off. I need a solution. A plan to rescue them."

"Even mean old Luther?" Rory snorted.

I collapsed on the bed and looked at him. "Yes, even Luther, and the others. I may loathe Crimm and Runecroft, but I can't condone what's happened, even to them."

Rory nodded. "I'm scared too. Mother Brona and Abigail need rescue. And nice Duke Nightshade. I like him. He gave me treats and didn't yell at me when I borrowed his gold cuff links."

"You stole them, sweetie," I said. "They were in your basket."

"Because they were shiny. I don't like Luther and Crimm Snot-Face, but we have to rescue them all. Being good is hard. Requires bacon. We need a plan. A good plan."

"I know. If Mother and Abigail don't take their medicine regularly, they may suffer a seizure or a mad fit. I am so worried for them both. Abigail is sweet and gentle, so like my mother. They must be terrified."

I jumped up and resumed my insane pacing. I longed for the comfort of my mother's presence. I went to my dresser for her wooden box holding my treasure. I opened the lid and gently took out her bouquet. I wanted to keep her gift safe. Even when we were at the palace, I kept it near always. The pink flowers tied with blue ribbons were still fresh.

"My grandmother, Sabine, charmed them for my mother when she went to the Academy with so much hope. Mother gifted this precious bundle to me when I began my own journey. Maybe we could use this to scry with?" I asked Rory. "It's a personal possession. It would add an enchanted spark to our search for Mother. Why didn't I think of this last night?"

"Sabi tired and angry. Thoughts scatter."

"How can you be so calm?" I asked, feeling jealous of my baby dragon. I took a deep breath and closed my eyes. "I read in the manual some pukis have a healing quality, but there wasn't much written about it. Most dispute the ability. Stupid people call pukis dragons vermin, but I know better. You're the best and most wondrous creature, but I believe you have more magic than we understand. Even Duke Nightshade remarked on it."

I clutched Mother's bouquet and looked into the round mirror on my dresser. I wanted to fuel some hope instead of despair. "Mother, where are you? Where are they hiding you?" I touched the mirror, wishing to see her face instead of my own reflection.

My fingers vibrated against the glass, and the mirror shimmered moonlike, brightening the room. I breathed deep as warm magic teemed through my body. Rory, alerted to mystic powers, flew to my shoulder. My hand flushed red. Spirals of silver leaves poured from my fingers, circling the mirror as the glass frosted with mystic heat. Startled by my magic's hold, I swayed, dizzy from the flow. Another image formed in the mirror, erasing my reflection. "Mother!" I cried. I banged on the glass. "Mother! Can you hear me?" She knelt in a cage, weeping. Then her head jerked up and she glanced around. "Mother!"

Braden burst into the room. "Sabine? What's wrong?"

"Get Veda, quick!" I shouted. "Before the magic goes away." Mother turned her head, and she saw me! She looked directly at me! "Mother, where are you?" I wept.

"Sabine," she called, scrambling to her feet.

"She hears me!" I cried. "Where are you?"

The magic vanished, leaving only remnants of a few silvery vines clinging to the wooden frame and a darkened mirror.

Veda and Kalem rushed into my room. My hand pressed to the mirror. I hugged Mother's bouquet to my heart. "You're too late. She's gone."

# # #

After a few moments of raging to myself, I simmered down. I went downstairs, feeling more despair than hope. I explained what happened in every detail as everyone listened with sober expressions.

Altheda brought me a cup of chamomile tea. "Drink this, Sabine, and no arguments."

"Coffee would be better," I remarked, sipping.

She put a piece of buttered toast in front of me. "Have some of this and we'll see."

I rarely defied Altheda when she used her firm tone. I sipped, happy she at least added lots of honey. "Time is not our friend," I said. "Both Mother and Abigail need their medicine. Damned Desta and Morgan know this."

"They've not won anything yet," Veda said, sitting next to me on the couch. "What happened gives us a chance to find them."

"What exactly happened to me? I can't even light a candle or elevate a cup with my powers, but vines spew from my hands when I'm angry or scared. Now suddenly I can talk through mirrors?"

"Have you ever experienced any sensations or magic reactions with mirrors before?" Kalem asked.

I shook my head, frowning. "Only as a victim, when the taman shade first attacked me. It emerged from the mirror. I didn't like mirrors much after that." I refrained from adding that I never liked my own reflection. My mother possessed graceful beauty, whereas I was small with weird eyes, pasty skin, and frizzy back hair. Luther often called me a changeling child when Mother was out of earshot. "Please believe me. I know she saw me! I know she did. I'm not mad. Well, maybe a little mad."

"We believe you," Veda said softly. "It may be deeper than that. You once told me you had an ancestor who was a mirror master. Such rare magic often skips a generation or two. It's possible you inherited the gift of glass. It's also possible your love for your mother bolstered your talent. Set it free. I never expected it, to be honest. It's a rare gift."

"I wasn't even trying to cast a spell," I said. "It just happened."

"The strongest sorcery has no incantation, no words or rhymes, just intent. You wanted your mother," Veda said, touching my cheek. "Pure magic conjured by a daughter's love."

I leaned against her shoulder, wiping tears from my eyes as Rory nestled in my lap.

"I agree with Veda," Kalem said. "I think you possess mirror magic. You formed a portal to the one you love most. No spell. No incantation. Our special talents are an inborn ability, like my shapeshifting and Veda's ability to transport herself. It generally activates in late adolescence. Your ability, locked up since birth, is just finally getting out. We scried all night and got nowhere."

"Does this explain the vines?" I asked.

"Miss Sabine, I don't think anyone knows how to explain those," Braden said.

I almost laughed. He was trying to distract me, but I needed to focus. "No, the silver ones I just made around the frame of the mirror."

Veda looked pensive as she thought about it. "I don't know. The silver leaves are unusual but may be part of the same mage skill that causes the green vines. We won't learn any more without practice and study."

"We don't have time," I said. "Has any other hopeful idea sprung up?"

"Braden had a brilliant idea," Kalem replied.

"If magic can't locate them, why not common sense?" Braden said. "When tracking a baseborn, we look for their haunts, where they live. Before now, we had no idea about who was connected. Now we have an idea to track down. We're searching not only any properties of Ashstone, Desta, and Baruti but also those belonging to the victims."

"Keeping several people prisoner requires lots of resources," Kalem said. "They need to be hidden away. Desta or Morgan would need access to a large and even isolated property. Then there are the issues of space, food and water, and security. We know Desta and Morgan are involved. We know who is missing so far. We checked the properties for Crimm, Ashstone, and Baruti in town. I have extended the search to their country estates. I have a team of wizards and soldiers searching for them now. I'm in the process of researching any additional holdings they may have outside the city. Morgan is rich and owns several properties. I just need to locate them. We will find them, Sabine."

I nodded as I clung to my fragile fragment of hope. "Yes. That makes sense. They have to be kept somewhere."

"When we find them, we don't want to spook Morgan into doing something desperate,' Braden added. "We need to make sure we can rescue those poor folks."

"We believe Morgan and Desta are the real culprits in burning down Fable House. We already know they murder without conscience," Veda added, "so any plan needs to be taken with care."

"So what now?" I asked. "We must do more than wait. A madman is holding them in a dungeon. I saw enough through the mirror as I witnessed my mother's suffering."

Altheda's forehead wrinkled in confusion as she raised her hand. "Sabine, I don't mean to interrupt, but what about Brona and Luther? How did they end up so far away from home?"

"Portals," Kalem replied. "It's the most logical way. Another way is through mirror magic, but both are dangerous. They would require high magic. I'm betting it's an inborn mage ability, but even those are tricky. Morgan may have power as a mirror mage, but his skill is erratic. Nightshade told me he was not an attentive student. He was impatient and raw. It is dangerous because if the mage does one thing wrong, it could be devastating. It could send the victim somewhere where they are lost forever."

"Mother isn't lost. I saw her in a cage." An unsettling memory shadowed my mood, and I looked up at Kalem. "When the keepers abducted me, I think they used a portal spell."

"Are you sure?" Kalem asked. "They drugged you with red dust. It's disorientating to your senses."

"Yes, because I sensed a definite mystical shift as they carried me, as though my insides were being pulled. Then we were at the mystic temple, which is across town from the palace. They could never have carried me there so swiftly. Does Morgan or Desta possess this type of mage power?"

"No, Morgan trained to be a mirror mage under Duke Nightshade," Kalem replied, looking pensive. "And Desta is a shapeshifter."

"Morgan and Desta probably aren't working alone," I said. "Narcissistic mages like them always have moldy minions who do their dirty work. What they've done requires help, even on a basic level."

The worried look on Kalem's face made me twitch. "What? Spit it out," I said.

"Several mystic keepers from the temple have gone missing since Baruti's arrest," Kalem revealed. "Not surprising, and we are hunting them down. But I think one of them had the ability to open portals. His name is Rupert. He was the first to go underground when Baruti lost his power."

Braden leaned in, his face puckered with worry. "Sabine, are you alright? You're paler than usual."

"Rupert was the leader of those men who took me. That toady-faced keeper! I wish I had kicked him in the balls when I had the chance."

"Sabi's magic saw Mother Brona," Rory said. "Can see her in glass. Mirror is still touched. Has seen the hidden place. Look again."

"What if I can't?" I asked, my stomach knotting like a steel corset. "If I fail—"

Braden sat next to me. "You can. You just shattered Morgan Ashstone's barrier a few moments ago with that mirror. We tried all night to get through and couldn't. Your magic cut through his shields to see your mother. That's a good sign, Sabine. Maybe little Rory has a point. We should bring that mirror down here and try again."

Everyone fell silent. Rory, cradled in my lap, looked up at me expectantly. I still held Mother's flowers. "Bring me the mirror."

Kalem smiled broadly. "Braden, bring down Sabine's mirror from the dresser. He took my hand and pulled me to my feet. "Now, let's focus on your magic."

Veda touched the bouquet. "I remember these."

"Mother's good luck flowers from my grandmother. I am beginning to wonder if they're cursed instead."

"Or maybe the luckiest blossoms in the world," Veda said. "They guided you to your mother. I see hope in them."

Braden carried down the mirror and put it against the wall where Veda directed. She spoke a few words of enchantment, and the mirror expanded to four times its size. The silver vines encircling the glass shimmered brightly and grew with it.

"Good idea," Kalem complimented. "If Sabine can summon her mother's image again, it will give us a wider view of the chamber and who else is there."

Veda's hand on my shoulder was firm. "Only you can do this, Sabine. Take your time and focus. Use the flowers. They are a connection between you and your mother."

I knelt before the mirror and took a deep breath. I touched the glass and concentrated.

The doorbell chimed, shattering my nerves. "What the hell?" I cried, sitting on my heels.

Veda rushed to the door, and a distraught Marigold Graven entered with her father. Hushed whispers among them made me mad. Kalem joined their circle of whispers.

"What is happening?" I shouted.

"Oh, Sabine," Marigold cried, running toward me. "I'm sorry, but we reported this at the palace. Alexander kindly told us Kalem and Veda were here. My poor Greeley has been taken! He's gone! Like the others!"

"What?" I mumbled.

"Forgive us, Sabine," Thomas Graven said, putting his arm around Marigold's shaking shoulders. "Her fiancé, Greeley Havelock, is missing. When we were recovering from being drugged and confined, we went to check on Greeley, and he was gone. His room still has his possessions, except for his prayer book. It is unlike the boy. No one has seen him."

"Sabine, I'm so sorry about your mother," Marigold murmured. "I know I don't have a right to ask for help. But we think my poor Greeley was taken too. I love him and he is gone." She sniffled into her handkerchief.

No one should be denied the one they love, not even Marigold.

"We came here not only to ask for help but to offer our own," Thomas said, "if there is anything we can do to help you find your loved ones."

Marigold's confused, red face, puffy from crying, looked down at me. "What are you doing on the floor?"

I touched the mirror and replied, "Finding my hope."

CHAPTER 28

T attered nerves hindered my efforts to connect with my mother again through the mirror. I didn't know how to cast spells. My magic was defensive or just pure chaos. For hours I struggled to beckon a potent sorcery I didn't understand.

Mirror magic requires skill and extensive training. I had none. I sorely wished for Richard Nightshade's guidance. Veda and Kalem were high sorcerers, but he was a master of this mystic art. Legs numb from kneeling for an eternity, I dropped my hands from the mirror in defeat. "Damn it!" I burst out, sitting back on my heels.

Braden handed me a cup of water. "It's alright. Just relax and start over."

"We don't expect you to be perfect. Compose your feelings," Veda said. "I know you're frustrated."

I drank some water and held the cup for Rory to take a drink. "Ready, Rory?"

My dragon nodded, flexing his tiny wings. I handed Braden the cup. "I'll try again."

"Just quiet your mind and focus on your mother," Veda said.

I looked up at my mentor. She had faith in me, whereas I was a bundle of doubt. Quiet my mind? No easy trick. My mind has never been quiet.

I pressed one hand against the glass and squeezed Mother's bouquet with the other, closing my eyes. *What did I do before when I summoned my mother's image?* I wondered. My wish was to see her, so I focused on that. My tension eased, and I glanced down to see Rory snuggled into my lap. His presence soothed me as I centered my mind.

"What if she's doing it wrong?" Marigold mumbled. "Sabine couldn't be a mirror mage. High magic takes years and years—"

"Hush now, Marigold," Thomas Graven whispered.

Blessed silence followed his words. I stifled a smile when I imagined Marigold's reaction when her father told her to hush.

Then it happened! Silvery vines sprang from my hands, encircling the enlarged mirror. Unlike the green vines, which possessed the strength of steel, these lay delicately like lace. My hand brushed against a bright leaf, soft as a rose petal. "Mother, where are you? Mother!" I called out. "Mother, I need you."

The mirror misted over. Mother's image unfolded before my eyes. "I see her! Do you see her too?"

"Yes," Kalem told me. "We see her."

Kalem was right about expanding the mirror's size. It showed a great deal more of the chamber imprisoning my mother. Now I could see the other captives in separate small cells behind iron bars. Locked in the same cell as Mother, Luther sat next to her wrapped in a blanket. Then Runecroft, his fine clothes dirty and torn, whimpering in fear, and Albertus Crimm, bitter-faced but not whining at least. I noted that, with the exception of Luther and my mother, they all wore blue metal binders on their wrists.

"They're wearing magelocks," Veda said. "Expensive to forge and enchant."

I searched the room like I was a bird observing from above. Abigail occupied a cell alone. Kalem gasped her name behind me, but he didn't distract me further. Unlike the others, her cell had a comfortable bed, blankets, pillows, food, and drink. There was also a privacy curtain for a portable latrine. Her eyes showed despair and fear. Then I found Nightshade in a tiny cell, a magelock binding his power. I could sense his fury and concern for his granddaughter. As Marigold feared, Greeley stood in a prison cell, his magic bound, but stoic and audibly praying. His devotion was clearly obvious. Marigold began to weep behind me.

I returned my view to my mother, unsettled by what I saw. She was lying on the floor, covered with a blanket. *Is she ill?* I thought. Luther huddled next to her.

"Mother! Can you hear me?" She lay sleeping, or I hoped she was sleeping. "Veda, she won't wake up! She looks sick!" I fought the urge to bang on the glass. "Mother! Wake up," I begged, leaning against the mirror. She did not wake, and desperation gripped me.

Luther's head jerked up, and he glanced around suspiciously. Who the hell's that?"

He was the last person I ever imagined I'd need for help. "Luther, you old sod! Can you hear me? It's me, Sabine."

"You've got magic now, missy? I heard about how Veda cured you. Fable magic hasn't died out yet. Well, use some of that magic to get us out of here."

"What the hell do you think I'm trying to do? What's wrong with Mother?"

"They took her away again. She always comes back like this, the fucking bastards. Been experimenting on her for days. These robed men come and take her away. All they tell me is the treatment will restore her magic. Each time Brona comes back weaker and weaker."

I feared they were using her for experiments. Damn them! "She's allergic to the medicine! This could kill her!"

"I told the bastards that!" Luther snapped. "They don't care. Been doing the same to me, except it doesn't hurt me like it does Brona. No magic, and my damned eye still twitches."

Shaking, I leaned my head against the glass. "Help me find you."

"They burned down our shop! Our home. Fable House is gone! They kidnapped us and burned it all." He began to blubber, and I needed him to think.

"I know. Altheda told us. I'm sorry. It was my home too."

Luther grimaced, wiping his eyes on his sleeve. "All they'll say is that she will be cured. I told them she's allergic to the treatment, but they don't listen or care. She's been getting more frail each day. More unsettled too."

Unsettled was his code word for her violent fits. As I thought about what they were doing to my mother, my temper surged.

"How are you even talking to me?" Luther asked. "Where are you? You close by, girl?"

Took him long enough to notice. "I'm speaking to you through a mirror. I didn't know I could until today. I summoned Mother by accident. I saw her, and she heard me too. Then she vanished. We need to know where you are. We're all looking for you. Can you tell us anything? Who is there? Can you give us names or a clue to where you are being held?"

"Old Jessup Fable was a mirror master. He was your great-uncle," Luther said with a grin. "You got the good magic, girl. Don't waste it."

"Nice family remembrance, but where are you? Are you near a town or know whose property it is? Anything to help us track you. Morgan has spells shielding his location."

"Morgan Ashstone. That's who has us. He's mad. I may be an old drunk, but he's downright cracked. He's got lots of folks working for him. Puffed-up wizards who used to swarm about the place in black robes. We're in an old castle. Don't know where though. Belonged to his grandfather, Morgan said, or did until he killed the old man in his sleep. He even brags about it. Mad Morgan I call him. He boasts about murdering most of his family just for the inheritance."

Charming. I thought my family relationships were cursed.

Brona lifted her head and touched Luther's shoulder. "Is that Sabine?"

"Mother!" I wept. "I'm coming for you!"

Morgan Ashstone's face appeared, blocking my view. My heart quickened as he glared at me through the massive mirror, his image blocking out everything else.

"I'm glad you are finally here," he said. "I was getting bored waiting for one of you to find me. Such a sweet reunion. But you're not yet proficient in the magic of glass, Lady Fable. Strange, I never suspected a little gutter wench like you would possess mirror magic. Such a valiant effort. However, I am the greatest mirror mage."

Terrified he would cut off my connection, I rose up on my knees, and Rory rolled off my lap. "Mother!" I cried. The glass flared brightly as Morgan's magic infected mine. I could sense his dark sorcery as my hand remained fixed to the mirror and pulled me into the glass. Hands grabbed at my shoulders and waist, even my feet, trying to pull me back. The desperate voices of my friends became distant echoes as Morgan dragged me into his mystical passage. The brightness shifted to shadows, and the mirror swallowed me whole. I flailed into the abyss of shadows. My heartbeat rapid and lungs starved for air, I couldn't even scream as I plummeted through the mystical vacuum.

#

I emerged from the void into the glare of light. My mortal flesh plummeted to cold stone. I rolled over onto my back, hollowed out and struggling to breathe. My shoulder and head hurt where I struck the stone floor.

I opened my eyes. Morgan Ashstone stood over me, smiling, foppishly dressed in his bright maroon coat and frilly white shirt.

"You're a reckless girl, Fable. I wanted you here anyway, so you're forgiven." Temple keepers flanked him like morose crows. "Desta is delayed, but I've arranged for him to come to us soon. He was going to bring you to me, but no matter. This was more fun. And we have lots of fun planned."

A familiar scream rattled me. *Oh no, she didn't follow me in!*

Marigold lay on the cold floor in her frothy lace and satin, wailing as two of the keepers pulled her up.

"Lady Graven is lovely, but she's not necessary," Morgan said, displeased. "She might serve as a better companion for my Abigail than you, Fable. However, her presence is troublesome, and my well-planned jails are already crowded."

"Please, don't hurt her. She's here by accident," I begged Morgan.

The keepers dragged me up and snapped a magelock on my wrist. Morgan's reply was a slap across the face. I've had worse, so I didn't even flinch.

"Not by accident. Your fault, Fable. It's your fault she's here, not mine." He ran his finger down the cheek he struck. "I can be generous if you obey me. I need you for my research. I will create a cure for my Abigail. Then Abigail and I can finally marry and live happily … Well, you know."

I was outnumbered and out-magicked, so I had to tread carefully. "Please, let me see my mother. She's sick. I just want to help her."

"In good time," Ashstone replied.

The keepers held my arms roughly. Rupert walked toward me, piggy eyes gleeful over my vulnerable state. "No little pets today. Shame. I was feeling a bit peckish."

Those were death words. "Still working as an underling, Rupert?"

Gloating, Rupert leaned down to my face so we were eye to eye. "Dwarfish, baseborn bitch. Powerless now, are we? But then, your weak magic was pathetic the last time you challenged me."

I snapped and kicked him hard in the balls. "Is that weak?" *I'm going to pay for that,* I realized.

Rupert doubled over as he clutched his raw privates. "Bitch," he grunted, blinking back tears. He lifted his hand to strike me.

"Don't touch her, you maggot!" Luther shouted from his cell.

Since when was Luther my champion?

Just then, Morgan made a gesture that froze Rupert's hand, literally. He screamed as he clutched his hand, frosted with blue ice.

"Now, now, Rupert," Morgan said. "Sabine is vital for my experiments. Behave." He then stood over me, too close for my comfort. "Manners are important, so we must set an example too. Lady Fable is feral and does not possess the grace of mageborns. Kill Lady Marigold."

Marigold gasped and fainted into her captors' arms.

Greeley, frantic, cried out for Marigold, beating against the iron bars. "Don't you dare touch her! Let her go! Scoundrels!"

"No, wait!" I cried. "I'm sorry. Don't hurt her. I'll be good. I promise. I lost my temper. It won't happen again. I just—"

"Just what?" Morgan pressed.

"I hate Rupert." I was honest. I suspected Morgan would not respond to begging.

Morgan tossed back his head and laughed. "I do understand," he finally said. "He is a loathsome worm, but he keeps my laboratory tidy." He paused, and with every second I thought I would scream. "I will allow you this one blunder, Lady Fable. Marigold is your responsibility. You must obey me. Promise? Marigold will be only the first fatality if you disappoint me again. Your mother will be next. And it will be your fault."

I wanted to kill him. But I nodded, defeated by his threats and power. Marigold revived, though she was hysterical.

Morgan smiled and whispered into my ear, "Good girl. But to enforce the fact I'm the one in power here, let me demonstrate what would happen to Marigold, Brona, Luther, and all the others should you fail me. To ensure your ladylike manners, Lady Fable, I have this."

He went to the far wall, where I noticed a tall shape covered with black silk. He stripped away the concealing shroud. In the glass prison, the taman shade swirled in murky shadows, a creature of fury and death. Marigold buried her head against my shoulder, weeping in terror.

"Yes, I reclaimed my lovely pet. Isn't she wondrous? Such raw mystical power! I had to retrieve her, of course. None of you understand how special she is. I alone have the power to control her. Let me demonstrate, so you understand the cost of failing me in the future."

He removed a red crystal from his coat pocket, fingering it in his hand, and whispered an incantation. The glass dome lifted, releasing the taman shade. In the background, I vaguely heard the fearful cries of the others and Nightshade's cursing.

The taman shade flew from her prison, a wailing shadow darting through the chamber. She did not assault anyone, so I hoped this was just a demonstration of Morgan's damned power. Ashstone pointed to Rupert, lying prone and helpless on the floor. Rupert howled as the taman shade attacked, her shadows obscuring him as he shrieked briefly before his death. She released Rupert's corpse and floated in the air above him, red eyes glowing.

"You killed him?" Marigold whispered.

"Yes, he was becoming a liability," Morgan said. "I am the only one allowed to torture my guests. But I am not finished." He rubbed the crystal and pointed at me! Marigold let me go like a hot coal and cowered on the floor. I could only stand there frozen as the shade flew at me in a fury. She hovered over me for a moment, then flew into her glass prison.

Morgan closed the dome. "You see?"

Dumb with shock, I could only shake my head.

"Of course you don't see. You are not aware, are you? You have no need to fear the taman shade. She's the reason you still live. Fey will not kill fey. Your silver eyes are fey born. Your ancestors were fey, long ago in the deep, forgotten past of our world. Your silver eyes are not just a unique anomaly. Such ancient powers are full of magic lost for centuries. Why the fates chose you is beyond me. You're common as dirt."

A cruel realization hit me. "You sent the shade to kill me when I first arrived at the palace."

"Yes! Very good. I sent my fey minion to kill you when you arrived with Veda at the palace. I wanted to punish Veda for not helping Abigail. I heard she had a new favorite companion she was helping, so I wanted you dead, of course. Then my pet refused to kill you. Later, I sent her after others, and she slaughtered most happily. But not you. She had you in her death grip more than once and let you live. The only logical conclusion was you. You were different. A throwback so rare. Your silver eyes are not just rare but reveal your ancestry. I came to understand you might be special. Old lore states fey will not harm each other. Then, after that nasty fight with your father, your magic exploded like a star. Your fey blood is the key to restoring magic. Fey blood, which will cure my Abigail."

He turned his back on me and walked away, waving his hand. "Lock Marigold and Sabine in the last cell. I will send for Sabine later, after supper."

They shoved us into a small space and locked the door. The keepers carried Rupert's body away. I longed to speak with the others, but several keepers remained, keeping an eye on us.

Marigold sat on the narrow bed in a corner next to me, crying. "How can you be so calm?" she asked.

"I'm not calm. The lives of those we care about are in danger."

"Surely we will be rescued," Marigold whispered.

"We must rescue ourselves," I told her. "We may not have a choice to do otherwise."

CHAPTER 29

Marigold's temperament wasn't conducive to the abuse of brutish madmen temple keepers. Or to being my cellmate. Her collapse into hysterical tears was inevitable.

"Please stop crying," I begged softly. "We've no idea if he's watching us."

I studied the chamber, a well-lit dungeon with cells spaced apart by several feet to prevent easy prisoner interaction, and five disgraced temple keepers standing guard at various posts. No windows. A sealed room with only one door, except for the mystical portal Morgan opened to suck me in.

Marigold blew her nose into her hanky and whimpered, "Watching us? Do you mean the guards?"

"I mean Morgan Ashstone. He's a mirror mage. Between his mirror magic and Desta Tabor's shapeshifting, it's not surprising they were always a giant step ahead of us."

My chief concerns were for Mother and Abigail. They needed treatment. Proper treatment. I had to save my mother from Morgan's experiments. I hoped my friends would find us. I confess I wasn't feeling very hopeful of about any option as Marigold cried incessantly.

"My love, fear not!" Greeley shouted through his bars. "Have faith the gods shall rescue us from this evil place. I love thee, Marigold!"

"Oh, Greeley, I love you!" Marigold cried, reaching through the bars in a futile romantic gesture.

Their declarations of love lasted long enough for me to beg for divine deliverance from them.

"Silence!" shouted an annoyed keeper, striking a staff against Greeley's bars. To his credit, Greeley displayed no fear, but prayed, though with a softer voice.

I longed to cry out for my mother, but I choked it down. The risk was too great. Her charmed flowers had been lost in all the trauma when Morgan dragged me through the mirror. I couldn't even see Mother from my cell. *Damn it, damn it, damn it.* I kicked hard against the bars. My foot hurt like hell, but it released some tension. It was that or pummel Marigold.

"What's wrong with you, Sabine?" she asked. "We were just expressing our love and affection."

I leaned my head against the iron bars. "We've been imprisoned by a raving madman, and the slightest offense will wake his murderous impulse. Do you want to die because you could not restrain your romantic moment?"

"No, of course not," she snapped. "I need some hope now. This place is grim and horrible. And it smells."

"And it's full of terror," I added, observing the glass prison holding the taman shade inside. She swam in her ether of shadows, crimson eyes flashing.

Marigold finally cried herself out and sat on the creaky cot, scratching her wrist under the metal binder. "What is this wretched thing made of?"

"You're only making it worse," I told her.

"But it itches!" she complained. "And it's so ugly. Mama says my skin is very delicate. This blue metal is not only uncomfortable but unattractive. Is it eating my magic?"

"Of course not. They're just binding our magic."

"Why would anyone create such abominations?"

For mages like Morgan and Desta. "For mageborn criminals and the insane."

"But I'm a good girl," Marigold mumbled.

"No matter. We'll have to make do without magic."

"Like a baseborn?" she asked with a grimace.

"Watch it," I said darkly.

"Sorry, I didn't mean it like that." She frowned, rubbing her arm. "So do you think it's true? Or is he just mad?"

I sat down on the bed next to her, too exhausted to fight. "What?"

"His theory about you possessing fey ancestry, silly."

"I think he's mad, whether it's true or not. I'll admit my magic does strange things." I thought about what Crimm said the fateful day my magic exploded for the first time in his office. Even he commented on my eyes and the fey legends.

"I'm sorry," Marigold said.

"About what?"

"I called you ghost eye when we were in school. I was mean. It was wrong of me."

"The past doesn't matter."

"You being morose, Sabine. Where's the Fable swearing and fighting spirit?"

"I'm being careful. My mother and Luther could well be next on the taman shade's menu. And don't forget poor Greeley."

I touched the cold metal around my wrist, moving it around. It didn't make me itch, but it felt weird. "Shame. About now is when one of my unpredictable bursts of sorcery would come in handy."

"Your green vines? They were most strange."

"They protected us from the taman shade when she attacked us. But I was thinking about something else—when my magic first erupted. Crimm and Runecroft can testify my fiery gush of magic was quite deadly. I don't remember anything after that. Only my anger. Braden told me they had to replace the carpet and repaint the walls to cover the scorch marks."

"A violent but unique display of sorcery!" Crimm shouted across the chamber. "I never believed Veda's potions worked. But I confess, you're proof her science can restore magic. Shame your pukis didn't see it. Such a small, irritating creature. So easy to miss him unless you look down."

Crimm took me off guard. He was speaking so strangely. Maybe he wanted to make amends before dying? Why mention my dragon?

"Crimm Snot-Face," Rory mumbled, poking his head through the bars.

Rory! I thought. I looked down at my feet, and there he was. He must have fallen through the portal with me! I glanced across the room, and Crimm nodded to me. Yes, I was dense, but I had a lot on my mind. He must have seen Rory and wanted to alert me before the guards saw him. Rory wiggled easily through the bars. I swiftly bent down to scoop him up.

A keeper became curious and walked over to check on us.

"Hide!" I hissed.

Marigold snatched Rory, sat down on the bed, and tucked him under her voluminous skirt and petticoats.

Her fast move prevented the damned keeper from seeing anything but did not remove his suspicion. "What are you two plotting?" he demanded.

I shrugged at him, feigning innocence. "We're just talking. Not much else to do. Some food and water would be welcome since we are going to be here a while."

"You'll be fed same time as the others," he said. "What you hiding?" he asked Marigold suspiciously.

"Oh, I'm in such agony," Marigold moaned, rocking back and forth on the narrow cot, hands on her stomach.

"Nice try. I'm not falling for such an old trick, girl," the keeper said.

"Show mercy! I just need to visit a private area for a moment."

"Use the bucket," he told her.

"No, it's not that," she said, tearing up. Fake Marigold tears I knew so well from childhood. "It's my moon time. I need something to catch my blood flow. You do know what a woman's moon time is? My monthly bleed is so heavy. And the cramps! It's so humiliating to talk to a man about this. I'll die from the embarrassment. I have nothing for it. Could you at least bring me some clean rags? Please!"

The keeper actually blanched and stepped back. "Stop talking! I'll bring you some rags." He marched away quickly.

"That was clever," I whispered, a little jealous I didn't think of it myself.

Marigold deftly wiped her eyes, beaming with triumph. "Nothing horrifies a man like reference to anything female." She lifted her skirts and handed a disgruntled Rory to me.

"Stuffy under there," Rory said.

"Hey!" Marigold protested.

"Thank you," I whispered.

Rory rubbed his face against my cheek. "Missed my Sabi."

"Rory, what are you doing here?" I whispered. "It's dangerous. How did you get here?"

"Dark magic pulled me in. When I came through, I winged to the ceiling and hid. They were busy with you, so they did not notice me. I stayed quiet, even when scary taman shade was loose. She saw me too but didn't tell."

Interesting. Did she consciously not reveal Rory or was she specifically driven by tasks commanded by Morgan? I cuddled Rory and was scared for him. "You're a brave dragon. But sweetie, it's unsafe."

"Maybe he can get out and find help," Marigold suggested.

"I don't want to leave my Sabi."

"I want you to hide," I told him. "Get out if you can. Find a way to let our friends know."

The dour-faced keeper returned. We tucked Rory under the blanket. The man opened the door and handed a wad of linen cloth to Marigold. "Here. Just don't ask for more."

She took the cloth with bowed head. "Thank you, kind sir."

He grabbed me by arm, pulling me out of my cell. "You must come with me. Lord Ashstone is ready to see you now."

I glanced back once as Rory peeked his head out from the covers, his eyes so sad. *Be good and stay safe,* I thought.

I passed poor Abigail, who bravely nodded to me from her cell, and then my mother and Luther. It broke my heart when I saw Mother's feverish face before the keeper pushed me through the door.

# # #

We climbed many steps until we reached the main floor of the castle. Carved stone walls and polished tiles spoke of wealth. I tried to get a glimpse of something helpful—a window or anything. The guard just dragged me along without a word until we entered a massive room with a huge burning fireplace, lush carpets, and heavy brocade drapes that blocked any view to the outside world.

"Bring her to me," Morgan ordered, sitting at the head of a long dining table covered with a white linen tablecloth and set with fine porcelain plates, crystal goblets, and golden eating utensils. A few candles were lit, but most of the room's illumination came from light globes placed everywhere in the room. Expensive.

"Lady Fable, you may sit down next to me," Morgan said, gesturing to the chair next to him.

I sat down, and my rough-handed keeper stepped back to guard unobtrusively from the background.

"There is plenty of food," Morgan announced. "I need you well-nourished for our work. I decided to invite you to sup with me because we have so much to talk about. What better way to get to know each other than with a lovely meal?"

My usual robust appetite shriveled, but I obeyed him. A silent servant offered roast beef, potatoes, greens, and gravy. I accepted it all and was even allowed a knife and fork to eat my food.

"Don't be surprised that you're allowed sharp objects," Morgan said, digging into his dinner. "You cannot escape. Your magic is bound, and if you do anything heroic and foolish, I will slit the throat of your dear mother."

I clutched my fork and cut my meat with vengeance, imagining it was his smug face. "I would never endanger her. Or any of my friends."

"Even Luther?" he asked, sipping red wine.

"Even Luther."

"You are a strange creature," he said. "Pour Lady Fable some water. I know she does not take wine."

He knows too much about me, I thought. A servant appeared and put a crystal goblet of ice water before me. I drank, hoping to calm my nerves. "You must have planned this for a long time," I said.

He smiled. "Yes. I would do anything for Abigail. Unlike your mentor, Veda Arcana."

"I thought Abigail, like my mother, was allergic to a key component of her cure."

"She is, but the reactions are not fatal. It just takes adjustment of the elements and how they are prepared. Veda was too cautious."

"But the two people who died under Veda's care?" I asked. "I thought her cure killed them. It's why she was banished."

"Oh, no. I killed them," Morgan said. "Punishment for abandoning my Abigail. You see, when I visited her, I saw them talking in their room about how they began to show signs their magic was returning. They upset me."

"Abigail is a sweet and gentle lady. I hate seeing her locked up with the others."

"I originally placed her in a lovely bedchamber, but she kept trying to escape or help the others. I gave her many comforts and even offered to send for Mrs. Doran. I had no choice but to keep my beloved confined. You think I'm mad, don't you?"

"You know I think you're mad." Looking him in the eye, I said, "I cannot lie to you, for you would know."

"Very wise of you, Fable. Geniuses are always accused of madness. I had no choice but to exact justice for Veda's wrongs to us. And for Nightshade's rejection of me as an apprentice and suitor for his granddaughter. I was able to get all of Veda's material on the disease from the keepers during the investigation. Baruti's keepers came over to our side some time ago. Desta helped ensure this. He is very loyal to me because I rescued him from the dreary monastery. Then we sought revenge on his father together. When Veda was being investigated, we copied all of her precious research. So easy. Desta's letter accusing Veda was brilliant. Baruti was so gullible." He leaned close and whispered, "The temple keepers were simple to deal with. Money purchased their loyalty quite easily."

I nodded, hoping my horrified emotions did not show on my face.

"Desta rightly wanted to punish his father and Crimm, who influenced him. They denied Desta the right to a cure, which I eventually gave him. Of course, Veda's original tome was missing some key pages, which Desta and I eventually found."

"You found the missing parts of her book?" I asked, curious because it would be crucial to finding a generic cure if we got out of this alive.

"I see I sparked your interest. Good. It took some time. Desta and I searched across many backwater provinces where she initially discovered it. It took some doing, but I eventually found them scattered in the most unlikely places. Because I had a copy of the original text, I knew what to look for. I found them over time in libraries, colleges, and even a museum. They were considered old relics or antiques. The fools who had them did not see how valuable they were."

"I must admit, I would love to see those missing pages."

"I agree. You must see them so you can be my assistant, especially since Desta is delayed. You will be witness to my greatness, but you will come to see I am just. Your delicate mother is required to ensure your good behavior. Marigold's appearance was unplanned, but your high moral code and Greeley's loving concern will keep even that irritating little bitch alive."

"So Greeley is one of your witnesses to glory?" I asked.

"Oh, no," Morgan said with a smile. "Greeley Havelock is going to perform the wedding ceremony for Abigail and myself. She will marry me, of course, when she comes to her senses and stops being so stubborn. I thought Greeley would be useful in such a case, and add to the mystery I have made you all play out."

Gods, he's mad. Totally mad. "I don't understand. But I'm still confused about fey blood as a cure."

"Of course you don't understand. You're not me. I'm a genius. Nightshade was too blind to recognize my brilliance. But I digress. This ancient and mysterious creature is proof of fey bloodlines. You have the silver eyes of that lost race. So rare—like your father's."

"He's not my father. Blood does not make family."

"True, but it can make magic," Morgan said. "And as Veda discovered, old tomes can be useful. When I was searching for a cure for Abigail, I found other old books and even some very interesting ones in my grandfather's library here. I inherited this property a year ago. Well, I did hurry my inheritance, but he was so old and senile that it was a mercy. But, he collected ancient books, many on dark magic. Very forbidden, very illegal. I never thought he would be so interesting."

"You discovered how to summon a taman shade," I said.

"Yes! Very astute, Fable. Taman shades are of fey origin. I will not bore you with the details of how I summoned her. Your magic is not yet strong enough to use such high magic." He took the small red crystal from his coat pocket, stroking it lovingly. "Needless to say, even I took a risk to bind this creature. But bound, she will kill anyone I ask her to, except you and Runecroft. But your blood has that fey spark. It's not just your eyes. You have more than Runecroft. He may have the eyes, but you possess something more in your makeup. You are a throwback, Sabine. I do not mean it as an insult, but your ancient fey bloodline is more active in your blood than you realize. Your blood will cure my Abigail."

"I don't understand."

"Veda cured you," he said. "But part of the cure was the result of your fey bloodline. I will prove it. Your kind is rare. From you, I will create a cure, and all the world will praise me for it. Abigail will be mine at last. You will help me in my quest for true love. Agreed?"

Dealing with a bloody lunatic is like dealing with a devil. Truth or reason does not matter to this lunatic. Trapped, I could only buy time for now. I looked at his mad face and prayed my expression was neutral.

"Agreed."

CHAPTER 30

After my dinner from hell concluded, Morgan's stern keeper took me back to my tiny prison. I was never so happy to be done eating in my life. I sat next to Marigold, and we waited silently for a few moments to make sure he was out of earshot.

"Where's Rory?" I whispered.

"Under the covers," Marigold answered, patting a small lump under the blanket. "He enjoys burrowing. How can we possibly go on hiding a baby dragon?"

"Very carefully," I said, lifting the blanket. He wiggled, his green eyes blinking from the warm shadows, but he remained quiet. "Good boy," I mouthed silently. Then I took a chunk of roast beef from my pocket and fed it to him.

"You had roast beef!" she accused with narrowed eyes.

"And it's sitting like a rock in my stomach," I replied. "I managed to stuff some in my pocket for Rory as Morgan pontificated about his plight as a misunderstood genius. Did they bring you any dinner?"

"Just bread and cheese. They are taking the prisoner motif too far. Don't they know who we are? It wasn't very good cheese and the bread was stale. And yes, I shared it with your dragon. Well, the cheese anyway. Not even Rory would eat the bread. He just sniffed at it and burrowed deeper. I think I offended him."

"Thank you," I whispered, handing her the last chunk of roast beef. "If you don't mind how it got here."

She pursed her lips, considering my offer. I knew Marigold had never wanted for anything in life until now. Survival had opened a whole new palate. She plucked the meat from my fingers and put it in her mouth, looking away from me as she chewed.

They did not leave us any spare water to wash with, so I wiped my hands on my skirt. "I must help Morgan with his experiments, or people will die. His charming dinner conversation emphasized my mother would be the first victim. Threats served with meat and potatoes. So I will do as I'm told for now."

"You had potatoes?" she asked, frowning.

"Bad potatoes."

"Liar. They will find us, won't they?"

I feared she was on the brink of another crying fit. I gripped her shoulders. "Of course they will find us. You must be brave now."

"I'm not supposed to be the brave one," she whimpered.

"You may surprise yourself."

She wiped her eyes. She removed the ribbons from her hair and took off her shoes. "I can't even wash or brush my hair." She pressed down in the creaky mattress. "Must being brave demand suffering on this narrow and lumpy bed?"

"It will toughen you up. I'll take the floor. Sleep isn't on my menu tonight anyway."

She lay down stiffly, carefully maneuvering around Rory's lump.

"Silence! Lights out!" a keeper shouted, and the lights dimmed a little in the chamber—but not enough to conceal any secrets or curious dragons. I sat on the stone floor, leaning against the bars, my mind a whirl of fear. I had to think, but rational ideas eluded me! Only Rory's soft snores eased my anxiety.

The next morning, Morgan Ashstone summoned me to his laboratory. I think it was morning. I had no idea what time it was, but the keepers began to dole out a meager breakfast of water, bread, and apple slices. I gave Marigold my share, except for some apple slices for Rory. My stomach still felt like an anvil resided in it.

The keeper unlocked our prison and roughly took me away. He steered me toward a broad, winding staircase and dragged me up four flights of stairs, pulling on my arm until I thought it would pop out of my socket. He pushed me down a hallway, and I jerked away, angry and breathless.

"Stop shoving me! I'm not struggling. Or do you enjoy abusing women?"

He grunted and finally thrust me through a door, then locked it behind me.

"Really? It's not like I'm going anywhere!" I shouted at the door, a useless gesture.

"I'm a careful man," Morgan Ashstone remarked, stirring a tiny cauldron at the far end of the room.

"Your keepers need to learn manners. What's the point of cooperating if I'm to be battered about like a bag of turnips?" I paused and finally realized just how massive and opulent the chamber was.

Morgan stood over a long stone table raised on a bed of enormous clear crystals. On the polished top bubbled several small cauldrons of copper, iron, and even red glass above blue magical flames to control the heat levels. "What do you think of my little workroom?" he asked.

I loathed Morgan but envied his mage laboratory. "I'm impressed." My baseborn origins screamed at the expense, but I coveted every item. Elegant rows of jarred and bottled powders and liquids from every imaginable source lined an entire wall. I could open up my own shop with this inventory. I inhaled the rich odor of plants and other organic ingredients, enjoying a familiar respite before I had to endure whatever Morgan had in store for me today.

I walked along the shelves, noting each jar labeled in elegant script. My apothecary side salivated. I looked up when I felt a warmth. Above me, a domed ceiling, crafted from blue stone and etched with many runes, radiated heat. At the heart of the dome, a circle of dark glass, or maybe crystal, glittered. I even studied the golden stone floor, painted with several mystical circles and symbols. I didn't recognize them from my weeks as Veda's secretary and mage student. I suspected they must be dark magic. Knowing Morgan Ashstone, they were definitely dark magic. Arched windows at least ten feet high, fitted with milky frosted glass, lined one wall.

"It's a magnificent chamber," I said. "You have everything a mage could ask for." *Except sanity and a moral center,* I thought, but I left that out.

"Yes, indeed. You are welcome to try to look out the windows if you like, but I treated the glass so no one can see out but me. And no one can see in."

"Clever," I noted.

"Please don't bother counting the hours until your friends come to rescue you. They won't find us in time. And if any mageborn crosses my wards onto my property, I will know."

The door unlocked and a guard brought in Abigail, in a much gentler manner than he'd used with me.

She rushed toward me and we grasped hands. Oh, Sabine! I'm so glad to see you, but I mourn the reason. Are you and Marigold alright?

How did you manage such a feat? Is it true you have mirror magic?"

"Dearest, your annoying little friend turns out to be a latent mirror mage," Morgan said. "Not a very good one though."

I hugged her with relief. "Well, for a first try I think I did well, minus the rough landing."

He directed us to a round table near the window set for an elegant morning tea. Even though I was hungry, Morgan's presence spoiled my appetite. I did relish the strong black tea. I hadn't slept, as iron bars made poor pillows.

"You must eat something, my dear," Morgan coaxed Abigail. "My personal cook made your favorite lemon scones this morning."

"How can I eat when people, friends and family, suffer in your prison, Morgan?" Abigail replied.

"You know there are penalties for disobeying me, my love," he said with a smile, handing her a plate with golden scones. "You have been refusing food, and it makes me most unhappy."

Abigail did not cry or fight further. She accepted the scone. I followed her example, afraid of tipping mad Morgan into a worse mood.

"Could Grandfather have tea with us?" Abigail asked softly. "I will eat as many scones as you instruct. I promise."

I poured more tea for her. "Perhaps it would ease Abigail's stress if she could see her grandfather, if only for a cup of tea. It would cheer her up."

"Please, Morgan," she pleaded, putting her hand on his arm. "It would make me so happy to see him."

"No," he said, and his tone did not invite debate. "He kept us apart. Aren't you happy to see me?"

"Of course I am," Abigail whispered.

"But soon all will be well, my love. Sabine has agreed to work for me to complete your cure. Then we can be wed. I'm a mirror master and possess more riches than Duke Nightshade. My worth has grown since I served as your grandfather's lowly apprentice. Can you not see how hard I labored to make myself worthy of you?"

"You are more than worthy," Abigail replied.

"And your grandfather was wrong about me," Morgan pressed.

"Yes," she said, nodding.

"Very good," he said. Then he got up, busying himself at his worktable. "I have another dose of your tonic ready as I prepare your cure to restore your magic."

Abigail looked at me, tears welling in her eyes. I gripped her hand briefly, and she took a deep breath. She wiped her eyes with her napkin and straightened her posture. I gave her another scone, projecting a calm I did not feel. "I think Abigail's appetite is improving."

"Wonderful!" he exclaimed, bringing a small vial of blue liquid. "Now drink this quickly. Then have more tea and scone."

She obeyed. I feared what he was concocting in his madness.

After a stressful breakfast, the guard returned to escort Abigail back to her prison.

"Abigail requires comfort and care," I told him after she left. "So does my mother. The dungeon prison you built may be clean, but it's cold and lacks fresh air. If my mother and I are key to your cure for Abigail's magic, they need comfort and care. I will talk to Abigail and make her realize she must obey you. Please!"

"Is that all, Fable? I rule this castle. I tried to keep her in a fine bedchamber, but she disobeyed me. How would you know what is best for Abigail?"

"Because I've had years of caring for my mother, who suffers the same fits and fevers as Abigail. I'm also a trained apothecary."

He seemed to consider my pleas for a tense moment. I prayed I had not ruined everything. If Abigail and my mother were away from that blasted dungeon, it might also give us options for escape. My foremost mission was to save them from the experiments of a ruthless mage with delusions of grandeur.

"Please," I whispered, kneeling before him. "Let me care for them properly. You may be the genius with the recipe, but I know how to care for your patients. If your love for Abigail is true, let me help them both through this. I will not make trouble. Please. You wanted me here so you could cure Abigail with my fey blood. Well, it's yours."

"It's mine in any case," he announced. "Your magic is scattered and weak! I will cure Abigail, and she will be grateful. You're here only because you carry fey magic in your blood and you're useful as an apothecary. Desta may know how to shapeshift, but he's almost as new to magic as you are. He's useless in the mage lab. Now, we are wasting time. Let's get to work."

"Very well," I said, standing up. "What about those lost pages you found? If I am to truly assist you, it would help to see the book whole."

He actually smiled, eager to share his superiority. I wanted to share my fist with his face. But I clenched my fists, praying my expression did not match my feelings.

"You need not conceal your hatred of me," Morgan remarked as he opened a cabinet. Then he removed the replica of Veda's book and laid it on the worktable. The copy was physically identical to the original in almost every way. Except when I touched the pages, the texture was not so crackly or old.

Damn it, my emotions must show on my face. "What do you mean?" I asked him.

"You despise me for one thing. I know your temper too. I've seen it in action. Such impressive violence in so small a person. You try to hide it, but you can't conceal anything from me. You may hate your grandfather, Luther, but you are more like him than you know. I know what you're feeling, Sabine. I see it on your face. Honest anger I can control."

I hated his words. I'm nothing like Luther. I hated myself for not hiding my feelings.

"Now examine the book. I was so clever in locating the lost sections." He laughed, almost giddy. "Veda wasn't smart enough to look for the missing pages of this manuscript, was she?"

I knew Veda had searched for the missing parts of her precious book! But I knew better than to contradict mad Morgan. It was inherently obvious his formula wasn't his own genius creation. He'd just adapted from this book, as Veda had to.

He touched the book lovingly. "When I finally acquired all the missing pages, I magicked them into the book in what I believe to be the correct order. The result is most illuminating! See for yourself."

I examined the book with care. As I reviewed the restored pages, I understood why Veda had such problems with her formula. "The formula she based her treatment on was only the first of many experimental blends the author of this text used."

"Yes! And that is how I can save Abigail."

"If Veda had access to this vital information, she would have come up with a more viable treatment years ago!"

"But your fey blood activated your magic in combination with Veda's formula," Morgan said. "It even says so, on the last page. This text refers to lost tribes of fey. So few were left in the world then, and now there are none. But it used to be a key ingredient."

Knowing how terrible people are, I feared the ancient fey had been victims for the magical properties of their blood. I read on, feeling concern as I detailed the formulations. "According to Veda, my mother is allergic to both unicorn root and dragon orchid seed. Abigail's sensitive to unicorn root, but the dragon orchid seed gave her deadly reactions. I also don't see any versions of the treatment that require fey blood. But there are two formulas that do not use either the dragon orchid or the unicorn root. Maybe we should try to use one of those? It would be safer for them both."

"Because those two ingredients make the cure potent. Fey blood was used in the distant past, but by the time this manuscript was written, the ancient ones were lost to us. I think the fey blood makes the mixture safer too. As far as unicorn root goes, Abigail is not allergic to it, and that's what matters. I've added unicorn root powder to her tonics daily, and she's been fine. Veda was too cautious. The book has pages on using dragon orchid in different ways. It can be deadly, but I'm experimenting with new methods the book suggests. I keep several dragon orchids in my hothouse. They are rare and precious. The unicorn root is more common, of course. I always keep one on hand for my experiments. It's over there next to the last window so it can have proper sunlight."

He guided me to the strange and rare orchid. "Aren't the red and black petals exquisite?" he asked. "So delicate, just like my Abigail. You're a heartier peasant stock, so you wouldn't understand. Follow me."

He returned to his worktable and I obeyed him. The tiny cauldron of silver bubbled red, and he extinguished the flame with a hand gesture. He took a potion bottle and poured some of his concoction inside. "I must take care with this and use it quickly. Hold out your hand."

I obeyed. He took a pin and pricked my finger. My blood dropped into the potion bottle. "How do you know my blood has any fey properties? How do you know it's not just a theory?"

"Remember when your soldier kissed you? He was actually Desta in disguise. Such a good joke. It was more than a silly prank. He was acquiring your essence for me."

The creepiness I felt expanded a hundredfold. "What did it tell you?"

"You are unique. I'm sure Veda noticed some irregularities too but did not understand. The book details it in another chapter. I do not have time to explain."

Two keepers entered with my mother. She was so pale and weak, they had to hold her up. My heart broke seeing her like that.

"Don't move," Morgan warned as he seized my arm. "I'm not finished yet." When he deemed my blood had spiced the potion to his satisfaction, he let go.

I rushed toward Mother, but one of the men stopped me. "No closer," he said.

"Do not worry, my darling," she whispered. "Just obey him."

"She's too fragile," I said. "What are you giving her?"

"Version three of the formulas from the restored pages. This one has the dragon orchid petals instead of the seed. And your blood, of course."

"The treatment almost killed her before."

"But it did not, so she may have just needed time to adjust. As I said, Veda was too cautious. Maybe if I had been around, your mother would be cured now."

Oh my gods, please strike him dead, I thought. Nothing happened, so I remained a godless heathen. "Please, she was bedridden for weeks after Veda tried her treatment. Some people may not be able to tolerate this cure."

"Remember your promise, Fable. If you displease me, your mother won't live long enough to be cured."

The keeper gripped my arm hard. I stood helpless as Morgan poured the potion down my mother's throat. He glanced over his shoulder, smiling. "Yes, your hatred is plain on your face. I understand hatred."

I fumed with rage as my mother passed out. The keeper had to carry her from the room. I looked at Morgan Ashstone's smug face.

You have no idea about hatred. But you will soon, I promised in silence.

CHAPTER 31

Morgan relished both the pain he forced on my mother and my torment of seeing her suffer. A thousand curses whirled in my head. I realized mad Morgan never intended to let any of us live. I think he realized he would get nothing more from me that day. He turned his back to me and ordered, "Take her away. Let Lady Fable simmer until she learns obedience." The waiting keeper shoved me toward the door.

When we reached the dim, chilly dungeon, I glimpsed my mother shivering in Luther's arms, his face twisted with anger.

"She needs help. Please," I begged. "Can't you see she's suffering?"

The keeper pushed me forward. "Keep moving."

Luther beat his fist against the bars. "What'd you bastards do to her? She can't take any more. It's killing her. She's delirious, you damn bastards!"

Desperate, I broke away from my keeper and ran to their cell. Frantic, I whispered to Luther, "Make her throw up."

"Get away, you stupid bitch," my jailer shouted, dragging me away by my hair. "Lord Ashstone said you'd be trouble."

"Let me go!" I screamed.

The taman shade shook her glass dome and shrieked, the sound splitting my ears. My abuser even let go of my hair, covering his ears from her penetrating cry. I stumbled back, but he grabbed me and slammed me against the metal bars. I felt my ribs crack with the blow. My face was a wave of pain. I collapsed, the wind knocked out of me.

Nightshade's hand grasped mine through his cell bars, his concern genuine as he held my hand. I staggered on my feet, dizzy and sick. "Leave her be," he demanded, but my jailer had no sense of decency. The keepers ignored him as they cheered the violent display. "She's hurt. Stop it!"

"Silence, old man! We don't take orders from you," my abuser said, laughing. Then he dragged me to my cell. "She brought it on herself. The little bitch needs to pay for poor Rupert." A keeper opened the prison door and pushed me inside, where I crashed into the bed.

A terrified Marigold wisely remained silent and out of their reach until they locked the door and walked away. Shakily, I dropped beside the bed, struggling for breath.

"Oh dear, you're injured," Marigold said shakily. "Where does it hurt?"

"Everywhere," I croaked. I felt the lumpy bed but no dragon. "Where's Rory?"

Marigold paled, wringing her hands. "I don't know."

"What do you mean you don't know?"

She cried, shoulders heaving as she collapsed next to me on the bed. "He's just gone. I took a nap while you were gone. I wasn't feeling well. I dozed off for a bit."

"For how long?"

"I don't know, but I woke up right before they brought you back."

"I don't think the keepers found him," I muttered, hoping that was true. "They would have gloated about it. I hope he keeps out of sight. They'll kill him if they catch him. These men know Rory is my pukis dragon."

"How do they know your pukis?"

"They abducted me and Rory in the palace. It's when the truthsayer invaded my mind for Lord Baruti. All these men used to serve Lord Tabor. It's a long story. They were bad men then, and they're bad men now. They just changed masters."

"My dear papa and Greeley have often spoken of the corruption here. It is more terrifying than I imagined. I thought Papa just exaggerated about how bad it was."

"No, your father's right. These men are nothing but vile sycophants. Their sole purpose is using brutality to enforce power, any power willing to pay for it. Being mageborn just gave them an edge."

"But they were temple keepers. They held a position of sacred duty," she said.

"Reality is bitter, but it's better to know the truth than believe a myth. We must escape. All of us. And locate Rory before they hurt him. Helping Morgan Ashstone is just a trail leading us all to death." My head ached terribly like it did before Veda's treatment freed my magic. Every breath I took was agony.

"You better lie down," Marigold said. "You can't even stand up straight. Try not to anger these tyrants. They enjoy violence."

"I can't lie down now," I said, moving off the bed and crawling.

"And why not?"

"Because I need the bucket," I gasped.

"Oh dear," Marigold cried as I heaved into the bucket. I couldn't breathe with the pain in my side. I thought my head would explode. When I finished, I lay on the cold stone floor, wiping away tears of frustration.

Marigold helped me up. "Escape? It's impossible. We're all mage-bound and locked in prisons."

It is indeed a cold day in the underworld, I mused as Marigold did me a kind turn and put me to bed. "I didn't say I knew how to escape yet. I'm not perfect," I said.

A shrill howl reverberated through the chill dungeon again. I held my ribs, gasping, as I glanced back at the trapped taman shade, swirling in her shadowy prison. "She's angry."

Marigold knelt next to the bed and handed me a cup of water with shaky hands. "The creature is always angry. The glass prison used to mute her cries. It doesn't now. Could something be wrong with it?"

"I'm sure mad Morgan just wants to frighten us. I do sense she is different."

"How can you tell?"

"The shade's fury is worse than before," I remarked. "It's a sensation. I can't explain it. She's not just circling in her prison like before, glaring at us with her red eyes. She's thrashing against the glass constantly. Her screams frighten even the keepers."

"Good," Marigold said, nodding. "Detestable men. They threaten us with violence as if we know anything but their viciousness here."

"Then we need to return the favor."

# # #

I must have blacked out. I opened my eyes to Marigold hovering over me, nervously patting my hands. I think she feared I might break, or die.

"Just how wretched do you feel?" she asked.

"Like I went ten rounds with a giant troll." I sipped the water she offered and slowly sat up, flinching with each move.

"Can you eat anything? It's only thin porridge this morning."

"No, I fear another trip to the bucket. How bad do I look?"

"Your jaw and cheek are badly bruised and swollen, and your hair's a mess."

I nodded. "Good to know."

"You been unconscious for hours. I feared you'd die right there in the bed last night." Her hands fidgeted, and she avoided looking me in the eye.

"What's wrong? I mean, besides the obvious hell."

"The keepers took them about an hour ago. They haven't brought them back yet."

"Who?"

"Duke Nightshade, Abigail, and your mother. I'm so sorry. I couldn't wake you."

"No," I said, propping myself up on my elbows. "I think he's escalating his experiments."

We fell mute when a keeper approached and unlocked our prison cell. Marigold paled but said nothing. I recognized the huge lowbrow grunt who'd brutalized me the day before.

"Master Ashstone orders you to come now. No trouble this time, bitch," he said.

Afraid you might lose? I thought. It's so easy to be defiant in your head.

He pulled me out of bed before I had a chance to move. I stayed mute and obedient as I was dragged on wobbly legs. I needed to think, not argue with vile sycophants. When I passed Luther huddled in his prison cell, I could only glimpse his stubborn, angry face. I wanted to shout that I would make them all pay. But I just winced in agony as that the guard pulled me along the corridor and up the long flights of stairs. I stumbled on the landing of the third floor, breathless and my ribs digging painfully into my side.

"You craving another beating?" he threatened.

"I can't breathe," I panted, bending over. I glimpsed a flash of blue from the corner of my eye.

"What you looking at?" he demanded, gripping my arm painfully.

"Nothing, just nothing," I said. "I'm sick and I have broken ribs."

"Your fault, wench. Lord Ashstone is waiting." His grip suddenly loosened on my arm and he slumped against the banister, rubbing his eyes.

I stepped back, seeing my chance to escape the keeper. I turned as another appeared, running up the stairs and wearing a black hood that concealed his face. "Wait!" this new one called.

Damn it, damn it, damn it! I cursed my sluggish pace and broken bones!

My confused guard mumbled to the newly arrived keeper, "Wait … I don't know you."

The black hood fell back, exposing Braden's face. He punched the keeper hard, and they tussled down the stairs, taking me with them. I managed to detangle myself and scurry up the stairs. I moaned at the nasty daggers of pain in my side. I didn't have the strength to move faster. The keeper stood and raised a magic buffer. The shimmering gray forced Braden back. I stumbled toward the keeper, and he grabbed my leg, pulling me down. I kicked at him, and his shield dissipated as he turned on me, raising his fist to punch me. Braden yanked him off me.

The keeper towered over Braden, who faced him with fearless bravado. Then the keeper lunged at him. Rory swooped down, a furious flash of blue attacking the keeper's head. He swatted at my furious dragon, cursing as he fell backward and nearly landed on me. Rory darted to and fro, scratching and biting his flailing arms.

Braden drew a blade from his robes and stabbed the brute hard. The man groaned, swaying backward on the stairs, and rolled a few steps to the landing. The blow was not hard enough to silence him. Nor was it fatal. The keeper gripped his bloody shoulder, trying to stand. Braden's boot smashed his face and finally knocked him unconscious.

"Damn, he put up a fight!" Braden exclaimed, kneeling next to me. "How badly are you hurt? You're so pale."

"It's my natural color." I glanced at the keeper to make sure he was unconscious. Braden gently helped me stand. A madness of relief swept over me. I and threw my arms around him, enduring a wave of pain from my ribs, but I didn't care. I was so happy to see him.

Rory dropped to his shoulder, holding a bright metal pin in his mouth. "My brave dragon!" I cried. Rory dropped the pin into my hand. "What's this?"

"Shiny," Rory said. "I helped Braden. Pin helped to pick locks."

"He's a good dragon. We found each other last night when I was keeping low," Braden said. Then he hefted the keeper over his shoulders and carried him like a sack of potatoes into a room nearby.

"Good grief, he's almost twice your size," I remarked, following him.

"I grew up on a farm, remember?" he said with a grin.

"Wait, how do you know where to go?" I asked, trailing him with effort. The chamber Braden entered was a small bedroom. Of course, a castle that size has many bedchambers. Another unconscious and bound keeper lay crumpled in the corner, sporting visible bruises.

Once inside the room, Braden closed the door and locked it.

"What's happening?" I asked.

"I arrived late last night. I had to scope things out and prepare after I broke in," he explained. "Wait, I need to make sure this new prisoner is tied up good and proper."

"You've been busy," I noted, impressed.

"Rory helped," he said, taking the silver metal pin Rory gave me and unlocking the magelock from my wrist.

"I'm the bravest dragon," Rory said, nodding and holding his head high with pride. "I missed my Sabi. When you were gone, I flew off. In the ceiling, I saw tiny tunnels in the walls. Braden called them air vents. I went looking for you. Also explored. Looking for our escape. Many nasty keepers about everywhere. I hid, and then I saw Braden. We plotted together."

My body ached like mad, but my joy and relief at finding Rory and Braden filled me with a spark of hope. Even my headache dissipated after Braden removed the magelock. I rubbed my wrist, and Braden took the offending cuff and bound the other keeper with it. "See how he likes it." Then he dusted them with powder.

"Sleeping dust?" I asked.

"Veda's special recipe. It will keep them unconscious for a few hours. Indeed, I used quite a bit since last night. Veda and Kalem sent me in with more than a blade and good luck. They gave me a bag of sleeping dust to smooth the way. I spiked their food and drink."

"So that's why the guard was so groggy," I said.

"I drugged the coffee and porridge in the kitchens. I thought the sleeping potion would have done the trick by now on everyone, but this one either skipped his morning coffee and porridge, or it just wasn't enough to put him out." He looked up at me, concerned. "How are you really feeling? After I made it inside, I spied on a few of them and heard them bragging about hurting you last night. You look terrible."

"I'm just a bit broken and bruised. I'll worry about mending when we free the others. Oh, gods, Morgan Ashstone took my mother and Luther. The duke and Abigail too. The rest are in the dungeon. They must be in his mage room on the next floor. My mother is so ill, Braden.

Ashstone is doing terrible things to her. Oh, I almost forgot. The taman shade is in the dungeon with the other prisoners. Morgan controls the creature with a crystal he keeps in his pocket."

"Good to know. We're all caught up then. We'll save them all. I promise, Sabine."

We opened the door and looked down the halls. We hurried up the stairs to the fourth floor and moved down the hall. "How did you even get inside the castle?" I asked. "The whole property is shielded by magic. Morgan told me if anyone mageborn enters his territory, his magic wards would alert him."

"I'm not mageborn, and I didn't cross here on foot. I flew in from the sky last night on your favorite gryphon, Mathilda. We landed on the roof. Morgan's patrols didn't even notice."

"I owe Mathilda a bushel of apples. Weren't there wards protecting the roof?"

"Morgan Ashstone's not so smart. The roof of this castle isn't shielded by magic or any wards. Otherwise, I wouldn't have gotten into this fortress. Poor Mathilda is feeling miffed though. She's been waiting up there all night. Old castle rooftops always have doors and passageways, else repairs and cleaning would be impossible."

"Are you sure the keepers aren't a problem now?" I asked.

"Most should be feeling the effects of the sleeping dust. The few left won't matter much when Kalem and Veda charge in with the wizards and soldiers." Braden's hand steadied me, "You're injured and sick, Sabine. Let us do this."

"I must save my mother and the others."

He nodded and relented to my stubbornness. "Lead the way then, but I'm not letting go."

CHAPTER 32

Morgan Ashstone's mage room door opened before I even touched the knob. Braden's hand on my shoulder hindered me from rushing in. "I don't like this," he whispered.

I paused, fighting my habitual impatience. He was right. Grave silent and empty, it was different from the last time I saw it. "The room's barren now. Yesterday it was filled with crystals, marble tables, shelves crowded with herbs and potions." Then I saw Richard Nightshade lying against the wall, a bleeding gash in his forehead. "Braden, wait. Over here!" I rushed inside, impulse overtaking sense.

Braden groaned. "You're trouble," he said, but he followed me inside.

"It's a family trait." I knelt over Nightshade. "He's still breathing, but we need to staunch the bleeding." I ripped a strip from my petticoat and bound his head as best I could. Nightshade's eyes flickered open. "What happened? Where are they?" I asked him, frantic.

"Abigail," he moaned. "He took Abigail and Brona. I must save them."

"Where? Where did he take them?" I cried.

Nightshade passed out in my arms.

Rory, perched on my shoulder, sniffed and grunted. "Don't like it. Let's find Veda and Kalem."

"You're right. We need to leave now," I said, relenting.

Braden lifted Nightshade in his arms and moved toward the door. Mystical essence prickled my skin, like pollen dust in the summer. And not in a good way. A gray barrier materialized, separating me from Braden and Nightshade. Rory yelped, flying above my head. Frustrated, I pushed against the sorcerous wall. "This feels like stone. I'm trapped behind this thing. Go!" I yelled to Braden. "Take Nightshade and find the others. You can say 'I told you so' later."

"I'm not leaving you!" Braden shouted.

I closed my eyes and extended my hands, focusing on summoning my magic. My hands warmed as they glowed, sending blue beams of magic at the wall.

"Anything?" Braden asked.

"It's pretty, but not deadly." I dropped my hands, frustrated by my unreliable magic. "Maybe I need to be angry to spark some power."

"Think about Albertus Crimm," Braden suggested.

'You're funny." My spine tingled, sensing a rise in magic behind me. I looked over my shoulder to the back wall.

A giant oval mirror floated above the floor, framed by the ornate detail of a winged serpent in silver. The glass gleamed black, glistening and shimmering with dark light.

"Don't touch it," Braden told me.

"I'm not touching it."

Morgan Ashstone stepped from behind the mirror. "Foolish little bastard. Did you think it would be so easy? How sweet! Your annoying little pukis found his way to you. Well, at least you won't die alone."

"I don't want to banter. Where's my mother and Abigail?"

"Let me illustrate," Morgan said, stepping aside. He waved his hand over the glass's surface. The black sheen evaporated like mist dispersed by sunshine, revealing Abigail and my mother within the mirror. They floated like fragile puppets, suspended in glimmering shadow, asleep in a dark tale.

"He's cast a black mirror curse," Nightshade groaned, rising to his knees. "Darkest of mirror enchantments, and deadly to those trapped by it. It's forbidden."

"Magic being forbidden obviously doesn't concern Ashstone," I remarked.

"Exactly! No magic should be forbidden. We are mageborn," Morgan proclaimed. "I know your friends are here. They brought soldiers and wizards onto my lands. I will not tolerate criminal trespass. Do you think they can defeat me in my own sanctuary of sorcery?"

Dear gods, he does love to pontificate. "What do you want?" I asked.

"I only want my Abigail. The rest of you, well, you can leave or die."

"You claim to love Abigail, but you would condemn her to a terrible oblivion," I said. "What about your cure? It's not working, is it? What did you do?"

Morgan's expression shifted. "She's just too frail. I tried a new potion this morning, and they both had such convulsions. I sent for you, hoping you would not be so defiant. Then I saw my enemies circling the castle. I had to keep Abigail safe."

"Free Abigail and Brona," I begged. "Let us help them. Veda can treat them."

"Veda will not touch her! She had her chance and failed!" Morgan raged. "She is mine! I rule here!" He softened, looking at her image in the mirror. "But Abigail likes you. You can join us. You could be with your mother. No change, no aging, just blissful eternity in shadow."

I noticed mad Morgan wasn't sending himself to the mirror's curse. Reason is never an attribute of a lunatic.

Veda and Kalem stormed the chamber, backed by a squad of wizards and soldiers. They stopped when they saw the black mirror and its prisoners. Kalem's anguished look reflected my heartbreak for my mother's fate. Veda's determined gaze was something I was all too familiar with.

Morgan grinned and said, "See, even these good men know better than to oppose my power. I will be merciful just this once. All may safely leave my castle and never return, or face the consequences. I will not make this offer again. Go, or must I summon my wrathful shade to demonstrate my power?" He took the red crystal out of his pocket and whispered into it.

"Oh hell, he's summoning the taman shade!" I shouted.

The shade manifested like a black nightmare, then tore through the room, attacking and screeching. The wizards formed a circle and summoned shields to blunt her assaults.

Kalem shouted to Braden, "Go now! You know what to do!" Braden nodded and backed out of the room. "Everyone else, leave! But stay close," Kalem ordered, his shield deflecting a nasty assault by the shade.

Most people backed out of the chamber as ordered, but Kalem and Veda stayed. She helped Nightshade to his feet.

"Excellent," Morgan whispered into the crystal, and the taman shade paused, a floating threat above them. "Better. It was getting crowded in here. See my power over this ancient creature? I am all powerful."

He was all insane, but he had the upper hand.

I noticed someone else come into the room. Luther. Haggard and bent over, he glared at Morgan. "I'm not leaving without my Brona and Sabine."

Luther never called me by my name! He called me a lot of other things. Imprisonment and experiments must have rattled his sentimentality loose.

"Your drunken kin has delusions of grandeur," Morgan said, laughing.

"I'm a drunk, but at least I'm not a crazy person," Luther spat.

Morgan tenderly touched the glass. "You condemn them to this fate. Brona can be her handmaiden in slumber, so she will not be alone. We will be together forever, my beloved." He glanced at me, "Say goodbye to your mother, forever." He put his hand through the liquid glass. He was escaping into the mirror!

Oh hell no.

I jumped Morgan from behind, and we rolled to the floor. Rory attacked his head from above with sharp little talons. As I tussled with Morgan, I glimpsed beams of colorful sorcery pummeling his shield, breaking it down. The wizards returned, adding to the offensive. The taman shade raged, circling from above, but not attacking anyone.

The frosted window glass shattered on my side of the wall. Rory flew up to the ceiling as I bundled my body into a ball, shielding myself from the spray of glass. Braden charged in on Mathilda the gryphon. Covered with broken glass and face full of cuts, Morgan jumped to his feet. But Mathilda snapped at him with her sharp beak before he could react.

Never piss off a gryphon.

"Fools! You will all die now!" Morgan cried, backed against the wall by Braden and Mathilda. He groped inside his pocket. His face paled when he couldn't find his damned crystal. He patted his ugly maroon jacket. "My crystal. Where is it!"

The shield wall finally blasted into mist, clearing the way for the others to move in.

"He doesn't have the crystal!" I cried as I frantically searched the floor. But I didn't see it.

Rory winged above my head, the red crystal gripped in his tiny talons. "Shiny. Found shiny."

"No! That's mine!" Morgan shouted. "Give it back, you wretched little reptile."

"He's a dragon," I said.

The taman shade shifted her angry red gaze from my friends to Morgan. Braden backed Mathilda away as Morgan panicked and bolted for the mirror.

Now it was my turn to panic. Unexpectedly, silver leafy vines streamed from my hands, not only framing the mirror but penetrating the mirror's dark glass. The vines blocked Morgan from escaping through it. My mystical vines threw him across the floor to the center of the room.

Everyone backed away as the taman shade descended. He screamed only once before the shade killed him. We all stayed still, fearful of what she would do next. But she did nothing.

I looked into the mirror and saw my vines wrapped around Mother and Abigail. Terrified I might hurt them, I cried out, "Veda, I can't control it! What do I do?"

Nightshade suddenly took my hand, gentle but firm. "Let me help you. The way of glass is old to me. Your instinct is bringing them back to the light. Focus on that. See, the vines are holding them aloft and carrying them back to us."

His mystical strength merged with my wild magic. Together, we pulled Mother and Abigail from the mirror's darkness. They fell to the floor, unconscious but whole. My vines dissipated to a silver powder. I dropped to my knees, shaking from the effort.

"Well done," Nightshade said, weeping. "You saved them."

Rory dropped the crystal into my hand, settled in my lap, and glanced back at the taman shade. "She's angry. Wants you to help."

The taman shade swept before me. I looked her in the eyes, fearful she would rip me apart. I sensed sadness in her, the same as when she was first trapped in the glass prison.

"Be careful!" Veda called. "You control the shade now."

I did not want to control her. Maybe she was like this because of what Morgan Ashstone did to her. Rory said she wanted help. So instinct drove my next move. "Give me your sword," I told Braden.

"Are you mad?" he asked.

"This is the only way, Braden. I know it seems crazy, but she has to be set free. I feel it in my bones."

Braden obliged and handed me the sword. I showed the taman shade the crystal and laid it on the floor. I took the sword, heavier than I imagined, and used the hilt to smash the crimson crystal into fragments.

The taman shade's darkness whirled like a storm cloud. The shadows of her being brightened as she transmuted before our eyes from a rage of shadow into a being of light. Her shrill cries softened to a heartbreaking cry of release. Pure light glowed around her, brightening the whole chamber like a sunburst. She shimmered with brightness, and her image—pale as the moon and so beautiful—swirled around us. Then her silver eyes looked upon me with kindness.

Dear gods, was she fey of my blood? She briefly brushed my cheek, and I felt a rush of love and warmth before she vanished in a burst of light.

"She's not angry anymore," Rory said, landing on my lap, preening his wings.

"She was fey," I whispered. "Had to be."

"Legends speak of the Cumas Ishtyr," Veda said. "They were spirit beings of fey origin. I never thought to see one in my lifetime. No one believes they existed."

"I believe," I whispered. "To bind and mutate such a magical being was heinous."

Then I shook off my metaphysical experience and focused on Abigail and my mother. Mathilda snorted and bumped my shoulder for attention. I stroked her beak. "Yes, you're a good girl!" I cried. "So brave."

"Hey, what about me?" Braden asked with a grin. He patted the gryphon's back. "Careful, girl," he said to her. "I think Sabine has some cracked ribs."

"Let's leave this dreadful place," Veda said.

Kalem lifted Abigail into his arms, Nightshade stayed close, and Luther carried my mother. Braden and Veda each took an arm, as though I could not walk. Well, my legs were wobbly, but I'd never admit that.

No one glanced back once at Morgan's dead body.

Altheda wept with relief when she saw us, smothering my face with kisses before taking her medicine satchel out to treat us.

I saw an army when I looked around. Soldiers and wizards, plus I think the entire Gryphon Corps, surrounded the property. I sat down on the stone steps of the miserable castle, exhausted. Soldiers and wizards ran to and fro. Luther and I watched Veda and Altheda tend to Abigail and Mother. Finally, they woke up, weak but alive. For an instant, Luther's hand gripped my shoulder.

Soldiers herded the fugitive temple keepers into a large wagon covered with iron bars. Bound by magelocks and guarded by stern-faced soldiers, they would never use magic again. Good. They could rot in prison.

Veda gestured to me. "Come, Sabine. Your mother is asking for you."

Mother sat up, holding her arms out to me. I rushed to her side and knelt before her. She took me in her arms, holding me tight. I didn't care if my ribs all snapped. She was hugging me! She had never touched me like this before. Her love was always distant, damaged by the violence she'd suffered. I wrapped my arms around her, sobbing like an idiot. I'm not sure how long we stayed like that. When we finally parted, she pushed my curly hair from my face and wiped my tears away. Then she looked at Runecroft. She stood and slowly walked toward him. I moved to stop her, but Veda's hand held me back.

Mother faced him, with no fear or pain, as she studied the man who'd hurt her. Runecroft fumbled uneasily before her steady gaze. My mother slapped him across the cheek—so hard even I heard the blow. His face turned tomato red.

"I spent my whole life paying for your sin!" she said. "I lived in shame because of your crime. You're an evil man. You raped me and used your family's influence to escape justice. Your sin did one good thing, Runecroft. It gave me Sabine, my daughter. She's a Fable. *My Fable.* I love her so much. You are nothing. I will never think of you again."

Even crusty old Luther grinned at her bravery. I think her bold gesture took a lot out of her, because she stumbled when she turned. Crimm stepped in and took my mother's arm to steady her.

"Thank you, good sir, but I'm much better now," she said politely.

Crimm bowed to her and glanced at me with a glint of respect.

Duke Nightshade offered my mother a blanket to ward off the morning chill, which I did not even feel. He gently guided her to a place to rest next to Veda, who was examining Abigail as Kalem held her hand.

"Your mother's bolder than I realized," Marigold remarked, clinging to the arm of Greeley Havelock. Her father, Thomas Graven, looked on them with joy.

"We are happy you're safe now," Graven said. "Thank you for looking after Marigold."

Greeley Havelock stated with vehemence, "My next sermon will reflect faith and perseverance. I learned its power in this purgatory and how we can defeat the darkest evil."

"I think many of us were stronger than we realized," I said, looking at Marigold.

"Those ugly bruises on your face are awful. Better ask Veda to fix you up," she said. "Papa, I'm so hungry. Did our rescuers bring any decent food? I'm so hungry."

And there it was, the old selfish Marigold returning.

I sat for a space in the sun, exhausted. Braden joined me, Mathilda following him like a devoted puppy.

"She likes you," I said, then laughed, stroking her beak.

"Only because she's fond of you. Mathilda refused to come along until I told her we were coming to rescue you. I never rode a gryphon before. I loved it."

"I think you're a natural," I said. "Your Griffin family name is very fitting. In all the chaos, how did you even find us? We were so busy, I forgot to ask."

"Well, one of Kalem's agents caught a rogue keeper stealing old tomes and books from the archives in the temple. The fellow may be mageborn, but he lacked baseborn common sense. Kalem showed him the error of his ways. That keeper about pissed his robes when Kalem explained the consequences of his crimes. He confessed and told us where Ashstone's property was, which was one of three we just discovered researching the records. This place is only ten miles south of the city. But the information made rescuing you a lot faster, though I saw you were pretty good at rescuing yourself."

"I was happy to see you, Braden," I confessed. "Not just because you were rescuing us."

"I missed you too. I hope your mum will be OK."

"We're Fables. We're tougher than we look."

"I thought you might want this back," Braden said, handing me my mother's charmed bouquet of flowers.

Elated, I took them tenderly. "Thank you! Where did you find them?"

"In the dungeon, lying in a corner. I think folk were too busy to notice."

Rory nestled on my shoulder, nudging my cheek. "Can we go home now?"

I laughed. "Yes, baby. We can go home." I looked at Braden and glanced back at Veda and my mother. I just wasn't sure where home was.

CHAPTER 33

Magic's currency changed my life, but not in the way I imagined. I found a different kind of family and a new home, where I could make things better—not just for myself but for others.

I am a mirror mage. A mystic fate I never dreamed of when I fantasized about becoming Sabine Fable, sorceress of her own tower in an enchanted wood. Reality is much more grounding, and less glamorous. Especially when you have to clean up after a pukis dragon and scrape potion off the walls when a spell goes awry.

Months have passed, filled with change and surprise. I've studied hard under the mentorship of both Veda Arcana and Duke Nightshade. We live on his estate in the country, sharing one of the lovely cottages. We also have a private mage lab in another. Because my magic studies are important, my mother took over my administrative duties as Veda's secretary. I was thrilled when she came to live with us. She is enjoying her independence. In the mornings we all have tea together. Rory enjoys having three women dote on him with bacon treats.

Kalem and his team of wizards found Morgan Ashstone's book with the restored pages. He found many other interesting documents and tomes as well, going back centuries. He turned them over to Veda to continue her research. Veda was giddy as a schoolgirl.

Premier Alexander Duchene is providing funding for our research now. This is wonderful because for years Veda had to pay out of her own pocket to research mage fever. We work together now to find a cure, not only to prevent the array of side effects people suffer, but to develop a treatment to prevent contracting the disease.

Luther returned home to Crimson Hollow. Because Morgan Ashstone burned down Fable House, Kalem pushed the courts, with Alexander Duchene's help, to award Luther and my mother a generous settlement from Ashstone's estates. Since the mad mage's death, there are no other heirs, as he seemed to have killed them all. The money is enough to support my mother for the rest of her life and for Luther to rebuild

Fable House. We offered, though I admit to having been hesitant, for Luther to stay with us and build a new Fable House in Túr Solas, but he wanted to go home.

"It's where my Sabine is buried," Luther told us. "I can't live anywhere else."

Altheda promised to keep an eye on him. Luther is staying sober and even writes to us. That's all we can hope for now. Maybe a fresh start would do him good.

Desta Tabor did not fare so well. The truthsayer said his mind was damaged. After a few weeks in custody, it was clear that the damage was more severe than anyone realized. His mind reverted to that of a child, unaware of his true past. He would never recover. He and his father, Baruti Tabor, went into voluntary exile, their magic bound and power diminished. But they looked happy. Veda told me they went to the monastery where Desta had been sent. She and I watched the two leave together.

Desta gazed up at Baruti, excited. "Where are we going, Daddy?" he asked.

Baruti held his hand, smiled, and said, "To our new home. We'll play lots of games and I'll teach you to read. Would you like that?"

Kalem often visits Nightshade House when he is not swamped with work. Alexander and Crimm appointed Kalem head of reformation in the temple. They decided there would no longer be one lord mystic ruling the mage castes. Now, a council with a member from each mage caste serves. Corruption infiltrated the temple for too long. A subject I know too damn well. I get a headache just thinking about it.

Kalem and Abigail are happy. I think the duke would like to see them wed, but we are not pushing them. Well, maybe a little, but we're being subtle about it.

On a scholastic note, Duke Nightshade and I are researching the healing powers of pukis dragons. We plan to write a paper together about it. Abigail is going to adopt a pukis egg. I'll help her raise and train her future dragon. However, Mrs. Doran is not thrilled about the prospect of having two puki around.

Over the last few months, I've noticed how fond Duke Nightshade is of my mother. They are shy with each other. He is attentive and kind. They are both lonely and deserve some happiness. Abigail and I conspiratorially find ways to bring them together alone. It's strange to be part of a world I often had contempt for. I spent my life resentful of people who possessed everything I was denied. I hated mageborns, nobility, and just rich people in general. I admit now there are decent mageborns. Magic and wealth do not always reflect the character of a person. Though, I might argue that point where Marigold Graven is concerned. Only time will tell if Greeley's kindness will rub off on her.

The summer is hot, but pukis dragons love warmth. Walking in the sunshine one day recently, I laughed as Rory flew around me, showing off, when I noticed a gryphon soaring overhead.

"Sabi, look! It's Braden and Mathilda!" Rory called, excited to see them. I waved and ran to meet them.

Braden landed Mathilda on the lawn and dismounted. "Rory! You're getting so big!" he said.

Rory landed on Braden's shoulder. "Yes, Mrs. Doran says I'm squirrel size now and just as annoying."

I scratched Mathilda's beak. She closed her eyes, enjoying the attention. "You look dashing in your new uniform," I said to Braden. "The dark blue leather suits you."

"I've completed my training, and I'm now a full commander in the gryphon corps. It helped to have the recommendation of Premier Duchene."

"Commander Griffin. I like the sound of that. Did they assign you Mathilda at your request?"

"No, I'm just one of the few people she won't bite."

Mathilda snorted, and Rory took advantage of her presence to climb on her back. Braden and I strolled across the lawn together for a space, enjoying the countryside.

"I haven't seen you for weeks," he said. "I know you've had a lot of catching up to do with your magic, and I was in training. But I missed you."

"I missed you too. It's been so strange."

"What's strange?"

"Being happy," I said. "And peaceful. Life has been peaceful, except for the occasional magical mishap. I grew up surviving. When you live like that, you don't think about the future."

"Now you have a future. I've been thinking a lot about things, Sabine." He took my hand as we walked. "I know we're not like most folks. We have things to do and adventures to chase. What I'm saying is there is no rush for us, but it doesn't mean we can't share the same path. I love you, Sabine. I'd never ask you to give up who you are. I've seen a lot of miserable people who do just that. I see a future for us if you are willing to trust in that."

"I do love you, Braden. I never thought I'd say that to any man. Trusting was hard for me, but I trust you."

He smiled broadly. "You know, I owe you a proper kiss."

I laughed. "What do you mean?"

"You remember. The shapeshifter who posed as me, and stole a kiss."

"Ah, well, I guess you do owe me."

We sat on the grass, and he leaned in to kiss me, but any notion of a quiet moment to kiss was disrupted by Rory flying down between us, a golden object in his mouth. He dropped it before me.

"Shiny," he announced.

"Is that a gold egg?" Braden asked.

"No, it must be from the kitchen. Mrs. Doran paints eggs with gold vegetable dye and keeps them in a bowl to distract Rory from stealing other things."

"It's pretty large for a chicken egg. Are you sure about that?" Braden asked.

The egg began to crack and move.

"Oh dear. I better find Veda," I said, jumping to my feet. Braden and I held hands as we ran across the yard, Rory flying overhead.

Other Works Published by TANSTAAFL Press

By author Verna McKinnon

The Bardess of Rhulon

Rose Greenleaf dreams of becoming a bard and making her mark on the world. Her mother, Gerta, sees her daughter as a hopeless spinster at seventeen, with abysmal cooking and sewing skills. With devious machinations worthy of the devil himself, her mother, Gerta, betroths Rose to her husband's new partner.

To escape the coming nuptials and prove her own musical worth, Rose's headlong flight runs her into the hands of slavers, a master spy, a dispossessed prince, and a soul-sucking changeling, and into the middle of an insidious plot to take over a kingdom—a much more preferable choice of perils.

By author Thomas Gondolfi

The CorpGov Chronicles

In a world where corporations suborn governments as a part of good business practice and unregistered humans can be killed without penalty, Tony Sammis, a mid-level corporate functionary, finds himself unwittingly a pawn in a guerilla war between a powerful cabal of business leaders and an elusive but deadly underground movement. His final solution to their biological terror mirrors Tony's own twisted sense of justice.

At this printing, there are four books in this series: An Eighty Percent Solution, Thinking Outside the Box, The Bleeding Edge, and Window of Opportunity.

The Toy World

Robotic AI toys are the dominant life form of Rigel-3. Sent there with hashed programs, the factories that created them are fighting a brutal Darwinian war. One of these factories, pushed to the edge of extinction by the fratricidal conflict, attempts a desperate gamble. Infusing one of its toys with the power of sentience not only begins the quest of a 2-meter-tall purple teddy bear and his pink polka-dotted elephant companion but also spawns of a new race with its own beliefs and needs.

There are two books in this series at printing: Toy Wars and Toy Reservations.

The Monarchy of America

Witch Stella Ochoa leads a double life in the world of 1880s Boston. During the day, she spells down coal dust from the sky. On occasion, she is called by her coven of witches, the hellfighters, to help them deal with escaped demons. Life as a hellfighter is glamorous and dangerous—and Stella always seems to be where the hellfire is the hottest.

At this publication, there are two books in this series: Of Demons and Coal and Courting Witchcraft.

Wayward School (standalone novel)

Elizabeth narrates her life to a priest from her jail cell. She has been convicted by a jury of her peers to be executed for saving tens of thousands of lives. He wants her story so that no one else will follow in her footsteps.

By author Bruce Graw

Demon Tales

Torval, Demon Third Class, Layer Four Hundred Twelve of the Eighth Circle of Hell, has been in the business of chastising sinners longer than he can remember. Delivering punishment is the only job he's ever known—and the only job he's ever wanted. After Torval witnesses something unexpected, his demonic Overseer demands that he take time off to resolve this personal crisis. And so, Torval the demon finds himself sent on vacation to Earth, the proving ground of souls!

There are two books in this completed series: Demon Holiday and Demon Ascendant.

The Fey of New York City

As the last faerie in New York City, Tillianita tends the land and beasts as best she can, reluctantly obeying her departed father's warning to avoid humans at all costs. But not all strictures can be kept for a lifetime.

When gremlin Sithlac makes a deal with another fey—one outside his selfish kin—it broadens his view of the world. It allows him to consider relationships rather than just the lonely pursuit of wealth at all costs. However, nothing is without a price, and thus with the sweet must come the bitter.

Lady Hornet (standalone novel)

Elizabeth Fontaine is a lonely, ordinary young woman in a world where superheroes struggle daily against evil. To fill the empty void within her soul, she becomes a hero fangirl, following every super's event, subscribing to multiple fanzines, and never missing the daily superhero talk shows. Until one day, when fate grants her the opportunity to leave behind her boring, dreary life and become what she's always dreamed of: a superheroine!

Elizabeth learns the hard way the meaning of the phrase "Caveat Emptor!"—let the buyer beware!

Anthologies series from TANSTAAFL Press
Edited by Thomas Gondolfi

Enter the ... (apocalyptic anthology series)

Over three books, authors from all over the world have created a wide range of apocalypses for your reading pleasure. Within the pages, you will find exceptional works involving malevolent fey, vindictive aliens, challenging crustaceans, dominating warlocks, ironic phone calls, thoughtless kaiju, frozen ecology, and more. Each of these maelstroms creates massive disturbances within human society.

While works of holocausts tend toward uniform darkness, the Enter the ... series contains a number of catastrophes that are humorous enough to cause hysterics, and others that are black enough to cause the devil himself to shrink away.

There are three books in this series that can be read in any order: Enter the Apocalypse, Enter the Aftermath, and Enter the Rebirth.

Witches, Warriors, and Wyverns

A collection of amazing authors from around the globe offer peeks into what fantasy societies and characters are doing when they aren't wrestling with earthshattering issues, such as preventing the takeover of the world by a horde of orcs, the devastation of the earth by fire-breathing dragons, or the reawakening of uncaring, multitentacled gods. Come read about what passes for normal life in a world populated with mythological monsters, magick, and legendary fighters. Visit with a selkie mother trying to feed her children, a giant with a taste for mangoes, a kinky warbear, a wyvern who can't find a mate, and many more.

www.ingramcontent.com/pod-product-compliance
Lightning Source LLC
Chambersburg PA
CBHW051338020726
47501CB00007B/2143